"Only heaven knows what the future holds for us. I have to keep telling myself this does not matter because 'We are Missionaries'! But I am not. Ralph is. I am Ralph's wife. The love that takes me to China is not the love that impels my husband. . . . But this is my life, freely chosen, and I must take what comes and squeeze every bit of joy out of it."
—Margaret Outerbridge

The year was 1938, the countryside of west China's Szechwan province a medieval blend of feudal obeisance and exotic folk belief. Into this world stepped Margaret Outerbridge. Her new husband, Ralph, had his medical work, contending with erratic traditional medicine to ease the grim state of health. Other members of the Christian Mission community in which she lived had their commitment to spreading the gospel. Margaret began as an outsider, seeking to maintain the façade of a North American existence in a society unimpressed by foreign notions.

Irresistibly, Margaret's new world transformed her. Her friendship with Banyang, the wife of a local landlord, at first formal and courteous, blossomed into an intimate bond. The two women shared their thoughts and emotions as wives, mothers and witnesses to Japanese invasion and social disruption. Banyang led Margaret beyond the moon gate, into the private garden of Chinese culture. Through her, we see the splendour of the last days of the landed gentry. We feel the anguish as a way of life is swept away by the Communist revolution.

In part this book is an irreplaceable eyewitness chronicle of the changes wrought by war and revolution on the people and the countryside of west China. In part it is a love story. But above all, this book is an account of the personal growth of a strong-willed, compassionate woman determined to live life to the fullest in the face of petty convention and human tragedy.

JOHN MUNRO has drawn from the palette of Margaret's experiences to create a colourful, well-rounded portrait of a remarkable woman. Using her own reminiscences, enhanced by other documents, he has written the story of a fascinating life in a turbulent time and place.

BEYOND

THE

MOON GATE

A China Odyssey, 1938–1950

by

JOHN MUNRO

Adapted from the Diaries of
Margaret Outerbridge

Douglas & McIntyre
Vancouver/Toronto

Wood Lake Books
Winfield, B.C.

Douglas & McIntyre
1615 Venables Street
Vancouver, British Columbia V5L 2H1

Canadian Cataloguing in Publication Data
Munro, John A., 1938-
   Beyond the moon gate
   "Adapted from the diaries of Margaret Outerbridge."
   ISBN 0-88894-684-8
   1. Outerbridge, Margaret, 1909-   2. Missionaries' wives -
China - Biography.   3. Outerbridge, Ralph, 1911-   4.
Missionaries, Medical - Canada - Biography.   5. Missionaries,
Medical - China - Biography.   I. Outerbridge, Margaret, 1909-
II. Title.
R722.32.O88MS   1990   610.69'5'092   C90-091172-7

Distributed to religious bookstores exclusively by:
Wood Lake Books
Box 700
Winfield, British Columbia V0H 2C0
ISBN 0-929032-18-7

Editor: Brian Scrivener
Design by Alexandra Hass
Front jacket painting and chapter opening drawings by Yü Tse-tan
Maps by David Lim
Typeset by The Typeworks
Printed and bound in Canada by D. W. Friesen & Sons Ltd.
Printed on acid-free paper ∞

*To Judy, Carol, Kerry and all those other Mish kids
who have made their contributions, great and small,
to international understanding.*

C O N T E N T S

The diary upon which this book is based was preserved for the eyes of Margaret Outerbridge's children alone. Margaret hoped that some day, reading it, they would realize that every generation faces problems which, however seemingly different, none the less must be faced with the same sort of honesty and courage.

When, shortly before her death in January 1984, she was persuaded to change her mind and allow this very personal document to be made public, I began searching for the right person to turn it into a publishable manuscript. Through a kind Fate and the good auspices of Mr. Darrell Zarn of Simon Fraser University, I met John Munro in April of 1986 and gradually Margaret's Diary has come to life.

During the process, not only has John become a budding Sinologue, but I have found my mind inexorably probed, squeezed and sucked dry to the point where today, I swear there is no one on this earth who knows me more thoroughly and completely than does John Munro. In spite of this, possibly because of it, not only has a book much to my liking emerged from his efforts, but at the same time, I believe I have found a lifelong friend. Thank you John, for both. I have been twice blessed.

There is so much I personally would like to share about Margaret, but this would be superfluous. It is all within the pages that follow.

RALPH E. OUTERBRIDGE
M.D., M.S., F.R.C.S.(C), F.A.C.S.
October 1989

"Onward, Christian soldiers,
Marching as to war,
With the Cross of Jesus,
Going on before."

The words and music of Reverend Sabine Baring-Gould's 1865 hymn must have stirred many a heart in that earlier age of muscular Christianity, when generations of Protestant Missionaries trooped the four corners of the world to spread the Word (and the "benefits" of Western civilization) among their less fortunate brothers and sisters. In 1938, at the age of twenty-nine, Margaret Outerbridge left a life of independence and North American comfort to become a recruit, albeit a reluctant one, to God's army. In fact, she was pressed into service through her marriage to a Medical Missionary bound for West China. There, in the back of beyond, she found a life she could never have imagined.

Soldiers of Christ were expected to endure, with appropriate decorum, whatever sacrifices their Mission required. But seven years, the usual term for those in the field, could easily translate into more hours of loneliness and despair than anyone should be asked to bear. This was particularly so for Missionary wives with no vocation of their own. Even those who felt the "call" to labor beside their spouses, often found themselves daunted by the everyday problems of hearth and home. Souls are not saved nor humanity served twenty-four hours a day. Questions of food, shelter, clothing, personal hygiene, sickness, disease, pregnancy, child care—every married woman's lot—could assume awesome proportions in remote jungle villages or war-ravaged Chinese towns and cities. When culture shock, hostile environment and physical danger were factored in, it was not uncommon for conviction to falter or courage to crumble. There were times when Margaret Outerbridge's life seemed to consist only of babies, bombs, noxious bugs and the horrors of assisting in an ill-equipped Operating Room which had become a court of last resort for the failures of traditional Chinese medicine.

By the time the Outerbridges set sail for China in September 1938, the world was moving rapidly to war. While Germany and Italy were still rehearsing in Spain, Japan pushed out from its puppet kingdom in Manchuria to extend its conquest from Kalgan (Chang-chia-k'ou) in the north, to Canton in the south, to Hankow in the west. By the end of October 1938, it held the rest of the Middle Kingdom under siege, hoping to break the resistance of the Nationalist government in Chungking by bombing the cities of West China to rubble. These, and the ensuing days of the Second World War, were dark and stressful for Western Missionaries stranded in unoccupied China, with neither any means to influence the events in which they were caught nor any clear picture of what actually was going on. Even when the tide began to turn in 1943 and Japanese bombers temporarily disappeared from the Szechwan skies, they could get no closer to home than Bombay. Only with the end of the War in Europe in June, 1945, and the elimination of the German submarine menace were the sea lanes from India consid-

ered safe enough to transport Missionary families back from the
Far East to New York. For those who remained in China or returned after the surrender of Japan in August that year, large-
scale civil conflict began where the Sino-Japanese War left off.

When the Outerbridges began their second term in Chengtu
in June of 1948, they found their personal situation as uncertain
as it had been ten years before, more so in that they had now the
responsibility for three young children. If Margaret had been
pressed into service in 1938, she now considered that she had
even less option but to follow her husband. Her commitment to
the life she had made with Ralph ultimately demanded she place
at risk herself and her babies for a cause in which she still had
no particular belief. Her story thus continues in revolution
where it left off in war, and her life was lived each day, as it had
to be, no matter how ominous the circumstances. Then came
the Korean War and China's intervention. By the time the
Outerbridges left for Hong Kong in November 1950, there
were 180,000 Chinese "volunteers" engaged against the West in
Korea and hatred of all things foreign was reaching fever pitch,
even in the more remote Chinese provinces. These were tumul-
tuous times for the Church in China and disconcerting, even
dangerous, for those who labored in its service. Margaret
Outerbridge's diaries, in addition to much else, provide a
unique portrayal of the step-by-step eradication of Christian
(i.e., Western) and other "reactionary" influences in Chengtu
during that first year of Communist rule. More subtly recounted
perhaps is Margaret's personal journey during that last "Year of
the Tiger."

While this work is in varying measure a Christian chronicle, a
war story, a medical case book, an exotic adventure and an ex-
posé of Mission life, it is also more than the sum of these parts.
It is a life lived. Had Cervantes written of Margaret, he might
have observed, "Every woman is as Heaven made her, and
sometimes a great deal better." For Margaret's is primarily a
love story, and unabashedly so. It was her capacity to love, as
bride, wife, mother and friend, that sustained her. And central

to this is a profound cross-cultural bonding between Margaret and the Chinese Buddhist *tai tai** who was her neighbor, in a friendship so true as to enshrine the very best of the human condition.

"Diary," it should be pointed out, is the format of this book, not its reality. I was given my choice of what to do with the Margaret Outerbridge diaries-cum-memoirs and, initially, I decided merely to edit them for publication. Given the eventual extent of third-person decision, alteration, reconstruction, compression and addition, however, biography is more the result.

Ultimately, an amalgam of seven sources provides material for this book. First, the "diary" itself (approximately four times the length of the final manuscript), which Margaret had put back together as best she could many years after the originals were written. Much had been lost, but with a judicious employment of excerpts from letters either by herself or her husband, she was able to reproduce a more or less coherent whole. She had begun her diary in the first place largely to be shared in place of letters home by immediate family in North America and, latterly, for posterity in the sense of providing the Outerbridge children a record of their China origins and early life. However, despite this "public" quality (which no doubt denies her "diary" ever telling *all*), her accounts are not inhibited in any noticeable way. Margaret was by profession a nurse; her father, two brothers and husband were medical doctors. She had worked in major North American hospitals in addition to assisting her father in his remote practice in northern British Columbia and Alaska and was much involved with her husband's medical work in China. Subjects many Missionaries found shocking were commonplace in her life and are treated as such in her diary. What is more, she was not a Missionary; she was married to one. Thus, while she may have seen her husband through rose-colored glasses, the same did not apply to anything

---

* meaning "Mrs., Madam, wife, the mistress of a household," a title associated with class distinctions in pre-revolutionary China.

else. To the disquietude of some of this manuscript's readers, both ex-Missionary and Chinese, Margaret described exactly what she saw, experienced, heard and thought. As in the most private of journals, it was her need to confide, to vent frustration, joy or other emotion that led to the actual writing, which gives it not only a clear and unmistakable voice but also an intimacy only diary can possess: characteristics which I found irresistible.

My second source was the original diary, such as had survived German and Japanese submarines and the ravages of time, plus the full collection of complementary letters to family and friends, including those by her husband. Third, some retrospective material which, like the letters, could be broken for story content to expand original diary entries or to create new ones. Fourth, Dr. Outerbridge's medical notes and case studies prepared for examination by the American College of Surgeons to detail case and technical references in the text. Fifth, long interview sessions with Dr. Outerbridge (Margaret died more than two years before this project began), which yielded invaluable personal amplification, insight and other essential information. Sixth, the helpful comments, corrections, recollections, personal documents and photographs provided by a number of former Missionaries, Outerbridge family members and Chinese associates and friends who read in whole or in part the manuscript in its later stages. Seventh, published secondary sources to check the accuracy of certain accounts of historical events and personalities or geographical particulars, as well as to provide incidental data for occasional bridging.

In allowing this biography to develop in first person singular diary form, I have sought to create a living portrait of an interesting and vital life. (Possibly even, by its example and in the eyes of those it touched, whether Western or Chinese, an important life.) In so doing I undoubtedly have taken greater literary licence than most historians or biographers would contemplate. While in this instance I would consider the question academic, it seems appropriate nevertheless to ask the point at which, in the reconstruction of events or the compression of individual experiences to achieve workable story line, I have pressed or momentarily crossed the boundaries of historical romance. How large a step have I taken, say beyond what my colleague, A. I. Inglis, and I endeavored as editors of volumes two and three of *Mike, The Memoirs of the Rt. Hon. L. B. Pearson*, which were themselves literary hybrids? In fact the distance is considerable, but inconsequential. For example, to whom or what does it matter that a particular social event occurred in the summer of 1940 rather than 1939 if in consequence a fuller (and ultimately more "accurate") picture of the Missionary community at play is drawn? Certainly, the same logic need apply to all details merely incidental to daily living. While in such circumstances footnotes seemed absurd, for the benefit of anyone interested, all original materials plus the various drafts of this book have been deposited in Special Collections at the University of British Columbia Library. As to the literary form or genre of this work, it evolved in response to the demands of my material and, no doubt, as a natural extension of my particular experience as a writer.

Finally, I would be remiss in the extreme were I to omit an expression of gratitude to those who have assisted in the successful completion of this book. First and foremost, Dr. Ralph Outerbridge, without whose support, encouragement and willingness to endure long, long hours reconstructing and critically re-examining these important years of his and Margaret's lives, this book would never have begun. (It is perhaps unfortunate that a balanced picture of his life does not emerge in consequence. But because this is Margaret's story, I thought it proper that he remain as she saw him.) Second, Dr. Outerbridge's many friends, former colleagues and family to whom I have referred above: among them, Dr. Gordon Campbell, Rev. Roy and Dr. Grace Webster, Katharine Hockin, Dr. Robert McClure, Art Edmonds, Alice Jenner, Bill Outerbridge, Hanna Fisher, Dorothy Watkiss and several who, because they still live in China, must remain nameless without assurances that crediting their contributions would cause them no inconvenience. Third, a number of my own friends, family and associates, including my former teacher, Professor Margaret Prang; Munroe Scott, the biographer of Dr. Robert McClure; Werner Aellen of Bay Productions Inc.; Mary McKeon, Helga Stephenson, Christine Hearn and E. G. Hemmings, readers and critics all. Fourth, my publisher Scott McIntyre, who has made this project his own; and the meticulous Brian Scrivener who fine-edited the manuscript. And last but never least, Dr. Outerbridge's secretary, Lois Howes, and my wife and editorial assistant, Joan Munro. Lois has rendered this project yeoman service by completely mastering a word processing system on her own to record, print and correct my many drafts. Joan typed my first drafts, researched specific items, proofread and allowed herself to be my sounding board. I am especially grateful that both were good humored throughout the several years it has taken to see this work to fruition.

John A. Munro
December, 1989

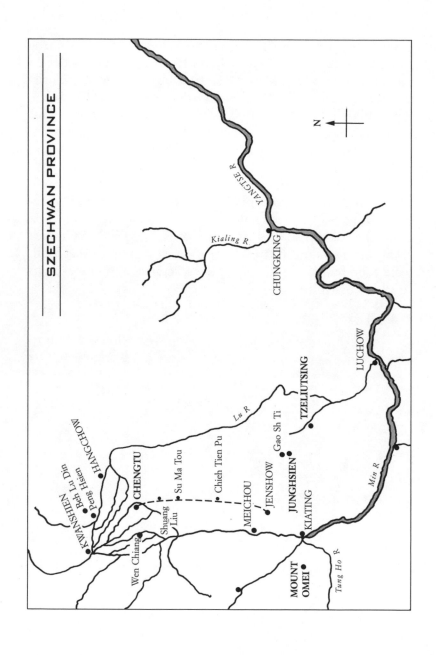

SZECHWAN PROVINCE

YANGTSE R
Kialing R
CHUNGKING
LUCHOW
Lu R
Gao Sh Ti
TZELIUTSING
JENSHOW
HANGCHOW
Beh Lu Din
Peng Hsien
KWANSHIEN
CHENGTU
Su Ma Tou
Chieh Tien Pu
JUNGHSIEN
MEICHOU
Shuang
Liu
Wen Chiang
KIATING
Min R
MOUNT
OMEI
Tung Ho R

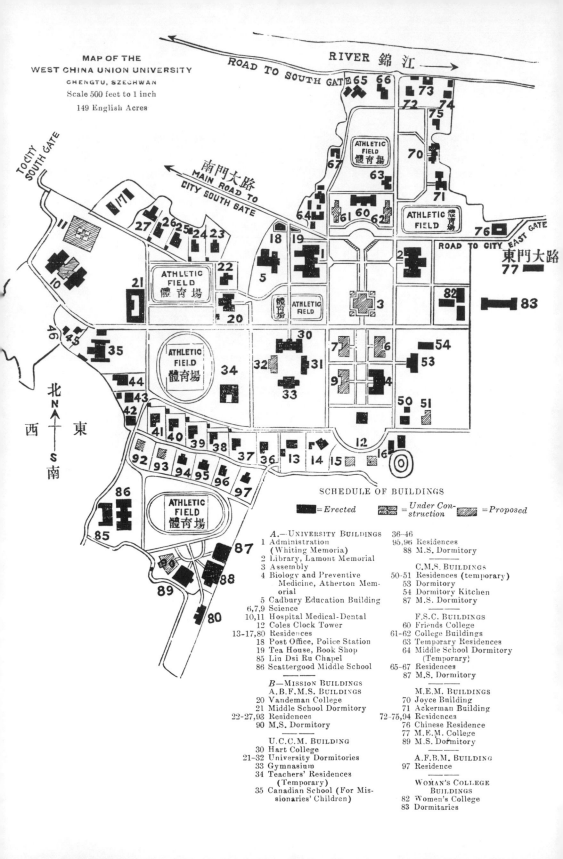

BEYOND
THE
MOON GATE

CHAPTER 1

Chengtu / Rites of Initiation

□ *SEPTEMBER 25TH, 1938:* This morning early, still some forty miles from shore, our ship entered the mud-rust waters which evidence the millions of tons of silt the Yangtse River disembogues each year into the East China Sea. One of the world's great waterways, the Yangtse is navigable by ocean-going vessels for a thousand of its more than three thousand miles and, in other times, we might have sailed on to the terminus at Ichang. In this second year of the bloody Sino-Japanese War, however, with opposing armies nearly eight hundred miles up river battling for Hankow, no such opportunity avails. Instead, we will stay on board the *Empress of Japan* when it sails tomorrow for Hong Kong. There we will wait passage on a French liner to Haiphong and thence by the Indo-China Railway to Kunming in Yunnan province, where we are scheduled to catch a Douglas monoplane to Chungking and finally to our destination, the ancient city of Chengtu, capital of Szechwan [Sichuan]*.

Our trip from the mouth of the Yangtse down the Whangpoo River to Shanghai was the most arresting twenty miles I have ever travelled. Every building had been destroyed! I'd seen newsreels and heard personal accounts of the Japanese bombings, the slaughter, the rape, the pillage and the plunder, but nothing had prepared me for this scene of total devastation. Even the trees are riddled and half torn apart. Shanghai, China's largest city, fell last November after four months of desperate fighting and hundreds of thousands of Chinese casualties. Today, however, the harbor is crowded with merchant ships of every imaginable flag. And warships: Japanese, American, British, French, Italian. We were saluted by the lot as we sailed majestically past.

□ *SEPTEMBER 26TH:* What I did not make clear in that portion of my diary begun yesterday is that Ralph and I are part of a Christian Missionary group (twenty-one in all) destined to spend the next seven years of our lives in Western China. But given the uncertainty that surrounds the War, only heaven knows what the future holds for us. I have to keep telling myself this does not matter because, "We are Missionaries!" But I am not. Ralph is. I am Ralph's wife. The love that takes me to China is not the love that impels my husband.

What is more, given the strength of Ralph's commitment to the ideals of Christian service, I suspect we'll never leave the Orient and that our life is going to be just like that of every other Missionary family: save, scrimp, sacrifice, with nothing material ever resulting from the effort. No beautiful home or prized possessions or elegant clothes. But I love Ralph so, believe in him, trust him and have such faith in his judgment that even this doesn't seem too great a price. This is my life, freely

---

* Where it seems of some advantage to the reader, the current spelling of major Chinese place-names, where these differ substantially from their historical equivalents in the text, will be provided in square brackets the first time they appear.

chosen, and I must take what comes and squeeze every bit of joy from it.

We have been married just three months and while I still feel as though my feet have wings, I am nevertheless re-experiencing the rather sobering emotion I had when I agreed to marry, a sense that life is taking yet another very definite road, another big leap, this time into the "x" quantity of that particular equation called our lives. Fortunately, our companionship is such that I am really terribly comfortable in my new state. I haven't had to make any spiritual adjustments of which I am aware, just social and material ones.

☐ *OCTOBER 2ND:* After a brief stay in Hong Kong, we are at last approaching Haiphong. The Indo-Chinese coastline is superb, spectacular in its needle-summitted mountains and pirate beaches, with golden-sailed junks fishing lazily in the foreground. There was a bit of drama in Hong Kong, for we did not know until the last moment whether we would depart or not. It all depended upon whether Britain went to war with Germany. Had this occurred, Japan might well have seized the opportunity to attack. When Chamberlain returned from Munich declaring "Peace in our time," however, we sailed.

☐ *OCTOBER 3RD:* In Haiphong, we stayed at the Hotel Europa. Due to capacity accommodation, Ralph and I took over the desk clerk's room. He being French, we found the place rather dirty and filled with risqué books and records. Given the piles of cosmetics and creams in his bathroom and the sissy clothes in his closet, I was rather surprised at the photos of nude women on the walls. We think he may have removed those he judged indelicate!

This morning, due to some confusion over our wake-up time, we arrived at the station to find the weekly train for China departed. Typical! This meant we would miss our connecting plane flights from Kunming to Chungking. After about an hour of negotiation, our entire party, *sans* half our baggage (which is to follow) was loaded into a motorized railway car. Mile after mile, we sped through what might have passed for carefully rolled lawns. In fact rice fields, tended by small brown men wearing nothing but G-strings and large coolie hats. And shimmering nebulous as a dream, distant mountain silhouettes. Beautiful.

We finally caught up with our train at Hanoi. And because our carriage smells of fresh paint, we can only hope the fleas, lice and assorted other noxious bugs will be fewer than anticipated. There is no dining car. We boil water for tea and cook our own food over alcohol lamps and don't seem to fare too badly. The railway itself is a superb feat of engineering, climbing through steaming jungles and over rivers and deep gorges that rival our most spectacular Alaskan scenery. What passed my window today was a jumble of tall palms, vine covered trees, bamboo groves, tumbling rapids, coconut palms, banana trees, fields of wild orchids and wonderfully colored birds. One long vine, hanging over a dark ravine, was a mass of small mauve flowers. And each village was an experience, as the browney red worn by the coast people gave way to the lovely indigo blue of the hill folk.

☐ *OCTOBER 4TH:* Last evening, we stopped in the mountains at Lao Kai. A brilliant sunset, gorgeous twilight, then sudden darkness and a full moon. As Ralph was assigned guard duty aboard the train to protect our baggage, I bunked in at the hotel with one of the other women and her daughter, under a large mosquito net. During the night, my companion suffered a gallbladder attack. I was developing a nasty cold (as is Ralph). And the room was alive with rats and salamanders. Not knowing anything about the latter, I was a bit apprehensive as they rushed around, occasionally falling off the ceiling. Needless to say, we didn't sleep very much, or well. Poor Ralph didn't do any better. When he switched off his torch to try and catch some shut-eye, the carriage came alive with clicking sounds, the source of which he quickly discovered when he flashed his light along the floor. Thousands of cockroaches had so crowded the space that they couldn't move without banging their hard shells against each other.

Lao Kai is at the border with China, where we had to pass through customs this morning. The officials were polite, but slow. We then continued to wind through the mountains, climbing steadily. At one stop it was market day. Several brilliantly attired Miao tribespeople crowded around members of our party in friendly curiosity. It was mutual. I noticed from my vantage point at the train window that their heavy black hair is coiled and held in position by large carved wooden combs. Otherwise, their heads are covered by elaborate, chequered turbans. One has the odd feeling of walking through the pages of *National Geographic*.

□ *OCTOBER 5TH:* When at last we began our descent to a plateau, divided as far as the eye could see into brown paddies, this leg of our journey was nearly over. At odd intervals, farmers thrashed rice sheaves over traplike grills, which tore the bursting heads. Flocks of ducks meandering to market across the harvested paddies searched out missed kernels. Water buffalo everywhere. Ox carts with solid wooden wheels of indifferent circumference. And soldiers carrying, of all things, shotguns!

At Kunming, we were met by Mission officials, cleared through customs yet again, then dispersed to various abodes to await flights to Chungking. Most went to hotels, but Ralph and I were sent with some of the men to a club, where we have to double up on a springless camp cot. No hot water, no mirrors and very questionable bed linen. In fact, I was horrified to find a black hair in ours. When I complained to Dr. Bell, he simply roared with laughter exclaiming, "My dear, you are in China!" No towels, no soap and indescribable outdoor bathroom facilities! Apparently we are lucky for this place compared with others is a paragon of comfort and cleanliness, or so I am told. I still think they are pulling my leg! We argued not, but our colds have taken over to the extent that both of us are voiceless, feverish and uncomfortable. Such close quarters under a Chinese *pukai* (a thick cotton quilt), a mosquito net and coarse-seamed sheets on a two-inch mattress definitely cramps my style. What is more, our servant has the disconcerting habit of hoisting himself up to look in over the six-foot partition that separates our cubicle from those of our neighbors before he knocks!

□ *OCTOBER 8TH:* Today, I went to wave good-bye to some of the Missionary women in our group. Ralph didn't, but asked me to take a photo of their twin-engine Douglas taking off. Alas, my camera was confiscated! Kunming is a training center for Chinese airmen (German, French, English and American instructors) and an important Japanese target.

□ *OCTOBER 10TH:* We were lucky. No Japanese fighter planes appeared to threaten our destruction. The huge Douglas (I had never flown in one before) was much like a modern bus. But it was rough, flying between the mountains and the cloud cover at 12,000 feet, as rough as any sea I've ever been on. Then, out of Yunnan province and into Szechwan, with the great Yangtse River curving below like a snake in convulsion. I was so fascinated by the changing patterns of cultivation that, almost before I knew it, we were over the confluence of the Yangtse and Kialing Rivers, circling Chungking [Chongqing].

The Mission House, where we are billetted, is a spacious, comfortable place that is home away from home to needy travellers. Located at the edge of the river battlement, it has an interesting collection of guests: a Russian (he is a little vague about what he actually does), the Eurasian wife of a man who brings pandas out of Tibet to sell abroad, an American working her way around the world, divorced and definitely "on the prowl," a German engineer and his wife, two newsmen, one from Reuters, the other United Press International and, to complete the picture, a German scientist with thick-lensed spectacles, untidy and absent minded.

□ *OCTOBER 13TH:* Last night, Ricky, our Russian fellow house guest, entertained eight of us at the Chungking International Press Club. The menu was Chinese, served with a rice wine, which I declined because it smelled like varnish. Before dinner, however, I accepted a sherry and found I was the only one in our group to do so! I thought nothing of it and proceeded to enjoy myself immensely. Just ready for bed about 2 A.M., we heard a frightful din outside. Eventually, the gateman roused himself and after a noisy altercation, someone entered the courtyard. There followed a knock at our door. It was Gordon Jones, who runs the Mission House. He said there was someone downstairs who wanted to see me. It was our Russian, very merry and brandishing a bottle of sherry for which he claimed to have searched Chungking so as to present me a farewell gift. I demurred (Ralph having already told me the error of my ways), but Ricky insisted and after all his trouble, I simply couldn't refuse. I felt like a criminal! Ralph considered the entire thing the result of thoughtlessness on my part and was at pains to point out, albeit gently, that indiscretions have a way of reverberating and being exaggerated within a community as small and particular as the foreign one in West China. I was a bit stunned and very ashamed of what I know not, but cheered by the fact that Rev. Jones considered it all a good joke. When I gave him the bottle (reluctantly), he said he would use it for shoe polish!

I could tell you about the loveliness of this riverside city in the first grey light of dawn (just a few hours later) as we made our way to the sand bar landing strip along the Yangtse to catch our flight to Chengtu. I could describe in detail the meat vendors, the night soil carriers or any of a number of things. China as I have seen it so far is more incredible even than Japan, revoltingly so at times. But my mind was totally preoccupied with the problem of living in a Missionary society where I would have to behave circumspectly at all times or otherwise disgrace my husband!

Despite air raid alarms, our flight took off on time and we arrived in Chengtu (pronounced Chen'du) without incident about 9:30 A.M., rode a rickety, weirdly fueled (I think wood alcohol) bus into the city, where we were met by Dr. Gordon Campbell, a dentist from Winnipeg, with whom we are to lodge. Casual, medium height, scant curly hair, blue eyed, he greeted us with a "How ya doin' guys?" I liked him at once. We rickshawed (he bicycled) to the West China Union University, the center of Canadian, British and American missionary work in West China.

The University (wcuu) was founded in 1910 to bring together the educational efforts and aspirations of the various Protestant Missions in West China: the American Baptist Foreign Missionary Society, the (American) Methodist Episcopal Mission, the Canadian Methodist Mission (now United Church), the Friends' Foreign Missionary Association (London) and the Church (of England) Missionary Society. Each denomination has its own college within the University along the lines of Oxford and shares responsibility for the much larger Union physical plant and administration of departments and colleges unrelated to denomination, such as English, Chinese, Agriculture, Medicine and Dentistry. Unlike a number of the Christian universities in Eastern China, the principal language of instruction at wcuu is Chinese, not English. As it now stands, the campus, about a mile outside the South Gate of the city, is large (154 acres) and very impressive. Combining some of the best features of Western and Chinese design, its many buildings are arranged to achieve order, balance and symmetry in accordance with the principles of traditional Chinese architecture.

We proceeded along "Canadian Row" to our new home, a big grey brick faculty residence with full ground-floor and second-story verandahs. (Apparently, every Mission household includes as many boarders as available space allows.) As the gateman let us into the spacious garden, two watch dogs came frisking out to meet us and the servants set off a wheel of fire crackers to wish us welcome and good luck. Gordon Campbell's wife, Mildred, also from Winnipeg, is small, vivacious, efficient, very modern and seems a good head. Also very pretty and five months pregnant. I was so miserable with my cold, sore ears and lack of sleep, I went immediately to my bed. Our room was itself a comfort after four weeks living out of suitcases. White walls, cream woodwork, tasteful furniture, a window overlooking the fields beyond our garden, clean sheets and no bugs.

By the time I awoke, visitors and invitations had started to arrive. One is invited here by chit. There are no 'phones. At 4 P.M. Mildred and I went by rickshaw to a tea in the city. Naturally, I was given the once-over by all present and I think did us proud in my one remaining clean outfit and on my best behavior. Everyone was charming and nearly all impressed me one way or another. Not many colorful personalities, but the tea was good.

Among those present: Mr. Hibbard, treasurer of the United Church Mission, a large, solemn, granite-faced man. His wife, dark, plain, ordinary and nice. Hilda Anderson, an American, also staying at the Campbells', clever, modern, mannish, chockful of personality. She is secretary of the University of Nanking, presently refugeeing here from the Japanese occupation (along with Gin Ling College, Cheeloo's Medical College and National Central University's College of Medicine and Dentistry). Mary Agnew, a large, blowsy, gushy redhead, dressed in too-bright pinks, who is a medical researcher and the wife of Gordon Agnew, head of Dentistry's Department of Oral Biological Science. The very nice, sort of "wifely" Emily Williams, a nurse from Winnipeg and married to Dr. Harry Williams, pathologist and parasitologist in the College of Medicine. A Mrs. Stinson, very earnest, very young and very "good." Her husband, John, a theologue, likewise. Then, Earl and Katherine Willmott and Lewis and Constance Walmsley. I liked them very much. Both the Willmotts teach in Mission Middle Schools, where their students are exclusively Chinese. Lewis Walmsley is headmaster of the Canadian School here for the elementary and high school-aged children of mainly the foreign community. All four know Ralph's parents and I have a feeling they are going to take a special interest in us.

□ *OCTOBER 14TH:* Frank and Nan Dickinson, former classmates of Ralph's parents at Mount Allison University, came to visit today. Personality plus, human, intelligent, understanding and enthusiastic, they are so far the most impressive of those we have met. Mr. Dickinson is the head of Agricultural Science at the University. He has just been given charge of Madame

Chiang Kai-shek's prize herd of fifty-five Holstein cattle (milk and butter are worth their weight in gold here) and is full of plans to use these animals to improve local dairy herds, something he has been attempting for years. A Chinese cow has only about a ten-to-twelve-cup capacity (a Holstein produces twenty-five times this). What is more, it won't "let down its milk" unless its calf is alongside. If the calf dies, its hide is nailed to a post in the stall for the cow to lick, otherwise no milk. Mr. Dickinson's ambitions include changing the psychology of Chinese cows!

□ *OCTOBER 27TH:* A succession of teas, receptions and dinners have brought us into contact with most of the two hundred foreigners connected with the University. Speaking of such, we have just met a wonderful person, Dr. Gladys Cunningham. She came to the Campbells' for dinner and stayed the weekend. A good obstetrician I am told, certainly a straight shooter and a barbed wit. Medium height, blond cropped hair, keen eyed, wise and shrewd. Not pretty, no nonsense clothes, but with a very definite style of her own. Another, Dr. Leslie Kilborn, came in this P.M. and stayed talking until his wife, Dr. Janet, sent their coolie to remind him of the time. Born in China and slightly crippled in one arm when shot by a soldier in the retreating army of a defeated war lord in Kiating in 1925, he is dean of Medicine at WCUU. His father, Dr. Omar L. Kilborn, and his mother, Dr. Retta G. Kilborn, first came to Szechwan as medical missionaries in the 1890s. Subsequently, Omar Kilborn led the campaign to create the University's Medical College, which offered its first courses in January 1914. Dr. Kilborn, senior, who was also an ordained Minister, believed the Medical Mission a potent agency for evangelism. He also believed it was the duty of the medical missionary to "multiply himself" by training Chinese Christians to be doctors. Now his son carries this responsibility and is at present supervising the construction of one of the most modern and extensive teaching hospitals in China.

□ *NOVEMBER 3RD:* There has been practically no sun the last three weeks. While the temperature outside is pleasant, we poor unimmunized newcomers pick up every cold bug around. When we are not at language school, which is our principal occupation until we can function in Chinese, Ralph spends his spare time working at the Hospital on campus, and I, mine, helping at the Woman's Missionary Society Hospital in the city.

Our Chinese language school consists of five hours per day, Monday through Friday, each alternate hour spent with a private tutor. No word of English is allowed. Szechwan Chinese requires four tones in speech. The first is a high, singing sound, the second low and flat, the third staccato and the fourth low with an upward slur. Ralph seems a natural in class. Our study is so intense that by the end of the week my throat is stiff and sore. Nothing a rigorous game of tennis, a hot bath and a good dinner doesn't cure, however. We have been given the Chinese surname, "Yao"—one of the original hundred Chinese names.

In many ways it is a thrill to have been dropped into a region where much has remained unchanged for hundreds, sometimes thousands of years. The irrigation ditch outside our window for example is part of a very old system that serves the entire Chengtu Plain (some 4,000 square miles known as the Red Basin). Before this, when the Min River, which runs diagonally across the province to the Yangtse, flooded, the results were devastating. In approximately B.C. 290, the Prefect of Chengtu, an engineer of extrordinary talent, Li-Ping, set about constructing an alternate channel for the Min, linked to a network of canals and ditches that at once solved the problem of flooding and converted this area into the most fertile in China. So it has remained. Never once in over two thousand years has Chengtu suffered famine.

There are about 60 million people in Szechwan today. 300 years ago there were virtually none. In the year 1645, after the fall of the Ming dynasty, one of the great despots in history, the rebel warlord Chang Hsien-chung, took possession of this province. His officers in the districts were given licence to kill and plunder as they pleased. In 1646, the militia and the gentry rose in protest. Chang, infuriated and believing that he had received a mandate from heaven through a dream, set about in a fit of religious mania to exterminate all who opposed him. Nor was he satisfied with simply butchering Szechwan's ruling classes. The poorest hamlet, the most secluded village paid its ghastly price. Soldiers were promoted to the rank of sergeant upon presentation of either 100 pairs of men's hands, 200 women's or 300 children's. And patents of nobility were available to those of his officers and men who demonstrated an even greater talent for slaughter. It is said that the inhabitants of the province were reduced from 3,500,000 to 7,000!

When the new Manchu Emperor finally moved to take control, Chang, forewarned, buried a fabulous treasure amassed from his victims and with it all who might reveal its whereabouts, then fled. He was later caught and executed, but for seventy years, the province lay waste, roamed by tigers from the Tibetan hills. Only by forced migration of landless peasants and convicts from other provinces was Szechwan re-populated. Thus, when one asks a Szechwanese the origin of his ancestors, he may reply from Hunan, Kwangsi, Hupeh, wherever, but never Szechwan. As to Chang's treasure, a local legend maintains that, "Between the stone ox and the stone drum lie one thousand times one thousand pieces of silver."

Despite Chang Hsien-chung, however, even Marco Polo, who travelled here in the latter part of the thirteenth century, would recognize Chengtu as it now stands. Apart from the rickshaws which have largely displaced whaggans (litters) in the city, a few automobiles and an overflow of population (now over 400,000) creating villages outside each of the city's main gates, nothing much has changed. Occasionally, one even may see a camel caravan, piled high with bundles of silk and other exquisite fabrics for which Chengtu has been forever famous, beginning its return trek to the mountain trails that lead to the "Jade Gate," the Gobi Desert and beyond along the historic "Silk Route." The city is about four miles square, surrounded by a high forty-foot-thick wall, with a second walled city (modelled after the Forbidden City of Peking) in its center, where one can still view the marble enclosures and reception halls of the Viceroy's palace. During the Three Kingdoms period (220–265 A.D.), Liu Pei, a descendant of the Han Dynasty Monarchs, held court here. It is now the site of Chuan Ta, the government university.

The other day, Ralph and I made a trip into the city on foot, entering by the South Gate which took us over the Marco Polo Bridge. It was fascinating. Everything is on the street. Mobile soup kitchens on cooks' shoulders. Flocks of ducks. Beggars in tatters, some crawling, knocking their heads on the ground, apparently too weak even to whimper. The seller of wool signalling potential customers with two sticks upon which he plays his particular vendor sound. Rickshaws, public and private. Tea houses, spice shops, silk shops, china shops. Just everything!

The drug stores intrigue me. Open to the street, their walls are lined with multi-drawered chests, each filled with things weird and wonderful: ginseng, bark, bulbs, snake venom, dried liver, bird tongues, tiger teeth and the prized aphrodisiac— ground deer antler. These are weighed out with great precision on Chinese scales (a type of counter balance unseen in the Western world) and carefully wrapped in pieces of rough brown "grass" paper (used for toilet paper in the foreign homes).

□ *NOVEMBER 7TH:* It is now confirmed that Hankow has fallen to the Japanese. We heard as well (information about the War here often reaches us long after it has ceased to be news in Europe or America) that Canton is also occupied. Chiang Kaishek has retreated to Chungking. Consequently, we are organizing for the worst: digging trenches, building shelters, organizing first aid supplies, instructing the older children when to round up the younger ones and so on. Doubtless nothing will happen.

Yesterday, we met a newspaper man named Hanson, who writes for *Asia* magazine. Just returned from living with the Communist Eighth Route Army in North China, he says their tactics are now entirely hit and run. Enemy drivers are killed, their vehicles stolen. Trains are derailed. Telephone wires cut. Whatever necessary to render Japanese occupation ineffective. Everyone is recruited. Small boys become passport examiners. Women occasionally are even made commissars! In the Communist-controlled countryside (that Tokyo reports quiet and enjoying Japanese rule), the peasants are benefitting from lower taxes, equitable rent and better living conditions. In return, they are easily recruited to the cause of their liberators. The humility, the poverty and the dedication of the guerillas impressed this reporter very much. Of course the Communists include some of the best brains in China, ex-professors from the Universities of Nanking and Peking and thousands of students.

□ *NOVEMBER 12TH:* A couple of Belgian nuns selling fine needle work came around today from an orphanage they run in the city. Very nice women. We spoke in French. I bought a beautiful tea cloth and six matching serviettes. The tea cloth has a two-inch border of handmade lace, cutwork corners and an embroidered center. I later went into Chengtu on my own for the first time. Jessie Parfitt had invited me to see her child welfare clinic. She and her husband, both Oxford graduates, are concentrating on public health here. Mil Campbell lent me her rickshaw for the trip. Of course, given my Chinese, we arrived at a Church instead of the clinic. A small confusion there. Jessie (reputed to be the most brilliant female ever to graduate in medicine from a British university) demonstrates each phase of infant and child welfare by printed poster and with stuffed dolls. I learned many things. Of course, the problems are immense. Women breast feed their children up to two and three years. If a mother cannot nurse her baby, it gets fed whatever is available. I personally have seen them literally spitting chewed food into their infants' mouths. Children and parents sleep together. In the gatehouse at Mil's, the gateman, his wife and two children live, eat and have their being in what amounts to two large windowless cupboards. Sanitation, as we define it, is unknown. And everyone spits copiously. On crowded thoroughfares, it is nearly impossible to avoid the barrage of expectoration.

Nevertheless, the streets and byways enthrall me. On my way to Jessie's, I saw two huge purple pigs being trundled along on a squeaky flat-bottomed wooden-wheeled cart, pulled by a sweating coolie and pushed by two enthusiastic youngsters. The pigs were dead, but so newly as to be still shaking in their very deadness. Further along, another coolie pulled two very alive pigs sitting up in a rickshaw, trussed together with bamboo ropes. Another lay tied across the shafts while still another swung from the back. All with their eyes sewn shut and squealing as only pigs can. A vendor of brushes stood aside to let us pass. On his shoulder pole every conceivable brush used in this part of China. Of course, he has his own distinctive call or sound, as does every vendor. Soldiers marching barefoot or in *tsao hai* (grass sandals). Fashionable rickshaws carrying very smart Chinese women. Rickety tied-together rickshaws filled with kids, their arms loaded with the day's shopping, reminding one a bit of Birnam Wood in *Macbeth*.

Often, when awakened early by the persistent high-pitched screak of wheelbarrows passing, we prop ourselves up on our elbows to watch. (We have very comfortable outside sleeping accommodation on a corner of the verandah off our room.) The wheelbarrow is Chengtu's most common form of transportation. Night soil, water, produce: everything travels this way— even people (the barrow is divided into two sections by a foot-high partition). I was delighted one morning to watch a three-hundred-pound woman being pushed, I can only imagine by her husband and pulled by her son. Overweight females are rare in the coolie class. This poor soul must have been hypothyroid.

☐ *NOVEMBER 14TH:* Sunday morning early, we splashed through muddy streets by bike (it had rained all night) into the city to our Men's Hospital at Si Shen Tse where Dr. Edward Best is in charge. At 8 A.M., we started rounds. While the cases were not particularly interesting, what we saw in the way of fighting the main sources of infection was most impressive! Flies are controlled in the diet kitchen by making the entrance very dark (black paint), "z" shaped and double doored. In the boiler room, one fire handles all three waters, distilled for intravenous, boiled for drinking and warm for bathing. The toilets, outside but on septic tanks, are flushed whenever sufficient hospital waste water is collected. Thus, the problem of flies between flushes. No one here would ever think of closing a lid if there were any (there are no Western fixtures, just holes in the floor over which one squats) and as beaded door curtains are a help not a solution, Dr. Best devised a mechanism whereby one's weight triggers a hinge beneath the floor causing a trap door to open below the toilet. When the weight of the person using this facility is removed, the trap door automatically shuts.

At the Woman's Missionary Society (wms) Hospital where I work in my spare time, I have come to like very much the Superintendent of Nurses, Miss "Tallie" Tallman, a graduate of Grace Hospital, Detroit. As I spend more time helping with charts and generally getting a better feel of the place, I am beginning to understand some of the difficulties of working even in what are considered the best of conditions out here. All five Mission hospitals in Chengtu are closely affiliated with the wcuu College of Medicine. Consequently, their equipment is at least on a par with that of most small hospitals at home. As to the Chinese nurses and students, like our own they seem to come in all shapes, sizes and dispositions. I've also had great fun with the two pædiatricians who live in residence, Helen Lousley and Jean Millar. Both are highly qualified (Jean is also an anæsthetist) and Canadian.

The other day after I had finished my various jobs for Tallie, another new friend, Alice Jenner (her husband Harley is an internist, she's a home economist), picked me up for some "window" shopping. Of course there are no windows.

Later, Ralph (who was raised in Japan) and I cooked sukiyaki for a party at Hilda (Red) Anderson's, who has moved out of the Campbells' to her own place, christened "Chrysanthemum Bowl." Practically all Red's guests were from amongst her colleagues at the University of Nanking, and a more witty, clever, courageous group I have never met, most having gone through both the horror of the Japanese destruction of Nanking and the saturation bombing of Hankow. One couple, married the same day as ourselves, Margaret and Jimmy Tang, we particularly liked. He is in agriculture and did post-graduate work at Cornell. Margaret is a New Yorker. Out here, as at home, mixed marriages are frowned upon and as Jimmy's family is prominent, I am sure their's will be a life of more trials and hurts than most.

Language school, I might add, is now interrupted quite regularly by air raid alarms. Today's was a little less frightening because we saw four Chinese pursuit planes go after the fifteen enemy bombers. (We are beyond the range of Japanese fighter escorts.) These, of course, did not stop three hundred pound bombs being dropped on the airfield to the north of the city. Buildings were destroyed, but no casualties. Col. Schultz, who represents Curtiss Aviation here, told us all about it. During the attack, we disobeyed all rules to wander about inspecting our neighbors' dugouts. It is in fact impossible to build an effective bomb shelter when the water table is only three or four feet down.

☐ *NOVEMBER 22ND:* The city proper suffered its first bombing today. We were at the South Gate on our bikes when it began and were caught in the general panic. First there was a high-pitched clamor from within the walls, increasing as the first blue-clad people emerged, to suddenly, like a flash flood, become a river of hysterical humanity. We were literally carried along as they raced towards the countryside. Women with babies, youngsters pulling at their mothers' gowns, old women hobbling on bound feet. Even beggars deserting their habitual posts. Despite this, there seemed also a general feeling of adventure. The excitement of the crowd, the planes overhead, the soldiers running about, the clanging of the alarm bells certainly started shivers of excitement up and down my spine. People would jabber at us in Chinese and we would reply in English, neither side understanding a word, but somehow feeling that we did. When we reached the campus, it too was alive with foreigners dashing for home on bicycles, in rickshaws or on foot, laughing and joking. Students, ankle-length gowns hitched up, sprinting for safety. Coolies, rickshaw pullers, servants huddled under trees and bushes. At home, I found Red Anderson and Mil in the bathroom, Mil in the process of washing her hair, excitedly discussing which ditch to run to. On the verandah, we watched an aerial battle over the radio station tower behind our house. The planes were so close we could see the faces of the pilots. Then, I decided not to leave at all and this is being written while the battle rages. In all, ninety bombs were dropped. When I asked our *danyang* (maid of all work) if she had seen the planes, she replied, "Oooh—I face down in hole."

☐ *DECEMBER 4TH:* We have been having a few days of incredibly good weather for this part of the world, even a tang in the air to bring memories of home. My ear cocks for the honk of wild geese winging southward. Just thinking of it, I again revel in the wet yellows and browns, the darkness of the evergreens, the dull red of the pigeon berry leaves and the occasional flame of Jack Frost's brush. I can almost hear the bang-bang of double-barrelled shotguns and feel the trembling of the beautiful liver-and-white springer at my side. Such an undisciplined mind is mine! So hard not to speculate in class why one of our teachers (Mr. Yü), while otherwise clean shaven, has allowed six coarse black hairs to grow out of a mole on his jaw.

School is still a fag! We in Szechwan are considered lucky because we have only four tones to deal with as opposed to the classical eight. Not only does a word in one tone have a pageful of meanings, but the same word in a different tone has another pageful! By our terms, there is no grammar nor rhyme nor reason to anything. Western scholars out here have been studying thirty years and are still at it! One makes so many embarrassing mistakes. For example, a word in one tone means wife, in another flag, in another rise and in another temper. We started characters this week. Previously, all our work was with phonetic script which now seems like child's play when up against a simple character of fifteen strokes! We hope to master 5,000 of these, but 1,000 in our first year will be acceptable!

When our head teacher, Mr. Pan, finds it difficult to make his meaning clear, he does pantomime. Great fun. Today, when demonstrating something we were being stupid about, he heaved a slippered foot up on his desk. I peeked under his gown to behold his long, bright-orange, jumbo wool underwear! I pay for these indiscretions by being unaware when asked a question.

It being Sunday, we went for a long walk with the Campbells. The boys got all dressed up. You should have seen them. Gordon, usually so casual, complete with fedora and cane. Ralph even wore gloves. They explained all the interesting things we passed. Acres of Chinese carrots, a red vegetable quite unlike our homeside ones, larger with, I think, a rather smoky taste. Chinese turnips, also different and so on. Together, we admired the swoop of kingfishers (so much more brilliant in their coloration than at home) and watched farmers netting wee fish in the irrigation canal. Long-haired red-brown goats seemed to wander at will. A mother passed with two small children. I have fallen in love with all these babies and it rends my heart when I think how quickly their carefree days pass, how early they assume the burdens of an unrelenting struggle for survival!

As I write this on the verandah, one of the servant children is playing near me fascinated by the typewriter. Runny nose of course, but cute withal. About three years old, he is a ragged wee chap. Dirty khaki cap on his head, stained padded blue gown pinned up at the back, his little bottom exposed, as he has on the seatless pants children wear out here until toilet trained. Very sensible in this soap-scarce land.

Yesterday, in town, I watched firecrackers being made. The Chinese invented gunpowder, but they used it for celebrations! I dallied to listen to the cooks haggling with the farmers. It is becoming fun now that I understand a bit. I also watched felt shoes being made, a sort of monk's shoe, padded and beautifully warm. I hope to get Ralph a pair for Christmas. He wants a tripod for his camera so perhaps it will be that. Although I could buy a small Tibetan rug for the same amount of money! Ah me. Then again, his one sweater is terribly moth eaten. We shall see. The candy man in this country is an artist. Toffee strung into dragons, fondant made into rickshaws. I wanted to take a dragon to the gateman's child, but according to custom, I should not. One loses face. Another way to do so is to say "Thank you" to a servant. One may say "Good," but not too often!

☐ *JANUARY 14TH:* One of my joys is the tea break at school. We usually skip across to a fellow classmate's place and often meet the servants coming home from their morning foray along the market streets. Not only do the cooks shop every day, one reckons accounts with them daily, at which time household problems and plans are discussed. The cook is the head man and in charge of the other servants. He takes his cut or "squeeze" from the groceries. This is normally ten percent of whatever is spent in addition to his salary. The table boy gets his squeeze from the milk purchases. One day last month our cook led the procession with a live goose in his arms, its feet trussed and beak firmly secured. The coolie followed, his arms laden with the day's provisions and a piece of meat on a string swinging beside his leg. Then, as Christmas approached, every household had a squawking gander tethered in its garden. Suddenly, silence. The Day was upon us.

It has been bitterly cold and, as I write, my feet are on a hot water bottle and I am wrapped in a blanket. The rain rarely falls nor does it snow. Consequently, even on the rawest day, we can stir up a little circulation with tennis if we start with several sweaters and gradually remove the layers. I watched Dr. Dryden Phelps, professor of Theology and English, playing today. He turned up in four different jackets, the top one of sealskin. These he peeled off as he warmed up, until I thought he was going to play "skinny." A servant picked up his things as he dropped them. He is a bit of a nut, although a mainstay of WCUU and the American Baptist Foreign Mission Society both in Christian education and in fund raising. We had dinner one evening at their lovely home (his wife Peggy is in Fine Arts) eating off "the Yale plates" inherited from his famous uncle, the former Lampson Professor of English Literature at Yale. Before leaving tennis completely, one of our more sophisticated Chinese professors turned up to play wearing a pair of striped flannelette pyjama bottoms. How could life be dull!

□ *JANUARY 15TH:* The last two weeks have been trying— language exams! In one way, my days absent took their toll, but in another I have finally licked the bug that has been plaguing me ever since we arrived. I feel as though I shall never be ill again! Things have slowed down a bit socially since New Year's, but even so we have had some good fun. The University has been hosting "The Christian General," Feng Yu-hsiang. In reality, he is a wily old hypocrite, changing his religion to suit the way the wind blows. Indeed, he is reputed to have baptised his entire army with a water hose, later distributing Bibles to every officer and man as compulsory reading. Such a chequered career: started life as a bandit, now lined up with the G'issimo, after working closely with Mao Tse-tung and spending some time in Russia. Although I could understand hardly a word, I went to hear him speak to the students. Talk about charisma! He held his audience in the palm of his hand, they laughed with him and they cried with him. He also spoke at our Church today.

We spent this evening with Olin and Esther Stockwell, American Methodists connected with the University. Mrs. S. is a gifted musician and he is a dear. All the people we particularly like were present and after a scrummy dinner and some music (Mrs. S. at the piano, John Stinson singing and Ralph playing his violin), we all joined the Agnews who were also having a party. Among others, Jimmy Yen was there. Known as "the famous Jimmy," he is a graduate of Yale and is in rural reconstruction, implementing basic adult literacy programs in the province. A tall rangy fellow, his face keen and clever (I would think some Mongol blood way back), he also has a lovely voice, and as the evening drew to a close, we sat around the Agnews' fireplace singing some of our favorite old hymns.

□ *JANUARY 17TH:* Because we are blockaded by the Japanese, we have to *chiang chiu* a lot. The words mean "make do" and I am beginning to feel that this and *chia bu do* (just about) and *chiang chia* (talking price or bartering) are the most used phrases in this part of the world. Speaking of which, have I told you about the *dongshi* men? In truth, they are sellers of junk, even by Chinese standards! A rascally crew, headquartered in the city's Thieves St., they visit our campus regularly, spreading their goods (*dongshi*) on faded, usually dirty cloths on the verandah outside the front door, where they wait patiently until noticed. Before I knew the language of *chiang chia,* these fellows saw me as an easy mark. But now I am becoming quite skilled at haggling. First, the wares are insulted and the seller's bona fides impugned, then one stamps off, to return reluctantly when the price is reduced just a little, to repeat the entire performance until a satisfactory figure is agreed. What fun! One never pays more than one-third the asked price, even when one finds an occasional treasure. Mr. Walmsley picked up a beautiful bronze of the Sung [Song] dynasty (960–1279 A.D.) the other day for fifteen local dollars.* And yesterday, I bought a lovely crackleware vase of exquisite line for only $2.50.

At school, we are each studying one particular aspect of Chinese culture. I am doing a paper on the founder of Taoism, Lao-Tse, and I find the research very interesting. Taoism may have degenerated through the centuries into a superstition-ridden religion, but Lao-Tse's original teachings seem very sound to me from a Christian point of view. Ralph is writing his essay on traditional Chinese medicine.

□ *JANUARY 19TH:* I had lunch at the Lindsays' today. He is dean of Dentistry. In fact he founded the Dental School, which

---

* Unless otherwise specified (i.e., American), all references in dollars are to Chinese currency (*yuan*).

is the only one in China. (They are in some way related to the Holt Renfrew clothing store people in Montreal, so have a little more cash than the rest of us.) Mrs. Lindsay grows orchids. (They have no children.) We started with fish, then went on to squab roasted under the omentum of a pig (very good), followed by salad, chocolate eclair and coffee. At teatime, I met a Mrs. Schroeder. She is a German Jewess, married to an apparently brilliant scientist who is also a medical doctor. They had to flee Nazi Germany, flee Shanghai, Nanking and Hankow. Now, their home in Luchow [Luzhou] has been bombed by Japanese planes returning from an unsuccessful mission against Chengtu. (Often, when the cloud cover protects us, other places get it in our stead.) She is a loquacious woman. At one point, Lewis Walmsley, who had not been sufficiently attentive to her monologue, bore the brunt of a terrific tirade against war in general and Hitler and Nazism in particular. Britain is her champion. She claims Jews the world over would come to Britain's aid if required. And that Jews never forget an injury or a favor! Her husband works for the Chinese government on bomb production, poison gases and such, about which she, of course, says very little. All very interesting.

After tea, we went over to the Walmsleys'. Ralph is their children's hero. When he plays his violin, they sit spellbound. Then to the Kilborns' for a late dinner, where we listened to the D'Oyly Carte Co. production of *Ruddigore* from London over the British Broadcasting Corporation's Overseas Service. Dr. K. said some very nice things to me about Ralph. Dr. Kilborn and Mrs. Walmsley are brother and sister, and Dr. Janet Kilborn is the sister of Dr. Robert McClure, perhaps the best known of all the Canadian Medical Missionaries. What a star-studded family!

□ *JANUARY 20TH:* This day is a very important one in the Buddhist calendar. The full moon celebrates the anniversary of Buddha's enlightenment. Consequently, it is set aside for the ordination of Buddhist acolytes. We had been invited, along with thirty high school youngsters from the Canadian School to witness this important ceremony at the Temple of *Wen Shu* (God of Wisdom) which hugs Chengtu's north wall. It was an experience that proved an education quite beyond our expectations!

Entering the Temple's main hall, one is confronted by a statue, known to foreigners as "The Laughing Buddha." He is one of the most important members in the Buddhist pantheon. To his right and left, temple gods who control the seasons and, on either side of the entrance, two particularly fierce creatures, Heng and Ha (marshals who lived at the time of the Chou dynasty at about 1000 B.C., deified for their prowess in war). Further on, a statue of *A-mi-t'o-fo,* the ruler of the Western Paradise and guide to Nirvana. Seated on a lotus flower throne, he has short curly hair, wonderfully exaggerated ear lobes and unusually long arms. For the masses, the importance of this god is his name. They believe the repetition of *"na-mo a-mi-t'o-fo"* has magic power, banishing darkness and fear and bringing understanding and light. In the Temple library, to which we were escorted as special guests of the Abbott, we saw many unusual and sacred treasures, the most revered of which is a beautiful pearl, representing the "remains" of the cremated Buddha.

The crowd of worshippers and guests, who included many visiting monks, some quite exotically attired, assembled for the ordination ceremony in the Hall of Meditation. In the center of this large low-ceilinged room, perhaps appropriately, stands a statue of the Goddess of Mercy, *Kwan Yin,* the goddess with a thousand arms. The excited murmur of the crowd anticipated the appearance of the novitiates. Then, the doors were thrown wide and 190 of them (of both sexes and ranging in age from old men to youngsters who didn't look more than ten) slowly filed in. Heads shaved, dressed in long black gowns, with stoles of orange and light brown caught at the right shoulder by clasps of special design, each was accompanied by two tutors (senior priests in saffron robes)—one to officiate and one to attend the candidate.

The third and final ceremony in their sleepless 72-hour initiation ritual had begun. The ordinands now took their places kneeling on circular cushions. Each shaved head had been marked with nine small circles drawn in black ink, on which the attendant priests stuck small cones of incense, held in place by vegetable glue. These they lit with tapers. And the smell of burning incense filled the air, adding an extradimensional quality to the background chants and drums. The acolytes, some with peeled oranges cupped in their hands, attempted to ignore the glowing cones, each silently repeating The Ten Precepts for a moral life under the supervision of his or her tutor. No cry or show of suffering is allowed. But we were within arm's length and could see the beads of sweat, the tightly clenched hands and sudden, involuntary shudders, all of which evidenced their considerable agony as the burning incense extinguished itself in human flesh! Incredible. The ashes were brushed away with feather dusters. The resultant scars, however, would be borne as badges of honor. (Each ordinand is obliged to shave his or her head every month with a straight razor, without the benefit of a mirror.)

□ *FEBRUARY 3RD:* On another religious front, we have just been to our first Mission General Council Meeting, where all fates (including ours) are decided for the coming year. Apart from a little back stabbing, the main controversy, which seemed to continue for days, was whether Rev. James Endicott would join the University staff or take over the Mission Middle School in Chungking. He has just finished six months service as special advisor to Madame Chiang Kai-shek. At one point during this hassle, Rev. Jesse Arnup, assistant secretary-general of the United Church Board of Foreign Missions and an old colleague of Ralph's father, stated that Missionaries are like manure. In a pile they raise an awful stink, but spread thin enough they do a lot of good! Naturally, Ralph and I were especially interested in the medical appointments. We are being sent to replace the Haywards in Kiating [Jiading], a lovely old city at the base of Mount Omei. At the confluence of the Min, Dadu and Quinyi Rivers, it is a busy trading center. More important, our Mission has a good hospital there and it is relatively near Chengtu. I can see it all now! The doctor's residence, I am told, is a good house with a lovely garden and a splendid view of the interesting river traffic.

After the meetings, a group of we younger ones went to the movies, which wonder of wonders, was something besides the usual "D" film, "The Three Musketeers." (American films are very popular here and attract enthusiastic audiences, despite the language barrier.) Then on to the New Asia "Coffee" Shop, for ersatz and *dianshin*, a sort of puffed rice stuck together with toffee. We rode home under a gorgeous sky. Perhaps I've picked up a few parasites or maybe it is just that we've had three Chinese meals in a row. In any event, I've been disturbing Ralph's sleep regularly, not to mention my own, with nightmares in which I am always chopped into pieces! I wonder what Freud would say?

☐ *FEBRUARY 16TH:* The great event in our household, of course, was the birth today of Donald Milne Campbell. Mil had a very rough time and since delivery has had pyelitis with terrific swinging temperatures. We were all typed for possible blood transfusions. I've been nursing her, my first such job in a Chinese hospital and an experience. It seems strange to be where one dare not put down a spoon unless on something that has been sterilized or to have to use such precautions with water. The regular nurses are of course Chinese and most of them darlings, quiet, quite efficient and very patient. Nothing hurries out here, so the rush of our home-side hospitals is absent.

☐ *FEBRUARY 18TH:* Tomorrow begins the Year of the Rabbit. I was at the hospital most of the day with Mil, but slipped out with Ralph and Mr. Walmsley to see if we could find some good buys on the street. Prices are down as all debts must be cleared before the New Year is ushered in. Gordon Campbell joined us. He is mad about opium pipes and bought four beauties, but at something less than bargain prices. This amused us for Gordon is a good Scot and normally very canny. My weakness is vases. Ralph bought a few pieces of jade. I've only seen one piece of jade so far that I'd like to possess, a bracelet of perfect translucency.

☐ *MARCH 1ST:* Mil is still in hospital, but gradually regaining strength. The Walmsleys had a party for the language school last night. For the record, I did us proud in my black velvet suit and beautiful diamond brooch and matching bracelet (presents from my dad and Ralph respectively). I put on a lot of rouge, curled my hair and did my nails. Even used my precious Chanel. Dr. Dan Dye, one of the most interesting characters out here, filled our evening with tales. He is an American, a member of the Smithsonian Institution and a regular contributor to its publications. An archeologist, a geologist, a mathematician, he is curator of the wcuu Museum. He is also the typical absent-minded professor about whom all the jokes could have been written, and a darling. He and his wife, Jane (an accomplished author in her own right), went to the Tibetan border country last year, where he became so fascinated with the ancient rock formations, he kept piling samples into his whaggan until his patient carriers "struck." He always talks in millions of years, but when he tried to explain the value of his finds in these terms, they thought him mad. A few years ago, he developed such a passion for Chinese lattice, he researched and published two books on the subject. He told us about the "armchair" graves, the culture of the Han dynasty (3rd Century B.C.), the earthquake lakes, a buried village he once found and about a piece of porcelain he discovered in volcanic loess that established the existence of certain trade routes into China thousands of years old. He even told us about the pestle and bowl method of grinding corn still used in remote areas. He is not in the least dry, but the mind boggles!

☐ *MARCH 15TH:* "God's protecting blanket," as one of our Indian doctors calls our cloud cover, lifted for two days and Spring is upon us. Endless fields ablaze with yellow rape, edged by purple bean. Masses of violets. Hedges of flowering almond. Exotic magnolia trees. Willows like thoughts taking form.

Peach trees in blossom. Roses everywhere. Even a few hyacinth. No tulips (they don't grow here for some reason). Our covering blanket returned, thank goodness, for sunshine also means air raids.

Mil is coming along slowly, poor kid. In the meantime, I am running the house with my limited Chinese. I attempted a birthday dinner for Emily Williams last night. What a flop! The chicken was neither tender nor properly cooked and three-quarters of an hour late. And after watching Ralph's efforts at carving the elusive "boid," Emily's husband, Harry the pathologist, took it upon himself to perform the necessary operation. Innumerable other things happened, only one of which had the benefit of being funny. The cook decorated the birthday cake a brilliant red (happy color). He copied the design from one of Mil's magazines, right down to the lettering in white icing, "Dodd's Kidney Pills." Ye Gawds!

Professor Leslie Cheng, one of the few practicing psychiatrists in China, took Ralph and a colleague to visit the Chengtu Insane Asylum. It occupies one half of a former Buddhist Temple outside the North Gate. (The other part is used as an orphanage.) Professor Cheng has neither responsibility nor authority there. It is run by the police, who receive $30 per month for support of each inmate, most of which the police superintendent's son takes as "squeeze." Ralph says he is sure the worst cases were removed from sight, but even at that the dungeon-like women's ward, a room half the size of our small bedroom, contained six inmates in a frightful condition of neglect. The men's ward was the same. When in excited states, these poor souls are chained to a post or tied double, their head and arms between their legs, and whipped to drive out the devils. There are only three modern asylums in all China. As to the orphans, Ralph saw a number down by the river breaking rock!

□ *MARCH 26TH:* These are cruel days. The Japanese air force is scientifically reducing each city they attack to utter ruin. We all wonder how soon we will get ours. The government has ordered that all city schools be moved to the countryside by the month end.

Mil has returned from hospital (plus wet nurse and wee Donnie). I've just done the baby's bed and it is adorable. I made the sheets, appliquéing a wee boy herding a flock of ducks across the top. Mil has to be very careful so we are all taking turns in the nursery. I had the fun of bathing Donnie under the danyang's and wet nurse's critical eyes. Then Mil and I escaped to join our riding club (bicycles). Later, at Church, we heard our Cambridge Anglican George Elliot, who attends Language school with us, hold forth. Recently, I asked him why he had entered the Mission field. He replied that when visiting Palestine, he discovered bed bugs would sooner commit suicide than bite him. I rather think he meant fleas. Apparently, while travelling by coastal steamer, he noticed one on his arm which instead of biting jumped overboard. Therein, his "call."

□ *APRIL 1ST:* We celebrated a successful day's shopping at Red Anderson's. She has access to foreign supplies and gave us a wonderful treat of ice cream with thick chocolate sauce. Two faculty members from Oberlin-in-China, a branch of Oberlin College, Ohio, were there as well. These men have refugeed with their students four times and are now taking up residence one hundred *li* (30 miles) from here. Incidentally, there are more good-looking men among the foreigners in China than one sees in a dozen moons at home. And these boys were knockouts! I almost neglected to mention that, despite the war, our streets are being flooded with Japanese merchandise. The white marquisette curtaining I purchased for our new home in Kiating is an example. Boldly stamped across the end of the bolt was, "Approved by the Japanese Government"!

□ *APRIL 7TH:* It is Good Friday and we have been out exploring on our bikes. Our first stop was a "dig" a mile downriver from the city, on an island called "The Stone Ox Dam." An old man recently presented himself at the government offices here claiming knowledge of the whereabouts of Chang Hsien-chung's great treasure. If untrue, he offered to "forfeit his head." The prospect of locating one thousand times one thousand pieces of silver resulted in fifty coolies being put to work and as the hole deepened, two foot-manipulated water wheels were set in place to keep their excavation dry. Weeks passed. Then a small quantity of silver was found. The day before yesterday, a stone ox about six feet long was brought up. Recalling the legend, all they have to do now is find the stone drum.

Another adventure took us to "The Opening of the Waters" at Kwanhsien [Guanxian], about 34 miles from Chengtu and 2,500 feet above sea level (thus, 800 feet above Chengtu). Each year in February the artificial channel of the Min River, which controls flooding and feeds the Chengtu Basin's intricate irrigation system, is dammed for a month or more, thus drying out the canals and ditches. This enables the entire network to be cleared of the past year's accumulation of silt, etc. Each farmer is responsible for cleaning that portion adjoining his field. This, however, is no longer "on pain of death," as it was in days gone by. When all work has been done to the Water Inspector's (Intendant of Circuit's) satisfaction, the dam may be broken, allowing the re-irrigation of the plain below. Thus, "The Opening of the Waters" ceremony.

In Kwanhsien's largest and most beautiful Temple, a sacrificial pig and goat lay before the image of Li-Ping. Buddhist priests, the Water Inspector, officials from the city of Chengtu and important visiting personages all took part in lauding the achievement of this great engineer, who, as I wrote earlier, had created the system some 2,000 years before. Various gods were implored, both to guarantee the supply of water throughout the year and to make the soil fertile. Then, the animals were carried down to be butchered and burned at altars on the river bank where thousands of spectators packed every space.

About noon, the official party arrived at an especially created riverside grandstand. A regiment of coolies stood ready. Bamboo tracking ropes had been attached to the base of one of the structures supporting the dam. More prayers were offered. Then the signal. The coolies picked up the ropes and with a great shout, tore the structure away. The tremendous pressure of the stored water did the rest. Much importance is laid upon the force of the water rushing into the system during the first few hours. In the old days, with the breaking of the dam, the Intendant of Circuit got into his whaggan and made for Chengtu as fast as his men could carry him. It was reckoned to be very unlucky for him if the waters reached the provincial capital before he did. Actually, it now takes about a week.

☐ *APRIL 23RD:* We have been having Chinese language exams again. While I have neither distinguished nor quite disgraced myself, Ralph has done awfully well. Fighting strep throat since our return from Kwanhsien, I've been lying low. Today, however, Ralph came dashing home to get me. There was an artist at the Canadian School who makes his living painting with his tongue. This is an art highly respected in China. Attended by two beautiful assistants, after some preparation, he emptied a shallow saucer of black ink into his mouth and began. I was just sick enough to find this revolting.

☐ *MAY 9TH:* Our amah came to me Thursday to say the gateman's week-old baby wasn't well. When I went out, I found the child trussed up like a small papoose (swaddling clothes are apparently the rule here), somewhat cyanosed (blue), no temperature but very feeble. Ralph's later examination confirmed umbilical infection. Inevitable. No dressings had been used after the cord was tied and the baby is never washed. My reaction is that no child in our responsibility is going to be treated like this, even if I have to care for it myself. But of course I can't. Ralph sent the baby to the WMS Hospital and asked Jean Millar who is, as I've mentioned, a very skilled pædiatrician, to do what she can. The gateman, however, doesn't want the child because she is a girl and will be quite happy if she dies. I find it all very depressing.

When our amah's little boy fell into the irrigation ditch the other day, our gateman pulled him out. Yesterday, I found her beside the stream with two lighted sticks of incense and an unbroken egg in her hand. She was offering thanks to the water god for sparing her child. One is constantly aware of one's ignorance in this strange and beautiful land. One simply doesn't understand the meaning or reason for half of what one sees. On the way home from Church on Easter Sunday, a month ago today, we were stoned by a crazed man. A nearby policeman just laughed.

C H A P T E R   2

Mount Omei / The First Test

□ *MAY 30TH, 1939:* About one hundred and thirty miles southwest of Chengtu, the Buddhist holy mountain, Omei Shan [Emei Shan], rises over ten thousand feet to its *Gin Din* or Golden Summit, so named because the ancient temple on this apex was once covered in gold leaf. There, caught in the mysteries and superstitions of his religion, a Buddhist devotee may behold a natural wonder known as the "Hall of the Patriarch" where, in the evening, when the cloud oceans gather below the summit edge, light is diffused and refracted in such a way that worshippers, staring down sometimes perceive their "second selves" in illuminated shadows. When this phenomenon of reflection (called "Buddha's Glory") appears at a distance, however, there are rare occasions when Buddha himself seems manifest. At such times, the devout prostrate themselves and those who sense a special call rise to leap into the arms of this illusion, dashing thousands of feet to the rocks below! Also, when the sun sinks westward and the night grows heavy on the cliffs, bright stars, called "Myriad Holy Lanterns," appear in the ravines to pay homage to Buddha. These, at least, we have seen. Obviously they are not stars, but no justification other than the religious is sought by the tens of thousands of Chinese who each year pilgrimage to Mount Omei, many taking weeks to make its ascent, some even crawling, as Moslems to Mecca.

Even without its mysteries, Omei is impressive, especially to those unused to the mountains of North America. To the Kilborns, for example, there is nothing more beautiful than the *Gin Din* and no grandeur in all the world to equal the Yangtse Gorges. But beauty is where the heart is, I think. And for the moment mine is here, in a summer cottage halfway up Mount Omei's verdant slopes. Indeed, I am writing this while a sou'wester roars outside. I hadn't realised how much I missed the wind and rain. The smoke has blown down the chimney and the dirt of ages has fallen through our tiled roof, but the air is filled with the wonderful sound of trees bending in the storm. I love it! I wish I could put on a pair of rubber boots, climb the cliffs and get soaked to the skin.

The mountain is a popular retreat for those escaping the intense heat of the Szechwan plains at this time of year. Many WCUU and Mission families lease land for cottages from one or other of the hundreds of Buddhist temples that dot Omei Shan's approaches. And our University has built facilities here for its summer programmes in Christian education. Consequently, when Japanese air raids necessitated the hasty removal of the Canadian School from Chengtu, this was a natural temporary location. The Mission Council Executive subsequently assigned Ralph and me as medical guardians to the children until they move to a more suitable location in September.

Our journey from Chengtu began ten days ago, after considerable preparation and a domestic crisis. As Mil and the baby were coming as well (with Gordon to join us in August), we simply arranged to move our household, servants and all. Consequently, we had to buy in enough staples to last three months. The cook took advantage of this unusual expenditure to increase his "take" (squeeze, as I've mentioned, is legitimate, but there is a sort of honor about the percentage). Mil, as the mistress of our household or boss lady (the *tai tai*), rather tactlessly chided him, instead of approaching this in the Oriental way by suggesting that if he bought elsewhere he might do better. The next morning, the rascal refused to go out on the street. He would cook but he would not buy. He felt badly about managing the *tai tai*'s affairs so poorly. Of course, none of the other servants dared to assume his responsibilities and we foreigners could not. There was no time to hire anyone else, so Mil practically had to beg him to continue and ended up "eating bitterness" (losing face).

For the purposes of transportation, all our provisions had to be divided into sixty-pound boxes or *shangzas*. Two *shangzas* constitute a load, one balanced at either end of a shoulder pole. We required twenty carriers just for supplies. In addition, Donnie Campbell's bed, a large box-like screened affair with drawers beneath and fitted with poles, had to be carried by two men. And Ruth Bannon, last November's bride and now a semi-invalid with Tb and a touch of pregnancy, came along carried on a chaise lounge with pots, pans, jugs and a breakfast tray hanging from its sides. What a procession as we made our way from the campus to the *dah mahtou* (wharf), about an hour's distance, where a junk awaited to take us nearly one hundred miles down the Min River.

We passed the time aboard playing bridge, reading or just watching the passing scene. For me, at least, those three and a half days had about them an air of fantasy. Every field was velvet-turfed. Every farmhouse picturesque. Each bridge straight out of the Middle Ages. And in the midday heat, even the poorest, most shiftless, smelly little village took on a dreamlike quality.

Finally, Kiating appeared on our horizon, its skyline defined by beautiful pagodas and the massive eighth century stone Buddha which towers 233 feet above the confluence of the three rivers (over two hundred people can sit on the feet of this wonder). Huge down-river junks and up-river rafts crowded the base of the red sandstone steps which provide access to the city above. As sufficient carriers were not immediately available to take us up the mountain, we had to impose upon the hospitality of our Mission until the situation straightened itself out.

Then the crunch! By this time, I was feeling exhausted and dizzy, and on the way up the steep steps to the Haywards' house, I fainted, then fainted several times more. The diagnosis is mitral stenosis. Although Ralph says I'll be better after a month's rest, it is nevertheless a shock to have one's heart go flooey. I feel so helpless. Part of it is apparently anæmia, for which I am to take powdered iron filings! I had had three weeks of nausea following my strep throat and then had developed a blood infection which left me covered with infectious emboli.

After a few days in bed, I was well enough to set off with our party for Mount Omei. We had now been joined by the Stinsons. For myself, I've never enjoyed travel so much. We women all rode in whaggans. This is a canvas seat slung between bamboo poles like a sort of swing, with another piece of bamboo suspended for one's feet and carried by two men. A canvas or cloth awning covers both passenger and carriers. Three men were assigned to me, rotating as they tired. I just leaned back like some medieval queen, as did Mil, Ruth and Isabelle Stinson, the latter nearly eight months pregnant. Ralph and John Stinson walked. Mil, looking very cute in her sailor pants and large straw hat, assumed the role of wagon master.

At village stops, our carriers refreshed themselves by sloshing down huge bowls of tea, re-fueling on enormous piles of rice, then relaxing with a smoke. I'd heard it said that almost without exception these men use opium. If ours did, I didn't notice and its sweet fetidity is hard to miss. Besides, they were beautifully muscled, powerfully lean and carried well.

As one travels, one cannot help but wonder why the Chinese have not long since been exterminated by the various parasitic and fly-borne diseases prevalent here. One answer is the popular belief that cold water is inhabited by the spirits responsible for pain and disease. In consequence, even in summer, tea is practically their only drink, and hardly anything is ever eaten that is not piping hot. (Many things we in the West have discovered only in relatively recent years, the Chinese have known for thousands!)

About 6 P.M., we reached Omeihsien, a thriving town at the base of the mountain and a famous seat of Buddhist culture, where, in a dirty little tea shop with a mud floor, mangy dogs, hungry chickens and goodness knows what else wandering around, we sat down to a dinner of fried chicken, potatoes and onions, topped off with cookies, stewed kumquats and tea.

□ *JUNE 4TH:* I am disturbed by talk that we won't be assigned to Kiating after all. Instead, we may have to accompany the Canadian School when it leaves Mount Omei in September for some frightful hole of a place called Jenshow [Renshow]. It's unfair to Ralph. The hospital there is closed. Thus, no equipment, no back up, no grants for poor patients, in fact no medical work. What a waste! Unfortunately, politics are not unknown in the Mission field. As for me, I was rather looking forward to seeing what I could do with the Haywards' house.

Our Chinese lessons have begun again and go on for five straight hours! When the weekend comes and that torture is over for a couple of days, you can imagine how we feel. Nevertheless, we are studying hard. I've just finished reading the third chapter of John's Gospel in the *Wen yen* (classical Chinese), struggling over those d--- characters. We went to Harry and Emily Williams for tea. (I still have to be carried everywhere.) Their cottage has a magnificent view: on one side, the plain as far as the eye can see, with the Min river curling across it like a silver ribbon and, on the other, the rich colored slopes of our mysterious mountain.

Dr. Luke Hsiao, a physician in private practice in Chengtu, brought his family up for the summer—charming people. (Our community is not exclusively foreign.) After settling them in, he started back intending to make the entire trip by rickshaw so he could do a spot of work en route. He was rolling along, deep in a book, when suddenly he found himself looking down the barrel of a big old-fashioned revolver. At the other end, a dirty-looking ruffian, accompanied by two equally nasty characters with long knives. They took his money, medicine, watch and all his clothes. Apparently, he begged so eloquently for his pants that they finally acquiesced. They then tied the doctor and his coolie to a tree. Fortunately, this little-frequented road produced a truck within minutes. The national treasures salvaged from the Japanese Rape of Nanking [Nanjing] and Peking [Beijing] are being secreted in our mountain's Temples. Hence his rescue.

☐ *JUNE 11TH:* A most beautiful day. I am writing this on the verandah. We have the nicest cottage on the mountain, but the most unrevealing as to view. My teacher was telling me that Mount Omei is thought particularly attractive because it is shaped exactly like a woman's eyebrow. He also told me there is a much-revered old monk at one of the Temples here who never moves from his sitting position and has been so long a complete parasite, his every need attended by his brother monks, that his muscles and sinews have become fixed and his fingernails grown to such length (one over six feet) that they are now encased in bamboo. For a fee, his nail covers will be slid gently upwards to verify their contents. To Buddhists, however, he is no mere curiosity. They believe his immobility has channeled all his energies into thought, making him especially wise and holy. Consequently, his counsel is often sought and highly prized.

Our cottage is roomy, with large open verandahs, a cozy dining room with a fireplace (the one that smokes) and a study, which serves as Ralph's examining room. There is a good kitchen and pantry, separate servants' quarters and three large upstairs bedrooms. Although the place is otherwise well furnished, we sleep on Chinese *zongbengzi* or rope-strung frames covered with *pukais* for mattresses, then made up as we would beds at home. I swear by the end of the summer I shall be like Bloody Mary, the English Queen who said that when she died, one would find "Calais" written on her heart. Well I'll have "rope," but elswhere printed! For baths, a round uncomfortably shallow, black lacquered wooden tub. We pay $7.50 a season for drinking water, which is delivered fresh each morning from a nearby spring. We think it the biggest treat on the mountain, for the wells in Chengtu get pretty awful and smelly. Barrels of rain water serve our other needs. We use wood for cooking and only use charcoal when ironing clothes. (If you have ever been in a Chinese laundry at home, you may have noticed that their flat irons look like small brass pots. Well, they are designed to hold pieces of burning charcoal to provide their heat.) We eat anything that presents itself. At the moment, two hens are clucking away under the verandah. Wild flowers abound: yucca, orange lilies, purple and white orchids and my two favorites, gardenias and hydrangeas.

Omei is a very social place, where people visit a lot. And some of the discussions are quite interesting, in fact disturbing, as the situation worsens both here and in Europe. The viewpoints of our Missionary colleagues run the gamut. The Endicotts are social revolutionaries. The Willmotts, theoretical communists. The Walmsleys, ardent imperialists. The Bannons, anti-British Eire-ites. Of one thing there is no question, the news on all fronts is just too appalling! Tallie says that there will be another Boxer-type rebellion here if the anti-foreign feeling continues to rise. Personally, I as yet know too little about China to speculate. But I do feel that Britain is honeycombed with rotten, capitalist pro-appeasers, something I have been upset by ever since her short-sighted policy during the Spanish Civil War!

Speaking of the Endicotts, they have been through a rather bad time in Chungking. Jim, who served in the last war, says the Japanese bombing is the most horrible thing he has ever experienced. Chungking is literally going underground, digging huge caves for shelter. Jim believes that Chengtu is next on the list of major targets.

☐ *JUNE 14TH:* Today we received a letter from Gordon Campbell confirming the accuracy of Rev. Endicott's prediction. Japanese incendiary bombs have demolished the heart of Chengtu. People in the streets were killed by the hundreds, a government hospital destroyed and frightful damage inflicted on the business area. Fires raged for twenty-four hours among the little grass and bamboo shacks where the poor live. Gordon says that no one had a chance to leave before the bombing started because for some reason the air raid alarms were not sounded. Five bombs hit the wcuu campus. The Japanese may have been specifically interested in destroying the radio tower about one hundred yards from our home, although I doubt it. No other bombs were dropped anywhere near a "military target." Besides it is so camouflaged with branches that it looks like some nightmare vision. One bomb landed amid a group of students at the river's edge, killing and wounding I don't know how many. Another blew out all the windows and doors at the unfinished medical complex, the machine shop, the Canadian School and nearby residences (Mrs. Liljestrand was wounded by the flying glass). Our house is apparently full of soot and fallen plaster. Across campus, one house was completely flattened. Nearby, a dwelling constructed of woven bamboo mats plastered with whitewashed mud was blown to bits and one of the girls living there, whom we knew and liked, was killed outright. Two other girls are in poor condition in hospital with shrapnel wounds to the head. A bomb fell beside the library but did not detonate. Had it exploded . . . ! Because the University Hospital, the Eye, Ear, Nose and Throat Clinic, the Mission Men's and wms hospitals were full to overflowing, an emergency campus hospital was established in the Administration Building. Gordon says the situation was horrible, children piled on heaps of straw bleeding to death and a constant stream of wounded coming in. The campus dispensary was closed and the need for morphia critical. (Why, I ask, couldn't they have broken down the door?) When Gord wrote, the full extent of casualties and losses was unknown. It is almost certain now that we will be refugeeing in Jenshow with the Canadian School children.

☐ *JUNE 18TH:* Our first anniversary party last evening was fun. We ate, played bridge (using a precious coal-oil lamp for light) and listened to records on the orthophonic. The place was decorated with ferns and Chinese temple lanterns of black wood and red silk. We gals put on long dresses and, treat of treats, opened a can of precious tomato soup to add to the chicken broth. We served cold chicken, duck and lots of other goodies. The weather, however, did not co-operate. A small typhoon blew up in late afternoon and those who did make it, arrived wet and disheveled and left early.

Ralph maintains I've changed quite a bit in this first year of marriage, but I think it's just wishful thinking on his part. He says I am far more tolerant of Missionaries and understanding and sympathetic toward their work. This is true, although I still have no time for the narrow, rigid ones. The important thing is that we are very happy together. Ralph is so much like my dad. He is lazy about the business matters of our life until I am nearly driven to distraction. Then he dives in and, in no time flat, clears up the mess. He just couldn't care less about material things. He believes the body needs food for energy, clothes to keep warm and will sleep at least once a day no matter where. This is not exactly my idea of living. About everything else, however, he is long-sighted, clever and, heigh-ho, long suffering. Guess it's love!

As I write, a pitiful little fellow, with a very bad hump on his left side (scoliosis), has just limped up the steep path. In his hand, a bunch of wild flowers for me. Standing on one foot, then the other, he shyly asks Ralph to cure him. Simple as that! The mountain people think Ralph is wonderful, for he has opened a free clinic for them and to date has had 100 per cent success. The habitable portions of Omei Shan are populated by the families of tenant farmers (who also lease their land from the Temples), but of a different type and dialect from those on the plain. They look almost Mongol, so probably are descendant from the original Szechwanese, for surely even the mad Chang could not have eliminated all these rugged people. The women are like those one sees in the fields of Japan, happy little beasts of burden. Or perhaps more appropriately, like O-Lan in Pearl Buck's *The Good Earth*.

□ *JULY 3RD:* Well, I am back in bed. I was tearing around too much and my heart has been kicking up again. And, it seems I am pregnant! The great event will take place February next, barring accidents. Yesterday, letters arrived from home. One included a clipping from the Toronto *Globe and Mail* reporting the bombing of Chengtu. Inaccurate, but the point is that they knew about it before we did! In the meantime, while my family are cruising the Alaskan fiords on my father's boat, the *Full Moon*, here I sit dying to be with them. I'm home-sick. Ralph thinks I would be better off with my parents, at least until I feel better and get over this mitral stenosis, but I cannot leave him. Things here are too dicey. I have contented myself by writing my mum for some satin ribbons for my hair, one peach, one red, one blue and one a surprise. I do hate not having pretty, feminine things.

About a week ago, Ralph found a level walk for the "crocks" (myself and Ruth Bannon) to enjoy that takes us out to a point which commands a magnificent view of the plain. There, we sit hour upon hour plotting the progress of blue clad farmers working among the fast-growing corn planted in every available niche on the mountainside or watching the browsing of a couple of very red cows. Errh Omei (Little Omei) rounds to a near summit, its gorges and valleys catching the shadows and mists and, thither and yon, blue smoke curls heavenward from charcoal kilns. We feel quite safe from bandits at the moment, for the Generalissimo and Madame Chiang are reported to be taking a short break at one of the local Temples. Consequently, there are soldiers on duty hereabouts, guarding roads, paths, etc.

I don't think I have made it at all clear that we are sharing our cottage with Mil, wee Donnie and Ruth Bannon. Thus, when we heard Ruth's mother was coming to stay for a while, we weren't exactly thrilled. Mrs. Sparling, however, is proving quite fun. A teacher at WCUU, where her husband, Dr. George Sparling, is president of the College of Religion, she couples the wisdom of experience with an outlook as young as her daughter's. And now Ruth's aunt is visiting with us as well. An itinerating Missionary gal and very interesting. She too is full of *joie de vivre* and, I suspect, a goddess to the poor devils among whom she works, the coal miners near Junghsien [Rongxian]. There, men are employed on twelve-hour shifts day and night, crawling on their hands and knees through small tunnels to dig and drag out the ore. Though they are paid well enough by local standards, after a few years they can no longer stand upright. As well, we are expecting Ruth's husband, Peter, a poetic Irishman, with a Ph.D. in English, who adores bridge. When Gordon arrives, which will be shortly, the house will be filled to overflowing.

We had a good party at the Williams' the other night. I was allowed to go by litter, and what a hoot. The Wilfords were there. Dr. Ted, second only to Dr. Kilborn in the College of Medicine, imagines himself irresistible to women. As we are all quite aware of this, we tease him along, much to the annoyance of his rather "battleship" wife, Claudia. Actually, I love her dearly, much more so than I do her charmer of a husband. Awfully good luck at the bridge table, where Harry Williams, who hates to lose, went down to ignominious defeat. As we wended our way homeward, Ralph and I couldn't stop laughing.

☐ *JULY 13TH:* I've been feeling so much better these past two weeks and am coming along so well with the translation of St. John's Gospel that I can now read all of it in *Wen yen*. I am also understanding the dialect of the downriver people. One of my dear old teachers, realizing my frustration with the language when I was ill, said comfortingly, "It is quite alright to go slowly, even better than going fast, but one must never stop."

We got weighed today. The Wilfords have a scale. 156 lbs. for Ralph and 135 for me. This is such an improvement, I was allowed to go swimming. No diving, but what fun swooshing down the kids' slide. There is a natural pool in one of the mountain streams which, with a little improvement, now serves the entire community. Although, I must say it has been rather diverting being an observer for a change. Sitting on the sidelines at the tennis court, for example, I overhear many interesting conversations. Claudia Wilford was sitting beside Johnny Gow the other day. Poor Johnny had a bad appendix operated on by Dr. Hsiao. Hsiao is a bit of a quack. Now, Johnny, previously one of our best tennis players, is hobbling around with a cane, a shadow of his former self. Claudia, of course, is noted for her avid interest in her husband's and everyone else's cases. She diagnoses them all. Indeed, Dr. Wilford refers to her in fun as "my colleague." Under her questioning, Johnny confessed that Dr. Hsiao was now giving him very expensive shots brought all the way from Germany (the Chinese are nuts about injections). "Not really medicine you know Mrs. Wilford, these co-ordinate my metabolic system and reduce the red blood cells." Claudia nodded sagely, "Yes, Johnny, a very good treatment." Also very funny, if one knows a bit about medicine.

The Fundamentalist women, so strict and narrow with their long hair, no make-up and dowdy dresses, don't know me yet and, as I sit and listen, we Canadian Mission people are the butt of their remarks. Cards are a sin, as is practically everything else, particularly the girls in tennis shorts, etc., etc. I feel sorry for them. None have any formal education. Husband and wife have to put in seven years each before furlough. "God will provide," they receive no salary and are sent to small isolated Stations to preach Hell-fire and Damnation. But I believe some of them very fine. One, who I think I would like very much, has the face of an angel. Another, whom we met the other evening, has been out three years with the interdenominational, evangelical China Inland Mission, and their course in Chinese is so tough, she has already translated the entire Bible!

□ *JULY 16TH:* I went to Church alone this morning because Ralph was looking after a threatening appendix. A friend of ours, Clarence Vichert, was taking the Service. The Vicherts are great people. Connie is a Vancouver girl and Clarence is from Spokane. She is very smart and always immaculate. Clarence looks like a non-dissolute, younger version of Bing Crosby (I think they went to the same school at one time). And they have three adorable boys. Anyway, Clarence, who is a scholarly sort of person, instead of a Sermon gave us a discourse on the religions of the world, warning that Christianity must not become the religion of a particular social order, because if that class structure fell away, Christianity would as well. It was a drowsy sort of day and I wasn't following too closely when, suddenly, an old girl (one of the Hellfire and Damnationers) got up. With her Bible clasped in one hand, her other clenched and shaking, she strode up to Clarence, turned, and told us what she thought of these new-fangled ideas and heresies. She then strode out declaring that she would never darken the doors of our Church again! Exciting, if embarrassing. I felt sorry for her, thinking it must have taken a lot of courage, but later learned she does this all the time!

I had to stop writing when the Canadian School kids came in. They have their discussion groups on Sunday evenings after Church, then drop over with any problems. They also plan and officiate at their own Church Services. Ralph gave the talk tonight, by invitation. They sing their favorite hymns and there is always something special in the way of music. Ralph often plays his violin and, one evening, a quartet sang Negro Spirituals out in the open air, which made them all the lovelier. The approach to religion shared by so many of our friends is such a good one. Nothing formal, just the working principles of Christ's teachings, presented in such a way as to make them all desirable and beautiful. There is such a wonderful lack of smugness, intolerance and hypocrisy. None pretends to be better than he or she is and all are so human!

□ *JULY 20TH:* We have become quite friendly with the Schroeders, the German scientist and his Jewish wife whom I mentioned meeting in Chengtu. She is small, dark, vivacious, passionately everything and very pro-British, with an explanation for all idiosyncracies of British foreign policy, including the Palestine business. He is a quiet, gentle man who, among other things, is interested in old Chinese documents. In one, he found that China had discovered America a thousand years before Columbus, landing in Ecuador. Long before coming to China, Dr. Schroeder was fascinated by Chinese ideographs. As a result, when he arrived, he could not only read and write modern Mandarin, but could manage the ancient grass writing as well.

His translations of old medical books have convinced him there is a fortune awaiting anyone who investigates traditional Chinese cures. For example, in ancient times, the Chinese treated Tb with the yolks of embryo eggs, something that at present is being tried out in the States. It is a question of isolating the active principles of the remedies and treatments known to be effective. Ralph and Dr. Schroeder are becoming such good friends, they hope to work together experimenting with some of his findings. Dr. Edwin Meuser, Dean of Pharmacy at wcuu (and the person who created one of the University's most successful and useful departments) has pioneered in this field and is, of course, responsible for the world getting ephedrine.

□ *JULY 26TH:* Mil received a paper from home describing the visit of King George and Queen Elizabeth to Canada, which was full of pictures of various members of the Royal Family. The Duchesses of Kent and Gloucester wore particularly smart hats I thought. When I showed these to our teacher, Old Yü, he pointed to the Duchess of Gloucester and said, "That woman is pregnant, isn't she?" "Why do you say that?" I asked. "Because she is wearing a veil on her hat. In China, if a woman wears a veil, she is pregnant." When this story circulates, I think there will be a marked reduction in the use of veils among our unmarried Missionary women! (Incidentally, I went to see Dr. Gladys Cunningham yesterday, and she clinched Ralph's diagnosis that, veil or no, I am pregnant.) Old Yü thought that Queen Elizabeth's hat was just like that of the Lolo Tribesmen!

Actually, the other day we met a Missionary from the Lolo country, where opium is the chief crop and the inhabitants are very wealthy. He was telling me that when the poppy is in seed, the coolies cut the side of the pod with an odd-shaped knife that leaves three small scratches through which a thick viscous fluid (raw opium) oozes. This is done six times at one- or two-day intervals before the opium is collected for export. That smoked here I think is mixed with mud or clay.

Our only experience with opium-related problems, however,

occured the night before last when our cook burst in on us after we had gone to bed, an act unheard of except in great emergency. He was in a state of such excitement it took us a few minutes before we understood that in one of the nearby farmhouses, a woman was now in a deep sleep, having swallowed opium following a lovers' quarrel. Ralph, after grumbling into a shirt and pair of shorts, raced off to help. No apomorphine in the house, no stomach tube, but at least he had some potassium permanganate and the cook took along a good supply of mustard (both emetics but not so effective as apomorphine). An hour or so later, I heard Ralph rummaging around for an enema kit. He had been all over the hill searching for apomorphine and a stomach tube but without success. In the meantime, he had left the girl to be walked by various of her curious neighbors. Indeed, all the farm families from near and far, even the children, had come to witness this drama. Those who couldn't get into her hut clustered around the door listening, as every move within was loudly reported by those with ringside seats. Ralph had forced the woman to drink bowl after bowl of mustard and water. In this, her neighbors helped by making swallowing sounds. And when she was supposed to vomit, all and sundry made retching noises. If it hadn't been so tragic, Ralph said it would have been very funny. Finally, when she became distended and still unable to vomit, Ralph realized the opium had paralysed her stomach muscles. Hence his frantic search for a tube of one kind or other. About two-thirty in the morning, I heard the cook and Ralph laughing as they came up the path. Of course, they returned laden with fleas which will plague our house for days. This afternoon, a shy Chinese girl appeared at our back door with a gift of ripe corn—the heroine of this tale.

☐ *JULY 30TH:* We have been having a feast of music. The Endicotts have some lovely phonograph records with them, but their machine is broken. Ours isn't, but we don't have much in the way of recordings. Last night, we sat outside listening to Mozart (I love the third movement of his 39th Symphony). Also Brahms' Symphony No. 1 and Handel's Sonata No. 4 in D Major, which contains a violin solo Ralph is studying. I have rather got to like the Endicotts. Jim is handsome and a bit of a flirt. Although he has always made a big fuss over me, I was never really taken with him until now because of his condescending attitude towards Ralph. This all changed when Colin, their house guest, the young son of Ho Beh-hen (one of the wealthiest men in China) contracted encephalitis. His condition was so serious that Ralph, who was himself sick and confined to bed, was carried down to their cottage by litter where he had to perform lumbar punctures and so on, staying beside the lad's bed until he was out of danger. It amuses me now no end to observe the awe in Jim's regard for Ralph (as opposed to treating him like the local nitwit). I have also learned to enjoy Mary, a self-conscious intellectual (the kind I usually avoid like the plague) with a rapier wit and a waspish tongue. I will miss them when they return to Chungking.

□ *AUGUST 8TH:* Our fame is growing. We are besieged by those wanting cholera shots and, for some reason, Mil and I are being approached to act as midwives. A rather ghastly Taoist superstition connected with motherhood is that if a woman dies in labor before her child is born, her soul is condemned to a lake of blood in the deepest pit of hell. There she stays, until a certain Temple gong is struck, each modulation of which moves the trapped soul an inch towards the side of the lake. As her relatives must pay and pay to extricate her from this torment, the most horrible methods are used to forcibly deliver the baby before a mother breathes her last. It doesn't take much imagination to realize the terror of women facing confinement in this country, where there are such high maternal and infant mortality rates. There is much that is beautiful in this ancient culture, but not its superstition and necromancy. Christianity at least helps rid people of these fears. At the same time, one is conscious of how far Christianity has strayed from Christ's original teachings. At least, I see it that way.

□ *AUGUST 19TH:* Ralph spent the morning tearing all over the mountain getting stuff ready for the Canadian School's swimming meet this afternoon. About 1 P.M., after a Chinese meal at home, I went upstairs for my siesta. I had just turned my face determinedly into the pillow when I heard the low roar of airplanes and the sound of heavy machine guns. Then the house shook with the fall of a not-too-distant bomb. In a flash, I was into the nearest piece of clothing and outside under a tree. Some three dozen Japanese bombers, high, high up, circled in the distance. They were firing at the beautiful Douglas passenger plane due in today at Chungking from Hong Kong. Later, people further up the mountain said it was thrilling to watch the Douglas, like some hunted bird dip, bank and dodge, as it flew over the "Gin Din" as though seeking to land. What we saw was dramatic enough for our household, in that we expect Gordon Campbell is aboard. He had taken advantage of an offer from Col. Schultz, the Curtiss Aviation man in Chengtu, to fly out a baby panda Schultz is sending to St. Louis as a gift. Gordon was thrilled to bits to have his return fare paid to Hong Kong, where he could do a little shopping for Mil (and practically everyone else). It's turned into a real adventure for him, first dodging Japanese bombs in Chungking and now this. Fortunately, the Douglas escaped.

But when Ralph and I went over to our outlook, which commands a distant view of Kiating, our hearts sank. A dark mist hung over the city, and what seemed a definite column of black smoke was rising, casting a pall over the white and fleecy clouds. We were also astounded. Kiating has a population of but sixty thousand and is of no strategic or military importance whatsoever. The strain proved a bit too much for me and I was ordered back to bed. In the meantime, Ralph went to find Dr. Hayward who is here on holiday.

Later, by the swimming pool, Ruth Hayward told me how much she and her husband had appreciated Ralph's offer to help. All the foreigners from Kiating are here at the moment but, as of yet, not one seems inclined to go to the aid of the people they are supposed to be serving (and converting), which is shocking! Although, to be fair, the Mission Hospital has two Western-trained Chinese doctors on duty and there are three or four others in private practice in the city. After the swimming meet, which went on as scheduled and was a great success, Ralph left to see if he couldn't organize an emergency medical team.

It was nine o'clock when he returned home and asked me to get some sandwiches ready, while he collected all the drugs, dressings, etc., he could find. Then he was off with another Canadian doctor, Irwin Hilliard, two Missionaries, Leonard Bacon and a Mr. Brininstol, and two whaggans full of supplies. Dark as pitch, the day already lost and Ralph no doubt completely fagged before even starting, they planned to walk all night. Ralph didn't take a mosquito net, they have no cook and Kiating at the moment is infested with malaria, cholera, encephalitis, meningitis, infantile paralysis, amœbic dysentry (which is deadly) and, of course, typhus. Tonight the city is a red glow. Incendiary bombs! Runners report the entire business center wiped out, our Mission Church destroyed, but our Hospital intact. The American Baptist Mission escaped, as did the refugeeing Wuhan University.

☐ *AUGUST 22ND:* Ralph returned late last night, haggard and thin, his facial skin drawn so tightly his head seems skull-like. He was almost too tired to be coherent, yet insisted on recounting his experience. With the blazing city before them in the distance they walked all Saturday night. Nearing Kiating about 7 A.M. after ten hours on the road, they encountered crowds still hurrying to safety with their bundles of personal belongings. Inside the town, people were digging through the smoldering ruins. Well over one-third of the city had been completely levelled. Charred bodies everywhere. Suddenly, someone started the cry (false as it turned out) that the Japanese planes were returning. Everyone began to run, the less agile literally trampled to death as the crowd, driven by sheer animal terror, desperately sought escape. Ralph and his three companions took refuge behind a crumbling wall. And as they watched in shocked horror, the full significance of *war* began to sink in.

The Mission Hospital was a frightful mess. The injured, many of whom had been dragged from under collapsed houses, had been dumped in the halls and there they lay on the shutters, doors or boards upon which they had been carried. All of the medical personnel who were supposed to be on duty were asleep in their respective quarters, apparently quite unable to cope and unwilling to try. The two doctors finally responded to the admonishments of our boys and came to work for a few hours. The nurses refused. Consequently, there was no one to clean up the patients, no one to arrange temporary beds, no one to tend to the million and one things that crop up in such emergencies. And of course, there was no sign of the physicians in private practice. The dispensary was locked. Ralph kicked in the door. An emergency station was set up for minor burns, fractures, shrapnel wounds, finger amputations, etc., where the two Chinese residents worked indifferently until they quit for the day at 3 P.M. Ralph and Irwin operated all day and late into the night (our two non-medical Missionaries gave anæsthetics). It was nearly midnight when relief arrived in the form of Jim Endicott and a Red Cross In China team from Chungking, consisting of two surgeons, an OR nurse and a dresser, all experienced in this kind of routine.

At daybreak, when our group was ready to leave, they couldn't find their carriers, who, as it turned out, had been pressed into service by the military to help carry the more than two thousand charred corpses to a mass grave beyond the city gates. Finally, this too was sorted out and they were able to leave for home.

☐ *AUGUST 28TH:* We have had a lot of fun this past week. Dinner at the Phelps', but first a swimming party. I was allowed to walk all the way. I still am exhausted at night, but every day less so. I've packed up my study books, having decided to devote myself to some general reading (in English) for a change. Ralph having joined me in this, we are having a great time. And yesterday I played a set of tennis, went to Harry's for lunch, walked to the swimming pool, then played bridge all evening. Gord the Scot, back from his panda adventure, is an astute bridge player, but Mil and I cleaned up on him and Ralph, which was a thrill. Thursday, on the BBC broadcast from London which gives the week's political events in review, it was reported that Hitler and Stalin signed a Non-Aggression Pact on August 23rd, and we have been pondering its significance relative to British as well as Japanese policy. It must improve China's position, but how we would like to get hold of some newspapers!

I have finally managed to over-rule one of Ralph's decisions (victory No. 1 in the history of our marriage). He is very much against my going back to Chengtu without him, but I want to have my teeth examined and a throat culture taken. I will be travelling with Mil and Gordon by boat (pulled against the current by coolie trackers). Five hours by automobile, ten days by junk! Fortunately, we have lots to read. Somehow, I'll get to Jenshow when I'm done. Ralph, in the meantime, will go overland with our trunks and other possessions.

☐ *SEPTEMBER 11TH:* We left the mountain early August 31st, travelling by whaggan. After a night at the Haywards' who, thank goodness, were sufficiently organized to feed and house us, we were lucky enough to find a good junk with a captain and crew who were not opium smokers. The trip up river was itself a fascination, dragged by our trackers through rapids, around difficult turns, through country that was truly as gorgeous as my hazy recollection of it. In the evenings, when we pulled up at some filthy little village, the men would go off to smoke and talk, returning about ten to start their fire, eat, then sleep till dawn. Occasionally, fights broke out, which were pursued with great vehemence, much spitting and earthy cursing beyond belief. Just for fun I picked up a few phrases. Our last day out, when we were being served a meal of stewed black-boned rooster (a great delicacy), we passed a beggar's corpse caught in the rocks of one of the rapids, his flesh black and falling from his bones. Ugh!

We arrived in Chengtu the evening of September 9th. Because of an air raid alarm, no rickshaws were available. So we walked the three miles to campus. The news awaiting us was not good. War had been declared in Europe more than a week before. Then I heard we were not welcome in Jenshow, that there was no place for us to live, that the Veals, the Missionaries with whom we were to lodge, were so disappointed we were not theologues coming to help them with their pastoral duties that they refused to have us! I was just too tired to take all this and decided I could not and would not take China any longer. I wept the whole night through. I was fed up with everything, even with Mil and Gord. What tipped the balance was the prospect of having to spend a year bunked in with some very uncongenial old maids and a bunch of school boys! My first visit after breakfast was to Helen Lousley to ask her to make reservations home for me when she made her own.

Helen proved the best kind of friend and got Dr. Gladys on the job. She examined me (I am due February 18th), asked some questions about things in general, then began to raise such smoke that the Mission Council Executive assigned us our own suite of rooms in the Veals' house (with our own kitchen, dinette and, what is more, a decent bed). So now the Mission has to supply the money for our freight! Three cheers for that piece of dynamite, Gladys!

□ *SEPTEMBER 12TH:* Ralph had given me $300.00 (American) to spend on furnishings, but I spent it all yesterday. Today, I bearded our ogre of a Mission Treasurer, Mr. Hibbard, reputed to be very grim and very tight. Lamblike, he lent me another $400.00. My purchases included two upholstered chesterfield chairs, a lovely *lan mu* (Chinese hardwood) kidney table, chiffonier and bed table, brass andirons, chrome framed mirror (just right over the dressing table) and a beautiful Tibetan rug (our nicest to date). I also bought a chaise lounge, chair and smart end table, all in split bamboo and a pair of old-fashioned flat-irons with detachable handles, the kind one heats on the stove. Most important, and after a desperate search, I found an amah to care for us. A healthy fifty-year-old woman who knows "queer foreign ways."

□ *SEPTEMBER 29TH:* The trip to Jenshow, about seventy miles due south of Chengtu, was largely uneventful except for a near accident when the mast of our junk caught in a tree while we were negotiating some rapids. I confess I found it odd to see the faces of our Chinese crew go ashen with fear. This, however, was the only exciting moment during eleven long hours on board. About 4 P.M. we landed to begin the second stage of our journey. I was in a party of parents escorting their youngsters back to the Canadian School for the Fall term. Twelve *li* (4 miles) inland, we put up for the night at a fairly decent inn. Of course, we carried mosquito nets and cots (which we cover with oil sheets to discourage bed bugs) as part of our normal baggage. Early next morning, we were off by whaggan, travelling hard in the rain. It was hill country, ancient and mysterious, the high cliffs above the road studded with little stone Buddhas. Because my carriers were opium smokers and shaky, I walked the last portion of the way and fell a bit behind. When the rest were no longer in sight, I was once again overcome with despair. And as I walked, I cried. Then I became aware of a figure sitting, waiting, by the side of the road. It was Ralph.

C H A P T E R   3

Jenshow / Job's Lot

□ *SEPTEMBER 29TH, 1939 (CONT'D):* Jenshow (pronounced Renshow) is a sleepy little town of about five thousand, a
few hundred houses strung along a narrow, colorless crease in
the beautiful dark-red hills. And although the children hail us as
"foreign dogs" and worse, their elders seem friendly enough.
More important, we are off the air route to Chengtu.

Within the walls of the Mission, the Canadian School (consisting of seventy-five students and staff) occupies the two grey
brick former hospital buildings and related residences which
have lain empty these last few years. Ralph and I have been assigned a commodious sitting room and a very small sleeping
porch on the second floor of Rev. Veals' house. Fortunately, our
abode has been recently calcimined and is relatively clean.
Really not bad for refugee quarters. As I mentioned, we have
been promised a dinette and kitchen of our own. The Walmsleys are attempting to get this stretched to include a small
bathroom, as one bath a week is all that the Veals allow (and

this a pail of hot water in the bottom of a tin tub). But I'm from Missouri, so I'll believe it when I see it.

I'll never forget my first meeting with our hostess, Edna Veals. A wisp of a woman with faded blond hair, she has a green face. Yes, green! Apparently she has been applying garlic poultices to it to relieve the effects of lacquer poisoning, which is extremely itchy. Hence the color. For a trained nurse, she has some very weird ideas. What is more, she and her husband are exceedingly frugal and, as we are obliged to board with them, my great trouble is getting enough to eat. And what slops they serve! Ever tasted boiled green dates without sugar? That kind of stuff. They are Oxford Groupers (inspired by American evangelist, Frank Buchman, who last year launched an expanded movement called Moral Rearmament) and always holier than thou. Mind you, I had decided in advance not to like these people.

□ *OCTOBER 8TH:* We live from day to day here. If we do not fear the coming of the Japanese planes for ourselves, for we are safe in this village, we fear them for what the fall of China may mean. Since the Declaration of War in Europe, we listen to radio broadcasts from London, Berlin and Hong Kong. Of course the news is censored and all we actually hear is propaganda. However, in conversation with various of the foreigners who abound in China (political scientists, newspaper men, etc.), it appears a distinct possibility that the British Empire will be annihilated. Consequently, happiness at the moment is of the moment and perhaps all the more delicious because of it. (I had to stop typing to catch a flea.) At home, my mum and dad are facing the departure of my two brothers into military service, facing as well perhaps some crisis that will knock annuities and bonds off the map and destroy their security. Thank God, Ralph still feels his job is here. I sound hysterical, but I am feeling tops, if a bit lumpy. We even seem to be getting along with the Veals, despite the food. I laugh when I think of my brother's remonstrance in a recent letter to exclude rich things from my diet. We live mostly on rice and native vegetables. But it seems to be agreeing with me.

☐ *OCTOBER 14TH:* I am quite busy. I start studying Chinese at eight-thirty each morning, then perform my household duties, have lunch, an hour's siesta, study 'til four, then help Ralph at the clinic (today typhoid injections). The other day, I gave my first anæsthetic in China to one of the students. And when one of Ralph's many local patients sent us what he modestly described as "two old hens and some very poor tight skinned oranges," we had the Wamsleys in for dinner. The hens proved young and succulent and the oranges juicy and delicious!

There are difficulties living in such a close community. Even Ralph, the unrufflable, shows signs when over-exposed. I'm glad I don't get on his nerves. I used to think he was a bit unhuman: he goes strong and silent if I blow up. Afterwards, when I've seen the light, he teases me about my rotten disposition. I fell running yesterday, so have scraped hands and knees. Fortunately, the baby ("Skeezix" for now) survived. Probably have a snub-nose!

The hill directly behind our house provides an excellent view of the surrounding countryside. The paddy fields now flooded lie like silver sheets. Everywhere, the crops of sweet potatoes and squash have been harvested and the dark red of the newly plowed soil contrasts against the rich green foliage of the ancient trees. The silhouettes are spectacular, reminding me in a strange sort of way of Wyoming.

☐ *OCTOBER 18TH:* We are now more or less settled and making plans for the things we still need. For drapes, we've bought local handwoven cotton of a natural lovely beige, a special "sport" for which the area is famous. This is being worked in a cross-stitch of indigo dyed thread. The pillows for our rattan chaise lounge and chair will be of the same material and also embroidered. These will calm the barbaric appearance of our Tibetan rugs. I am dyeing the skirt of my dressing table with a local tea to achieve a similar shade and may also have cross-stitch put on that. We are planning a carved "cloud lattice" fire-screen and are designing our own book cases to fit beside the small fireplace.

We have received a letter from John Stinson in Tzeliutsing [Ziliujing] bemoaning the frequency of air raid alarms and how he and Isabelle spend most of each night under the kitchen table. Their compound has been peppered with bombs, with extensive damage to the medical buildings. He estimates that bombs landed within twenty feet of every foreigner and no casualties. Sounds incredible to me, make it a hundred feet and it's still too close. He begged Ralph to give him a little encouragement and the two of them would enlist. We laughed at John's idea of comparative peace and quiet! Besides all this, the poor kids had their blankets stolen, a great loss out here. How one's perspective changes!

☐ *OCTOBER 24TH:* We are trying out a new language teacher, or at least I am. Chiang is a clever young lad, well educated (a Middle School graduate) and the son of one of the local Christian pastors. We heard of him through Mr. Veals. Because he has epilepsy and is hard to handle during his seizures, however, he is considered a family disgrace, a *fengdze* (possessed of devils), and when at home has been literally imprisoned in an attic room, fed through a slot in the door, etc. Ralph managed to get in to see him, found his affliction relatively mild and has been giving him a grain of Luminal every day to keep his condition under control. The trouble is, this drug is very expensive here, so I have asked my dad to send some from home. When Chiang entered our sitting room this morning for my Chinese lesson, his face was alight and he was oh so clean. His English pronunciation isn't good, but this will improve. I know he will try very hard and be very patient. Ralph says I am letting my heart run away with my head.

☐ *OCTOBER 28TH:* It would be difficult for anyone at home to realize how cut off we are from the world. Ours is the only radio here and when the battery wears down, we have to send it a two-day trip by carrier to Chengtu, wait a couple of weeks for it to be re-charged, then have it returned. Expensive!

The surrounding countryside is becoming a cotton belt. Apparently, the main cotton growing area of China is in the hands of the Japanese. Consequently, the price of cotton has skyrocketed and the farmers of the inner provinces are attempting to make up the shortfall. Sweet potatoes, rice and *tung yui* (tung oil) are also important to the local economy, as are experimental fruit orchards and salt wells. The entire district, however, is bitterly poor withal and it appears we may be facing a drought. The Jenshow area doesn't benefit from the irrigation system that supplies water to the Chengtu plain.

I love the *tung yui* trees. Very tailored in appearance (about the size of a scrub maple), they have twisted elephant-skin-like trunks, their bright scarlet and green foliage hiding nuts (somewhat larger than walnuts) from which a valuable oil is obtained. We are told that, in the spring, they are covered with beautiful large white blossoms of gardenia texture, slightly tinged with pink. The nuts are harvested in November, their oil extracted by a primitive type of press, the required pressure obtained through a series of wedges. (The crushed shells and pulp are used as fertilizer—everything in China is recycled.) Tung oil is used for lacquers, waterproof varnishes, paint, for waterproofing cloth and paper and, of course, we burn it in our lamps.

☐ *NOVEMBER 4TH:* Prices are soaring. The cheapest oil we can buy for lamps or cooking is now $1.00 a gin (approx. one lb.). It was $.15 until recently. Coal-oil is not only a great luxury, but a rarity. (Our artificial light problem is solved by retiring early.) Everything else costs more as well, but I've been able nevertheless to do something about our colossal board bill. A rather dicey procedure actually, telling our "hosts" they were overcharging us. I volunteered to help manage the place and suggested we pool expenses. The Veals, to my surprise, agreed. Unfortunately, our cook, a very temperamental fellow, is always either walking out on us or fighting with the other servants. In all, they are a poor lot. I do wish we could get along without them.

□ *NOVEMBER 8TH:* Work has been started upon our small suite. I call it the "wart" because it is to be tacked on to the corner of the existing structure between the up and downstairs verandahs. When complete, however, it will give us a ground-floor kitchen and a tiny dining area large enough to hold a table and four chairs. This is in addition to our second-floor sleeping porch and large living room. And surprise, surprise, we are to have a reasonably large bathroom which will boast a black wooden tub, a toilet, also black lacquered, a cupboard and a long table for changing the baby. The two levels are to be joined by narrow stairs which will have three turns.

□ *NOVEMBER 19TH:* The Veals are away, tra la, tra la! I had a dinner party last night for eighteen of the women I have met here. Ralph, of course, skipped. Among my guests, Pearl Chiang and her staff from the local girls' school. Pearl is a peach and speaks English beautifully. Her sister, Martha, a complete "rip," so we had lots of fun. My favorites, however, were the Gin Ling Women's College girls (the female portion of Nanking University) who are refugeeing nearby. They are organizing reconstruction work in this district. Dr. Irma Highbaugh (Ph.D., D.D. and goodness knows what else) is their "boss man." One of their projects about which I feel strongly is preserving the beautiful old cross-stitch designs and needlework skills of the Jenshow district. Dozens of women are working for them, adapting their old blue-thread patterns to modern use and at the same time learning how to read and write. The children, who accompany their mothers to the college, are taught games. I love going over to practice my Chinese on these little kids. The Gin Ling faculty also provide a midwife service and a clinic three times a week for minor complaints. (Ralph is the only doctor around.)

The Gin Ling nurse gave me a small green fruit (looks like an apple) that she says is used instead of santonin for round worms. I asked Mr. Chiang about this. He said it works but has to be taken before the 15th of the month when the worms are pointed upwards! (Now that Mr. Chiang is officially a teacher and paid as such by the Mission, his rank demands formal address.) She also gave me a remedy for toothaches. First, the bark of a particular shrub (she gave me a sprig) is brewed. Then, meat is added. The resultant broth is supposed to cool the blood and stop the pain. As to whether she believes this actually works, I cannot say. In any case, like Dr. Schroeder, we are taking notes. On a more "scientific" level, we recently did two cauterizations of the cervix with a nail heated over an oil lamp.

Today our cow started an awful moo-ing! She was tied outside my window. Finally, I went downstairs and tackled the coolie to find out what was wrong. As my Chinese seemed inadequate to the task, I called in one of the Canadian school teachers. Unfortunately, her dialect is Northern. It took the combined language skills of six foreigners before we understood that the cow is in heat! Now what do we do?

☐ *DECEMBER 10TH:* I must tell you about Chen *shien shen* (Mr. Chen), another of our language teachers. He had fallen in love with a girl in Tzeliutsing, but his mother would not allow the match. Arranging marriages in this country is the prerogative of the parents not the children and she wanted a local daughter-in-law to help on the farm. No entreaty would move her. I had been worrying about this affair of his heart and almost robbed our wee savings of $100 to further the path of true love! However, family reverence is very strong in Szechwan, so Mother had her way. We went to his wedding today.

Despite arriving half an hour late on principle (nothing here ever starts at the appointed hour), we were the first of the guests. At the Minister's house (the Chens are Christians), we met the respective mothers-in-law and the *kai shou jen* (the official go-between or match-maker). The bride's mother, in a satin jacket and black trousers, her tiny bound feet in beautifully embroidered shoes, was as neat as a pin and obviously enjoying herself hugely. She sort of smoothed her clothes lovingly in a way that reminded me of a couple of elderly women I know at home. His mother was not particularly well dressed, but had an interesting, intelligent face and was obviously very much in charge. We presented our gifts of money to the groom with appropriate compliments and retreated to the Church, which proved a *lao rei* (noisy) place with kids everywhere, running, gawking and giggling. Country folk in town for market day jostled for vantage points, as much to stare at us as at the bride and groom. It is the custom here for the groom to escort his bride down the aisle, but as the old reed organ began to play "Here Comes The Bride," I saw Chen stop, feel his pocket and disappear. After a short delay, I assume to locate the ring, the music began again. Then in fussed Pastor Gin, cute as ever, his face a mass of anxiety. The mothers-in-law and the *kai shou jen* sat facing their guests on a slightly raised dais. The first item of business was the National Anthem, during which I nearly disgraced myself by laughing at Pastor Gin's pantomime as he tried to get one of the old ladies in the congregation to stand. He looked as though he were warding off a swarm of bees. Ralph particularly enjoyed the announcer, who, standing where one normally reads the lesson, gave this otherwise "foreign-style" wedding a very Chinese flavor with his play-by-play description of the ceremony. He had great round glasses over which he peered when about to read, a wee red nose, a plumpish face and a very grand fedora. I thought him adorable. The Service was followed by some polite and definitely impolite speeches by friends and relatives. Then all retired to the feast. We declined as it meant staying the rest of the day. Ralph, as "doc," can always get us away gracefully. Our servants thought us quite insane. Miss the ceremony, of course, but the feast, never!

☐ *DECEMBER 23RD:* Four nights ago, a Nanking University student (their agriculture department is here as well) was brought in with a history of acute abdominal pain over the previous twenty-two hours. The signs were classical and the diagnosis simple: a ruptured duodenal ulcer. But life was slipping away. Even in a modern hospital after 15 to 20 hours, his chances would be only 50:50. As the school was about to go on Christmas break, Ralph decided to operate here. The kids, of course, were very keen. The boys helped Ralph clear a couple of classrooms, one for surgery and the other for recovery. The girls and I prepared the gauze packs and dressings which we sterilized by baking them in the school oven. Surgery started at 7 P.M. Dr. Wilford, who had driven the Mission truck down from Chengtu to pick up the kids, assisted Ralph. Rev. Veals poured the anæsthetic. I was circulating nurse. Rev. Bridgeman, visiting from Junghsien, held the lamp.

If you can visualize a small bare room, the patient laid out on a kitchen table, an inexperienced man giving anæsthetic, the only light a Coleman held at a safe distance from the inflammable ether, Ralph's precious instruments (a gift from my dad) spread on a desk top, the dressings charred by a too-thorough sterilization, the doors and windows pressed high with curious humanity both white and yellow. It was good fun. Ralph is a gentle surgeon, but Dr. Wilford belongs to the "mop and plow" school and I shuddered to think of the poor lad's post-operative pain. Our intravenous was the trickiest bit of business for we had to improvise to make the distilled water and had only ordinary salt to add. But miracle of miracles, there was no adverse reaction. I've given him daytime care, Ralph has slept beside him every night and everyone here has been very very kind. Lewis Walmsley brings in a beautiful new scroll to hang at the foot of his bed every day (a Chinese custom). Of course, Ralph is now *din hao* on the street and has been deluged with patients, hare lips, crossed eyes, the entire bit!

The following day, the dental clinic from Chengtu arrived to take care of our various needs. It is strange sitting in one of these portable dental chairs, the slow drill operated by a foot pedal. Gordon Campbell and Harry Williams (who came along for the ride) stayed with us. We played bridge every spare moment, something we don't often get a chance to do. Indeed, when we first arrived, I was told cards were forbidden!

And today I am rich! Four letters from home, one particularly precious from my brother Fred. At tea-time, much to

Howard Veals' delight, Ralph quoted some of his cryptic comments on life in general and me in particular. When Rev. Veals forgets he's a pastor or *mousi* (we always say "mouse") and becomes a human being, he can be utterly delightful. In such close quarters the idiosyncracies of the various ill-assorted foreigners get on one's nerves a bit. Life seems a constant struggle to keep above the pettinesses and smallnesses of jangling personalities, and we seem to be succeeding, due in large measure to Ralph! I should also mention that at the last of our weekly open houses for the Canadian School, which provide occasion to teach the children some home-side courtesies, the woman hater among our boys told Ralph, "Boy, you sure got a bargain—your wife is swell."

☐ *CHRISTMAS DAY:* When the school children went off for their holidays, we moved in with the Walmsleys for a break of our own, which has made ours a real Christmas. On the Eve, their children ready for bed, we sat around the tree while Constance read, "The Night Before Christmas." Later, we listened to carols over the radio and violin music on the gramophone. We filled stockings and did all the things to prepare for Christmas 1939. Today, as I watched and listened to the youngsters, memories of Christmases long past flooded my mind.

☐ *JANUARY 6TH 1940:* The New Year got off to a bit of a hectic start when Ralph decided we had to open up our patient to drain a huge secondary abscess that had formed in his abdomen. Of course, we had no drainage tube. Ordinary rubber stuff had to be softened. It took me all morning to prepare our makeshift OR. We began with a local anæsthetic, but ran into so many adhesions, Rev. Veals had to come down to administer ether. Miss Haddock, the Canadian School Matron, circulated and I assisted. We started at 2 and finished at 4 P.M., so you can imagine the difficulties, not to mention the mess. However, there was no post-op discomfort, appetite returned quickly and yesterday he was finally well enough to leave us.

The culture of this place is so rich. I wish you could see the beautiful blue cross-stitch work on the cotton cuffs on our amah's gown. She is too old to do anything so fine now, but every girl here learns this at her mother's knee. And as a young woman prepares for marriage, she makes a valance for her marriage bed of rough hand-loomed cotton embroidered with these meaningful designs. Speaking about our amah, she wears glasses, a misnomer actually for the lenses are made of quartz and are worn for medicinal reasons. They could hardly improve sight!

☐ *JANUARY 14TH:* No sooner had the children arrived back than Miss Haddock had a sudden rise in blood pressure which resulted in a ruptured aneurism and cerebral hæmorrhage! Ralph immediately took off 300 cc's of blood. I am so proud of him—he seems to be able to cope with just about anything. He was with her night and day, until a nurse finally arrived from Chengtu. The aneurism, however, is still leaking and we are very worried about "Miss Headache," as Ralph affectionately calls her. When the Mission in Chengtu sends down the station wagon for Miss H., we will return with her, as I am getting near my due date and have no intention of having my baby here.

☐ *JANUARY 28TH:* We came up to the Chengtu last Thursday. We were properly "sunged" (bid farewell) the day before by the Canadian School kids at a formal tea where the boys in Scout uniforms served and were unusually shy. Jean Millar and Tallie Tallman had come down with the Mission wagon: Jean to relieve Ralph (you will remember she is a pædiatrician) and Tallie, my friend the Superintendent of Nurses at the WMS Hospital, to accompany us back. Fairly late the afternoon before our departure, Ralph met a Chinese lad on the street to whom he had given worm medicine the previous day following a 4-plus ascaris (round worm) smear. He was feeling "worse." When Ralph brought him back to the school, he found a "red hot" appendix which demanded an immediate operation. Jean thought the appendix had perforated, Ralph believed it gangrenous (he was right). Because there was no room at the

school, they "vegetablized" him with sedatives and put him in
Rev. Veals' study for the night. The following morning, we took
him with us to Chengtu.

It was quite a trip. The station wagon is comfortable and
sturdy, one of those one sees transporting dogs at the hunt in
Country Life. Miss Haddock was on a stretcher in the rear of the
wagon. Ralph sat on my overnight case using his back as a brace
to keep her steady. Tallie, who is a small woman, perched beside our other patient. I was in the front with our White Russian
driver and the Chinese nurse who has been caring for Miss H.
Thank goodness for perfect weather. Miss Haddock became
violently carsick, as did her nurse. Tallie couldn't breathe, as she
has a rotten cold and clouds of dust drifted over those in back.
The countryside has been so dry and parched this year, there is
great fear of famine. Our Chinese patient just stared glassily
ahead. Given his performance at the wheel, Vallasheen, our
driver, was obviously feeling weary of life. The dirtiest, ugliest
looking man I have ever seen, he had spent a sleepless night in
the cold car. The Chinese inn where he was quartered had been
too foul even for him. From time to time, we had to get out and
put planks (every motor vehicle carries an assortment of emergency equipment) across the creaky bridges for safety. One had
disappeared entirely forcing us to ford at rather a bad spot. Negotiating the hill on the other side of this stream was particularly
tricky. The grade was about 45 degrees, with a switch-back so
sharp that those of us able had to place stones under the tires to
keep the car from rolling back as Vallasheen maneuvered it foot
by agonizing foot. Of course, given my condition, I had to take
every opportunity to pop behind large rocks. On one such occasion, I encountered a Chinese gentleman of our acquaintance
who was travelling by whaggan to Chengtu, but in this part of
the world one doesn't experience the mortification one would at
home. The countryside was lovely withal and I, at least, enjoyed
the trip thoroughly.

Eventually we reached the Min river and as we neared
Chengtu, I realized how many things we had missed in Jenshow:
the screeching wheelbarrows, the gay streets, the different look

of the farm people, the neat fields of yellow rape and purple bean, the flatness of the plain and its innumerable irrigation ditches. Shortly after passing the Thunder God Temple, swinging wide to pass a rickshaw, we landed in a ditch well concealed with drying cabbage leaves! We had to hike the rest of the way to campus, arriving about four-thirty, where our friends and colleagues rallied round as though we were visiting potentates.

We are staying with the Cunninghams, Drs. Ed and Gladys. They have a fairly modern house, low ceilings, nice big fireplaces, large windows overlooking their garden, right next to the Men's Hospital. It is a total luxury for one hailing from Jenshow. Lots of nice hot baths, comfy bed and electric lights. What joy! I've been feeling absolutely super. Yesterday, Gladys gave me a thorough check-up. She says that if she did not know my history, she would never suspect last summer's heart lesion. I have about two weeks to go.

☐ *FEBRUARY 6TH:* There was a meeting of the Mission Executive last evening to "officially" change our station from Kiating to Jenshow, where we are to remain for another year. In some ways I'm disappointed, but in others we do know some nice people and have a secure supply of milk. In addition, a Chinese doctor and nurse are being sent to relieve Ralph of outside cases so that he can get on with some serious language study. Next year, we are to go to Tzeliutsing, the salt center of China, where the Mission has a large hospital. They appear to want Ralph because of his tact, which they feel essential given certain complications in the administration there. My fear is that his work will be entirely administrative and I don't approve of that. Our experience to date, however, has taught me not to get too excited.

It has been quite a social round. Had lunch with Mil today. She has some new dishes that make her table very smart. She has been servantless this last wee while. Her greasy old cook is now one of the leaders of the anti-foreign agitation here. Gordon is running the household messages, as the gateman has gone as well. Mil is doing the cooking, a tough job, involving refining of one's own sugar and salt, not to mention buying the food. And to add to life's complications, her wet-nurse is going dry. She has had Edgar Snow as a house guest and says that regardless of what other people say, he's a wash-out. He talks with a cigarette hanging out of his mouth and gives all the gals that "come up and see me some time" look. On a pleasanter note, the Madame and G'issimo were recently in Chengtu to get some dental work done. Gordon Campbell worked on Madame Chiang and "Hash" Mullett on the G'issimo. Mil says that Madame C. is charming, makes one feel like an old friend, has a beautiful simple hairdo, cleverly applied make-up and is always gorgeously gowned.

Later, we went to a lecture by Dr. Eugene Chen, a South China man, on the history of eye treatment in China. He has done a couple of corneal grafts and Dr. Ed thinks very highly of him. Tea at the Smalls', where I met Lily Hockin, a Missionary just returned from Canada. I was dressed up like a Christmas tree, lots of lipstick, nail polish, perfume and my best clothes. I didn't make a very good impression. Mil and I left early to watch Donald being put to bed. He is adorable. Small, fair, red cheeked, always dirty, tears all over the place and with a smile for everyone. That night Mil and Gord had the Bannons, the Williams and Dorothy Fox in for bridge. Dorothy is a Toronto General Hospital nurse who somehow got here without going through "The Angel Factory" (the Deaconess Training School in Toronto). Consequently, she is regarded by some as suspect. I was in wonderful form and Harry Williams, the bridge fiend, my partner. The devil possessed me and I found myself doing things just to see the blood vessels bulging on Harry's forehead. You know, raising his one diamond bid to five, just like that! We came out ahead, but Harry had a bad time of it.

The streets are filled with excitement. Tomorrow is Chinese New Year's, the beginning of the local holiday season when everything closes for a couple of weeks. Over the past year, Chengtu has become so sophisticated with the flood of down-river refugees that even I am aware there is less observance of the old customs than during our first New Year here. The kiddies, however, remain awe-struck and pop-eyed as they contemplate the special joys of the brilliant paper and bamboo toys for sale everywhere. Horses, boats, kites, lanterns and noisemakers, all fearful and wonderful to the little ones. And many of their elders appear to find it difficult to attend to business. The varnish-like smell of Chinese wine wafts through the byways, its tell-tale coloring on the passing faces. The atmosphere is much like Christmas Eve at home. I found myself saying, "*gung shi*" (Happy New Year), even to merchants who had roguishly bettered me.

However, I am not sure there isn't more anti-foreign feeling around this year. The night before last, I walked out to meet Ralph and somehow missed him in the crowd. And because of a rickshaw strike, I had to walk back. Naturally, I was awfully tired, and as I waddled along, a bit frightened to find myself the target of children with firecrackers! Also, I think I may have been called "child of a goat" on a number of occasions which, you will admit, is not very complimentary, however irresistible the pun (although "foreign" and "goat" are distinct characters, each is pronounced "*yang*" and in the same tone).

Speaking of language difficulties, one night very late, a man came to the house to ask Dr. Ed's help. His "*Niu dze*" was having great difficulty in giving birth. Dr. Ed explained that obstetrics was not his specialty. Consequently, Dr. Gladys followed this farmer to his house, where instead of his suffering wife, she found a cow that had retained its placenta. I can only imagine what she said to Dr. Ed on her return! The words for "cow" and "woman" sound similar to a Western ear. Despite these confusions, there are many beautiful expressions in Chinese. For example, the two forms of "thank you": to acknowledge a gift, "*do hsieh*," and when someone has done you a kindness, "*fei hsin*" (you have expended your heart) which I just love. To tell a person not to worry, "*fang hsin*" (lay down your heart).

☐ *FEBRUARY 18TH:* Another Sunday and here I am sitting up typing and feeling great. But what a week! Last Monday, Dr.

Gladys decided were I not in labor by the following evening, she would give me castor oil to help things along. The question was whether this would be more effective mixed with orange juice or brandy. I opted for orange juice, not wanting my taste for cognac eternally spoiled. Tuesday, after a day of preparation, washing woolens, hair, etc., we went to a party at *Shin Hongdze*, the WMS Hospital residence, in honor of Tallie who is returning home on furlough. Dr. Gladys had been making me diet, but I said, "*swanlo*" (to heck with that), and tucked into everything in sight—jellied consommé, roast pigeon, chocolate sundae, the whole bit! Then at 10 P.M., my castor oil. Miss Wellwood, a hardy old Woman's Missionary Society gal, came up with a glass of good port to take away the after-taste and we left the party in high form. Ralph, Gladys, Ed and I joined arms as we picked our way over the rough roads, singing all the crazy old songs we could remember. By the time we got home, I was oh so sick. (I've since told Ralph there's a plot to put me off alcohol for life.) My contractions, however, started before midnight. First thing Wednesday, we experienced an air raid. Everyone was very busy as the Hospitals and Churches were crowded with wounded. Dr. Gladys didn't think I would deliver until Friday, but I was determined to have my baby that very day (Valentine's), so I kept taking quinine. By late afternoon, I knew something must happen and, about 8 P.M., I went to the WMS Hospital by rickshaw. They tell me our little girl was born just before midnight.

I will spare you the details, but I think those were the worst moments in this previously carefree life of mine. Its amusing aspects I will share. Miss Sawyer, Bostonian warhorse of the nursing game and recent refugee from "God's Country" Honan to this wild, uncultured, untutored and unloved Szechwan, gave me the anæsthetic. She is good, knows it and tells everyone else how rotten they are. Then in the middle of things, Japanese bombs knocked out the power station. Ralph dashed off to find a flashlight. And thus did Miss Outerbridge enter the world. After the delivery, with explosions all around, I was taken to a bed in the basement. Thank goodness the baby was beside me, for

the place is infested with rats! Of course, I was too excited and
thrilled to sleep. You should see her. At first I thought the contrary, but she's quite lovely, her mouth a rosebud, her hair a wee
bit curly, her nose a button. But darn it, she is awfully like me! I
wanted her to look like my husband or my father, but I got
"me"! The next few hours, I lay in heaven. Such bliss. No pain.
No tummy! Not even the exploring rats chewing through my
overnight case bothered me. The next morning, with Miss
Sawyer in command, I was bundled onto a stretcher and along
the crowded streets to the Jolliffes' home on campus, where I
am to complete my confinement. Curious faces poked into mine
as we filed along, but it was all an adventure ending in the peace
of a quiet room, a lovely grate fire and a comfortable bed. On
the table against the wall is a large white pottery vase holding a
branch of gnarled *tie jou hai tung hua*, flowering quince (translated, "the iron-footed flowering tree"). Sweet peas, yellow
roses and lilies surround me.

Just to be silly, we canvassed the community for a Christian
name for our baby, sending out a *chwan dan* (round robin letter). This called forth a riot of suggestions, serious and otherwise, including Zenobia, Ralphetta and Tugluck. All the time I
wanted "Judith." Finally, I realized she was meant to be
Dorothy Judith. Her Chinese name will be "Yuin Fuh" (Ever-
lasting Happiness), the nearest I can get to "Happiness All
Round," my dad's honorary Tsimpsean Indian name.

□ *MARCH 10TH:* Time passed all too quickly in Chengtu.
Ralph left the 25th of February for Jenshow to resume his duties
and to get our house set up before Judith and I arrived. Dr.
Gladys bullied the Mission officials into allowing the station
wagon to take me home, but when we had a spot of rain, the
men, anxious to back out of their commitment, declared the
roads too dangerous. This meant I'd have to go overland by
chair, a two- or three-day journey staying at filthy inns! Then a
runner arrived with news that Bruce Dickinson, who attends the
Canadian School, had had an emergency appendectomy and
needed his mother. Mrs. Dick decided to go down by car and

offered me a ride. At this point, my amah, who had come up to join us just before Judith's birth, told me she would not be returning. I was upset until I realized it was all a bluff for more money. This is an unheard of thing for a "green" servant, but the Chinese are great gamblers. However, because the tremendous inflation has meant hardship for everyone, I gave her a small raise and she came along quite happily. As it turned out, we were only able to travel half way by car. Thereafter, we used rickshaws. The only time Judith cried was when we stopped at a teahouse and I had to change her. Men, women and children crowded around (very politely), timidly touching her clothes and remarking on how nicely foreigners keep their babies. She was very hungry, but I didn't want to nurse her in front of these strangers. Everyone was very concerned and considered me cruel, even our rickshaw men. When at long last, we sighted the familiar banyan trees and the old pagodas on the hilltop, we expected to find Ralph to greet us and kids on bicycles to escort us (a Canadian School custom). But when no one appeared, I was sure the Dickinson boy had taken a turn for the worse. In fact Bruce was doing beautifully. The runner from Chengtu with the message confirming our departure had yet to arrive. (He did, poor fellow, moments later.)

□ *MARCH 23RD:* Ralph organized a surprise party to celebrate my birthday this week. The high school kids had a tea in my honor (and Judith's), complete with cake, flowers and little presents. Later, the adults assembled at the Veals' for dinner. Howard even wore his tuxedo! I wore my dark-rose velvet hostess gown and silver slippers. In the midst of the festivities, Alice Jenner and Mrs. Bridgeman arrived from Junghsien (two days overland). Alice has been ill on and off for the last two years and had been in bed the last month, so was completely done in. Notwithstanding, she donned a lovely blue chiffon dress and joined the party. Ralph and I had donated coffee, canned asparagus, cocoa, candles and, biggest luxury of all, cheese to give the party a truly Western flavor. And Ralph gave me an "heirloom piece," an exquisite banquet cloth which he himself designed, using many of the beautiful lacy phoenix cross-stitch patterns about which I've written. It had taken many women months to complete. In all, a lovely day!

I am feeling a lot better, liver shots and a change in iron tonic. What is more, the "wart" is finished. Our wee dinette has a bamboo ceiling, white walls, a light varnished floor and large windows now framed in patterned red cotton curtains (because there is a beautiful red pomegranate bush just outside). I designed the sideboard, necessarily shallow with open fretwork and drawers below. It is all unobtrusive yet very gay. The garden and far hills are so beautiful, we take turns sitting where we can see them best! The bathroom is upstairs over the kitchen and is the nicest in Jenshow (and I think as nice as any in Chengtu if it hangs together). Must close for now. I have a date with Ralph. We often wander up the hill behind our house to lie on its jasmine-flowered slope and stare at the stars and moon. If we are early enough, Ralph reads to me. Tonight, we will just talk.

□ *APRIL 14TH:* Judy's two month birthday. She smiles, laughs, plays and enjoys every person who comes her way. I had been having a difficult time nursing until one morning at breakfast, the danyang set before me the most evil smelling broth one could imagine (dried fresh water shrimp, rice wine and sugar). "Please drink the soup, it will make your milk come," she said. It tasted as it smelled, but I downed it. Embarrassingly, I simply spouted!

We attend the local Chinese Church, which is very good for our language skills (as well as our souls). The old custom of separating the sexes by a wall has been done away with, but with the exception of ourselves, the women still sit on the right and men on the left. The congregation is a great mixture of students, farmers, merchants, women from the fields and so on. Easter Sunday was very amusing. (I feel just as sacrilegious as I sound, but even dour Rev. Veals laughed when he got home.) First, Pastor Gin insisted the choir come up the two aisles, girls on the right, boys on the left, with Pastors Gin and Chiu leading the way. This was too much for poor, shy Pastor Chiu. He was so overcome with embarrassment that upon reaching the chancel, he leaned his head against a pillar and, to our horror, proceeded to be sick to his stomach. Then, there were the Damon and Pythias of the street merchants, a great tall, button-nosed, bespectacled, fur-hatted individual with gold crowned buck teeth and his wee tubby black-satin-capped companion, who appear at every function, including Church, together. During Communion, Damon, the big man, took the wine, smelled it, put it back, then helped himself liberally to the bread. I felt so guilty at finding it all funny that when I got home I read the Easter Story all by myself and in the proper spirit.

☐ *APRIL 21ST:* Jim Endicott is again working with Madame Chiang as an advisor to the New Life Movement, which is designed to combat the political corruption which permeates every aspect of government here. The Movement is based on the principles of Christian love plus the four Confucian virtues, *Li, I, Lien* and *Ch'ih* (courtesy and good manners, justice and uprightness, frugality and integrity, modesty and self-respect). Jim spent a few days here last week and was full of interesting things concerning the Chiang Kai-sheks. Jim says Madame loves fun. At a rather exclusive Christmas party, which was all very proper until the Generalissimo retired about 10 P.M., games such as blindman's-buff began. Jim thought it comical to see otherwise dignified Chinese officials at such sport. And as Madame Chiang waxed merrier, one commented with almost a sigh, "Madame is very American."

☐ *MAY 5TH:* Last night, when I went out on the porch to check Judith, she shrieked when I touched her. She was so feverish, I was paralysed by the frantic notions racing through my head. Her back was so sensitive, at first I thought the amah might have dropped her. Then of intussusception. And then of some other awful thing. In this country the possibilities seem limitless. This morning, she is fine. For myself, I've never been so fat. I weigh 158 pounds. I don't think I am becoming a hypochondriac, but when I exercise I've been getting dizzy with sawmill-like roarings in my ears. It is back to the old iron filings again!

Poor Rev. Veals! He has been my *bête noir* ever since our arrival. He thoroughly disapproves of me, although we do a heck of a lot more for the school kids than he does. He may have meant to be funny the other day when he said, "Unfortunately, I have no authority over you unless, of course, you do something that necessitates your being put out of the Mission." I felt like replying, "What, for example? I'll get right on it!" but thought of Ralph and bit my tongue. The Veals' sleeping porch adjoins ours, separated only by a thin partition. Ralph and I had to stick sheets into our mouths the other night for fear of disturbing them, as we sat in bed drinking toasts to distant friends and relatives with "sherry" from the dispensary. Goodness knows what it really was, but we felt great!

☐ *MAY 18TH:* It is my dad's birthday in this country of one day ahead. We are again at Mount Omei for the summer. I haven't been very well lately. Having to force down food and mingle with people proved such an effort, my long-suffering husband finally put me to bed. And poor Judith is back on supplementary feedings. It was so hot before we left Jenshow she was vomiting, refusing to nurse and had diarrhœa. The pædiatrician who examined her here decided she was suffering from "starvation." The little darling is now a picture of health. You can imagine how I felt though.

☐ *SEPTEMBER 8TH:* I'm sure we will look back on this past summer with pleasure, but at the moment my feelings about it would pass for the temperature chart of a malaria patient. The lows were various illnesses. Both Ralph and I had amœba (an intestinal parasite), the treatment for which is very hard on the heart and requires prolonged bed rest. My weight dropped to 120 lbs. which was as unbecoming as my earlier 160. The high points were the get-togethers with our various friends, old and new. At times, our social life seemed almost frenetic. But it all was natural enough when one reflects on what each of us had to return to. Those from Chungking to Japanese terror bombings. Those at wcuu to the difficulties of maintaining a good teaching program on a campus now crowded by six refugee universities and plagued by air raids. Others to their often lonely dangerous Stations and thankless jobs. And none knew if we would ever see Mount Omei or each other again.

Initially, we planned to go to Chengtu by bus so that Ralph could get a thorough medical check-up before we returned to Jenshow. These buses are charcoal burners and are so crowded that people literally bulge out the windows and ride on top amidst the baggage. Such travel can be quite an adventure as Connie Vichert and Lily Hockin discovered when bandits attempted to stop their bus. When the driver refused even to slow down, a hail of bullets killed several of the passengers, including Connie's amah who was sitting right beside her. Lily had a bullet pass twice through her half-raised arm both above and below the elbow. Connie is the same girl who, along with Alice Jenner, was robbed on Mount Omei last year. They were left strung up by their wrists. On another occasion, she had a placenta prævia and was being rushed (a misnomer if there ever was one) by junk to hospital in Chengtu when bandits boarded them. The *futor* (head man) protested that Connie was dying and if anything happened to his boat or passengers, Britain would go to war with China! The brigands backed off. Perhaps we were just as well travelling overland to Jenshow by whaggan.

Actually, we had a pleasant trip down. No one else was as lucky. Not a drop of rain the entire three days. The first night we reached Chia Chiang, famous for the quantity, but not quality, of its paper production. We stayed at the small Chapel there. The place smelled to "high heaven" as they were feeding silk worms, but we had a bedbugless night! Our carriers made good stages and we slept in another Chapel the following night. This too was relatively clean. Ferried six rivers in flood, but nothing dangerous. The countryside is always interesting. The seasons in China are so short and varied that every time one travels there is planting or harvesting in progress. I like one of the Chinese names for Szechwan, "The Granary of Heaven." As we approached Jenshow we saw the effects of a flash flood, devastated houses, ruined crops and, in the village itself, mud and water still sweeping down the main street. There were water marks twelve feet high on some of the shops. Outside the school, the river had swept all before it, gardens, walks, bridges and about thirty feet of the compound wall. Worst of all, our roof had leaked and when I went to wash Ralph's precious winter woolies, they fell apart!

Our trip back was made all the more interesting by our travelling companion, Irma Highbaugh, a terrific American woman who, as I've mentioned, is head of the rural reconstruction work of Gin Ling College. She told us the Gin Din had been linked to the Swiss Alps during the Ice Age and that was why Swiss edelweiss is found on its summit. She showed me the Jewel flowers of which there are two hundred varieties in the mountains around Omei. Besides being a fund of information, she is a very good sport, lives "Chinese" all year round, enduring all sorts of inconveniences (to put it mildly). The night we arrived back, Irma found her place flooded out and the suitcase, containing her most precious clothes and jewelery, stolen. The man who robbed her later killed himself, but this didn't help much.

The Walmsleys took us in and made us comfortable. Next came some unpleasantness with our servants and to make a boring story short, except for our amah, they all left, taking some of our possessions with them! It has been such a relief to be alone and do our own work for a change. And so it goes. We will have to get new staff, but we shall be very careful and much more sophisticated about those we hire. Constance simply laughs at my self-recrimination for being so stupid about the last lot.

☐ *SEPTEMBER 13TH:* If I'd realized today was Friday, I might not have waved so gaily when Ralph left for Chengtu by bicycle this morning with Olin Stockwell. He has to get his check-up. He lost sixteen pounds this summer and it isn't certain whether his amœbaiosis is cured. Personally, I am feeling tops, whatever was wrong with me cleared up when I weaned Judith. I've started music again (one evening a week doing choral work with the kids) and a well-baby clinic, which will do wonders for my Chinese. The rest of the time I look after our darling and enjoy my home. I would be exceedingly happy though if I didn't have to worry about someone to carry water from distant wells, someone to start the morning fire, someone to wash all our floors once a day, someone to dump the toilets.

☐ *SEPTEMBER 29TH:* When Ralph returned from Chengtu, he reported that Donnie Campbell was very ill with bacillary dysentery of the dreaded "Shiga" type which is almost 100 per cent fatal to young Westerners. Reports became progessively worse and a week ago Donnie died. I hopped a whaggan for Chengtu the day we received the news. When I arrived two days later, I found Mil and Gord absolutely devastated, almost in a state of shock. The Service at the University Chapel had been in the capable hands of Mary and Jim Endicott. It was one of music and apparently particularly beautiful. The Campbells seemed very much to want me to stay with them even though theirs is always a houseful, this time an American couple from New York called Sarcissian. "Sarky," the husband, is interested in promoting a rug industry here. And another guest, a Swiss working with the Chinese Air Ministry, who told me he feels he would be of more use in Europe and is going to enlist in Britain. Despite the circumstances, it is refreshing to get away from the usual doctor-teacher-minister syndrome.

Friday, Chengtu received a very bad bombing. One of the Japanese targets was our hospital complex and I just made it to the cellar under Jolliffe's house before bombs started dropping all around us. It was hard to sit in that stuffy place, the air alive with sound, and not know exactly what was happening. Thank God there were no major hits on campus, just windows and doors blown out. Then the wounded began to arrive. About four hundred in our area alone. I went out with one of the doctors to give first aid. He would examine, tell me what to do, then move on to the next case. If I didn't catch up, he would mark his instructions in code on the patient's forehead. A nearby school received a direct hit. There were no survivors. One of the tragedies was that people fleeing the city were killed by bombs intended for us, many by concussion. We found them lying apparently unhurt, but dead!

The next A.M., after three medical appointments, the last one with Dr. Gladys at the WMS Hospital, I went out to the campus for a two-hour session in the dental chair. At eleven, the air raid warnings sounded, but I was all done up in a rubber dam and Gordon was darned if he was going to stop before he had finished. We arrived home just in time to make it under the dining room table with the others as the bombers swept overhead. We looked rather like a flock of ostriches with our heads hidden and our bottoms sticking out. This time the west part of the city caught it. After lunch we attended the curiously impersonal wedding of a pair of Oxford Groupers. Why can't they just practice what they preach and leave the rest of us in peace? It was good, however, to see all my friends at the reception. Then to Ruth Bannon's for tea and more gossip (there is always plenty). Later, we read a play at Mil's with the Willmotts and Endicotts.

I was in rather a rush to get away from Chengtu, and as I could get neither rickshaw or whaggan, I had to travel "hard class" by junk to Su Mah Tou, about fifteen miles from the halfway mark, where Ralph was to meet me. We left at daybreak, standing room only. Sometimes it takes all day depending on the speed of the river. I had consulted Mil about what would be the best plan re the inconvenient essentials of daily life when travelling alone. Her solution was "carry a potty in your basket." The local custom is to hold on to the circular overhead covering or "pong" and squat over the water. But not me. I knew I'd fall in! Fortunately, when we landed to take on more passengers, I managed to get to a public lavatory, a description of which I will spare you, but it too was an experience! Talking about smells, back on board I had a bunch of candles made out of rancid beef or water buffalo fat swinging over my head. And all sorts of odiferous things were being cooked in a brazier, including the Szechwan *lah dze*, a very hot pepper. Fortunately, we made good time. Ashore I was able to get a rickshaw and despite the rain arrived at Chieh Tien Pu at dusk. I really didn't expect Ralph because of the miserable weather.

I managed to get the only relatively clean room in the inn, put up my cot and mosquito net, and was just going to have a meal when in dashed a runner with a parcel from Ralph containing a thermos of coffee, a sweater, a blanket and note saying he couldn't make it, the roads were too bad. Fifteen minutes later Ralph staggered through the door, covered with mud from head to foot. What a reunion!

☐ *OCTOBER 20TH:* Our new cook, blast him, has been caught watering the milk. He has also been stealing our precious sugar. We buy it raw at $1.50 a pound, then refine it, losing more than half, depending upon how dirty it is. On top of this, he was squeezing more than is allowed. However, I am much more capable of handling these situations than before and all this will be shortly straightened away.

Things are really tightening up. Many of the Americans have left for home, although Canadians seem still to be coming out. There is talk of moving the University further west to escape the Japanese air raids. The dear little Convent where I have so many friends among the Belgian sisters received a direct hit the other day. I've not heard details of the casualties. If there is a move to send Canadians home, it will be mothers with babies first, but I have no heart for it. I would rather stay and take my chances with my husband.

☐ *NOVEMBER 13TH:* This week has been a disaster. First, we experienced an earthquake. I woke about midnight to things rattling in the room. My first thought was to save our precious mirror over the fireplace so I jumped up, yelped at Ralph to do likewise and made a dive for it. He refused to respond, even when we had a second and stronger tremor. Then, when getting out the beautiful banquet cloth Ralph gave me for my birthday, I found it falling apart! The linen had been over bleached! Not by me, but by the people who sold it. I was devastated, as was Ralph. He had put so much heart and money into it. Finally, the part "foreign" cow which we bought last month to ensure Judith gets whole milk and plenty of it (putting us severely into debt) gave birth to a dead calf and retained its placenta! It took Ralph two hours with his arm sunk up to the shoulder to get the placenta delivered by hand.

☐ *NOVEMBER 24TH:* The amah who worked for the Veals had been carrying on an illicit love affair with their coolie and, if you please, using my amah's bedroom! Edna fired them when she discovered this. But now my funny old woman refuses to go to bed at night, without first getting the goose we have tethered in the front garden to put under her bed. Geese are very good "watch dogs" and she has no intention of being surprised! If you could just picture this ugly old dear solemnly thudding on her little bound feet to her room each night with this large protesting bird under her arm. Wish I could paint it!

☐ *CHRISTMAS DAY:* We went to the Chinese Service. Like a Buddhist temple, people come and go as it suits them. Children wander in and out. The Pastor's wife patrols the aisles trying to maintain order, a role Mrs. Gin obviously enjoys. I have mentioned our Pastor Gin before. He has a little statue of the Laughing Buddha of which he is very fond and, on this particular morning, he had it sitting on the pulpit. Poor man simply can't understand why Howard Veals gets upset! Further, he insists upon singing the doxology ("Praise God from Whom All Blessings Flow") at the end of the Service. It amuses me to watch Howard's jaw tighten every time this happens. Repeated explanations and requests for a more conventional order of Service seem only to bring further departures.

☐ *DECEMBER 27TH:* Today we went over to Gin Ling College to see a new bit of advertising about midwifery which was very funny. Irma Highbaugh had invited the women hereabouts to come, bring their children and visit. Her audience captive, she then put on her play. It centered on a woman in labor (offstage and screaming) and the filth, ignorance and superstition of country midwives (two old crones in consultation on the stage). As the screams grew worse and more soul tearing, a neighbor came in to talk about the advantages of modern methods and asked, "Why don't you call in Miss Wang? She is that new modern midwife who has just come to Miss Highbaugh's place. What, you don't know Miss Highbaugh? Why, everyone knows Miss Highbaugh. She is the tallest woman in the world."

□ *DECEMBER 31ST:* A page for myself this New Year's Eve, 1940, a "rose" for the winter of my life. Fate has dealt so kindly with me that I wonder upon what merit it is meted, especially when I think of those many people ground under the "conqueror's heel" and contemplate the daily enrichment and growing joy of our life here. The death of Wee Donald, whose life was "a dancing flame" and whose parents, dear friends, are left grieving, has made me realize we have but the loan of Judith and must enjoy every moment of her stay with us lest one day we too shall have to content ourselves with memories. We are looking forward to April when, with the advent of a playfellow for Judith, another wonder will unfold. One of the exciting things about the maturing process is one's growing awareness. My resolution for 1941 is to count my blessings.

I am waiting to go to dinner with our "Culture Club," a vain attempt on my part to interject something beyond religion into our social lives. Tonight, Howard Veals, whose turn it is to give a book review, is treating us, if you please, to his analysis of "The Book of Job"! A little thick for New Year's Eve! Oh well, pregnancy isn't particularly conducive to "partying" (not that there are any to go to), so perhaps I am lucky to be tucked away in this forgotten corner of the world waiting for our *mousi* to intone on the problems of good and evil and man's inability to understand God's judgment.

CHAPTER 4

Junghsien /
Through a Glass, Darkly

☐ *JANUARY 4TH, 1941:* What a way to begin the year! I've been in bed the last couple of days recovering from a small operation to relieve a strangulated hæmorrhoid. As opposed to the Chinese custom of hanging a beautiful scroll at the foot of my bed, Ralph cut out an "Anusol" advertisement from the *Canadian Medical Journal* featuring a picture of the old gentleman who couldn't sit down!

Mil Campbell arrived today from Chengtu with the Canadian School kids returning from their winter break. We had a marvelous time catching up. She is continuing to Junghsien by whaggan (the motor road, such as it is, ends here), a two-day trip over narrow flagstone paths seventy miles to the south, to visit our mutual friend, Alice Jenner, who, as I've mentioned, has not been well for some time. When Alice stayed with us at Mount Omei last summer, she too was bed-ridden with amœbaiosis. And Harley, her husband, has active Tb.

☐ *JANUARY 9TH:* No sooner had Mil departed than Dr. Gladys and Esther Stockwell showed up with the news that the

Mission Council has decided to send Ralph and me to Junghsien. The Jenners are going home to recover their health. This is
really quite wise as Alice is eligible for furlough, even if Harley
isn't. Among those to be transferred along with us are Alf and
Margaret Day. Margaret (née Meuser) is also pregnant and due
about the same time as myself.

□ *JANUARY 26TH:* Ralph returned yesterday from Chengtu,
where he enjoyed himself thoroughly. Everyone makes such a
to-do when either of us visit. Jean Millar in particular loves to
fuss over Ralph. She once told me she wished I'd hurry up and
die so she could have him! Fortunately, I doubt I'll ever have to
"push up daisies" to save face on her account! Ralph also met
"The Heroine of Shanghai," the girl who carried the standard
to the Lost Battalion. What carnage Japan has wreaked upon
China.

To more immediate matters, it appears our situation in
Junghsien is not going to be any cup of tea. By all reports the
Mission Hospital is a mess. When Harley Jenner was sent down
eight months ago to assist on a half-time basis (because of his
Tb), the acting Superintendent and only other physician, Dr.
Loh (a Peking Union Medical College man), took offense. He
refused to discuss any of the Hospital's problems. And this despite a mounting debt, no money for drugs, no credit at the local
shops, desperately low supplies and rampant theft of Hospital
property. What is more, because Harley was on half-time, Dr.
Loh decided "face" required he only work the same hours. No
doubt we can expect real trouble when Ralph replaces him as
Superintendent.

Mil came back from her visit with Alice to confirm everything
that Ralph had been told and more, including a garbled version
of an old story, but reported as if it had happened quite recently. In fact, it was in 1927 that the then Mission doctor,
Percy Tennant, created the "incident" which has become part
of the anti-imperialist, anti-foreign legend in this part of China.
During surgery one morning, his Chinese nurse fainted. Not
able to use his hands (for obvious reasons) to move the woman

while operating, he pushed her aside with his *foot*. When news of this got out, it was interpreted by the local Nationalists as racial violence and a disgrace to the Republic of China. Local Kuomintang (ruling party) officials demanded Tennant make a public apology before the national flag. The Chinese nurses at the Hospital threatened to strike. The outcry was such that Dr. Tennant was forced to leave Junghsien. Indeed, this ended his service as a Medical Missionary in China. And fourteen years later, the story is still being told as if it had happened yesterday. In this country, no one ever forgets or forgives an insult, real or perceived. Nevertheless, it should be fun to try to make a go of it. I am not so Missionary-minded, however, that I'd never raise my head again if we got run out of China.

☐ *FEBRUARY 27TH:* The days before our departure from Jenshow were hectic. Ralph did most of the packing. I looked after the commissary, Judith's arrangements and personal things. On Valentine's Day, the community had a lovely party in Judith's honor and she received cards from everyone. The children all assembled in the morning, serenaded her, then gave her a "Royal Bump." In the P.M., she had her birthday cake with one candle (which she insisted on eating). She made all the proper noises and loved the fuss, going from one kid to another with as many smiles for the next as she had had for the last. I must have been very thirsty for one of the school girls asked, "Marg, would you like a seventh cup of tea?" Our Gin Ling College friends brought Judith a small silver locket and chain, which she adores. Later, the community presented us with a lovely study of the Jenshow hills by Lewis Walmsley. It was a busy, exciting, but sad time.

At a local Mission committee meeting (each Station has a degree of autonomy in deciding matters that affect their community and work) just before we left, Ralph asked permission to take one hundred of the unused bed covers which lay in the attic of the former Hospital. From what we'd been told, patients had to supply their own bedding in Junghsien. To my complete surprise, there was stubborn opposition to our request. Then, the normally quiet, twittery Edna Veals tipped the balance in our favor even though this meant taking sides against her husband. It's hard sometimes to believe that we are all working for the same cause.

The actual trip was a nightmare! First, we got off to such a late start we had to spend two nights on the road instead of one. Second, because we had a poor *futor*, the carriers with our food and bed rolls were allowed to get so far ahead of the whaggans that we never saw them again. Had I not kept back some canned milk for Judith, I don't know what we would have done. This was particularly so our second day out when all the shops were closed for Chinese New Year's. Finally, Ralph and I were cross with each other. Indeed, neither of us has mentioned the trip since.

I will never forget that second evening stumbling through the pitch black (we had no torch or lantern) in the Gao Sh Ti hills (about fifteen miles north of Junghsien). We were cold, hungry and quite prepared to break into the first foreigner's summer cottage we happened upon. Our carriers were grumbling, even though by this time I was walking. I was afraid the men would slip and drop me and harm my unborn baby. I was starting to feel desperate, when we happened upon a little Mission school for the mountain children. Even now I can scarcely believe our luck. Four marvelously hospitable people took us in, gave us hot water (our first en route) to bathe Judith and wash ourselves and a clean place to sleep. They are very poor, but the next morning shared their simple meal with us. Lo *chieh chieh* (Older sister Lo) who runs their household (and everything else) simply overflowed with thoughtfulness and kindness. We were very touched by the experience and left refreshed both physically and spiritually. And I, at least, found the rest of our journey relatively pleasant.

□ *MARCH 3RD:* One hundred and forty miles due south of Chengtu, Junghsien (translated "City of Glory" and pronounced, You-in-sheean) is very old and very conscious of its history. This walled city of some 60,000 souls in the heart of the coal mining district is county seat and administrative center for forty-eight surrounding market towns. And unlike Tzeliutsing (where we expected to be stationed), it has not been bombed, even though the new "motor road" from Chungking has increased its importance. Along this route, Tzeliutsing is 30 miles to the east and Kiating 60 miles to the west. As yet, I haven't been outside the Mission compound which lies inside the northwest corner of the city wall.

The Jenners' house, which is soon to be ours, is the smallest, cheapest and ugliest in the Mission. And, of course, there is the sheer physical confusion of us moving in when they are madly packing to leave. Then there are the usual obligatory farewell and welcoming feasts. This last week has been a muddle. Everything seems so depressing. Alice feels badly about abandoning me in such circumstances, but fortunately her servants have decided we pass muster. I fired our cook in Jenshow for drunkenness and our old amah decided to return to her family in Chengtu. We would have been in a bit of a fix had the Jenners' lot not liked us.

The cook, Fuh Hai-yuin, is certainly the best I've encountered in China. Of course he runs the show so far as the other servants are concerned. He is efficient, honest as can be, doesn't care one hoot about face, has a great sense of humor and is simply swell to get along with. My fear is that he will be enticed away by the offer of a higher salary. His wife is our danyang. She is a green country girl, bright as a button, but slow and thus far confined to dusting and the heavy washing and ironing (Ralph's hospital whites and the table and bed linen). The amah, Dzan, is in her fifties, a Christian, reasonably well educated, although I gather she was sold into slavery as a girl. She cheerfully works from dawn to dusk looking after Judith's and our clothes, sewing, mending, helping the cook, looking after the dog and cat and so on. So far she has shown herself to be loyal, clean, conscientious and kind. "The Dragon," Lung Puyuin, is our coolie. He cleans the floors, helps the cook, works in the garden, carries the water and goes out with Ralph on night calls. He is particularly devoted to Judith and often carries her about in a basket on his back (much to her delight). The gate-man runs our errands, delivers notes and helps in the garden. Finally, my teacher, Miss Wan, who came with us from Jenshow doubles as Judith's nanny. Mr. Chiang is here as well, but he is now Ralph's teacher (so well did my experiment work) and has in addition been given a couple of administrative jobs for which he is suited at the Hospital.

Household establishments in China tend to be large, much like in Victorian England. Ours would be considered minimal. We don't have servants because we are rich. We are anything but (although the Chinese seem to assume that every foreigner is wealthy). We have them because we need them. There are none of the home-side conveniences every North American house-wife takes for granted. Everything here involves considerable physical labor and servants enable us to get on with the jobs for which we are trained, our reason for being here in the first place. They can also be more trouble than they're worth, as I discovered in Jenshow.

Our foreign community seems to contain a lot of "concentrated" personalities who insist upon giving us "concentrated" advice. They make me tired with their old talk. You would think we had no brains of our own. And first and foremost among them is Mrs. Margaret Bridgeman, a very talented and creative woman who more or less runs everything here (public health, Well-Baby Clinic, training school for girls and so on) except the Hospital. Violet Stewart, another WMS field worker and re-cently of Honan, is full of beans as well as goodness. She has had the most amazing adventures escaping through Japanese lines to refugee in this remote province. We like her very much. Miss Lulu Rousse is just as you would expect a Lulu to be. Large, slate-blue eyes in a wondering face, very "Mish" in dress, deeply in debt because she insists upon adopting every needy child, sweet, kind and tiresomely full of advice. Finally, Miss Steele, a very level headed sixtyish person. Something like Dr. Gladys, a quiet, no nonsense woman and I would think the backbone of the Station. Ourselves you know too well.

☐ *MARCH 24TH:* Where shall I start? Alice and Harley left
last week and I have been very busy trying to get things un-
packed and straightened round. We bought a lot of the Jenner's
furniture and household things which when combined with
what we moved from Jenshow more or less fills our eight rooms.
If I wasn't so pressed for time, it would all be rather fun. Unfortunately, we have some entertaining to do and I am expecting
house guests next week. And Ralph is at the Hospital the entire
time. In addition, I am helping Mrs. Bridgeman at the Well-
Baby Clinic which operates once a week. The Hospital and
other Mission agencies serve an area population of 600,000. I
find the work fascinating, but the circumstances of many of our
clients are heartbreaking. The Sino-Japanese War (now in its
fourth year) and this year's drought which has ruined 80 per
cent of the local crops (there has been no rain for over five
months) have so driven up prices (rice is now $120 a *dou*) that
people are starving to death. Men, women and children have
left the land to carry coal from the mines ten miles to the north
of us to Tzeliutsing. Working from first light to last, the children
and nursing mothers in this endless procession of suffering
humanity earn barely enough for two meals a day. There is so
much need and we have so little money with which to help!
Nevertheless, we manage to give some of the neediest infants a
milk made from soy beans, peas, calcium lactate and sugar,
which is very nutritious. Originally, we used wheat instead of
peas, but this tended to give the babies diarrhœa.

One of the very few funny moments at the clinic occured the
other day when the mothers and their babies were being inspected by Mrs. Bridgeman. The routine is that as each files
past, Mrs. B. whips open the mother's gown, takes a breast, ex-
presses it to determine the quantity of her milk supply. One
woman with a very emaciated baby came up. Out came the
breast. No milk. "Ah," said Mrs. B., "no wonder the child is
starving." "But," the woman protested, "I am her grandmother!"

At the other end of the economic and social scale, I met a

rather charming *tai tai* at one of Jenner's farewell feasts, a Mrs. Hsieh or Hsieh *tai tai*. (I am now accustomed to hearing myself called Yao *tai tai*.) Mrs. Hsieh is married to a banker and is the daughter of the chairman of our Hospital Board, Mr. Liu. In a private moment, she asked Ralph if she could consult him about some medical problem she is having, which augurs well as her family and Dr. Loh are very friendly. I think I would like to get to know her.

As I mentioned, Ralph is at the Hospital most of the time, where he is now the only doctor. Dr. Loh tendered his resignation when Ralph replaced him as Superintendent. Further complicating Ralph's life is the discovery that Dr. Loh, the Hospital Registrar, Mr. Wong, and the two Chinese nurses were part of a ring supplying a drug shop in the town with stolen hospital stores. Although their involvement is common knowledge on the street, nothing can be proved. So Ralph immediately took charge of the pharmacy, changed the locks, inventoried the supplies, carefully weighing and recording each drug in stock (a very time consuming and tedious process). As there is no one to replace the nurses, it is a question of gradually placing them in a position where theft is no longer possible while convincing them they are completely trusted. Apart from this, Ralph thinks Miss Li and Miss Yuin very capable. On the other hand, he fired two of the four male student nurses (there are three female students as well). One was caught walking out the gate with hospital linen, the other strongly suspected as the party who stole the hospital microscope. Then he fired the cook, the biggest thieving rascal of the lot and the Registrar's nephew. He hoped Mr. Wong's loss of face in this would cause him to resign. No such luck. Dr. Loh has since threatened to put us out of business and was no doubt behind last week's general staff walk out. Only Miss Li decided to stay and see things through (although Miss Yuin has now returned). Ralph paid them all off and told them not to come back. The consequence of all this is a rather nasty anti-foreign feeling on the street. The only time I've been outside the compound, we were followed by angry, cursing crowds.

Ralph, however, feels the Hospital has potential and is impressed with the quality of its construction and layout. There are two wings (one for women, the other for men) joined in an H by the OR and Admin. office. It has wide halls, well lit wards and a physically separate Out-Patients Department and kitchen. If he can straighten out the personnel problems, get in some money and supplies, introduce a little efficiency and tend to some necessary repairs around the place, he may have a chance. It is rather shocking to one from the Western world to see hens running through the wards and patients surrounded by family preparing their food. The buildings need paint, the windows glass and screens, the OR would be immensely improved by a sky light (we have no electricity) and there should be a separate Delivery Room to minimize infection. Of course, anything is an improvement over operating on a kitchen table in Jenshow.

☐ *MARCH 18TH:* I am a bit blue tonight for Ralph has an amœbaiosis flare-up and can't take treatment again until he gets off his feet. The only news from Jenshow since we left is that one of the students came down with encephalitis and died within a few days. It made me realize once again the responsibility we had been carrying.

The Days finally arrived. Margaret is a very sweet girl, but I really can't get excited about her husband. Another theologue, he is boyish, nice looking in a proper way, prominent Adam's apple, precise and I'm afraid a bit smug. I get the urge to poke him or something. What is more, although they have no duties other than language study for the year, their house is larger than ours, in better repair and the Council has given them more money than we received for settling in.

I had a dinner party for twelve to introduce our new Public Health Nurse, Dorothy Fox, to the Medical and Mission personnel. Fuh did it beautifully. He arranged an old-fashioned bouquet as a centerpiece with streamers of morning glory interlaced with nasturtiums. I had freesias and sweet peas on the mantel and everything seemed to blend in the light of our four pewter lamps (peanut oil) on the table. The Chinese love bright colors. He served soup, fish, chicken, salad, pie, cake, biscuits and coffee. Because the Chinese serve many courses we usually have quite a few desserts so that our guests feel sufficiently honored! *Ai yah*, "face"!

☐ *APRIL 19TH:* I take my typewriter "en lap" to write the few things I can remember from the hundreds of bits and pieces I've been attempting to "storehouse" these last couple of weeks. Dr. Gladys came down on March 30th with Margaret Day's mother. They had quite a trip. Mrs. Meuser is an extremely gracious woman and very correct even in the most trying of circumstances. Gladys, on the other hand, can become very impatient. At one stop en route they were hot, weary and in need of a bit of a wash before their meal. When a basin of hot water was fetched for this purpose, curious villagers, I suppose quite naturally, gathered to watch these foreign females at their "toilette." Gladys asked them to leave, but to no avail. Consequently, when she was done, she simply tossed the dirty contents of the basin over her shoulder and into the crowd. Mrs. Meuser was horrified!

By the time they arrived, I was feeling pretty low. I guess it was just that I really had no one to talk to, no one to walk with and Gladys in her wonderful way supplied everything required. She knows exactly when to love or bully or scold or encourage. We walked miles every day. She also went through some of the worst of the Hospital headaches with Ralph, making it all an interesting game of chess. I lay awfully low on April Fool's Day, the day "Kerry" was due and the one day "he" would not be welcome. Then we waited . . . and waited. What a delinquent baby! Finally, Gladys ruptured the membranes and at 2:30 A.M. on April 8th, after twelve hours of fairly easy labor, Carol was born. I had been so counting on a boy it took them a minute or two to break the news to me. Of course I knew by their silence. Ralph chose her name. I had named Judith so it was his turn. Her actual first name is Frances after my Mum. Carol was less than nine pounds, not fat, very long, and so different from Judith. She has a nose, which Judith had not, and a very firm mouth and chin. Her head is much smaller than Judith's, not much molding, smaller fontanelle. Beautiful hands though, with lovely long fingers. While adorable, she has been wrecking our sleep ever since her arrival.

The Sunday before Carol was born, poor Judith ruined her beauty from her mouth to her umbilicus. We were sitting around after breakfast discussing the pros and cons of doing something to hasten my delivery. Fuh had just brought in a hot pot of coffee, when Miss Wan came downstairs with Judith on their way out for a walk. As we exchanged pleasantries, Judith clutching at the table edge unfortunately grabbed the mat under the coffee pot. I come out in gooseflesh every time I think of it. It was dreadful! We put her into a burn bed where she spent two days and nights trussed up so that she couldn't disturb the tannic acid compress. Fortunately, there is only one small area of third-degree burn on her chest. This all happened the same morning the Registrar walked off with the Hospital seals, adding another bit of interest to the general scene! The seals or "chop" are used as one's signature is on a cheque, loan or legal document at home.

Judith's reaction to Carol has been interesting. The first time she saw her in bed with me, she started screaming and wouldn't come near us. A couple of nights later, when she came in after her bath all shining and sweet to say good-night and have me sing her a little song (she is the only one in the family who appreciates my voice), her reaction was the same. She started screaming, "*bu yao*" (don't want), and burst into tears. I was by this time a bit stronger, so I took the struggling, heartbroken Judith into my arms. She was determined not to be loved, but I held her firm. Then, after a few minutes, she turned around, put her head on my shoulder, her arms around my neck and sobbed and sobbed. Of course the poor wee thing was still sick with her burn. But we are friends again.

☐ *APRIL 26TH:* I am back in bed. The delivery went okay, but unfortunately I had a lateral placenta prævia and a rather bad hæmorrhage. All in all, I am pretty useless. Just have no strength. But I'll get it back! I am taking iron tonic, calcium and occasionally liver by hypo. Ralph is working so hard I don't see much of him, but he does his best. Actually I'm rather discouraged with everyone these days, except for Dzan and Fuh. I asked Fuh the other day if he could make us some candy. I had such a longing for something sweet. He looked at me gravely and said, "Yao *tai tai*, I don't think we can afford it." Isn't it wonderful to have someone who cares?

☐ *MAY 4TH:* Mrs. Hsieh, whom I mentioned earlier, came round to visit the other day. As it turns out, we are neighbors. Indeed, our houses are a mere stone's throw away. Now that I am finally emerging from my confinement (which was approaching the traditional Chinese forty days), I hope to see her often. She is so charmingly open in sharing her thoughts and experiences, I think you will find her story rather interesting.

As I've indicated, Hsieh *tai tai* belongs to the aristocracy here. (So far as I can gather, Junghsien has always been a city of feudal landlords who rent out their ancestral holdings to tenant farmers on a share-crop basis.) But I suspect she would be a remarkable woman regardless of station. For example, she was educated at the Mission Girls School here, but has remained a Buddhist. Although she and her husband, Hsieh Chao-chuan, make their home with her mother-in-law, hers was not an arranged marriage, but a love match. Also, both believe in monogamy (which is a relatively new concept in China). It was in this latter connection that she had sought Ralph's professional advice.

She is again pregnant, but on four previous occasions has failed to carry to term. As Hsieh *tai tai* is about my age, she and her husband are under considerable family pressure to produce an heir. Given the Chinese view of marriage, which among other things demands male issue to carry on the family name and serve their ancestors in the Temple, if Hsieh *tai tai* cannot manage a live birth, then tradition dictates a secondary wife to do the job. This both Hsiehs find repugnant. Indeed, Mr. Hsieh recently made a pilgrimage to the temple at Mount Omei to pray for a son, undoubtedly paying large sums of money to the Buddhist monks in the process. Then along comes this Christian doctor. . . .

Ralph's first concern when he examined her was to rule out syphilis as a possible cause of her miscarriages. This disease is so widespread in this part of the world, it is not unreasonable to expect that anyone might have been infected. Hsieh *tai tai* was not. Finding nothing in particular amiss, Ralph thought progesterone (a supplementary sex hormone inhibiting ovulation during pregnancy) might bring her through. The question was where to get some. Then I remembered Marnie Copeland, a friend in Chengtu with a similar problem, mentioning something about this when I saw her last September, so I wrote to find out if she had any extra. She did. Now Hsieh *tai tai*, who is due in late September, proudly walks about with her little tummy stuck out as far as possible. I wonder if they thank God or Buddha or Ralph?

Of course, we spent most of our visit talking about babies, my two and the fantastic preparations for hers. It is the custom that the first child's clothes come from the mother's mother. These will be traditionally Chinese. She has asked, however, to make copies of some of Carol's (actually hand-me-downs from Judith). She also admired my two beautiful rugs, newly arrived and the first produced by the China Industrial Co-operatives. This was "Sarky's" venture and I ordered them when I met him in Chengtu at the time of Donnie Campbell's death. They are a natural sheep's wool, hooked, with a heavy nap and a border clipped in the Greek key pattern. Hsieh *tai tai* tells me this is quite close to the Chinese thunder pattern.

□ *MAY 10TH:* At the Hospital, Ralph fired the Registrar (with three months pay) and appointed Mr. Chiang in his stead. The immediate effect of this was a month-end surplus of $1300! He then asked the Chairman of the Hospital board, Liu Nien-mong (Hsieh *tai tai*'s father), if he would use his good offices to secure the return of the Hospital seals still in Mr. Wong's possession.

Mr. Liu, in addition to being a prominent citizen and a scholar of note, is head of the local Elder Brothers Society (a secret organization that, among other things, metes out justice according to its own shadowy code). The seals were returned. Dr. Loh, however, has been doing his best to sully Ralph's reputation (a word here, a whisper there). One result is that a number of cases, including a ruptured spleen, a ruptured urethra and two strangulated hernias left Hospital because the relatives of these patients refused to sign permission for surgery! When a little beggar boy died in our care (we and a couple of others were paying for him because there is as yet no money for charity cases), his father was encouraged to sue. Ralph rejected the suit, claimed he could be tried only by the British Consul and thus insulted the Judge and infuriated the District Governor. I thought this a mistake at the time, but maybe not. Certainly it was coincidental with someone setting our Out-Patients building on fire. Fortunately, the blaze was discovered in time to save our drug supply (the pharmacy is in the same premises). On the other hand, the former Registrar chose to challenge his dismissal in open forum at the tea house.

The tea house, especially in the smaller towns, is more than a place where men meet to discuss the affairs of the day over bowls of tea. It is a time-honored institution which for 2,000 years has served the interests of local justice. When a serious dispute arises between individuals in the community, the party claiming injury may call his alleged malefactor to a public confrontation at one of the larger tea houses. Once a time is agreed and a headman or referee selected, the news is broadcast so that interested citizens may duly assemble. The challenger speaks first without interruption. Then the defendant makes his case. There are no time limits. Next, the referee seeks clarification of any obscure points in either position. The disputants are then obliged to answer all questions from the floor. Finally, those assembled decide on a solution, which usually represents a compromise between the opposing sides.

Thus, had Ralph refused Mr. Wong's challenge, it would have been considered a grave insult to local custom, perhaps even an "incident." Instead, he responded by suggesting that the proceedings take place at the Hospital where his language difficulties would be less a disadvantage. The public would be welcome and Mr. Wong could bring as many supporters as he wished. Ralph would ask Rev. Bridgeman, whose Chinese is excellent, to help him should he require this. The former Registrar agreed, I think because he and his friends expected that if they gave Ralph enough rope he would eventually hang himself by somehow so enraging anti-foreign sentiment that, like Dr. Tennant before us, we would be driven from the town. I must confess I feared the same result, having been exposed to such resentment, even hatred here.

What neither Mr. Wong nor I had calculated was the Oriental aspect of Ralph's character. Even I tend to forget that Ralph was born and raised in Japan where his father is with Kwansei Gakuin University in Kobe. Was I ever proud of my guy! He was cool as a cucumber and looked it, dressed in his white sharkskin suit (his only one) and red tie. Before the meeting began, Ralph cordially greeted Mr. Wong. Listening to his antagonist's litany of grievances, he didn't blink an eye, just sat there calmly cooling himself with his black laquered fan. When asked why he had fired the Registrar, Ralph agreed that Mr. Wong had rendered the Hospital years of faithful service and expressed the Mission's appreciation of same, but pointed out that it was established Chinese practice for a new man to bring in his own assistants, people he had previously known and worked with. Not once did he so much as allude to the real reason for firing Mr. Wong. This was much appreciated as everyone knew about the thefts. Custom had been maintained. No one lost face. The former Registrar's people were satisfied and the situation resolved without the fat even coming close to the fire!

☐ *JUNE 22ND:* It's my mum's birthday, bless her. Ralph and I celebrated our third anniversary on the 17th. We dined alone and, although we normally have meat but once a week (which is all we can afford), he bought a kidney and I somehow managed a tin of asparagus. We felt as though we were royalty. We had candles and a lovely old-fashioned centerpiece with hollyhock blossoms at the four corners of the table mat. I wore a long, flowing desert dress. Ralph said I looked awfully nice. Afterwards, we drew the curtains, turned on the radio, found some soft music and danced! They are so sticky here, Mrs. B. would certainly have had plenty to say had she known. The other day she told me to get down on my knees and ask God to forgive me for my stubborn pride! Coming from her, I found this most amusing.

Ralph's is a particularly tough job and all the more so because he believes that our hospitals, no matter their size, should be models of efficiency and service. We are teaching and demonstrating to an awakening people eager to grasp and adopt all they see that is good and progressive about them. He is also distressed because there are no funds to feed our charity patients. Quite rightly, he is convinced the main thrust of a Mission hospital is lost unless it has within its power the opportunity to give medical aid to the destitute who come to its door. I think he is coming to the conclusion that a balanced budget doesn't mean much if to attain it the Hospital ceases to be a Christian institution of mercy.

Nevertheless, the practice of medicine in this country is intensely interesting, if at the same time frustrating. I have mentioned something of the appalling ignorance and superstition connected with the human body and its care. Of course, this brings cases we would never see at home where the average man and woman are comparatively well educated, medically speaking. To take a common example, we are sufficiently aware of the potential dangers associated with acute abdominal pain to send us flying to a doctor should we experience this. Here, we rarely see an appendicitis before the appendix has ruptured, formed an abscess or developed peritonitis. The other day, Ralph operated on a woman weighing one hundred and seventy-six pounds, ninety of which was a tremendous ovarian cyst to which she had been anchored for three or four years. And she lived just across the street from the Hospital!

We compete with dozens of local "doctors" for whom no license to practice is necessary. Knowledge may have been passed down from father to son or, if one can read, it is a simple enough thing to purchase one of the old medical classics written a couple of thousand years ago. Then, all one has to do is hang out one's shingle. Most Chinese admit we are far ahead of them in surgery, but they stick with their own doctors when it comes to internal disorders. Often we are no more than a court of last resort for those for whom traditional medicine has not worked and our hospitals frequently treat cases mutilated by Chinese physicians. Not long after we arrived in Junghsien, a woman came to Ralph with both breasts sloughed off after applying the "medicine" prescribed by a Chinese doctor for swelling and tenderness a few days after she had given birth. Following a month in our hospital and extensive skin grafting she was able to return home. There are so many cases of this kind. A Chinese doctor assumes no responsibility for his patient or the results of his treatment. Accepted routine and custom are such that any lack of skill is never exposed. Thus, our struggle is not limited to the treatment of dysenteries, malaria, puerperal fever or any of the other "Sentinels of Death." Of far greater importance ultimately is the struggle against ignorance and superstition.

□ *JULY 12TH:* We reached the hill resort of Gao Sh Ti about two weeks ago. I came alone with the two babies, Miss Wan, Fuh, the "Dragon" and the danyang. The trip, although only twenty miles, was full of mishaps. I had to walk most of the way in the blazing sun, no food en route, endless delays, etc., etc. Since our arrival, the temperatures have been so high everyone is suffering from prickly heat. One can only imagine what Ralph is enduring on the plain. Our cottage is constructed of two-foot-thick dried mud blocks which have been recently whitewashed. It is small and there is not much furniture, but the verandahs are nice. Our stove is also made of mud bricks and it took Fuh two days to get it working properly. Needless to say our food is simple (everything we eat is cooked in a single large wok) but plentiful and the children are thriving.

☐ *AUGUST 10TH:* It is a lovely Sunday morning marred only by the explosion of distant bombs. I have been remiss in keeping this chronicle, but with two grown-ups, two children and three servants to tend to. . . . (I had to let Miss Wan go. Inflation is wrecking our family finances and we just couldn't afford her salary.) Ralph is here, restoring mind and body in the quiet and peace of the pine-covered hills. He finally secured a young Chinese doctor and a student to assist him at the Hospital, which means he is getting quite a decent holiday. With this arrangement, he only has to go down one day a week, unless there is something our new Dr. Hsu feels he can't handle. Carol, four months old yesterday, is lying on our bed fascinated by the typewriter. Judith is off on the Dragon's back in her *bei dao*, a bamboo woven chair which he straps over his shoulders. She is a laughing sunbeam these days, developing beautifully and always dirty. Yesterday she had eight baths and a complete change of clothes each time. Her first English phrase, "petty moosic," as she sits on her little potty chair and stretches her arms in appeal toward the silent gramophone. (I hope she will not always identify "petty moosic" with this activity.) She now helps her daddy put on his shoes, loves fitting bottles with corks, covers to cans, lids to other things. The servants adore her and we, typical parents, are convinced she is very clever.

The foreign community here is not particularly social, so we are getting a lot of rest. We sleep outside on the wide verandah and are becoming quite fond of the Chinese rope beds, about which I so complained our first summer at Mount Omei. I am still nursing Carol, even though (as with Judy) this leaves me completely pepless. However, "straight from producer to consumer" makes a lot of sense in this country. Time out while I upend Judith who has just swallowed a date stone. Too late.

☐ *AUGUST 18TH:* We have been having a bit of a problem with break-ins which, however annoying, are understandable, given the poverty that surrounds us. You should see the booby traps Fuh sets every night in the kitchen. Any thief would run for his life. Besides this, the community have hired a small band of men to make rounds at night to see that all is well. They are a ferocious looking crew and it gives one quite a start to suddenly wake up and see this lot literally beside one's bed. One gets used to it, but when Ralph is away, which is most of the time now, I imagine kidnappings and what not. Actually, my sleeping arrangements have become a small Mission scandal. I invited my servants to sleep in the cottage with me, something that is never "done" (they have their own adjacent quarters). And, bless them, they agreed.

There is one woman up here who drives me up the wall. Talk about insensitive! She insisted on staying at our house en route to Gao Sh Ti in June even though I was ill. She is so tactless and thoughtless that by the time she and her husband left, our happy ménage were at one another's throats. She is married to a very nice and rather good looking Minister (she caught him on the rebound, his fiancé couldn't face China). Now she positively insists upon "Mothers' Club" meetings. I am sure in her heart of hearts she is hoping to bring a little light into my darkness. She discusses child psychology, habit patterns, play methods etc., etc., etc. So far I've knitted a sweater.

□ *SEPTEMBER 6TH:* This week has been one of bombings. Usually we take them as a matter of course, but the Japanese navy has stepped in to finish the job of breaking Chinese resistance before launching a southward drive. Every day forty-five bombers in squadrons of nine whizz over our heads to drop their death on the innocent citizens of the surrounding cities. Most of these places don't have so much as an anti-aircraft gun with which to defend themselves. The air here is so humid, we can actually feel the detonations, even at long distances. The other day the planes overhead were so low the servants were scared. I moved Carol's bed to a relatively safe place, but couldn't find Judy until I heard her screaming. There was nothing the matter with her except the atmosphere of fear.

I have decided to stay up here until it becomes too cold to do so any longer. Prices continue to rise. Meat is now $10.00 a lb., sugar $4.00 and vegetable oil $5.00, if and when you can find them. Our new 50 lb. bag of flour ($210.00) is full of worms and Fuh says it should be thrown out. I agree, but we will eat it and ignore the worms. Talking about Fuh, I must tell you a funny story. The other day I was out in our combination chicken coop and outhouse, when the outside latch slid tight on me. I was just wondering how loud I'd have to shout when along came Fuh. He opened the door and tossed in a chicken. (The servants have their own outhouse.) Because the door was locked from the outside, he of course didn't know I was there. At the sight of me, he was so embarrassed he inadvertently relatched the door in his hurry to get away. I called and called, but he wouldn't come back to let me out. Finally, when I demanded he do so, he realized my situation. Fuh has a marvelous sense of humor, but we both restrained ourselves and with what dignity I could muster, I strolled out a free woman. While I was relating this adventure to my much-amused husband, however, I heard great giggles coming from the kitchen.

□ *OCTOBER 3RD:* I hated coming down from the hills last week, though towards the end, when I was there with just the children I had some pretty down periods sitting on the cliff edge looking forward to who knows how long in our small Station, with Ralph away most of the time, no one really to talk to and nothing to read. I thought seriously about going home. I am not really all that important in Ralph's scheme of things. Indeed, he seems to manage very well without me. There were also times when I felt I'd like to jump, but Judith is so lovable and Carol so responsive (bless them), both seeming to live for the moment I'd poke my nose around the corner, I just couldn't.

At the moment, for want of anything else, we are re-reading Shakespeare. During meals, with books propped before us, we do this aloud. Chopsticks have the advantage of freeing a hand to turn the pages.

We received the most depressing news today. I mentioned meeting Jimmy and Margaret Tang when we first arrived in Chengtu. We really got to know and appreciate them at Mount Omei last year. Jimmy was the most perfect gentleman I have ever known. We heard today that on a trip down the Min River with our dear friend Gordon Campbell, their junk overturned in a rapid and Jimmy was dragged to his death by another drowning passenger. Gordon narrowly escaped. Also that Fred Owen, one of the best and most amusing friends a person could have, has drowned in the Yangtse below Chungking. He too leaves a lovely wife and two wee boys. It has been hell in Chungking this summer. Dive bombers hitting the hospitals, caving in air raid shelters, even attacking summer cottages in the nearby hills. This same letter told us of another friend who is going home with œsophageal cancer.

Between you and me, our neighbors are nothing to write home about. I am simply thankful that I'm not like them. The Days are pacifists. When war is discussed and Mrs. Bridgeman asks Alf, "And what would you do if Margaret were brutally attacked?" "Nothing," Alf replies, looking very self-satisfied. Then Margie pipes up, "And I'd be proud of him too." What babes! We have our share of heated arguments. Given my own broken Chinese, it is probably unfair to comment on Mrs. B.'s, but there is nothing funnier than listening to her attempts to explain contraception to the Chinese women who attend our clinic. It worries me sometimes that I am no more "Missionary" than I ever was. I feel I have learned a great deal, but that my experience in China has been more a cultural exchange. Perhaps this is why Mrs. B. does not want me to take over the baby welfare work when she and her husband leave on furlough. She claims it would give the "Hospital" too much authority which properly belongs to the "Church," all of which is tripe! She wants Margie Day to do the job. Margie is a home economist and a natural for taking over the cross-stitch work. Oh well, the Mission field does not always bring out the best in people.

I've been working a bit at the Hospital as Dorothy Fox, who originally promised to lend a hand from time to time, for some reason has gone sour on us. She is exceedingly bitter in her criticism of everything we do. I only wish I knew why. I feel particularly badly as I had hoped to have a friend of my own sex here to love and share things with. But Dorothy needs this more than I do! Nevertheless, it is good to be back in harness, even though nothing straightforward ever seems to come our way. One of our recent cases involved a very pregnant woman who had a four-inch bone hairpin in her urethra. There is little doubt that this was a case of attempted abortion, although our patient flatly denied this. Indeed, she claimed only to have mistakenly sat on it! Another involved a woman with a ruptured ectopic pregnancy. Because she had lost a terrific amount of blood before coming in, her condition was critical. When her peritoneum was opened and found to contain a large quantity of fresh blood, however, I suggested we try an auto-transfusion. Ralph had never seen this technique, but I recalled assisting on one in Alaska. Consequently, we proceeded to mop about 600 cc's of blood out of her abdomen, strain it through a gauze filter into a flask of sodium citrate solution and put it back into her by intravenous. It worked! Ralph was intrigued. We often study together before we embark on a job, although I am not as good an OR assistant as I once was. Surgery is done under such a strain out here that one gets very weary near the end of an operation. We are so short of catgut and dermal that Ralph twists the bleeders if he can and we use street-bought silk for suturing the skin. We lack so much that is simply taken for granted at home (often even gloves), but our results have been pretty good. Actually, I loved it when I was working full time in the wards (the regular nurses had diphtheria). But imagine not having tablets and having to measure out the powder and wrap it into wee grass paper parcels—this I did find trying.

Have been a bit depressed about my garden. The horrible banana palm which never produces bananas is as healthy as can be, while my beautiful fruit trees so lovingly planted and cared for are dying. And someone removed most of our persimmons before we had a chance to taste them. As to flowers, we haven't a one and it irritates me that none of our neighbors has offered us any from their myriads. The servants must have discussed this with some feeling, for when Vi Stewart happened to look out her window at the WMS house the other morning, there was Judith with the cook's market basket over her arm in among their flowers helping herself. Then she calmly walked over to their well and spat in it! (So typically Chinese.)

☐ *OCTOBER 12TH:* Mrs. Hsieh, thank heavens, has been delivered of a healthy beautiful child, a daughter, Hong-di. And the Hsieh and Liu families are simply ecstatic. I went out on my bicycle yesterday to visit her. The country house in which she is staying is typical of the Chinese wealthy here. Courtyard after courtyard, servants and family of several generations all living together. None of the opulence one associates with the Orient, rather a spare, not too clean comfort. Hsieh *tai tai* has a fine balance of East and West. For example, she brought her "winter bed," a foreign-made inner-spring mattress, with her to her friend's place. She finds it warmer at this time of year. But during the summer heat, out comes the traditional Chinese leather-covered rope mattress.

Ralph, of course, did the delivery. When he does these home confinements, Miss Yuin accompanies him with a sterile bundle, as one would at home. If the patient is wealthy, private litters are sent for them. These are black box-like conveyances containing a comfortable seat, room to stretch one's feet and a curtained window on either side (much like those depicted in the etchings of 17th century London society). The carriers are so smooth one can drink a cup of tea while riding.

Since returning from the hills, I've cleaned house and had a great time re-reading every letter we've received from home over the last three years. I've also been doing a bit of entertaining. I had a tea for the few Chinese women I have met and with whom I hope to become friends. We are starting what we laughingly call a *Tai Tai Hwei* (Ladies' Club). The only rule is that it is never to become serious! Then I had a formal dinner for the foreign community, actually a dress rehearsal for one I am planning for the District Governor.

It is important to do a certain amount of feasting one's influential friends out here, but it is hard when we have less then $100.00 (American) to live on for *three* months, even with an exchange rate of twelve to one. I refuse to cut out meat and eggs entirely and of course we have to have milk for the children. (We did not bring our cow from Jenshow.) Prices have now reached about the same as they are at home and with our servants' wages, we are going into debt. But I am learning to economize. I do a lot of the work around the house now that I am feeling better. I remake old sweaters, use glue to wash woolens and a native nut for hair and silks. Because wool has been impossible to get this last year, I bought a yellow machine-knit suit from a Missionary returning home and ripped it. This takes patience for one gets nothing but short pieces because of the seams. Dzan and I then wove the ends together, poured boiling water over the lot to take out the curls and "presto," some beautiful fine yarn for children's clothes.

In addition, I have been having the Chinese nurses (we now have three) over with Dr. Hsu each week to discuss professional problems, plans, etc. I always serve sandwiches and tea as we sit around our dining room table very informally, arguing and have a great time. While there is still something of a language barrier of course, my big problem has been getting the nurses to take me seriously. You see when I was so ill this Spring, I couldn't hold a thought in my head and was always confused and dependent. At the time, I believe they thought me quite stupid. That has all gone, thank God, for it was hell while it lasted. I now enjoy adding my training and experience to the common pool for what it is worth. This naturally has brought criticism upon our heads from the foreign community who feel we are losing face or dignity or whatever, but Hospital *esprit de corps* is building and we are acting more and more as a team.

☐ *OCTOBER 26TH:* Judith is developing apace. She tried to carry Carol today. Fortunately I was on the spot. She can now say "Amen" to her prayers. I took her out to visit the other day in her white beret, little blue coat, blue viyella matching dress with lovely cotton smocking, white shoes, lovely fine socks and beautiful white galoshes, all gifts from home. It was a cold wet day so the Dragon carried her in her beloved *bei dao*, in which she sat like an infant queen.

The wedding of Dr. Gilbert Hsu, Ralph's assistant, and Chloe Sung, a nurse, Junghsien 1942. Chloe is wearing Margaret's wedding dress.

The Mission compound at Tzeliutsing, 1944. The large complex in the background is the Hospital; in the foreground are missionary residences.

The Hsieh family with Gerrie
Hartwell, superintendent of nurses,
Junghsien, 1946.

Margaret with Carol, Kerry and
Judy, Tzeliutsing, 1944.

Ralph with Clarence Vichert, a missionary friend who accompanied the children to safety in North America.

Gordon and Mil Campbell, colleagues and friends in Chengtu.

The Li Hen family, colleagues at West China Union University, continued their friendship with Margaret and Ralph at some personal risk during the Communist take over.

Drs. Leslie and Jean Kilborn, medical faculty at WCUU, with their daughter Mary, an RN.

Ralph's farewell concert, shortly before departure, Chengtu, 1950.

凡木菇則其地潛惟檣不然葉茂於水中䕺
腐能肥田甚於糞壤故田家毒稊之淨風
茇。如白楊也
中仁尊兄大人居 趙熙

Scroll by revered Junghsien callig-
rapher Chao Hsi, presented to Ralph
Outerbridge in appreciation for his
medical work.

☐ *NOVEMBER 9TH:* I was invited to the Hsieh home for tea. As one enters its black heavy doors, it depends upon the nature of one's business as to how far one progresses through its various courtyards. About fifty feet in there is a lovely moon gate, with well-tended gardens beyond. Their house is graciously unostentatious, actually foreign in appearance. I believe it has been built within the last ten years. The baby, if I haven't mentioned it before, is a darling and Hsieh tai tai is very proud. Hong-di's clothes were brought out for me to inspect. How beautiful they are! She has the most gorgeous "piglet" cap of black satin. This has an elaborate pig's nose at the front done in gold thread and stuffed out to be very realistic, satin and jade ears and around the rim the eighteen *lohans* (deified figures in Chinese mythology who had achieved Buddha's enlightenment) also in gold. This is but one of a dozen or so equally interesting bonnets. I particularly loved a summer one, just a black satin band which widens at the front to cover the anterior fontanelle. This sports a little pig tail of braided silk so cleverly embroidered into the band that it looks truly as though it were a natural growth. And so many shoes!

☐ *NOVEMBER 15TH:* Even with my wonderful Fuh, the house sometimes gets me down, so I hop on my bike for an hour's change of atmosphere. This does wonders for one's equilibrium. Also I won't allow raised voices in my presence. The cook and the amah, however, have the Szechwanese *hoper peechi* (firecracker temper) and occasionally one can just feel the tension building. When this happens, I buzz off. They have a wonderful fight and by the time I return, all is sweetness and light.

☐ *NOVEMBER 23RD:* It is the custom here for the *tai tai* (me in this instance) to carry the keys, the most important of which is to the supply cupboard. But Fuh has proved himself in so many ways that I have long since taken to giving him the keys whenever he needs them. This has scandalized (what doesn't) our foreign neighbors. Although every servant gets a bit of "squeeze," to my delight, not only has Fuh played fair, he has been helping me keep my head above water. We are paid by the quarter, but this money which is supposed to last us three months now melts away almost overnight. Consequently, Fuh and I discuss the local market and decide what we are going to buy. Then he goes out and spends our entire salary on oil, rice, sugar, whatever, which we store in the attic. As we need money, he sells these supplies at current prices. To prevent rats menacing our investments, Fuh has brought along two large, otherwise harmless snakes. These shy things now live overhead and I've become used to hearing them slither about. When someone coming from home brought out an old overcoat that had belonged to Ralph's Grandfather Baker, Fuh managed to sell it for an entire winter's supply of sugar.

□ *NOVEMBER 28TH:* Guess what—my *New York Times,* so desperately out of date that my subscription has expired, is beginning to come through! It arrives in batches, but what a lift to be able to read it from cover to cover, to look at the fashions and dream of copying them, to remember that one once was carefree, went to parties and had fun. I've written the *Times* asking whether they would send it free if in return I submitted short pieces on some of the interesting things we see.

□ *DECEMBER 7TH:* Last Sunday, Ralph and I organized a Worship Service. Initially, I outright refused to help, even though it has distressed me deeply that there is so much pettiness and backbiting among the foreigners here. We are all depressed and worried of course, but this should be a time of mutual trust and help. So finally I agreed. There is a lovely little Chapel in the Mission, but our two ordained Ministers don't like taking Service. Ralph and I cleaned it up and the community gathered to sing, pray and reflect. Alf Day and Dorothy Fox sang solos. Ralph played Schubert's "Serenade" on his violin and told a story that left everyone's throats a bit tight. I read the Lesson and I guess rubbed it in. *First Corinthians,* Chapter 13:

"Though I speak with the tongues of men and of angels, and have not charity, I am become as sounding brass, or a tinkling cymbal.

2 And though I have the gift of prophecy, and understand all mysteries, and all knowledge; and though I have all faith, so that I could remove mountains, and have not charity, I am nothing.

3 And though I bestow all my goods to feed the poor, and though I give my body to be burned, and have not charity, it profiteth me nothing.

4 Charity suffereth long, and is kind; charity envieth not; charity vaunteth not itself, is not puffed up,

5 Doth not behave itself unseemly, seeketh not her own, is not easily provoked, thinketh no evil;

6 Rejoiceth not in iniquity, but rejoiceth in the truth;

7 Beareth all things, believeth all things, hopeth all things, endureth all things.

8 Charity never faileth: but whether there be prophecies,they shall fail; whether there be tongues, they shall cease; whether there be knowledge, it shall vanish away.

9 For we know in part, and we prophesy in part.

10 But when that which is perfect is come, then that which is in part shall be done away.

11 When I was a child, I spake as a child, I understood as a child, I thought as a child; but when I became a man, I put away childish things.

12 For now we see through a glass, darkly; but then face to face: now I know in part; but then shall I know even as also I am known.

13 And now abideth faith, hope, charity, these three; but the greatest of these is charity."

CHAPTER 5

Junghsien /
Beyond the Moon Gate

☐ *JANUARY 18th, 1942:* The big event in our household was the birth just before Christmas of a son to the "Dragon" and his wife. Some months before, he had confided to Ralph his sadness (he is such a gentle man) that all three of his children had died in infancy. When questioned, he revealed that his mother, who had looked after them while his wife worked in the fields, has Tb. Ralph told Lung (the "Dragon" is a literal translation of his name) that the next time his wife became pregnant she should have her baby in hospital where she would be taught how to protect it from infection. In fact, she was already expecting and due for confinement about Christmas. As her time approached, we suggested he bring her to live in the servants' quarters so we might be at hand from the moment of her first contraction. One night we were awakened by the shouts of Lung dashing madly up the walk with a baby in his arms, the placenta swinging like a pendulum as he ran. She had delivered that quickly! Thank heavens he hadn't attempted to tie the cord. This is traditionally done using a lace from the oldest, foulest grass sandal available.

The popular belief is that the placenta can only be drawn out or "down" by an object that has spent its life on the ground. The consequence of this practice is so often tetanus that the Chinese refer to it as "the seventh day madness." There is no more pathetically horrible sight in all the world than a week-old baby unable to eat, its jaw locked shut, its little back arched so that only its heels and head touch the table beneath it, its wee body wracked by tetanic spasms. One poor old dear arrived at our OPD the other day carrying her niece's eight-day-old child, who, she said, had refused his mother's breast for the past forty-eight hours. Ralph told her the infant had tetanus and would live only a day or two more. As her eyes filled with tears, she told him that five times previously a baby born to her niece had died within ten days. All Ralph could do was to promise that next time, if her niece came to the Hospital to deliver, it would cost her nothing. We have now begun to gather information on infant mortality in this area and regularly ask post-menopausal women who attend our OPD how many pregnancies each has had. The answer may be twenty to twenty-five, but the number of living children, two or three. There are so many deadly diseases, it is a wonder any survive. I guess this is why those who do are so resilient.

I kept no record of this Christmas past and have no very clear recollection of it. We have been so busy, the foreign community here so small and peevish and ourselves increasingly involved with the society we serve. But doubtless it was pleasant, with Judith and Carol at least aware it was a very special day. We must have had the traditional goose. Fuh does this like a Peking duck, the endless bastings making its brown and crackly skin the best part. He also has a way of removing the insides of mandarin oranges without seeming to disturb the skin. These we use to decorate the tree along with chains of colored paper and strings of popcorn.

There has been growing steadily a sincere friendship between me and Mrs. Hsieh. I am sure this began because of her gratitude at finally having been delivered of a live child, but we are "sympathique." At first this was more instinct than anything else for my language skills were confined to the "nitty gritty" of everyday life. Indeed, I have learned more Chinese from the servants than from any of my teachers and our talk is exclusively domestic. Hsieh *tai tai* has been very patient in this regard, gradually expanding my exposure to aspects of Chinese culture and equipping me with the necessary vocabulary to cope with each new piece of knowledge. For example, a Chinese poem, popular for about 900 years, reads:

> The scholar has reaped the reward that is due,
> And homeward returns on his wearying steed;
> When the blossoming apricots come into view,
> He urges his charger to bear him with speed.

But for me to understand it, I had first to know that the apricot is an emblem of the fair sex and that the slanting eyes of Chinese beauties are often compared to apricot kernels. We have become such good friends that I have been invited to call her by her familiar name, Banyang (eighth aunty), as a child of the family might. We call her husband, Robert, but not yet to his face. This relationship is developing into the most precious experience for both Ralph and me in China.

What else? Carol has four teeth. Judith is talking. Ralph doesn't expect to be mobilized (I don't think I mentioned he had registered for active service with the British Consul in Chengtu). The possibility of Szechwan being invaded by the Japanese seems slight now that they are so busy elsewhere. The Hospital has taken on a semblance of order. Patients are many. Our reputation on the street is growing. The Bridgemans are leaving and the Websters, whom we like, are coming to take their place.

☐ *JANUARY 31ST:* Margaret Day and I set off on a small adventure last Monday. We rode atop a coal truck the thirty miles to Tzeliutsing to visit friends. Ralph and Alf thought we'd earned a rest from responsibility for a few days. The next morning an exhausted Alf Day arrived on his bicycle (the road is unbelievably rutted and hilly) with an urgent message from Ralph. Carol was very ill. She'd been a bit off color when I left, but Ralph didn't think it anything serious. I was lucky enough to catch a ride and was home by lunch, feeling as guilty as I've ever felt for leaving in the first place. Poor little dickens had what looked like typhoid: a violent dysentry, pus and mucus in her stool and a temperature hovering between 104 and 105 degrees. Ralph had nasal feedings under way and the kid had had a couple of interstitials, but she was so toxic as to be unconscious. One or other of us was with her day and night waiting, praying for some sign that she was fighting back. I kept thinking of Donnie Campbell, but after what seemed an eternity, she began to snap out of it. Oh for some sulfaquanidine! I'm going to write my dad for a small supply even though the only way of getting letters home is by air "over the Hump" to Calcutta, then by ship around the Cape of Good Hope to Britain and hopefully on to Canada.

☐ *MARCH 1ST:* Carol is her own gay little self again. She is trying desperately to talk and will earlier than Judith we think, for Judith is always chattering away at her. Earlier today we went to the local Chinese Church, and because the servants were all off doing something or other, we took the children. Dzan Simoo (our amah), who tends to be a very officious little character, bustled in about halfway through the Service to get them because she felt it was time for their lunch. Before leaving she ordered Judith to say "Bye bye Mummy," ditto "Daddy." Mrs. Hsieh was with us, so Judith was ordered to say "Bye bye Banyang." Then "*hsin li*" (bow), then "do a kees" (blow a kiss), all of which is Dzan's idea of deportment in a foreign child. There was no use trying to stop her. That would have created even more confusion! The Hsieh's have done us the honor of inviting us to become the godparents to their precious baby. The Chinese for godmother is *gan mer* (dry mother). The formal ceremony may raise a few orthodox Mission eyebrows because the Hsiehs, as I've mentioned, are Buddhists.

It is a glorious day. The Dragon is beating the rugs. Judith is eating her lunch in the garden beside me. I am sitting near two splendorous *mei hua* (flowering plum) trees. Their blossom is China's national flower. Banyang was telling me that Lao-Tzu, the founder of Taoism, was born under a plum tree. The valley, a curving series of terraced rape fields, is now a golden blaze. The bees are busy and the air is filled with the elusive fragrance of rape and purple bean. The bean flowers, small purple clusters, are always in bloom with the rape. Truly, the world seems very peaceful today. Ralph and Alf Day decided, money or no, to go to the annual Mission Council meetings in Chengtu. It will take them four days by bike if the weather stays good. I know they will have a wonderful time. Indeed, most of the Station has gone on one excuse or other, so their irritating presences are for the nonce removed. Personally, I am having a lovely time for I have let routine go to the four winds and am living a cotton-wool wrapped existence enjoying my children, the sunshine and my few Chinese friends. Notwithstanding, my days are filled. A spot of spring cleaning, a spot of study, a spot of English teaching, a few hours out in the country and presto, the day is gone!

Yesterday, Margaret Day and I went on a picnic with Banyang and three other *Tai Tai Hwei* friends. It was their turn to provide lunch. Judith came along on the Dragon's back. I didn't know where we were going, but wandered contentedly through the fields laughing and talking, gradually nearing a rather incredible Buddhist Temple built into an entire hillside, its architecture fashioned to the shape of the Laughing Buddha and domed with his face, proportionately huge and golden. On an adjacent ridge, we entered the stone-walled garden of a country home belonging to one of our friends' uncles. The courtyard was a mass of pink and white *mei hua* bloom and another flowering tree that the Chinese love, the *moli hua*. Its particularly fragrant flowers are like small white roses but about the size of ten-cent pieces. Judith especially adored it when the caretaker allowed her to ring the bell in the most exquisite private Buddhist Chapel I have ever seen. The setting sun, reflected in the endless flooded rice paddies, gave the surrounding countryside a crimson hue as we sat to our delicious tea of *bao dzes* (much like apple dumplings but filled with either a meat mixture or a sweet one made with rose-petal-flavored sugar) and ripe fruit. Later, when we slowly wended our way homeward along a moonlit path, servants preceded us holding branches of *mei hua* into the gentle breeze. Its fragrance filled the air, the petals of the lovely *moli hua* in our hands completing this bouquet. One of my friends has purchased a small silver-mesh case, especially designed for perfumed petals, to pin on her dress.

☐ *MARCH 15TH:* Judith picks up Chinese much more easily than she does English, although there are some of our words she particularly loves, "T'poon" being one, "Bun-unn" (button) another. Her favorite Chinese expression at the moment is "*dow gow*" (pray). The other day, dressed only in her underpants, she stood on our upstairs verandah exhorting all who passed to "*dow gow, dow gow, dow gow.*" We thought this rather a good sign as she had been caught swiping tomatoes not too long before.

There is a faint possibility we may be moved to Tzeliutsing. I keep my fingers crossed, for although our house here is falling apart, the houses there have been blown half to bits, with no hope of repair until after the War. Besides, in that they have been bombed so often, there is the constant strain of expectation. Certainly, it would be a marvelous opportunity for Ralph to be in charge of surgery in what is our third-largest hospital in Szechwan. He would love it, but I wonder if he is quite ready for it. Besides, his work here is not complete.

I think I now have some idea of how the Queen must feel, living a goldfish-bowl existence. In our small city, everything we do, every move we make travels the street so quickly the entire town often knows what one or other of us has done before we have a chance to share the experience at home. This, I suppose, is natural enough. But, in addition, we have been watched with gimlet eyes by the pro-Dr. Loh group, who have been waiting to pounce at Ralph's first mistake. It was to the particular delight of these people when recently we became a public laughing stock. One afternoon at OPD a man was brought in bleeding profusely and accompanied by a large crowd of excited people. His ear had been lopped off by Mr. Wu, the bus depot manager, who caught him picking pockets (the customary penalty for such and rather better than the Mohammedan one). Ralph treated his injury and admitted him to hospital, much to Miss Yuin's discomfiture. She maintained he was a criminal and a threat to the other patients. Ralph reassured her by taking away all the thief's clothes and possessions and locking them up in the Administration office. It is the custom for a patient to retain these in a small cabinet beside his bed. He reasoned the man wouldn't want to leave without them and further that he couldn't get up to much mischief if he had to flee dressed only in a hospital gown. It was the next morning at rounds that Ralph conceived the idea of trying to re-construct a new ear for him. And so the pickpocket stayed on, a quiet fellow who caused no trouble. Early the fourth morning, however, we were awakened by the most awful row from the male wing of the Hospital. When Ralph went over, he was greeted by anger and consternation. There was little doubt our thief had gotten up in the middle of the night to systematically raid the lockers of the other nineteen patients on the ward. We assume he bundled everything of any value into the sheet now missing from his bed and escaped over the compound wall with the help of the bamboo pole we use to prop up the middle of our clothes line. The street simply rocked with laughter at our expense. And speaking of such, Ralph was financially responsible for every missing article, real or imagined. Our Hospital Board, their families and our few friends in the city all scrounged around for stuff they did not need until finally we were able to make restitution in kind. Only in retrospect can one see the comic side of this affair.

☐ *MARCH 27TH:* The other day, the ladies from our *Tai Tai Hwei* felt free enough to tease me about my Chinese, telling me about some of my boo boos with their language. "You see," said one, "you have learned it from your servants, so you are often very vulgar!" What fun. Banyang, of course, is becoming my dearest friend. I don't think I have ever described her to you. She has the peach-shaped face considered beautiful here, but with an unusually high forehead. Actually she has a very mobile countenance, full of expression and good humor. I also think she's very clever and generous. When she drops in to visit with "Jennifer," as we've nick-named our goddaughter to be, she usually brings some thoughtful gift, perhaps a ring of flowers for my hair or a little tea about which she carefully instructs me. Did you know that when serving tea in China the spout of the tea kettle must never face one's guest? Mastering Chinese tea culture is at least as complicated as becoming an expert on French wines, perhaps moreso. Of course, I now feel very free to pop over to her house, which is just across our back wall, where gradually I have become *persona grata* with her mother-in-law, *Lao tai tai* (Grandma, literally "old lady"), who rules the Hsieh roost with great discipline. Wizened, with pulled-back grey hair, bright brown eyes and very poor teeth, *Lao tai tai* keeps an array of beautifully fashioned silver tooth and ear picks on a small ring pinned to the lapel of her gown. One is shaped like a miniature eagle's claw. These fascinate me. The old girl and I now regularly have tea and eat peanuts. When first I visited, my peanuts contained but one nut per shell. Then, as we grew to know and like each other, I began to get two. When Ralph visits, however, he gets three peanuts per shell. According to Banyang, *Lao tai tai* personally sorts every nut and one tells where one stands with her by the kind she serves.

While Fuh is a great cook, it is Banyang who has taught me about some of their delicacies. Once, for supper, she gave me a steaming bowl of lovely chicken soup with a pigeon's egg poaching on top. For breakfast, one might be served rice and several kinds of wonderfully cured bits and pieces (duck tongues for example) or a hen's egg in a sweet and sour sauce. The unripened walnut and chicken dishes I have sampled are also excellent, but take ages to prepare for each kernel must be meticulously peeled of its green inner skin. And spring rolls wrapped in a very thin wheat flour crust like a *bao dze*, but filled with spiced meat and a certain kind of just-sprouted leaf for maximum tenderness.

One is invited to "formal" dinners or feasts here by a red guest list or *kai dan*, which one signs if able to attend. The feast may be called for 2 P.M. but normally takes place much later. Actually, this is the reverse of the Western custom where dinner is followed by coffee or tea and conversation. Here, conversation, tea and sunflower seeds precede the feast. Consequently, one usually arrives a little late. At the dinner itself, the guest of honor would be seated mid-table facing the entranceway, so that he might take note of everyone coming into or leaving the room. Were he sufficiently important, his cook might be invited to prepare the meal to ensure his master's satisfaction. Thus was his safety assured in earlier times. The host always sits opposite him, his back to the door. There may be twenty-four dishes served at one of these dinners and it is important to go easy on the early ones. And every hamlet, town and city is famous for at least one culinary treat. Jenshow, for example, is known for a small fresh-water crab creation the equal of which I have never tasted, and Junghsien for its wonderful soy sauce and pig tendon. The tough tendons are reduced over several days to a gelatinous pulp, which is delicately flavored and served in a delicious soup. I should add that soup (which must be spooned towards one's self, not away as we do) is always served last, sometimes with a chicken swimming in its broth. Except for this (for which porcelain spoons are provided), one uses one's chopsticks both to eat and to serve oneself, whether to pull the flesh off a wonderfully crisped fish or to take some *ba bao fan* (eight precious ingredients in sweet glutinous rice) or whatever. The second-to-last course is rice, and it is considered impolite to leave so much as a single grain in one's bowl! Difficult for a novice. To some degree, the messier and noisier one's performance at table, the happier one's host for this tells him how much his hospitality is appreciated. The host eats very little, but spends his time circulating, sometimes actually serving a particular delicacy or other to his guests. Under no circumstance may he complete his own dinner before his last visitor is sated. When finished, one puts one's chopsticks parallel atop one's bowl. The person on one's left then places them on the table, at which point your host will say, "*chin kuan dzo*" (please sit wide). In other words, one is free to go to the courtyard or wherever to digest or ruminate. The woman of the house may or may not appear, but never joins the feast. She is mistress of the kitchen.

☐ *APRIL 7TH:* The Bridgemans are gone but not forgotten. Before they left, we purchased their two part-foreign cows, both supposedly enceinte, for $6,000. As it turns out, the older of the two is not and never will be and is only good for the glue factory. When I consider that they got this cow for nothing in the first place. . . . What a gyp! As expected, Mrs. B. turned over her needlework girls to me and her Well-Baby Clinic to Marg Day (we switched as soon as she was out of sight).

In any event, our younger cow has now given birth to a heifer and freshened. She has a thirty-two cup capacity (exactly two American gallons), which not only assures us a secure milk supply but has given Fuh much face in the town in that the average Chinese cow produces only enough for its offspring. We had a great scare though, given our investment, a few days after she calved. She became so sick we thought she was going to die. Ralph attempted to treat her, but of course hadn't the foggiest. He prescribed a warm bran mash and when that didn't work a large dose of Glauber's salts. To effect the latter, Fuh had to pry open her mouth while Ralph poured in the mixture, the two of them massaging it down her gullet. By nightfall, she was no longer able to stand. It was at this point that Fuh summoned the courage, knowing how we feel about Chinese medicine, to ask permission to call in a Chinese veterinary. Ralph agreed, thinking that if it didn't help, it couldn't hurt. When the vet arrived, he made a rapid diagnosis and began sticking long steel needles up her nose and along her back. These, he explained, would let out the noxious humors. He then prescribed a potion, said she would be fine by morning, collected his fee and left. Sure enough, by the time we woke up, our cow was not only back on its feet, but had broken free to cavort with the neighbor's bull. Ralph observed wryly that the vet obviously had prescribed too much Yang and not enough Yin.

Certainly, we are better acquainted with the failures of traditional Chinese medicine; our OPD and Hospital wards are filled with them. Recently, Ralph, returning from Tzeliutsing on his bicycle, stopped for tea in one of the villages along the way. While there, an acupuncturist set up shop on the sidewalk outside. Of course Ralph stayed to watch. The scene he described had the flavor of a patent medicine show at home. A crowd of interested villagers gathered to listen to the pitch, look at his charts of the human body and watch various of their neighbors being treated. A husky farm boy, who appeared to be suffering from tuberculous glands of the neck, was the afternoon's feature attraction. The Chinese doctor picked up what looked pretty much like a ten-inch steel knitting needle. He spat on it, ran it several times through his filthy straw sandal to remove the rust, wiped it clean on the sleeve of his gown and lubricated it in his oily hair. He then passed the point of his needle up the patient's nose and with a single mallet blow drove it a full inch through the ethmoid plate into the brain. This was done so quickly, the young man just stood there looking rather stupid and blinking back the tears. When it appeared he was about to faint, the needle was removed, the fee collected and the patient pushed back into the awestruck crowd. A week later, Ralph stopped at the same tea house and in the course of conversation asked the proprietor if he knew what had happened to this lad. He did. Within two days of his treatment, the boy's neck glands had virtually disappeared. On the third day, however, he became ill "with a hot disease and began to rave with demons." He died the next evening. When the acupuncturist was contacted, he indignantly insisted that he had driven his needle through the spot and to the depth dictated by the ancients. Could he help it if his patient was so full of malignant and malicious humors that they plugged the very opening made for their escape!

☐ *APRIL 12TH:* The main street of our city is dominated by its teahouses, open to the street, where men congregate and all the gossip and news are circulated and digested. Dogs and chickens scrounge the dirt floors for tidbits, but the usual fare is simply tea. A bowl is dropped before one, a pinch of green tea added, then a stream of boiling water is poured over the guest's shoulder from a large copper or tin kettle with a long thin spout. This really takes skill, but I have never seen anyone scalded. One rests, one sips, one listens, one talks and before one's bowl is empty it is refilled (but further tea is never added). Various mobile craftsmen (shoemakers, tinsmiths, candy vendors, etc.) often sit outside to listen in on the conversations while plying their trades. But Chinese women and children are welcome only on those rare evenings when a travelling story-teller is performing.

We have market day twice weekly. The rural phrase for husband is *gan chiang di* (go-to-market person) and that for a wife, *sao guo di* (keeper of the hearth). I love the street when it is thronged with farmers, vendors, tradesmen and servants buying for their respective households. Each farmer is allowed six square feet of sidewalk for his produce. Local transport is mainly by wheelbarrow or shoulder pole. Meat is brought in live and of course there are all kinds of fresh vegetables, fruit, etc. The vendors have the usual array of merchandise, including split-bamboo baskets of every shape and form, palm-bark capes to wear in the rain, woven bamboo mats for sleeping, slightly thicker palm-bark mats for mattresses. One of the most interesting tradesmen is the man who mends broken dishes. Using a fine bit fixed into the end of a stick and rotated by a string on a bamboo bow (much like a boy scout making a fire), he carefully drills tiny holes into the bottom of the plate on each side of the break, into which he then hammers narrow flat brass staples. These not only join the break so completely that the dish is whole again, but the mend is watertight and virtually invisible. Crowds gather at any excuse, but the "medical men" attract the largest as they perform their "miracles." Above the din, occasional bells signal either a Buddhist priest begging for alms or a line of four or five blind men passing as in Biblical times, one leading the next, hand upon shoulder, the front man ringing the bell. The people are good natured, laughing and joking. Of course when foreigners appear, we are regarded simply as extra entertainment and as I understand more and more Chinese, the remarks our presence elicits become funnier and funnier, although invariably rude.

☐ *MAY 28TH:* Ralph usually operates in the morning, with a busy Out Patients in the P.M. If there is an emergency, two of the coolie staff dash out with a stretcher to bring in the patient. We have had quite a few nasty cases of men and boys gored by water buffalo lately. Normally peaceful, this animal occasionally goes berserk. I've been told this is usually coincidental with a small amount of exudate oozing from its ears. Sounds like a parasite of some sort. Ironically, their victims' cases are usually complicated by the inevitable round worms which inhabit the human bowel. In one instance, a farmer was carried thirty-five miles with eight feet of small intestine protruding from a three-inch hole in his lower right quadrant. In another a twenty-year-old was gored close to his anus. After four days of not being able to void or move his bowels and in continuous pain, he went to a doctor in private practice in the town who catheterized him, removing a considerable quantity of bloody fluid. When the bladder was almost empty, the metal catheter was removed. But on trying to get it in again, the doctor could not do so. Consequently, he sent the man to us. As it turned out, this patient was suffering from a complete rupture through the lower end of the extra-pelvic urethra. He was in hospital for over three months.

Then there are the normal run of acute appendicitis, strangulated hernias, hysterectomies, etc. Maternity work is usually done at home for superstition decrees that a woman not cross her threshold until forty days after delivery. I hear that the more enterprising obviate this by using a window. In any event, it is generally only cases the local midwives have given up on that come our way. These foul creatures account for 70 per cent of the women in labor Ralph sees being infected before admission to hospital. We had one the other day, a woman allegedly in labor six days, twenty-six years old, primipara. She had been manipulated by dirty midwives, one of whom had used a knife to perform a mid-line incision of the perineum! She was distended with gas, urine was leaking from a torn bladder and the anterior wall of the vagina torn away and protruding. Ralph found upon examination that the baby was still alive, head not engaged, in fact the woman was not in labor at all!

The G'issimo's recent proclamation of the death penalty for anyone caught smoking opium has led to a great number of poor souls seeking admission to our Hospital where they undergo gradual withdrawal over several weeks. One interesting sidelight: when a wealthy patient is cured of the ailment that has been bothering him, and Ralph is asked for the bill, he demurs, "Why sir, it was an honor to treat you." The poor fellow is then put in the embarrassing position of having to save face by making a donation instead, usually more than he would have been charged.

☐ *JUNE 7TH:* Ralph is in Tzeliutsing (pronounced dze-liu-jin) for a month relieving Dr. Sheridan, who has taken his wife to the hills for a well-deserved holiday, their first in two years. Ralph is very excited about this for the hospital, as I've mentioned, is large, well equipped and better staffed than ours, despite its bomb damage. He is getting six times the surgery he gets in Junghsien. Many of the emergencies seem to occur at night, but at least Tzeliutsing has electricity. Ralph says (his letters arrive daily) that he looks at their drug supply and is almost sick with envy. He and my friend Tallie, who was transferred to Tzeliutsing when she returned from furlough, are reorganizing the dispensary. Also, there are several doctors in private practice in the city who occasionally call him in on consultation. I miss him very much and have decided to spend the rest of this month in Junghsien hoping he will be able to go to Gao Sh Ti with us when the Sheridans return.

☐ *JULY 3RD:* Ralph is finally back. About time too! Carol was beginning to call the Dragon, "Daddy." However, it now appears we will have to go to the hills without him after all, if we are to escape the heat and the danger that cholera will spread from Chungking where there's been an outbreak. Of course we will take the cow and her calf. For this they will be fitted with grass sandals exactly like the ones we all wear (except made for a hoof) to prevent them slipping on the flagstone paths. It should be quite a procession. Too bad we don't have a couple of pigs and a goat!

Banyang and I saw each other every day when Ralph was away. Mr. Liu, her father, who spends a good deal of time at the Hsiehs', now treats me like one of the family. On one occasion, he even got out a precious bottle of Spanish Sherry for me. And another day, he took me to visit one of the Buddhist Temples. As we walked around looking at the garishly painted and menacing god figures so overwhelming in their size, I asked, "Surely you don't actually worship these images?" His reply solved many riddles for me, "Mei Dei [my Chinese name], these are for the little people to help them to visualize what Buddhism is all about." I like their Temples, always open, no formality, children running about, people coming and going, the monks never too busy to take a wee one by the hand and wander with him answering his questions. To get back to Banyang, she was just about as excited as I was when Ralph returned. The afternoon of his arrival, I found her in my kitchen in consultation with Fuh. Then, just before bedtime, we were presented with hot drinks. When Ralph asked what they were, Fuh said simply that Hsieh *tai tai* had instructed him to prepare them. *Ai yah*, aphrodisiacs!

☐ *AUGUST 9TH:* I am writing this at Gao Sh Ti. It is a lazy Sunday morning. Mary and George Birtch and their two children are with us and at the moment. We are having a very good time, although I was pretty lonely and homesick until Ralph finally got away. It is so hard to find things to interest one when there are no books, few people one enjoys and so on. The cottage we occupy is large, rambling and in poor repair. We spent five hundred dollars before coming up just fixing leaks, etc., but when the first rains came, a portion of the ceiling fell in. Like the cottage we had last summer, it is made of thick mud blocks and is surrounded by wide verandahs. It has a small barn out back for the cow and her calf. The kitchen is just a lean-to with a couple of *gohs* (woks) on braziers and a funny little oven made by the tinsmith which seems to work fairly well in Fuh's capable hands. I should mention that we haven't seen a Japanese bomber all summer.

Judith has just returned from the children's Church Service. They have been learning about Daniel in the lions' den. She was Daniel, and Ralph Birtch, just her age but with a terrific voice, was a lion. She has grown about six inches this year, a tall wee monkey and very sweet. Carol is running everywhere. She feeds herself almost as well as Judith and in some ways is better trained. A good vocabulary in English as well as Chinese, she has brains *de hen* (very much). You would love her bright golden hair, vivid blue eyes and incredibly dark lashes.

George Birtch is considered one of the bright lights among the younger theologues, all kinds of scholarships and a couple of years in Scotland. Mary is very attractive and a good sport. We have played bridge, picnicked, wandered in the moonlight, sung old songs, all interspersed with good conversation, getting a lot off our respective chests. One evening, we organized a community folk dance. George's Missionary aunt was persuaded to play her accordian. The oldsters sat around the bonfires and watched while the rest of us danced ourselves silly.

□ *SEPTEMBER 21ST:* August passed too quickly and we returned to Junghsien in early September, regretfully, for another year. I am writing this on a very busy morning. You should hear the bedlam in the kitchen. Both children are very hungry and Carol in particular is demanding food! Monday here is much like at home, washing, cleaning, etc. At the moment, we have house guests, so of course there is even more washing than usual. This we do with a scrub board in wooden tubs.

Now that mail is getting through again (for a while we had difficulty getting it from Station to Station, never mind continent to continent), it is interesting to learn that those at home are rationed. If I do not sound sympathetic, I certainly am. One rather forgets, however, what it is like to live in a country where anything beyond staple commodities can be purchased. I have but one pair of silk stockings which I have been wearing very carefully for over a year. We don't buy anything except food. Wool is selling in Chengtu at $1400 a pound. We are grateful to have enough to live on, enough to wear, a place to sleep and our family intact. Actually the simpler life becomes the better I like it. One bowl, one pair of chopsticks!

□ *OCTOBER 4TH:* The children grow apace. Carol now has all the teeth she will be getting for a while. She is very vociferous and full of beans, won't go to sleep at night until I tuck her in, hates vegetables and will only eat them if one of us feeds her. She usually wears a little pleated skirt and puffed sleeve blue blouse or white sweater, all of which I have made without a pattern. Her most prized possession (a birthday present from Margie Day) is a very beautiful scrap book, each page in which has one picture carefully cut from some magazine. Carol loves this book (she has no other) and always takes it to bed with her. One day when I went in to waken her from her afternoon nap, there she lay looking very contented, the book open at the page which had featured a cornflakes advertisement. This she had carefully picked off and eaten!

These last couple of weeks have been a strain. Our dear friend Mr. Liu is very ill. Banyang's step-mother, however, is old fashioned and refused, despite his being chairman of our Hospital Board, to have a Western doctor consulted. Instead, she had in the most prominent of the hundred-odd local herb, acupuncture and cupping types. Each prescribed his remedy. Mr. Liu became weaker and weaker. They all said he was going to die. Banyang, as a younger daughter, hasn't much authority in her father's home, but she has a great deal of enterprise and courage. She defied the rest of the family and on the eleventh

day of his illness came to us in her distress asking Ralph to examine her dad. So he did. (Actually, this was the one and only
time either of us ever entered Mr. Liu's house.) Ralph diagnosed
typhoid fever, but refused to treat him unless he was admitted
to hospital. His wife would not hear of it. Mr. Liu's eldest son
was away and out of reach, as were his three other sons, so
Banyang, contrary to all custom, assumed responsibility for her
father's life or death. At the Hospital, the entire staff was put on
special duty. Ralph slept by his bed. Mr. Liu was coddled and
cared for like a premature baby. Banyang has had to fight tooth
and nail with various members of her family just to give us a
chance to save him and we are holding our breaths.

☐ *OCTOBER 17TH:* Quite a lot to report. First of all, Mr. Liu,
dear frail old man, has gradually pulled out of it, is sitting up in
bed, eating soft foods and will be discharged in a week or two.
Banyang's face is great, although she has lost pounds through
this ordeal. I haven't mentioned she is also very pregnant,
thrilled to pieces and hoping for their much-longed-for son.
Ralph expects her to deliver around the middle of November.
Since her father was admitted to hospital, she and Ralph have
been in close consultation. And when she isn't at the Hospital,
she is with me. At first, I didn't understand how serious a gamble she had taken, but gradually the full story has come out. In
the absence of her brothers, her eldest sister's husband was the
next in line to make the decision about Mr. Liu. He could not
bring himself to contravene his step-mother-in-law's wishes, so
Banyang acted alone, an unheard of thing for a woman in her
position. This has provided the entire district with a fascinating
drama. Had Mr. Liu died, custom and public opinion would
have gravely censured and perhaps ostracized Hsieh *tai tai*! Am
I ever glad we proved worthy of her trust.

Dr. Hsu, Ralph's assistant, is marrying the most attractive of
our nurses, Chloe Sung. They are both very poor and have
turned to me for help. If I'm going to be a mother figure, I'm
going to have to stop pulling out my grey hairs. I've borrowed
from here and there to make their big moment a success. The

wedding gown is my beautiful white satin night dress, which has a small train. With appropriate lingerie and a little lace bolero jacket, she should be quite elegant. The veil, which belongs to one of the WMS girls, however, is pretty tacky having gone through bombings and floods. I really wish we could do without one, but the bride-to-be loves it. Actually, the Hospital is standing most of the financial strain, hosting the feast, etc. Judith is to be flower girl and I shudder to think of what may happen. The bridal couple are to spend their wedding night at our house before starting out on a short honeymoon.

□ *OCTOBER 25TH:* The Hsu wedding took place yesterday in the Mission Chapel. Only the senior staff, the foreign community and the Hsiehs were present. Our Chinese Pastor performed the ceremony. Gerrie Hartwell, our new Nursing Superintendent, mangled the wedding march on a small portable organ and Judy was in her element! That old amah of ours, whom I threatened almost on pain of death to be quiet and not interfere, was allowed to take Carol. Judy wore some beautiful coral beads my dad gave me when I was about her age and my little turquoise ring, a lovely crisp pink voile dress, white socks and shoes, a garland in her hair. Filled with her own importance, she preceded the party down the aisle, throwing rose petals to all and sundry, smiling, waving at friends and generally having a wonderful time. Gilbert Hsu looked as depressed and scared as any groom I have ever seen. Chloe, as is required, looked very sad as well. Alf Day sang a solo. Ralph gave away the bride, I the groom. Then we all went to the Hospital where our combined cooks had prepared a huge feast which included everyone in the Mission from the coolie staff on up. Many were the jokes (very earthy ones) and many the speeches. At last it was over and we returned home with the bridal party and a few close friends. When I went up to the guest room to see that all was well, someone (darn that Dzan—for I'm sure it was she) had turned down the bed and had scattered blood-red rose petals suggestively on the sheet. I didn't remove them, feeling that perhaps this was part of the drill. Banyang later told me that it's the custom to send the bloodstained sheets from the wedding night to the bride's parents. If these are not suitably soiled, they lose much face. She also tells me there are seventy-two ways to make love in China and that most men have copies of a book graphically illustrating each position (some of these painted by famous artists). I would like to see a copy.

☐ *NOVEMBER 12TH:* Ralph recently released a patient whose stay in hospital had been just over four months. This was as bizarre a case as one might encounter, even here where the grotesque is commonplace. Six years earlier this man, with suicide in mind, swallowed a pipe, with a small metal bowl, a ten-inch bamboo stem and a metal mouthpiece! All this time it had lodged in his stomach. He came to OPD only when it finally ruptured the stomach wall and a red and somewhat painful abscess developed. Initially his case seemed a fairly straightforward procedure. The abscess was opened, the pus evacuated and the pipe withdrawn through the incision. But when the wound did not heal, a second exploratory operation (obviously we have nothing so modern as x-rays) revealed the partial destruction of the ninth rib. When it still did not heal, a third operation found the eighth rib had a hole the size of a nickel punched out of its lower margin. With portions of the two ribs removed, there were no further complications.

The wealthy Church in Montreal where Ralph was "designated" as a Medical Missionary in 1938, several months ago donated *thirty* Canadian dollars to our work (enough for one bushel of rice), their first such recognition of Ralph's existence in China! Ralph has been hoping to find a specific use for their meager contribution that might squeeze blood from a heart of stone in spurring them to a greater commitment to our Mission. In this regard, he remembers well their warm response to an address one evening in early 1938 by Doctor W. E. Smith, who had retired after long years of service in West China, much of it in Junghsien. One of his stories concerned an old beggar who had appeared on our streets in 1927 accompanied by a terribly crippled four-year-old girl. Smith's audience was appropriately shocked when he told them this child had been maimed by the old man, who cut the tendons in her left limbs to improve her value as an object of pity (a practice not unknown in England in an earlier age). Retribution (presumably Divine), however, lay just around the corner. The old man and little girl had been begging quite successfully for several weeks when one day a high official happened past in his litter. The child waved and seemed to call a familiar name that reminded him of friends in Kueiyang who had been attacked by bandits the year before, their house burned and everyone killed except for their little girl who had mysteriously disappeared. When he had last seen them alive, she too had called him "*Ba Ba*." He at once stopped his conveyance and had his men seize the old beggar, who despite loud protests that the child was his own granddaughter, was quickly tried and convicted of kidnapping and mutilation. His sentence, to be taken outside the North Gate of the city to an abandoned quarry where he was to be stoned to death by the children of Junghsien. A punishment to fit the crime.

Fourteen years later, shortly after our arrival here, we were being entertained at a welcoming feast, where Ralph was seated beside a Mrs. Jung, a Mission lay worker, who has lived here for many years. Ralph asked her about this story. She not only recalled it clearly, but believed this girl, now in her late teens, to be still at the local government orphanage. When Ralph wondered aloud if it would be possible after all these years to help her by surgery, Mrs. Jung was intrigued and offered to find her. Subsequently, arrangements were made to bring the young woman into hospital for a thorough examination. Certainly, she had a marked deformity in her left limbs, but she had been born a spastic hemiplegic, a condition quite beyond any surgical remedy. There wasn't a scar on her body!

□ *NOVEMBER 14TH:* Banyang has given birth to a second daughter, Ying-di. Ralph and Miss Yuin were in attendance. By all reports it was a fairly easy labor and Ralph says that she does not seem overly disappointed at the result. She will try again for a son, and again and again if necessary.

□ *NOVEMBER 24TH:* With eggs two dollars each and ourselves the proud possessors of four live chickens (Banyang gave
us two, grateful patients did likewise), we decided to build a
small chicken coop in the back corner of our garden. Our sleeping porch overlooks this area and the other night we were
wakened by excited sounds from that direction. Fearing someone was trying to steal our clucking treasures, we lit pewter
lamps, slipped on kimonos, ran downstairs and out, pausing
only to grab a couple of kitchen knives. The moon was bright
and I couldn't help being amused by our long threatening
shadows as we hurried across the yard to investigate. Three
dead chickens lay on the dirt floor, necks broken, and one was
fast disappearing through a small tunnel under the wall. (Fuh
says the culprit was a wildcat.) With our now characteristic
Oriental fatalism, we hung the birds to bleed and went back to
bed. In the morning we put our heads together with Fuh and
decided the "signs" were favorable for a long-planned feast. So
out went the *kai dan* to the District Governor, the most prominent members of the Hospital Board and, of course, Dr. Hsu
(ten in all). We worked hard all day. Fuh is not only a good cook
but an artist, so we banked the table with garlands of fresh
flowers, displayed the silver shield a grateful patient had given
Ralph praising his skill and so on. The menu was Western with a
Chinese flavor, making it as interesting as possible, followed by
coffee and talk in the living room. I stayed in the kitchen, where
custom demanded. Fuh later told me that one of the men, confused by the presence of the small cream pitcher, picked it up
by the handle and took a small sip from the spout! Don't laugh.
I have made similar breaks in Chinese etiquette. We all do when
introduced to a new culture. The Governor made a very flowery
speech ending with, "And our gracious host has given us coffee
to drink! Do you realize that this luxury is now $25.00 gold a
pound on the street? It shows the great regard in which he holds
us." (Fuh had made the ersatz to which he always adds any old
coffee grounds he can find. It is tasty, but it certainly is not coffee!) Ralph of course had to reply in kind, but to my horror
ended with the story of the wildcat's visit. This amused every-

one no end. Mr. Liu was well enough to come, still very frail but gaining daily.

□ *DECEMBER 13TH:* I have just returned home from a trip to Chengtu. Despite Ralph's encouragement, because of my earlier experience with Carol, I was reluctant to go, but it was wonderful. I was like a kid from the country going to New York. I hadn't realized how much I needed a break. At first, I found I couldn't even talk to people like I used to. All I could do was cry when anyone asked me about Junghsien. One of my friends looked at me and said (the Chinese can be brutally frank), "Margaret, what has happened to you? You look ten years older!" Of course, Mil and her friends were wonderful to me. There was always something happening and it wasn't long before I was dancing every night at the Canadian School where the RAF boys refugeeing from Burma have their parties, doing old-fashioned stuff like the Lambeth Walk. We were all lonesome and disorientated, but their conversation meant so much to me, hearing about the War and their experiences. I particularly lost my heart to Dr. LaFrenais, a charming Scotsman living with the Campbells, always fun, but never losing his sang-froid. I talked so much about him when I came home, Ralph had a nightmare in which LaFrenais and I ran off together! Somehow a precious healing took place for me in Chengtu. I had become so depressed with our isolated life. The Mission men have their work which is always challenging, but their wives either crack up or go to seed unless they too have a profession to pursue or a deep commitment to our work here.

□ *DECEMBER 27TH:* We had a splendid Christmas this year. I found a lovely design for miniature bunk beds in one of the old magazines and had them copied for the children's dolls, complete with bed sheets and patchwork quilts. Their dolls also got new outfits. We painted the girls' two Chinese chairs a bright red and had a lovely table made to match. And in Chengtu I bought and borrowed children's books. Judy and Carol were thrilled with everything. The WMS crew came for Christmas breakfast. I then sent the servants and all to Church. We went to the Hospital for a noon meal and at 3:30, the Mission children plus the two Hsieh girls, Jennifer and "Marilyn," came to a party here. Santa distributed gifts and the proud parents plus the WMS'ers had tea. In the evening we went to the Days' for a community dinner. And yesterday Ralph went up to Gao Sh Ti to be present at the Boxing Day celebration of our dear Chinese friends at the Mission school. He returned feeling the effort had been very much worthwhile. I almost forgot to mention that to complete Christmas Day I discovered nits in Judy's head, followed shortly by a similar find in Carol's. But life is like that I suppose.

C H A P T E R 6

Tzeliutsing / An Act of Love

☐ *JANUARY 17TH, 1943:* Am I ever glad I'm a nurse! Ten days ago, with Ralph somewhere on the road from Chengtu and Dzan in hospital getting a bad leg fixed, Judith came in to me, curled up on my lap and said she wanted to go to bed. Her temp. was 104 degrees and mounting. I spent the night by her bedside, sponging, pushing fluids—you know the drill. It was morning when she finally dropped into a troubled sleep. After breakfast, I got the young woman who is helping me at the moment to take Carol over to the Websters' to play. Back with Judith an hour or so later, I became conscious of screams and hysterical voices coming up the walk. When I ran downstairs, there was poor wee Carol shrieking with pain, the entire right side of her face raw. And her eye! I nearly lost my head.

I later learned that, against all rules, she had followed the Websters' puppy into their kitchen, where she attempted to retrieve it from under the stove. Chinese ranges are lower than the home-side variety and the Websters' cook had left a pot of oil on to boil. When Carol screamed, however, no one reacted.

Thinking perhaps the pup had nipped her, moments passed before anyone realized what had happened. And because her blue wool "aviator" cap was not at once removed, her burns are worse than they otherwise might have been. My hand was shaking so badly when I tried to sedate her with half a Dover's powder (opium and ipecacuanha), I gave her too much. Dear Fuh just took one look and started to run the seventy miles to Jenshow, where Ralph, we knew, was planning to spend a day or two.

Dr. Hsu came immediately and was wonderful, spending what seemed an eternity on his knees patiently and gently removing every vestige of burnt skin and swathing Carol's little head and hands in cod-liver-oil-soaked bandages. (I was going to save her curls, but the Dragon threw them out.) It worried me that I had never heard of using cod liver oil for burns, but Gilbert had just read an article on it, so I had to trust his judgment. Providentially, when the Red Cross supplies arrived, I was working in the pharmacy and swiped a couple of quarts for the kids. (Ralph insisted I pay for them. What a guy!) When Carol lay unconscious in my arms, however, her breathing more and more depressed (due to the large dose of sedative), I almost hoped she would not survive. Although I would carry the cross forever, I felt neither she nor I could bear to have her confront the world, with all its cruelties, so scarred and maimed.

In the meantime, Fuh kept running. When he could go no further, he hired someone else to carry on. And so the word went out. No details. Just that Carol was terribly burned. Poor Ralph! It was a blessing Gordon Campbell was with him. Covering the seventy miles as fast as their feet could carry them, they were so exhausted and sore by the time they arrived, I thought I'd have to put them to bed as well.

Carol had a very rough week with a great deal of swelling, toxemia and pain. The poor wee soul was totally blind for the first few days. Fortunately, most of the third-degree burn is on her head not her face and, thank God, she will not lose an eye. She is feeling a lot better and soon will be running around again, although resembling a little soldier. Judith, who was ill with tonsilitis throughout Carol's crisis, is an angel of a patient. It worried her so when she couldn't keep down the sulfa drugs I gave her. Both children are so dear.

☐ *FEBRUARY 19TH:* It is official, we have been moved to Tzeliutsing. I, however, have absolutely refused to go before the end of summer. If we move now, we won't have enough money to go to the hills and the babies must have this change. So I have put "my foot down." (It appears I have potential as a "battle-axe.")

Dzan has such fun dressing the children. When we returned home last night, Judith announced, *"ngo shih hsin guniang"* (I am a bride). Her hair was parted in the middle with pale turquoise bows on either side and crowned with a coronet of plum blossoms. Eyes shining, cheeks matching the flowers, she was wearing her turquoise-blue turtle neck jersey with a pink pullover. Carol was dancing around croaking "pretty, pretty, pretty." We now let Carol up twice daily to let off steam.

☐ *MARCH 5TH:* Carol's bandages came off today and we are able to assess the degree of her disfigurement: a three-inch hairless swathe across her skull from crown to right temple, temple included. Ralph says we can have a good plastic man bring the scalp together when we return home and will start massage as soon as we can to keep the skin loose.

Ralph spent the last ten days in Tzeliutsing and returned on Monday. This, I'm afraid, will be the pattern of our lives until we move our household in September. When he is away, however, I have time to read and think about things other than the eternal problems of ways and means. As to the latter, I think I have solved this once and for all. The cook and I are going into the profiteering business. I am going to begin selling various of our personal possessions for equity. Fuh will do the brain work and get a percentage of what we make, as will all the servants (it's the only way we can keep up with their wages). This will shock our fellow Missionaries, but I can't sit by, as so many do, fold my hands and say, *"mo fah"* (it can't be helped).

☐ *MARCH 13TH:* I think I'd best explain this sales business. The Nationalist gov't has fixed our rate of exchange at $16 Chinese to $1 American, despite the fact the actual value is about a couple of hundred to one. This is a typical Chinese way of maximizing foreign reserves, minimizing foreign debt and squeezing out the foreign institutions. It is costing the various foundations and Churches that support the Mission a fortune just to keep us going. Also, since extraterritoriality has been abrogated, we have to pay taxes on Mission property which previously had been exempt. Fair enough if we got a reasonable exchange. Of course, on a personal basis, we can send money home at 16 to 1. When the Jenners left, we bought their furniture and household effects at a fair price. It was wonderful for us because we had very little. But given the present inflation, everything we own can be sold for many times its original cost and at what the Chinese still consider a relative bargain. The Mission officials at home are somewhat confused by all of this. On the one hand, they hear about our desperate need and, on the other, individual Missionaries are banking large quantities of gold. Ralph and I are worried we may not have been fair with the Jenners so are planning to split any profits on the sale of their former possessions with them. Further, so that we won't fall victim to the greed we have witnessed in some of our fellows, we are putting 10 per cent of everything aside to help with charity cases at the Hospital.

Ralph is hoping to be accepted into one of the best medical graduate courses in North America when we return, which will keep us home-side for two years. The Mission has agreed to give us an extra, albeit unpaid, year of leave. If all works out as planned, he will be the next professor of surgery at wcuu, as Dr. Wilford will be close to retirement when we come back (if we come back—a dream I hardly dare dwell on). He has also begun to write up some of the fifty detailed and the one hundred shorter-form case histories necessary to qualify for his facs (Fellow of the American College of Surgeons), which is an important form of professional recognition. I am sure the examiners are going to find them fascinating. For example, although there doesn't seem to be much in the way of prostate trouble in this part of China, there is a relatively high incidence of cancer of the penis, perhaps due to a general absence of hygiene and the fact that circumcision is virtually unknown. Whatever the reason, he has recently had three cases, involving two partial amputations and a complete radical. The latter entailed splitting the scrotum open down the mid line and removing the complete body of the penis, leaving about three-quarters of an inch of urethra protruding beyond the triangular membrane, which was brought out and sutured at the base of the wound. A mass block dissection of the glands of both groins was necessary as well and, later, when the scrotal wound became infected, the left testicle sloughed out.

☐ MARCH 20TH: Early this morning I missed Ralph from my side. Cries of "Happy Birthday Mummie" or in Carol's case, "Happy Burfday Mummie," announced the arrival of my 34th. In came Judith with a large bouquet of sweet peas and a small white parcel tied with red ribbon. Carol a close second, also carried flowers and an envelope. A pale Daddy followed in pyjamas and dressing gown. We all had fun for the next few minutes opening and examining my presents, a tin of "Essence of Taste" (monosodium glutamate), a great luxury (Fuh will be ecstatic) and a much appreciated beautiful handkerchief. Breakfast was a gala affair. We opened a tin of sausages from the Campbells. Then our Miss Yuin came in laden with *bin tang* (rock sugar, considered a real delicacy), some *mian* (noodles) and a small dish of pork. Later, Mrs. Meuser and Margaret Day came over with flowers and candy and stayed for tea. By the way, Margaret did have her baby boy and is he ever a darling! Then at six, we all went to the Hsiehs' to a party in my honor. As my birthday this year coincides with China's national Flower Festival, Mr. Liu made several very charming speeches in this regard.

☐ MARCH 21ST: Our lovely old city has been occupied by the infamous 18th Route Army, brigands whose business is opium, not the defence of China against the Japanese. Based in the Tibetan foothills, they have recently played havoc in Luchow, Den Gin Gwan and Tzeliutsing, interfering with the salt traffic, collecting illegal taxes and protection money and opening opium shops. The warlord commanding this lot has used his vast revenues to make his the best-equipped army in China. From what Ralph has told me about the situation in Luchow, the Generalissimo had to divert some of his best troops to dislodge them through a show of superior force. One can only hope he will do the same for us. The object, so far as one understands Chiang Kai-shek's tactics here, is to force them back into the hills without starting a civil war.

□ *MARCH 28TH:* Banyang was in Chengtu when the soldiers decided they wanted to quarter some of their officers in her home. They had taken the keys from her mother-in-law, but Banyang entertained the General's *tai tai*, made a big fuss over her and the keys were returned. I'm a bit annoyed at her lowering herself to gain the favor of the wife of this infamous man. Third wife at that! When Ralph and Robert Hsieh are away, we girls spend most of our time together. It seems to me Banyang can do anything, although I worry that her heart is too great for her strength. Jennifer, whom I also affectionately call "*San Mei,*" as she is my number-three daughter, often comes over to play and our two just love going to the Hsieh's, where they get to feed the goats and goslings, ducklings and the chicks. I've mentioned Banyang's mother-in-law, *Lao tai tai.* She is parsimonious to a degree except when it comes to Mah-jongg, at which she drops a small fortune. The Chinese are inveterate gamblers and Mah-jongg (normally played with 136 dominoes, called tiles, which take the place of playing cards) is one of the most popular diversions around.

Opium is now freely available on the street. Banyang says one can smell it in many of her friends' homes. If our experience follows that of Tzeliutsing, the shops are almost giving it away at present. When enough people get "hooked," the prices will go up and the entire countryside will go berserk. Whatever is necessary to get enough money to satisfy one's addiction: from petty thieving (our summer cottage at Gao Sh Ti has been broken into) to selling wives and children. At a feast we attended last evening, opium cigarettes were passed out as one might serve cocktails at home.

☐ *APRIL 3RD:* The Vice-Commander of the 18th Route Army (he calls himself the "wise commander") has been making great overtures of friendship to Ralph. He has been to the house a few times and is on the surface an amiable, interesting person (a northerner, tall, quite good looking and with a fair command of English). Possibly it suits him to keep in well with the doctor and Hospital people in case of hostilities. One day he asked Ralph to lance an abscess on his horse's nose. Ralph agreed and so instructed Miss Yuin. Later when he went to collect the surgical tray, he found the obstetrical room converted into a private facility, flowers, a rug on the floor and matching bedspread and curtains. Very presentable indeed. "What's all this?" he asked. "Well you said you were operating on the Vice-Commander's mother, so I thought she should have a special room." What a joke! (Horse and mother are the same word in Chinese except for the tone.) His steed was put instead into the Webster's garden, its legs tethered to trees with about twelve men to hold it down. The creature was so terrified that when Ralph tried to give it a hypo of novocaine, it threw its handlers to the four winds. They then tied it more tightly, more soldiers sat on it, three on its head and neck, covering its eyes. Ralph skipped the anæsthetic, put in his knife, applied a dressing and that was that.

☐ *APRIL 16TH:* I wish you could see my vase of beautiful peach blossoms. "Its fragrant leaves, how richly green,/ Its blossoms, how divinely bright." I've wondered, however, if the crops out here aren't lower in calories than their North American counterparts. One seems to have to eat more. In any event, I am always hungry, especially when Ralph's away. Like

Aristotle, Fuh believes women are but the slaves of man. Consequently, all I get is what the kids don't eat.

I went to a Prayer Meeting last night and got in dutch when I asked how one could attach a personality to God. Everyone turned on me except Miss Steele. One of the giants of yesteryear, she works like billy-o. Rather fundamentalist, dislikes men, but a darling under that leathery hide. As to the other wms ladies, Florence Fee, who is supposed to be a scholar, has no sense of humor, is grim and disagreeable and, poor dear, seems to be ill a lot. Miss O'Neill, late of Honan, is rather nice, if narrow, but doesn't function very well. Finally, dear Gerrie Hartwell, our Sup't of Nurses, who is very generous and hard working, but erratic temperamentally and a religious crank. When at times I long for single blessedness, I've only to look at them to thank God I got married. I feel like a pig writing these things because they are all earnest and righteous. Perhaps I'm the queer one!

□ *MAY 12TH:* We had supper at the Hsiehs' last night, a simple but delicious meal of noodles in a meat soup, cold smoked meats, peanuts, rice *shi fan* and pastry cake. Although Robert was away, Banyang amused us with a couple of stories about her husband's adventures in Chengtu. He is a good looking chap, "with big eyes and an innocent face," to quote my dear friend. Looking at him, one would never guess that he is a wealthy banker. He was getting a shave and hair cut one afternoon when a couple of handsomely gowned young women paused to look in on the barber shop which is open to the street. The more attractive of the two appeared quite taken with Mr. H., remarking on his lovely hair, how hers was ugly and had lost its curl ("*dieu le*") which has a double meaning and may be interpreted as a sexual proposition. When he ignored her inference, she and her companion appeared to lose interest and departed. According to the barber, Mr. Hsieh had just been invited to make love to the third wife of the richest man in town. Apparently, it is the custom for such women, when bored, to take to themselves some poor but handsome youth as a gigolo. Tonsorial establishments in China are leisurely places, and an hour or so later when Robert emerged, the women were waiting for him, one by her motor car, the other by her rickshaw. "Such a beautiful child, let us take him home and feed him," the one remarked. Her companion rejoined, "If mine were as fine a home as yours I would certainly invite him." They then loudly exchanged addresses so that he might understand where he might be "fed." He just strolled on to the hotel where he and several other wealthy Junghsien businessmen share adjoining rooms. All except Mr. H. have taken mistresses and are stepping high, wide and handsome. The Hsiehs, however, are so devoted to each other that Robert would never two-time Ban-yang. She, of course, is very happy about this, particularly because "in the spring all men are alike, they are restless and must make love," or so she says.

That Dzan! I mentioned that at one time she was a slave. It appears she was also a courtesan. Ralph told the story of the time he was alone last summer when Dzan came up to our bed-room, dressed only in a discarded pair of Alice Jenner's tennis shorts and a very loosely tied blouse. Apparently, she had been drinking and determined to "comfort" the lonely master! Another time when I was still at the cottage, Ralph was entertaining some of the local worthies. The day was hot and in swished Dzan, who was supposed to be serving the food, in something totally inappropriate, her hair a soft wave which she wears in a sort of page boy, protruding teeth in a huge smile, to join the conversation. This may not mean much to a Westerner, but let your imagination take you to a very old and conservative part of China where women are always gowned and know their place. I wish I had enough Chinese to really get her story. The poor soul has bound feet. Consequently, her legs are very thin and deformed. As she has no arch, she clumps when she walks. But she is absolutely irrepressible.

Foot binding has almost disappeared in China, again largely due to the efforts of the Missionaries. It dates back in history to Yao Niang, a very beautiful concubine at the court of the pretender Li Yu (A.D. 970). I am not at all clear about whether her feet were naturally deformed or deliberately compressed to form an "arch resembling a new moon." In any event, she teetered about in very small shoes, which somehow became the fashion and ambition for all women. Baby girls' feet were bound at birth, toes pressed under the arch. As the children grew, malformation developed to the point where all weight was taken on the heel. Even women of the peasant class had bound feet. And how they must have suffered! While on the subject of old and dying customs, we occasionally see men with pigtails coiled around the top of their heads, a leftover from the Manchus and abolished by Sun Yat Sen.

☐ *MAY 18TH:* I should tell you about the adolescent girls I work with at the Mission. They are recruited from the very poorest in society. All are undersized from starvation, having lived off roots, wild berries and vegetables while bending their little bodies to carry coal from the nearby hills to Tzeliutsing and living in windowless rooms or caves. They come in dirty, hungry sullen little rats and leave fat and happy with a good knowledge of cross-stitch embroidery, plain sewing, knitting, a little household science and asepsis, plus some idea of the care of children. All take their turn at the Well-Baby Clinic. Also, each is exposed to Christian teaching. A Chinese Bible woman comes in several times a week to read them Old and New Testament stories as they work. When they are ready, Banyang helps me find them jobs as servants in the town.

☐ *JUNE 5TH:* We were visited unexpectedly last week by two members of our Consulate, both charming, bringing us a pound of coffee and the sulfaquanidine my dad sent out through an old friend of his, our new ambassador to China, General Victor Odlum. (Actually, the General's rank is Minister, but there are too many of these in my text.) As is my custom when people come directly off the road, I asked our two guests if they would care for baths (thus giving me the opportunity to check their clothes for bed bugs). They accepted and the senior of the two, a military chap by the name of Wooster, went upstairs to wash away the dust and grime of a hard day's travel. In the meantime, we had prepared tea around the fire in our study. When Ralph Collins, the political officer, took his turn, he seemed gone an unusually long time, so I sent Ralph upstairs to see if he was okay. He was. So was Judith. She was swinging on the bathroom door, entertaining him. Collins, poor fellow, stuck in the tub was trying to shoo her away. Ralph, much amused, asked if there was anything he could do. "Yes," replied Collins, "you might dispense with the child!" It is always so good to talk with someone from outside and we had a very interesting time together. They were eager to know all about Ralph's work, looked about the city and were fascinated with the military situation here, although relieved that so far the foreigners have not been threatened.

The closest I've come to actual danger was one day when we were invited by the warlord to a mid-day feast. I feigned illness. He is such an evil man I did not wish to "break bread" with him. Ralph, of course, had no choice. He was not long gone when there was a terrific banging at the front door. Fuh came rushing upstairs where I was playing with the children to say that two soldiers had arrived to escort me to the feast. I was furious. I wanted to refuse, but they were such ugly looking ruffians and their rifles so shiny and powerful! So I dressed and was marched down the main street. I'm certain everyone we passed had a field day of speculation! I had the frantic idea as we passed Banyang's gate of seeking sanctuary, but knew this would only bring trouble. After I arrived, to be greeted by my host and seated, the first dish served had snake meat in it! Ralph gave me an amused glance and I behaved as befitted the wife of the Sup't of the Hospital, etc., etc., etc.

Miss Steele got off in a cloud of dust yesterday. The girls at the Mission school, smart in immaculate uniforms, marched her out of the city. The city Magistrate, who is responsible for local government, paid her all honor in a speech of appreciation for her devotion to the cause of women's education, etc., took her photograph and paid for her rickshaw to Chungking. She is a

very fine person and I hope she has a decent trip home. I feel
the Magistrate is trying to get our girls' school under his control.
He's a decent fellow and I particularly like his wife, but it appears he has a plan to integrate all our facilities under his administration. There are many Chinese who feel the time has come
for us to depart. Certainly, I go along with this in certain areas.
Perhaps the education of women is one.

☐ *JUNE 12TH:* Dr. Bill Service, who came out from home last
year to take up an appointment in the Faculty of Medicine at
wcuu, visited last week. Both he and his wife were born in
Chengtu where their fathers also taught at the University, Bill's
in Medicine (1914–1930) and Norma's in Dentistry (1914–
1932). Bill had done special work on burns and their treatment,
so he and Ralph undertook Carol's first-stage operation. This
consisted of removing a ¾-inch strip of scar, undercutting and
loosening the edges and drawing them together with retention
sutures fastened through six two-hole buttons to prevent the
stitches from breaking the skin. Carol was a brick. Didn't even
whimper when getting her hypodermic. Bill gave her the
anæsthetic and she went down happily. Ralph did the actual
surgery, judging there to be a definite advantage in Carol having
the same surgeon for each of her operations. These little girls of
ours are special when it comes to courage.

☐ *JUNE 20TH:* During the night the 18th Route Army
vanished from our lives, headed north, but leaving a legacy of
opium addicts to contend with cold turkey cures or face the
consequences of the law, death.

☐ *SEPTEMBER 15TH:* In a week we will be leaving the hills of
Gao Sh Ti to say our farewells in Junghsien before proceeding
to our new home in Tzeliutsing. It has been a long summer,
longer than most. Ralph has not had any real holiday, just a
weekend here, a few days there. The Cunninghams were going
to come for a month; indeed, they started out three times, but
the roads proved impassable. Ernst and Tina Schroeder, our

German scientist friends, were here for a fortnight from Luchow. They work side by side and, as I think I've told you, are on the frontiers of medical science in many of the cures they are investigating. We have become very close friends for people who see each other so seldom. Also, General Odlum surprised us with a short visit. We managed a reception in his honor, where he was a great hit among our news-starved summer community. And, what a ladies man, he charmed me completely! He was, however, hard on all the men I thought, particularly on Leslie Kilborn, for the moment temporary Second Counsellor with the Canadian legation in Chungking, who has had to shepherd the General about and seemed pretty fed up with him. Of the other interesting people passing through: Edgar Snow, whom I've mentioned before; Joyce Homer, who authored *Dawn Watch*; and Dr. Marion Manley, who with her intern, Han Su Yin, wrote *Destination Chungking*. Fuh has spent most of the summer in Junghsien getting everything arranged for our move to Tzeliutsing, leaving us to endure Dzan's uncertain cooking and carefree ways. Banyang, however, managed to spend three weeks in August with me. She brought Jennifer (Hong-di) and the baby, Marilyn (Ying-di) and we all had a super time. (I should add that Ralph and I are to be Marilyn's godparents as well.) She showed me how to do green dates the Chinese way. Each date has to be scored with a razor about sixty times before one begins the complicated process of curing them. I have the recipe, but know darn well I'll never use it. Too much work!

☐ *OCTOBER 29TH:* We came down from the hills five weeks ago today to spend two days in Junghsien where we were royally feasted. Everyone was very nice to us and seemed sincerely unhappy about our leaving. The children particularly enjoyed the bus trip to Tzeliutsing, which was a new experience for them. It was one of those weird charcoal-burning affairs, packed to the gunnels and beyond by a largely good natured crowd. Dzan, however, got sick to her tummy. We arrived to find the house in order. Fuh had the rugs down, beds made, mosquito nets hung and flowers everywhere. Even hot water for our baths. What a peach!

Tzeliutsing (which means "self-flowing well") lies among bare rolling hills covered by a man-made bamboo jungle of salt well pylons, related apparatus and pipe lines. This bustling city sits atop a huge salt sea that has been a source of great wealth for over two thousand years. At the present time the Tzeliutsing salt wells produce over three hundred thousand tons yearly and provide employment for nearly a million people. During the Han Dynasty (202 B.C.–A.D. 220), although coinage was used, salt was legal tender. Even Marco Polo, more than a thousand years later, refers to its use as money. And the tax on salt has been an important source of government revenue for much of the Middle Kingdom's history.

Each salt well is about one-and-a-half feet in diameter, two to three thousand or more feet deep and may have taken anywhere from three to twenty years to drill. Although many are now run by coal-burning donkey engines, thousands are yet to be converted. In a traditional operation, a spliced bamboo tripod slightly more than one hundred feet in height is built over the well. (The bamboo used in Tzeliutsing has been especially developed and is from six to eight inches in diameter.) The bucket, also made of spliced bamboo, is exactly one hundred feet in length so that when pulled to the top of the pylon its lower end just clears the well head. The half mile length of woven bamboo rope required in this operation is wound round a huge, sixty-foot-diameter windlass. Four water buffalo, trained to circle to the left (they would baulk if driven to the right) provide the necessary power. Once the brine has been raised and emptied into a large vat, the buffalo are detached and the bucket descends by gravity. As it does so, the windlass, revolving at an ever increasing speed, begins to shake and scream. To be within a hundred feet of this is like stepping into a tornado. Colored bits of cloth hooked into the rope indicate the bucket's depth and as it reaches its destination, the windlass is stopped by a contrivance not unlike the brake band on a car wheel. This too is made from bamboo split into a flat ribbon about two feet wide, which when tightened against roughly two-thirds of the windlass's circumference, gradually brings it to a smoking, shrieking halt. The entire routine takes about three-quarters of an hour. Amazingly, one becomes accustomed to the constant din.

Natural gas, which is often the product of the "dry" wells, is used to evaporate the brine. In that the Chinese have yet to acquire the technology to transport natural gas, the brine is piped instead, sometimes a distance of up to five miles or more, through an elaborate gravity-flow system. The pipes, naturally, are made of the large-diameter bamboo, the smaller end being fitted into the larger and sealed with a tung oil and lime mixture, which acts as a cement. To prevent splitting (the pressure within the pipe may be as much as a hundred pounds per square inch), inch-wide ribbons of ⅛-inch-thick split bamboo are closely wrapped around the pipe, the ends looped under one another, then cinched up with a wedge. Frequent "boosting" stations (bamboo towers which lift the pipe into elevated curves) aid gravity in speeding the flow. As one can imagine, the city is literally a maze of pipes in all directions.

At the gas wells, the brine is collected in vats and fed into huge cast iron "woks" (six or eight feet across) under which a controlled flame burns constantly. As evaporation takes place (a process that takes a day or more), soybean juice is mixed in, which causes sediment to rise and allows impurities to be skimmed off. The purified salt is then carefully weighed under the watchful eyes of government officials into woven bamboo baskets. If these are to be transported to their destination, as many are, one at either end of a carrying pole, the surface of the salt in each basket is carefully molded and marked in red dust with a Chinese character. Thus the slightest pilfering will destroy the shape of the character and the carrier is liable for the loss.

Just a week after our arrival, I contracted meningitis and truly thought I was going to die. In my lucid moments I kept trying to figure out how my dad could get here before I breathed my last. It was very painful. I could not stand vibration of any kind nor even the sound of a human voice. Not even morphia would contain it. Thanks to my dad, we had extra sulfaquanidine. It didn't work, but we sold enough of it to buy some sulfadiazene ($60 American for six pills). However, try as I might, I could not keep them down. But where there's a will, there's a way. . . . Well, either the disease had run its course or what was left of the sulfadiazene did the job. Half my face is still a bit paralyzed, my smile's a little lopsided and I have to be careful how I eat. Anyway, enough! As you can imagine, all this took a lot out of Ralph who, despite the huge load he is carrying at the Hospital, nursed me completely for three weeks. Poor darling.

I was just on my feet again when we heard that Barbara Ward, an eminent economist and British Labour Party candidate, was to arrive the following day. I volunteered to put up one member of her group and agreed to host a dinner. So a nice Mr. Enoch Williams, a Welshman attached to the British Embassy in Chungking, came to stay. Miss Ward is a rather florid, fortyish English type. In private, she is rather hesitant in speech, but the men say her public delivery is excellent, to the point but discreet. She was accompanied by a Miss Chen, prominent in the New Life Movement, who acted as interpreter (and gov't spy). When we managed to get Miss Ward off by herself, she was very interesting. She is serving on several important committees in Britain, one being Ernest Bevin's on the distribution of labor. She mentioned spending a night at I Pin, the model village near Chungking. Lady Seymour, the British Ambassador's wife, accompanied her and was bitten to distraction by bed bugs. Miss Ward is apparently one of the lucky people immune to such pests. Lady Seymour's comment went something like this, "Those who think that the life of an Ambassador's wife is full of glamor should see me now!"

Banyang arrived just after the British departed. She had heard I was very ill and had come up to see what she could do about it. Finding me in pretty good form, she stayed about a week. Hers was a diplomatic mission as well, for she wanted us to meet the influential people of this wealthy city. Each day, she brought five or six guests for tea, one of whom has actually visited me since. This particular *tai tai* brought along a country lass for me to inspect, "I am getting too old to look after my husband's physical needs so he is going to take a concubine, what do you think of this girl?" I tried not to show surprise and made a few complimentary remarks, "She is certainly young and in obvious good health," etc. What a riot for one brought up in the West! Banyang thinks it wonderful the way I accept customs so different from our own. Of course I feel the same way about her.

I've never been happier in China than I am now. Psychologically, I think it is that I am a gregarious person and Tzeliutsing is such a change from depressing old Junghsien. More people, lots of interesting house guests, our furlough just around the corner. And with the opportunity to sell things, our financial burdens are lighter. What is more, about-mid April of next year, I may have our longed-for son. He would complete our family, and we do want to enjoy our babies while we are still young enough to do so.

□ *NOVEMBER 28TH:* Carol had her second operation last week. Of course, Ralph did the surgery again, but Cecil Hoffman gave the anæsthetic and what a switch. When she had her first operation last June, Bill Service did it with such gentleness that there was no after-trauma. Cecil, however, put her down screaming and struggling. I could have killed him! I really think I shall never tolerate him again, even though he is my obstetrician. I know I shall never go to him. I wish I could get up to Chengtu and have Gladys deliver me. Carol's surgery, however, appears to have been a success.

Ralph continues to find his work at the Hospital very stimulating. On staff, there is an internist, an ear, nose and throat man, an eye man, and a man to assist Ralph in surgery. Two dentists are expected daily. Cecil does the Obs. and Gyn., in addition to his duties as Superintendent. Ralph is Chief of Staff but remains Superintendent of our Hospital in Junghsien, to which he journeys by bike once a month for administrative and surgical duties or whenever emergency demands. Ward rounds take place weekly and staff meetings once a month at which time one of them gives a paper and the deaths of the intervening period are discussed. As Ralph is still working on the case histories for his FACS, there unfortunately isn't much room left for language study.

We had a "garage" sale the other day at the Baby Welfare building. The local Chinese simply clamored for foreign-made articles. Ralph's old felt fedora sold for $1200 and a long-discarded pair of spats for $300. The wealthiest man in town bought all my imported crystal and silver plate, plus my double damask linen banquet cloth and twelve serviettes for $65,000! Even when exchanged at the new rate of 27 to 1, this is a bonanza. The man brought the money round to the house in ten dollar bills. You should have seen me after he left. I dug my hands in and flung them to the ceiling, showering myself in filthy lucre.

☐ *DECEMBER 27TH:* The Saturday before Christmas, Dora Ann Stinson, Judy and Carol had a party for all their little friends. Banyang brought Jennifer and Marilyn from Junghsien. Isabelle Stinson managed to find some crêpe paper and we made caps for everyone. The centerpiece was Santa Claus driving in state, but drawn by six birds (the best we could do). There were place cards and wee gifts for everyone. Isabelle looked after the games and I the food. It was a great success! On the Sunday, I had the seventeen graduating nurses in for tea. Fuh and the Dragon made cedar-bough wreaths decorated with holly-like berries. The tree was equally festive with strings of popcorn, hollowed-out small oranges and paper chains. I got out my best tea cloth and Tallie, who is the Sup't of Nurses here, poured. As usual, Fuh produced wonders from the kitchen and all ate hugely.

At last Christmas Eve arrived. We filled stockings for our children and Fuh's little boy and presented the servants with soap (a great luxury) and material for new gowns (very expensive these days). In turn, the servants gave us the traditional live goose. We had a simple meal around the fire. Then Ralph went to play his violin at a concert and I had the fun of putting the children to bed. I read them the "Night Before Christmas" and tucked them in. Carol was almost beside herself with excitement and just too cross for words. A little fanning of her *pi ku* (seat) helped restore her equilibrium. Christmas began early with the stockings. Ralph's gift to me was a beautiful length of white silk and mine to him a new watch strap. Later we made the rounds wishing everyone a Happy Christmas. Then off to Church. At four o'clock, the community tea, which was followed by the children's concert, so long anticipated and practiced. I hate to confess our children behaved like morons. Although they knew their songs, they wouldn't sing. They just stood there looking stupid. Maybe next year. . . .

□ *JANUARY 20TH, 1944:* Ralph has gone to the Mission Council meetings in Chengtu, as have most of the other members of our community. Last Sunday, Cecil Hoffman and I were invited to Mr. Dzen's for *mian* and bridge. He is the head of the Salt Gabelle (National Salt Administration) and the most important person in Tzeliutsing. He has a foreign-type house, situated on a hill top commanding a view of the city and the river (a tributary of the Yangtse). It was fascinating playing bridge with experts for a change. The cards are dealt, you pick them up and are expected to bid instantly. If not, someone drums his fingers on the table saying, "Yao *tai tai*" (my name). It is a question of hastily counting your losers. I must say I played with greater care than I ever have before. Didn't do too badly, considering.

We have been selling some of our milk to various of our neighbors. When I complained to Fuh that some of our customers were no longer coming, he replied, after an embarrassed moment, "I hate to tell you this, *tai tai*, but the girls have been cursing and insulting them." I was furious and told him that if this was the case then I held him responsible for where would they learn these things unless from the servants. He rejoined that the other kids in the compound had taught them to swear. I decided I'd do a spot of listening and, of course, he was quite right. I had a good tough talk with all the Mission children.

□ *FEBRUARY 10TH:* Another Chinese New Year is upon us, this time the Year of the Monkey. Our first was the Year of the Hare, then the Dragon, the Snake, the Horse and last year, the Ram. At present, I am helping Ralph prepare some of his case histories. He lets me accompany him to take progress notes as he makes rounds. It gets me out of the house which is good for all of us. I am getting pretty heavy, but even so seem to be in reasonable physical shape. As I observe the medical problems on the wards, it is to re-encounter everything elsewhere described. Parasites of every kind. Venereal disease. Malaria, although fortunately little of the malignant variety. Tuberculosis manifesting itself in ways never seen at home. *Lai dze* or scrofula. Poorly set fractures causing gross deformities, again never seen in the West, in this century at least. Tumors. Osteomyelitis of the bone, untreated and far advanced. Eye infections. Blindness caused by trachoma with scarring of the eyelid, thereby turning it in so that the lashes rub the cornea until it becomes opaque. Gunshot wounds. Trauma from bombings. Skin burns. Encephalitis. Meningitis. And I haven't even mentioned the horrors one encounters in Obs. and Gyn.

Although the bombed out portions of the hospital have been re-built thanks to generous grants from the Canadian Red Cross ($12,000 American) and the WMS ($10,000 American), we have no money for beds, etc. Among other things, we need 3,470 panes of glass. (Our own home lost all its windows during the bombings as well. We use oilcloth to keep out the elements.) We also require $100,000 for electric wiring. Paint would be too much to ask for. In the meantime, we do what we can to get by. Ralph, for example, has just finished making a suction apparatus out of some old organ bellows! He is trying it out tomorrow on a harelip case. Next week he is going to try to build a distilling apparatus out of some other discarded equipment. Despite the fact the Hospital is full (Ralph did thirty-five majors last month), inflation has resulted in our debt increasing at about $5,000 (Chinese) a day! We did well over $60,000 charity work last year, but the Hospital should be doing this every month. No

Christian institution in this country should be forced to treat only those patients with the wherewithal to pay. We do have two orphans in the Hospital at the moment. One has had a leg amputated because of bone infection and deep ulcers due to cold exposure. The other lad has a serious knee infection. Neither could afford even food, but their condition was so desperate we had to admit them.

Banyang, Jennifer and Marilyn have been visiting me again. Banyang says all the portents point to the fact that we are about to become the parents of a son. She is having a beautiful satin cape made for "him" in purple because it is our royal color, with five-clawed imperial dragons embroidered thereon. The Chinese dragon is not the gruesome monster of medieval imagination, but a genius of strength and goodness. It has been the emblem of Imperial power since the Han dynasty and may be used by princes of the first and second rank. This augurs well for "Kerry," I hope. We have no one out here as close to family as the Hsiehs. They have helped us no end, even lending us $20,000 when we were so broke we didn't know what to do. I paid it back as soon as I had my sale. At Christmas, they sent us hams, sausages, smoked duck tongues and chicken livers and those wonderful dates about which I have written, shoes for me in padded velvet and presents for the girls. It is wonderful just to know we have such friends. Besides, they are great fun. It is considered unhealthy by the Chinese to speak of anything sad to one who is "enceinte." Consequently, even though she has recently lost her step-mother, Banyang is much too thoughtful to share her troubles (I think she may be pregnant herself). We just talk or visit her friends or play with the children.

☐ *APRIL 25TH:* I think I've made it abundantly clear that I have little use for Dr. Hoffman. Apart from the way he treated Carol, as my obstetrician he never once examined me. He has stirred up trouble among my servants, accusing them of stealing, invading their quarters to search for whatever he imagined they had taken. What is more, he has made Tallie's life a misery at the Hospital, undermining her authority as Sup't of Nurses

and so on. So Tallie and I decided that if possible we would deliver my baby ourselves. I decided not to tell Ralph about this. It
would simply complicate his professional relationship with
Cecil. On the afternoon of April 16th, I went into a normal
labor. Tallie was at my side. I had just entered the second stage
when coincidentally (I assume) Marie and Cecil turned up. Although huge, my son, Howard Kergin Glen Outerbridge (Kerry
for short), delivered easily compared to his sisters. I am fine. For
weeks I was sure I was going to have quintuplets. He weighed
eleven and one-half pounds. He isn't fat, just large. He has a fair
amount of golden straight hair, slate-grey eyes (so were Carol's
whose eyes are now a vivid blue), 22 inches long, 22-inch head
and 21-inch chest. We can't believe our luck. Our family is now
complete! The girls accepted their brother with open arms and
now oversee his care.

As soon as the news reached Junghsien, Banyang made a
spectacular entrance at our front gate! She had travelled by
rickshaw to the city, stayed with some friends, then hired a litter
to which she had tied twenty live chickens, gifts from well-
wishers in Junghsien. We also received what seemed like a thousand red-colored (happiness) eggs. After looking Kerry over
carefully, Banyang explained the significance of some omen
manifested in our garden the day Kerry was born. The servants
have been babbling about it ever since. When two birds of different species travel together, according to legend, something
auspicious has taken place. This is what had so excited Fuh,
Dzan and the Dragon. The male was a beautiful white bird with
a long tail.

□ *JUNE 3RD:* Do you know that, except on rare occasion,
since leaving home I haven't washed a dish or prepared a meal
nor ironed a blouse? I have a wonderful cook, the best in this
part of China, who is most happy when I am ill and he can run
the show. The only time we get into trouble with one another is
when I nose around too much. My big job is keeping the family
clothed and healthy and our personal budget balanced.

We receive some awfully funny notes from the city Magistrate from time to time. Do not think for a moment that I fault his English, as I am all too aware of the awful hash I make of Chinese. All this to the contrary, I cannot resist recording this one. "Dear Doctor: This court has filed a suit for compulsive intercourse. I request your hospital examine this appellor named Sun Shu Fen whether she is yet a girl or not. If she is not a girl I want to know whether her hymen has been broken in what time about and either she committed criminal conversation or not in what time about, and either she committed criminal conversation or not in last two weeks. I hope your return to us a medical certification with reference to the preceding statement. With many thanks, etc."

□ *JULY 14TH:* It is a glorious morning after an unseasonable heavy rain. At dawn, the Snow Mountains of Tibet were visible, as was Mount Omei's Golden Summit. It's hard to believe this will be our last summer here at Gao Sh Ti. Next year at this time, we will be home with loved ones we won't have seen for seven years. It is still early. The children are off playing in panties and shoes (snakes abound) and it isn't time for Kerry's bath. Ralph sits nearby studying a beautiful surgical atlas lent us by our dear German scientific friend. The air is perfumed by gardenias, which grow wild on the hills. The cicadas and the cries of the children break the silence. I can hear Carol singing.

We came up a week ago from the blistering plain. This year, because I was so tired, I travelled by litter with three carriers. Previously I had always walked up from Junghsien. Thus, from each and every tea house en route, the curious would call to my men, "Who are you carrying?" "Yao *tai tai*." "Why is she travelling by whaggan?" "Haven't you heard? She has great face. This year she gave her husband a son!"

□ *AUGUST 4TH:* Ralph went back to the plain and the heat on the 1st. I would have gone with him if Banyang and the two girls had not been coming up. I am so lucky to have her, but I do make enemies too, darn it! I was told off by one of our fellow Missionaries the other day for asking for something he had borrowed but not returned. I comforted myself that he wasn't worth worrying about, so dried my tears. There are rotters travelling under the cloak of Christianity, which to me seems the greatest of profanities. Another thing, so many sent out here to lead are intellectually and spiritually inferior to those they presume to teach. And I resent their arrogant attitude toward the Chinese. I desperately hope we won't have to return and that Ralph can find a job that satisfies his idealism at home.

☐ *AUGUST 30TH:* It is a wet cold day and I am writing this beside an open fire. Judith is asleep on the bed beside me and the room is strung with lines of drying clothes. Yesterday, she fell in the stable, cutting her knee badly on a broken glazed-crockery water container. Practically everyone had returned to the plain and I had to sew it up myself—with ordinary thread! Poor kid was very brave as we had no anæsthetic, but today she took a turn for the worse. I've sent the Dragon down for anti-tetanus serum.

☐ *AUGUST 31ST:* The Dragon returned from Junghsien last night. Remembering a patient of my dad's who nearly passed out from a protein reaction to the serum, I prepared a syringe of adrenalin and put it on the mantelpiece. I administered a wee bit and watched for the result. She seemed to take it well, so I gave her a bit more. Suddenly she went into shock. Dzan, who was with me and thought Judy was dying, threw her apron over her head and went into hysterics, knocking the precious syringe of adrenalin to the floor. I was terrified. Fortunately, I remembered my dad giving his patient artificial respiration. I did the same and after what seemed ages she came out of it. I still have my precious little girl, thank God!

☐ *SEPTEMBER 25TH:* Judith recovered. She has a bit of a scar, but my surgeon husband, who came up to spend a few days before we went back to Tzeliutsing, complimented me upon the way I had handled things. And now we are very busy preparing to go home! In less than five months, we will be on our way. Our passport pictures have been taken (the usual grim convict-looking ones), our visas for travel in China are being processed and our house is looking bare, as we have been selling everything we can spare. There are many things that we have promised to people when we leave and they are paying us in advance.

On our way back from Gao Sh Ti, we "officially" became godparents to the Hsieh children and the Hsiehs to ours. Banyang and I had discussed every aspect of this at great length when she was with me on the mountain. Of course Ralph and Hsieh Chao-chuan (Robert) were equally enthusiastic. In the West, becoming a godparent is often a mere formality, more of liturgical than dogmatic importance. In China, however, this is a very serious commitment for it means literally that if anything should happen to the parents, the godparents will take over the care, education and so on of the children. Of course we are honored that the Hsiehs hold us in this regard. We stayed with them until the day judged most auspicious. Then we all dressed in our very best. Kerry in his "royal" clothes. The Hsieh and Liu families assembled. There were exchanges of very special gifts. For example, Kerry received a twenty-four-carat gold ring and piece of white jade of symbolic significance. (The gifts on both sides were comparable.) Scrolls of good wishes, long life, prosperity and happiness were hung everywhere. The high point was when we were conducted into the Hall of the Ancestors where we bowed in respect to the scrolls of their forebears and the Hsiehs, in turn, bowed to us. As expected, we have been criticized by the Christian community for indulging in Ancestor Worship. It simply doesn't seem that way at all to us. We merely paid honor to the ancestors of our godchildren. And why would we not? Afterwards, there were fireworks, a great feast and many speeches. We are now part of the Hsieh and Liu families and very proud of this. Our God will not frown upon us for this act of love.

□ *NOVEMBER 2ND:* From the sublime to the ridiculous, shortly after we returned to Tzeliutsing, Dzan dressed Kerry in his "royal" clothes and took him around to all the servant quarters in the compound. We hear that she induced him to urinate whenever possible, the distance and arc of the stream duly impressing all onlookers. Apparently, this is a sure sign he is to be a great man. Drat that woman!

☐ *NOVEMBER 24TH:* We have been spending a fair amount of time in our "cellar," the unfinished filthy hole under our house. The Japanese have launched a final offensive against Szechwan and we are suffering air raids again. Normally a Chinese city is incredibly noisy: dogs barking, people talking in loud voices, hawkers calling their wares, etc. And Tzeliutsing with its screaming windlasses is noiser than most. When the air raid siren starts, however, there is silence. Not even the dogs make a sound. We have been so badly bombed in the past that the feeling of fear is almost palpable. As I write, the girls are in the kitchen driving Fuh crazy. He is refining sugar today. The ten pounds of raw sugar are boiled in a huge pot of water. After adding a bit of milk, the impurities are skimmed off. Then, just as it is about to harden, it is taken off the stove and vigorously stirred with a large wooden paddle until it once again becomes recognizable as sugar, but of a much lighter color than before. Well, the kids are all over the place, swiping handfuls.

☐ *DECEMBER 1ST:* Our dear friend, Mr. Liu, arranged to have Mr. Chao Hsi, Junghsien's great scholar, write and dedicate a scroll to Ralph as a farewell gift. To Western eyes, it may appear to be nothing more than a series of large ideographs. However, it is not only a superb example of the calligrapher's art but a beautiful tribute to the worth of Ralph's contribution in Junghsien and a sincere expression of the Liu and Hsieh families' love. The following unfortunately is very much a literal translation:

> Every tree which bears leaves forms a shade
> And the ground beneath becomes less fertile
> Except for the Alder
> Whose leaves fall to the ground and blanket its feet.

Soaked by the rain they rot and turn to fertilizer
Far more efficient even than the dung of animals.

Thus the farmers like to plant the alder
For when the winds blow its leaves rustle like the Poplar.

Obviously the Alder tree is meant to represent Ralph. Reference to the Poplar is not so easily understood. The *T'ang Si*, an ancient book of 300 poems written in the T'ang Dynasty (618–906 A.D.), contains a famous verse that portrays the sound of the wind in the Poplars as being one of such utter sadness as to evoke the thought of Death. Since that time, Chinese poets have used the image of rustling Poplar leaves to symbolize the sadness of good friends parting.

□ *DECEMBER 12TH:* We are gradually tidying up our affairs. We have gotten out of the milk business. It has been a great joy to give our precious Fuh our lovely little part-foreign cow, again with calf, which potentially makes him a rich man. My dad sent a pound bottle of luminal which we will give to Mr. Chiang to keep his epilepsy under control. I didn't tell you that just before Chinese New Year in 1943, he led a revolt of the junior staff at the Hospital in Jungshien. He is an intelligent young man and the fact was that we had not given him enough to do. Because he had so mastered his duties as Bursar/Registrar, he had a lot of time to read and think about the writings of various social reformers. I suspect he was looking for a cause when he heard the rumor (all institutions are energized by unfounded gossip) that Ralph planned to have the pig we were raising on hospital scraps killed to feast the senior staff. Without reference to all his experience with us nor bothering to enquire if this were true, he organized a strike of the coolies, cooks and ward aides. I have never seen Ralph so angry. He had Chiang up on the carpet and blistered him stem to gudgeon. The pig had indeed been intended for a feast to celebrate the Chinese New Year, but one to include everyone, even the patients. Well, Chiang called off the strike. Everyone went back to work and all was forgiven.

☐ *DECEMBER 18TH:* Today, we received orders from the Mission Executive to leave immediately for Chungking to catch a flight to India. There is fear that if we wait, we will be trapped by the Japanese. Fortunately, we have things pretty much in order. Arrangements are being made for Dzan, the children and me to travel by bus. Ralph will follow as soon as he can after finishing his jobs at the Hospital. Charlie Bridgeman, who has been living with us for the last several months (his wife remained in Canada), will take over our house and its remaining contents. When we leave Chungking, Dzan will return to live with her daughter. The Dragon is going back to his mother's farm.

☐ *DECEMBER 25TH:* We made it to Chungking without incident. Unfortunately, there was no place for us at the Inn or anywhere else. None of the foreigners here had been alerted, and no one was prepared to take us in. Eventually, we were shunted to the servants' quarters of a Canadian Minister's house across the Yangtse River from the city, where we are obliged to sleep on the floor in a drafty, dirty room. We had all picked up bad colds en route and Dzan is in a state of high dudgeon (I'm in a state of shock) that we can be treated so cavalierly. There is an empty bedroom in the house, but we have not been offered it. We are allowed, however, to use their bathroom! Today, as I was washing out some of Kerry's diapers, I heard our hostess talking with Mary Birtch, whom I'd always thought of as a friend. "What is this Margaret Outerbridge like?" she asked. "Oh," Mary replied, "she's fun, but she doesn't wear well."

CHAPTER 7

Chengtu Again /
A Woman of Substance

☐ *JUNE 5TH, 1948:* It was six full months before we were allowed to sail from Bombay to New York and nearly three years
more before we again saw China. In the meantime, Ralph successfully completed his post-graduate course in general surgery
and passed the examinations to become a Fellow of the Royal
College of Surgeons (Canada), which is really an earned post-
graduate degree, as opposed to becoming a Fellow of the American College of Surgeons (which he also received in recognition
of the surgery he had performed over seven years in China and
in North America). There is much I could write about this
period, but I won't. I was a housewife, the mother of three children, each of whom in turn entered school and lost what remained of their Chinese ways. We lived in substandard,
Mission-subsidized housing. Our budget was tight. Ralph was
hardly ever home. I endured without him. My friends of
yesteryear were now strangers. So were my brothers. I discovered that one cannot pick up the pieces after seven years,
and this both surprised and pained me. They had all been so im-

portant, a part of my definition of "home," their memories sustaining me in difficult situations. Now, I would have them no longer. My parents were more than half a continent away. I needed both my dad and Ralph, but when on occasion I had to choose between them, there was no pleasure in the realization that I was more part of my husband's family than my own. For the first time, I understood and felt close to my mother. Finally, Ralph's commitment to the Mission's work in West China grew even stronger. I had never been a legitimate part of the Missionary community abroad and I was even less so at home. Zealots don't amuse me—they never have. At thirty-nine, after ten years of marriage, with nothing to show for it, I didn't want to go back to Chengtu, but what were my options? Had I refused, Ralph would have felt obliged (in part the *quid pro quo* of the United Church Foreign Mission Board providing us meager existence in Toronto for three years) to complete his second term in China without me. I wondered sometimes how in the world I had made such a bed for myself.

I first met Ralph in 1935, when he was working for the summer as a medical student in the small United Church Mission hospital at Port Simpson (where British Columbia and the Alaska Panhandle meet). My father, Dr. W. T. Kergin, who practiced medicine in Prince Rupert, a several-hour boat trip to the south, was the Hospital's consulting physician and surgeon. I was a graduate nurse, but had the best of both worlds in a comfortable combination of dependence and independence, working six months each year in my father's office and the other half as a special duty nurse at the Toronto General Hospital. Ralph was going into his last year of medicine at the University of Toronto. As you know, he was born of Methodist missionary parents in Japan where he was raised, and had visited Canada only twice prior to his enrollment at U. of T. in 1929. Perhaps naturally enough, given the context of his upbringing, Ralph decided when he was still in high school to become a medical missionary in the Far East where the need for such Christian service was desperate. Nevertheless, in that he was not and never had been a theology student, I was surprised to learn he had spent his previous summers working for the United Church as a lay preacher in out-of-the-way places in Western Canada. My dad, however, was fascinated. Coincidentally, both our fathers, inspired by the Social Gospel of the Christian Student Movement, had felt the call to serve in China when they were newly graduated. Instead, circumstances led Ralph's father to Japan and mine (for the first years of his career) to serve the Methodist Church among the Indians in Port Simpson. And as if this didn't give us enough in common, both my older brothers, Bill and Fred, were doctors as well.

At the time, I hadn't the slightest inkling I had met my future mate. Although I was twenty-six, I wasn't looking for a husband. I had had a number of offers, but I liked my life the way it was. And being a missionary (or married to one) had never crossed my mind. So far as I'd ever given the subject of holy wedlock a moment's serious thought, I rather expected the style of my existence to continue pretty much as it was, with a lovely home, prized possessions, trips to Europe, shopping on Fifth Avenue and winter holidays in Hawaii or Palm Springs. What I didn't know at the time was that under all Ralph's quiet demeanor there lives a man of iron determination. His agenda included the acquisition of a wife before he returned to the Orient and he was compiling a list of suitable candidates. Of course I overstate the degree of his cold calculation. It is true, however, that in those few instances when he found himself getting serious about a girl, he felt obliged to objectively assess her potential for surviving a missionary life. I don't know why he thought I qualified.

Initially, I didn't see that much of Ralph back in Toronto. He was studying hard and I had my own circle of friends. This began to change during his year of internship. I felt comfortable with him. One didn't have to spend all one's time either protecting one's "honor" or pretending to be a good sport. I don't recall being swept off my feet. Neither of us ever had any money to speak of. Of course, my problem was extravagance (my father always made up any serious shortfalls). Ralph, on the other hand, was obliged to count every penny. When I was with him, however, this didn't seem to matter. Nor did it concern me that I was two years his senior (my mother, after all, was seven years older than my dad). At some point, our good fellowship turned to something more intense. After I returned from Prince Rupert in the Fall of 1937, I went to visit Ralph in Montreal, where he was doing a year of general surgery at the Royal Victoria Hospital as a final preparation for his work in China. This, however, was certainly not in anticipation of a proposal of marriage, not even when one romantic evening he filled my arms with flowers and hired a calèche (a horse-drawn carriage of a type unique to Quebec) to take us up Mount Royal's gentle slopes. Nor would I have guessed as we clip-clopped along, content in each other's company, gazing up at the night's first stars, that buried among the stems of my bouquet was a wee box containing an engagement ring. In fact, I was taken by complete and utter surprise when, on bended knee, he asked the question. With the lights of the city blinking below and the huge electrified Cross of Mount Royal shining its message of Salvation from the hilltop above, I said, "Yes." Later, we slipped into St. James United Church to sit and contemplate the enormity of the course upon which we had embarked.

Even had the battles of the Sino-Japanese War not been raging, my parents would have had grave doubts about this plighting of troths. Probably so did Ralph's, who were still in Japan (Ralph hadn't been home for over eight years). I had second thoughts myself, especially as the day of our wedding drew near. I was at home in Prince Rupert and Ralph still in Montreal when I wrote him about my misgivings. I don't know why I was reassured by his reply of April 16th, 1938, but I was: ". . . I often am surprised that you don't get that way more often. To ask a girl to give up all the lovely things and wonderful friends she is used to, to go across half the earth and settle down in a God-forsaken place among a strange people and surrounded by untold hardships of every kind with a queer old soak who loves her to distraction, takes not only courage but gall of the first magnitude! To accept such a proposition takes far greater courage and to such a woman I raise my hat; to the particular one in question, I bend my knee. You say that at times you are overwhelmed by a feeling of the magnitude and the responsibility of the proposition. Marg., at times my own unpreparedness for this tremendous task is born in upon my mind with such reality that I shudder to think of it. You speak of having a 'cool questioning reason that must have a logical answer', and for that reason you find it hard to accept in 'blind faith'. I can understand that perfectly. I have the same difficulty though I feel that justification for adopting our future life work is grounded a little more firmly than on 'blind faith'.

"You see, being brought up among the Oriental peoples, I, quite naturally I suppose, grew to love them and to understand them. Their hardships, their poverty and their suffering made a great impression on my boyish mind. Finally, when I stood on the threshold of Manhood, I came to the conclusion that the life work from which one receives the richest gains is that to which one gives the most. It was really on that somewhat selfish principle that I decided to become a Missionary doctor in the Far East. Throughout the past eight years the vision of the great need of these people which I might some day be able, through the guidance of God, to in a small part relieve, has constantly been before me to keep me to my task. You can call it 'blind faith' or 'Divine Guidance' or anything you like though I prefer the latter.

"I know you have always wondered at our somewhat strange pre-engagement 'courtship', Marg. Reading the above you understand how tremendously important this business of choosing a wife was. It meant either a making or a breaking of my whole life. You don't realize how wonderful it is to know that I have found the right girl. You ask me how I know? I can't tell you—I just know. Call it 'blind faith' if you like.

"I realize, dear, that most people think the thing we are doing is, as you quote in your letter, 'foolish' and 'sacrificing' but I can't seem to think of it in that light. To me, it is a need crying out to be met; it is a man-sized job, with no sissy trimmings, which will demand all we've got to give it; it is a life work which, I am persuaded, will bring for us great happiness. So you see, I too have figured it all out in a 'cool logical manner' and that is the conclusion which I reached, after a great deal of thought—a conclusion which has not changed an iota since it was first conceived.

"Of course, Marg, you must realize that the whole course of your life has suddenly been turned into a new channel. You cannot expect to grasp the meaning or the purpose of that change fully in one gulp. Even I, who have lived out there in that atmosphere, so often pass through my moments of doubting. But the whole thing boils down to this—I am so convinced that the results will be worth the effort, that I am willing to stake everything, even to dragging the one I love most in the whole wide world into it too, in order to make that effort. Until you too can come to that same conviction, dear, I'm afraid that you will have to accept the whole proposition in blind faith. . . ."

Ralph's big day came two weeks later on May 1st, when all his early dedication was crowned at Montreal's St. James United in his "designation" (a sort of ordination) as a Missionary. Participating in this ceremony, which took place during the regular Sunday morning Worship, were Mr. Goodwin, chairman of the United Church's Quebec Conference, Dr. Monroe, the Conference Secretary, Rev. Ross, a Missionary recently returned from Korea, Rev. Bruce Hunter, the Minister at St. James, and Rev. E. N. Baker, Ralph's grandfather (all appropriately gowned and seated facing the congregation on the chancel dais). At the beginning of the service, Ralph (also gowned) was ushered to a front pew. The liturgical order was as usual until after the Reading: *Isaiah* 16 (perhaps selected to remind Ralph that God is always a Force on the side of His chosen no matter how inhospitable the lands in which they wander). Then the Church luminaries stepped down to the font enclosure where Ralph now stood before them. Rev. Hunter formally introduced the proceedings, after which Ralph was questioned as to why he felt he had been "called" to the office of Missionary. Ralph then knelt while his Grandfather Baker read a prayer, following which each of the Churchmen laid their hands upon Ralph's head and blessed him and his calling in the name of God. When he arose, Mr. Goodwin presented him with a beautiful inscribed Bible (Moffatt's translation), a gift of the Foreign Mission Board. He made a short speech, speaking layman to layman, recommended the Bible as a textbook and daily guide and advised Ralph to remember, when caring for all his patients, Christ's comfort to His Disciples in *John* 14:2, "In my Father's house are many mansions: if it were not so, I would have told you; I go to prepare a place for you." Then everyone, including Ralph, reassembled on the dais and Rev. Ross gave the sermon on his work in Korea, using as his text *John* 4: 34–35, "Jesus saith unto them, My meat is to do the will of him that sent me, and to finish his work. Say not ye, There are yet four months, and then cometh harvest? behold, I say unto you, Lift up your eyes, and look on the fields; for they are white already to harvest." When he had finished, Grandad Baker rose to say a few words. He told those assembled he had experienced conversion seventy-one years before and that for sixty-five of these he had been in the active Ministry. He reflected that in the course of a life time there are really just a few outstanding moments. This was one of them: the opportunity to hand the torch to his grandson! Then Ralph spoke, telling why he was going to China as a Medical Missionary and asking for prayers and support. Finally, before bringing the Service to a close, Rev. Hunter asked the congregation to consider Ralph their own Missionary. (Obviously, they didn't take this injunction very seriously. You will recall my mentioning their miserly gift of thirty dollars when we were in Junghsien.) I wasn't there to see any of the above, but Ralph wrote me a play-by-play account of what he described as a "beautiful" experience and "the most impressive service I have ever attended."

And while I read every word and was happy for Ralph, at the time I was preparing for my own "big" moment. Consequently, the significance of the event he was describing escaped me. And, for better or for worse, we were united before God in Prince Rupert on June 17th, 1938. That same evening, we left by coastal steamer for Vancouver to catch the *Empress of Japan* for Yokohama. It would be over seven years before I again set foot on my native soil. I had been told what I was getting myself into, but the words had no meaning. I was in love.

We spent the next two months in Japan with Ralph's family. (Both his parents have been with the Kwansei Gakuin University since 1912.) It was a joyous reunion and a very happy time for me as well. My diary for this period fairly bubbles with enthusiasm. The Outerbridges could not have been kinder. I was especially taken with Ralph's young brother Bill, who turned thirteen that August 10th. (I should mention that I already knew and liked Ralph's sister Dorothy, a Home Economics teacher in Toronto.) Because the summers in Japan are unbearably hot, we spent most of our stay at the Outerbridge cottage at Nojiri Lake. Sailing, swimming, hiking and tennis were the order of most days, although Dad O. (the family calls him "Pop") and I did manage one game of golf. Those of the foreign community I met were civilized, cosmopolitan and often very talented. And what I saw of Japanese life was fascinating. In retrospect, our holiday served me as a very gentle introduction to the Orient and made China, when we arrived, a little less shocking to my Western eyes than it otherwise would have been. It also gave one a positive introduction to Missionary life. This, of course, is exactly what Ralph intended.

I found Ralph's dad selflessly hard working, intelligent and supportive. Often on our walks, Pop would instruct me in the great religions of the world. He, of course, had graduated in theology from New Brunswick's Mount Allison University, was an ordained Methodist minister and had served a couple of years as a missionary before taking up administrative and teaching responsibilities at the University (where he is now president). His father before him had been a Methodist Minister who served various parishes in Nova Scotia after leaving his home in Bermuda (where Ralph claims there are more Outerbridges—both black and white—in the 'phone book than Smiths). Pop met Ralph's mother, Edna Muriel Baker (the family calls her "Gay") at university where she was studying music. Her father, Grandad Baker, was the principal and founder of Belleville's Albert College for young men. From the beginning, they shared (it would have been remarkable had they not) a commitment to spreading The Word. I liked my mother-in-law immensely (and still do), admired her ability to take everything in her stride, her good humor and, to a large degree, her taste in furnishing, etc. Her home in Kwansei is a dream. She is in charge of choral work at the University and is herself a trained mezzo-soprano. With Ralph and Bill on their violins, our neighbor Dot Swetnam at the piano and Gay singing, we had some marvelous evenings. The only time Gay and I had a disagreement that became at all heated was over the qualities or lack thereof of Dot's German boyfriend, and this was something I really didn't care about. My one trauma that honeymoon summer came when I received a cablegram informing me that all my personal possessions (clothes, effects, wedding presents and special purchases for seven years in China, including baby and children's clothes and shoes to age six in anticipation of our "family") had been destroyed in a fire on the docks in Vancouver. I felt numb. When we calculated the dollar loss, it was considerably more than Ralph's salary for an entire year!

Coming back to Gay, Ralph regards his mother as the ideal missionary helpmeet and, no doubt, hoped I would learn something from her in this regard. I doubt I did. We are such different personalities and the particulars of our circumstances were to bear precious little similarity. In that the possibility would probably never have occurred to her, she could not give me the advice I ultimately needed: do not get between a missionary and his God—if he has to make a choice, it may break his heart, but he can not choose you!

So here we are again in Shanghai. We arrived on May 20th and have only just succeeded in getting our household effects (which have been here since the end of April) through customs. This has involved Ralph and several other men working all day, every day, to unravel miles of red tape through a maze of Chinese bureaucracy. In the customs building, you pass from one desk to another, one department to another, following your import papers. The list of your dutiable goods is checked by one pair of hands, double-checked by a second, triple-checked by a third, stamped by yet another, dated by a fifth and on it goes. Ralph says that on the worst day, his papers were stamped or chopped by nearly seventy different officials. And we have been among the lucky. Some have taken over three months to get their stuff through this process. It is painfully obvious that one of the reasons everything is made so difficult is because the Chinese do not want the foreign communities to re-establish themselves. More fools we, say I, for forcing ourselves upon them!

Personally, I have never experienced such rudeness, and rudeness from a Chinese is calculated. A pedicab (a bicycle-drawn rickshaw) man will agree to take you somewhere for a certain price, but when you arrive he will hold you up for more. One day when Judith and I were out and I made the mistake of not alighting directly at our door, this happened to me. The driver first threatened. I refused to be bullied. He then started punching me. I was furious and all the more stubborn. A curious crowd started to assemble. One man said, "Give him another $10,000." Even though this was only a couple of cents American, I couldn't do it. I explained in Chinese and English how I had made an agreement we both understood. A general discussion followed. Then one of the onlookers said, "Missy, you right, man wrong, you go home." And that was that! I love the old Chinese sense of justice and their "tea house" way of settling disputes. In the old days, the driver would have been beaten for laying hands on a foreigner, but now that we have no protection, the old hatreds are everywhere apparent. I have met some foreigners, held in Japanese prison camps during the War, who now dislike the Chinese more than they do their former tormentors.

Shanghai is difficult to describe. It is certainly not the China we know. The Bund, with its row of stately multistoried buildings, could be Vancouver or any other large port city. One of the most beautiful of its edifices is the Hong Kong—Shanghai Bank. Particularly impressive are the two huge bronze lions couchant, which guard its entrance. Their paws and tail have been rubbed by those passing until they are smooth and shining.

One day, I asked a Chinese gentleman of my acquaintance whether the locals felt there was some medicinal property in this bronze. He explained that the lions had been hidden at the onset of the Japanese invasion in 1937 so that they would not be melted down for shell casings and had but recently re-appeared. Now when people pass, they stroke the lions to keep them happy, somehow believing their presence will prevent more war and suffering. The city is crowded beyond belief. Its pre-War population of 3½ million has increased by fifty per cent. Amazingly, there is little evidence of the War or Japanese occupation. Two friends, one Polish, the other Russian, took us for a drive past the concentration camp where they had been incarcerated, now a peaceful little cluster of houses and shops. The theater where hundreds of Chinese had been killed by Japanese bombs has been rebuilt and plays to packed houses every day as though nothing had ever happened. The shops are loaded with everything one could wish to buy. Expensive, desperately so if your American dollars are exchanged at the official rate of 480,000 to 1. Few Chinese actually do this, but use the black market, where one can get about 1½ million to 1. Several foreigners caught doing this, however, have been severely fined. Between these two, there is a preferred rate which may be used by Missionary organizations, schools, etc., of 880,000 to 1. This morning's paper says these organizations may soon be able to obtain black market rates through accredited banks. In that the rate fluctuates constantly, one exchanges only as much as one needs each day. Even though we'd heard about all this before our arrival, it came as a bit of a shock when our friend Marnie Copeland met us at the jetty and handed Ralph $14 million "to do you for a little while." The city is loaded with U.S. Army tinned food. Shiploads of war surplus including cheese, bacon, chocolates and nuts. Word has it these supplies can be obtained inland, so it looks as though our diet may be a bit more interesting than last time.

We have been staying at the Army and Navy YMCA in the heart of the business district, the only accommodation available. It isn't bad. Adjacent rooms, shared bathrooms (Male and Fe-

male) with the other floor guests (showers, basins, etc.). Everything spotlessly clean. The servants on the floor are kind and
interested in the children, who have been the best little sports.
Carol, the fastidious, however, is literally nauseated by people
expectorating on the streets.

We don't know what is going to happen politically. Can the
Nationalists hold out against the Communists? It's hard to get
any clear sense of the overall situation. Certainly, this is a period
of great change. Even Shanghai seems unusually hectic and
evanescent, due perhaps to the Chinese taking over so much traditionally managed by the British and Americans. But there is a
feeling as well of vast subterranean forces at work. A day or so
after the student riots at St. John's University, when the children
and I were out for a walk, the earth suddenly trembled. The
sound of a soft explosion followed. A mushroom of smoke (like
the atom bomb on a small scale) rose above the newspaper
building on the opposite side of the street as it slowly fell apart.
We think the cause is anti-Americanism, but this is only
speculation. Even the old China hands find it confusing, so
don't mind my dumbness too much. Our friends estimate the
chances of Szechwan falling to the Communists at about
fifty:fifty. We recognize the gamble, but are optimistic. Our situation is far different from that in 1938. We have a nice home to
go to, everything we need, and we are not green. Besides, we
really are no longer all that far away. I can fly to Hong Kong,
then across to San Francisco and be home in less than a week if
need be.

□ *JULY 4TH:* On the morning of June 10th, we slipped out of
Shanghai Harbor, up the Whangpoo and into the Yangtse on
the Motor Ship *Min Shen*. This was her maiden voyage (her
owners called it her "virgin voyage") and a stroke of good fortune for us. Normally, the dirt and overcrowding make such
travel unpleasant. By custom, after the normal complement of
tickets is sold by the vessel's agents, the captain then sells deck
space on the side to "yellow fish," a term that refers to all passengers on a boat, train or bus who have not paid the regular

fare. (This expression finds its origin in a species of tiny fish which travel upstream with a minimum of effort by swimming in the wake of larger fish.) In addition, any soldier can force his way aboard. Consequently, when the ship is ready to sail, one is literally confined to one's cabin, for there is no space to move anywhere else. Not long ago one vessel capsized in Nanking harbor due to the uncontrolled crowding of soldiers and "yellow fish." Knowing all this, it was just by chance Ralph dropped in to see the manager of the Min Sung Co., which has the largest passenger service operation on the river. They told him about the *Min Shen*, a super-deluxe class, sailing all the way to Chungking with a government guarantee there would be no deck passengers allowed. This seemed too good an opportunity to miss, even when its departure was postponed a week (during which time the price of everything jumped 90 per cent. Money is such a nuisance. Unless one carries a suitcase full, one simply cannot make the simplest purchase.)

The *Min Shen* is 120 feet long, with a shallow draft, twin screws and three rudders. Her engines were retrieved from ships sunk in Shanghai harbor, one British and one from a Japanese battleship. The hull was put together by hand, the plates bent by hand, each rivet driven home by hand. The superstructure, except for the General Electric fans in the staterooms, is entirely of Chinese materials. There is an attractive promenade deck (with chairs) and the dining room converts to a lounge between meals. Each of the twenty first-class cabins is 8' × 10', with two comfortable spring beds, a table between, a clothes cupboard and a fold-out wash basin. The linen was new, as were the mattresses (what a relief, no bed bugs) and everything spotless. Even the passageways were lined with flowering plants in attractive pots. The officers and men in stiff new uniforms simply exuded pride—pride in their lovely ship and pride in the fact she was an achievement of modern war-torn China. Captain Harnish (English father, Chinese mother) has been navigating the river for fifty years and is considered the best there is. By special request, he came out of retirement for the *Min Shen*'s maiden voyage. He told us he never feels better than when drinking Yangtse River water. Yuk!

I do agree, however, that of all the world's great waterways, none could offer a greater feast for the eyes than the Yangtse. Its lower reaches pass through flat, heavily cultivated country which has a population density of some 2,400 per square mile. The tiny "postage-stamp" fields were lush with yield. The river itself is as much as four miles across, progressively narrowing as it winds its thousand miles to Ichang, except when it opens into small lakes. We were disappointed at not getting a chance to explore Nanking. Instead of docking (it was feared, government guarantees to the contrary, we might be boarded by soldiers fleeing west), we anchored several miles down stream, replenishing our fuel supplies from coal-laden junks. We then proceeded to Hankow, steaming day and night.

The river is the busiest of thoroughfares. Large junks loaded with rice from Changsha. Others with sugar, raw cotton or wheat from wherever. Smaller ones, under full sail heading upriver, hugging the shore to avoid the full force of the current. Stern-oared sampans providing local ferry service. As the days passed, we began to notice the changing styles of river craft. The experienced eye will note the type of rudder, the elevation of the rear deck, the design of the bow, the cut of sail, etc., and know where the junk was made, where it plies its trade and its cargo. Watching the ever-changing shoreline, with the white-gowned farmer patiently following his water buffalo or the fisherman casting his nets or the scholar resting for a pipe beneath a shady tree, one would never dream this country has had anything but peace for the last 4,000 years. In the evening, as the brilliant colors of the sunset faded, bluish smoke would curl from each thatched hut. Then the country folk would come out to sit on the dikes and discuss the day's events.

On Sunday, the fourth day of our journey, we drew near Hankow. The area from Hankow to Ichang (Yichang) had been experiencing Communist hit-and-run attacks for some time and one could observe small units of Nationalist troops dug in every few hundred yards, keeping watch along the river bank. There are actually three cities at the junction of the Han and Yangtse Rivers, Wuchang, Hanyang and Hankow. The port of Hankow, which is accessible to ocean-going ships, was opened to foreign trade in 1858 and is the most important commercial center in this part of China. I, however, do not know why our Captain decided it would be safe to dock there.

Bob McClure had been posted to the Hankow Union Hospital in November 1947, where he and a young Canadian surgeon, Doug Dalziel, have established the only cancer clinic in Central China. Doug was there to meet us when we came ashore and whisked us off in an ambulance to spend the day at his home in the Hospital compound. We had a great time swapping stories before returning to our ship at about 8:30 P.M. to put the children to bed, as we were due to sail at midnight. To our consternation, we found that in our absence some three hundred wounded soldiers, desperate to get to Chungking, had rushed the ship's guards, almost killing one and severely injuring the others and had settled down on the deck like a cloud of locusts. They had with them all their worldly possessions and were packed so closely, sitting or lying (depending on their condition), it was impossible to make one's way without continually stepping on someone. With difficulty we at last reached our cabin and squeezed inside. It was very hot and the air was fetid with the odor of unwashed bodies and suppurating wounds. The poor devils outside our window must have had advanced Tb because they coughed up sputum all night!

Of the one hundred and forty-five paying passengers, only twenty-eight were foreigners: we five, twelve attractive young American Baptist fundamentalists who had been forced to abandon their mission in Shansi [Shanxi] province, four Mennonites (also evacuees) and three American vips. These latter, two U.S. Navy wives (one the spouse of an Admiral) and a Captain Linder, the naval architect responsible for the *Min Shen*, were passengers quite unlike the rest. They were friendly enough in a superficial way, but didn't deign to dine with us, having brought on board a private supply of food which they kept in a locked fridge in one of their cabins. What is more, they tended to be a trifle coarse—loud and seemingly always with a drink in hand. Unfortunately, the three of them had been out partying and were quite inebriated by the time they returned an hour or so before our scheduled departure from Hankow. As they surveyed the scene on deck, they became furious. And when the soldiers would not clear a path for them, Captain Linder began throwing and kicking their duffel out of the way.

Tempers flared. One of the soldiers whose bedroll had been kicked aside accused the Captain of stealing something from him (a typical Chinese reaction to losing face). Others vowed vengeance, denounced the United States, etc. Each of our uninvited guests was armed to the teeth and our American fellows could not have been more provocative. I was particularly upset with the two females who kept opening their cabin doors to hurl drunken curses at the soldiers in the passageway. (Performances that did nothing to enhance our Western image!) We watched all this from the darkness of our cabin and for about half an hour we fully expected bloodshed, possibly even ours! Finally, one of their officers arrived to defuse the situation. He talked to his men for a long time, explaining the Americans were under the influence of alcohol, etc. Gradually passions cooled, but it was close! The children slept through the whole thing.

In the circumstances, Captain Harnish refused to cast off. It took three days of patient negotiation and many speeches to convince any of the soldiers to leave, during which time we stayed with the Dalziels. My impression of Hankow was that of people living with their suitcases packed, ready to flee at a moment's notice. There appears to be no general confidence that the Nationalists can stem the Communist advance. Perhaps this is why the soldiers were so determined to stay on board. Eventually, half of them agreed to other transportation. The remaining one hundred and fifty were to stay with us to Ichang. Our three VIPs, however, quickly departed for Shanghai, leaving us the key to their refrigerator (unfortunately someone pulled the plug and everything spoiled) and for some reason giving their booze to the Mennonites (who promptly gave it to us).

So it was at midnight, June 16th, that we started again up-river. It was hoped that by leaving at this hour we would pass safely through the most dangerous portions of the Yangtse battleground. The next two days were uneventful, but not pleasant. We had to keep pretty much to our cabins, and the heat and the stench were terrific. It would be difficult for someone at home to imagine what one hundred and fifty wounded Chinese soldiers can do to a beautiful new ship, the paint soiled beyond description, the deck indescribably filthy with discarded refuse and slippery with spittle. The Chief Purser took one look, broke down and wept! At Ichang, thirty well-armed police immediately came aboard, apprehending three Communist agents who were working to exploit the discontent of the men. Shots rang out, one soldier was killed and great confusion ensued. We saw the agents dragged, their arms tied behind them, to the wharf where the police proceeded to beat them brutally with rifle butts. They fell to their knees begging for mercy, but were led off up the hill no doubt to be shot. In the meantime, the wounded soldiers realized their joyride was over and peacefully transferred to a waiting river tramp. This accomplished, we steamed across the river to coal.

It was by this time evening, so we put the children to bed and went on deck to watch. It was all very efficient. A human chain from the barges to the ship passed the coal from hand to hand in bamboo wicker baskets. In the meantime, as we tugged at our anchor, the brown river water whipping by at four or five knots, small sampans crossed and re-crossed bringing supplies or articles for sale. And before our horrified eyes, one carrying cigarettes, candy and such missed the boathook hold and turned turtle. Before we could reach the stern of our ship (a mere fifty feet away), the contents of the little boat had been scattered at least a quarter-mile down stream. There was no sign of its crew. Four more victims for "the Yellow Dragon"! No wonder the Chinese hold this river in such respect—and dread.

One of China's most famous poets wrote, "The road to Szechwan is more difficult than the ascent into Heaven." To me it is small wonder the province has remained isolated throughout Chinese history and smaller wonder still the Japanese had not the courage to push their way to China's wartime capital, Chungking. The river drops 200 feet from Chungking to Ichang and is in places confined to a narrow cleft not more than a hundred yards wide as it rips its way between granite towers some ten thousand feet in height. June is an ideal time to navigate its passes, for the river is then swollen by summer rains. Amazing as this sounds, it had risen sixty-three feet by the time we went through. Four miles north of Ichang, we entered the first of its gorges. Our ship, now hugging one rocky face, now easing across the torrent to avoid a hidden danger, now into a dead end only to turn at right angles, sometimes barely moving despite the throbbing of her powerful twin engines, slowly took us from one breathtaking scene to another. And perched like eagles' eyries on the jagged cliffs above, small temples, adding a particular Chinese quality to nature's awesome beauty. We passed through the Ichang Gorge, the Ox Lung Gorge, the Horse Lung Gorge, the Wind Box Gorge and the Witches Gorge, where caverns are believed inhabited by evil spirits and dragons. One is reported to contain a centuries-old iron coffin with a lid too heavy to lift. A particular rock is reputed to have once held a large magic ring which, when seen by a traveller, assured safe passage around the next, very dangerous bend. This ring was never to be touched, but when one Doubting Thomas insisted, it turned into a snake and disappeared. I should add that junks journey upstream through the gorges at the end of bamboo ropes pulled by up to twenty or more trackers bending their backs and chanting in rhythm while their feet wear an ageless trail. In the earlier part of this century, everyone en route to West China from Shanghai travelled by junk, a journey of six to eight weeks duration.

At last Hupeh province was behind us and we entered Szechwan with its familiar hills, its fertile fields and its blue peasant dress (the indigo plant grows abundantly here). And on June

22nd, we rounded a bend and there, on the wedge of land between the Yangtse and the Kialing Rivers, the war-scarred city
of caves, Chungking! The *Min Shen*, again pristine, sounded its
whistle. Sirens in the city answered and firecrackers blasted
their welcome. Our journey was over. Every delay, every inconvenience, every risk had been more than repaid by all we
had seen and experienced.

We had scarcely cast anchor when Ralph's name was broadcast over the ship's loudspeaker. He was to report to the bridge.
Talk about guilty consciences! We immediately assumed this
was a customs matter, that somehow someone had discovered
we had a radio, purchased in Hong Kong, on which we had not
paid duty in Shanghai! (A young diplomat with whom we became friends on the ship from North America had taken it
ashore for us.) Obviously, we would never make good crooks.
Of course, it was nothing of the sort. When Ralph arrived, he
was introduced to some very important looking gentlemen who
turned out to be the mayor and aldermen of the nearby model
city, I Pin. They were expecting to meet Ralph's cousin, Ted
Outerbridge, the head of the International Red Cross in China,
whom they hoped would agree to inspect their hospital and add
it to the list of those receiving free medical supplies. Ralph explained the confusion, but volunteered to go with them should
they desire this. No doubt to save face, they accepted. Consequently, our freight and baggage were immediately chopped
through the Chungking customs check. (Our radio was safe!)
As it turned out, Ralph was sufficiently impressed with their set-
up to write his cousin recommending their request be granted.

While the children and I proceeded by transport plane to
Chengtu, Ralph took the overland route in order to collect those
furnishings, rugs, trunks, etc., we had left in Tzeliutsing. House
106 on the West China Union University campus is our new address. The Cunninghams had set up camp cots for us and had
engaged the nucleus of a staff, so we were able to move right in.
Our beloved Fuh Hai-yuin was dead, Dzan and The Dragon un-
traceable. Roy Webster drove the Mission truck from Tzeliutsing, with Ralph sitting atop the load. At one point, a low-

hanging telephone wire caught him across the face. He does look odd. The resultant burn gives his mouth the appearance of being twice its normal width. Fortunately, they were not travelling at more than a few miles per hour. Then, on a particularly bad section of road, the truck overturned, dumping everything into a flooded paddy field, where it lay for forty-eight hours. No one was hurt, but oh, my stuff! (Chinese dyes are notoriously unfast.) Besides this, our goods from Shanghai had been stored under a leaking tank of formaldehyde. Talk about stench! Also, as we unpack, we are discovering many things missing, presumably stolen by the customs staff in Shanghai, including our only clock and a spring-filled mattress. Finally, the Missionary who took over our house in Tzeliutsing had helped himself to the best of our chairs and one of our stoves when he moved on to his next Station.

At present, the place is a terrible mess. The tinsmith is trying to put our stove in working order, busily soldering old tin cans to make the stove pipe. A carpenter is building cupboards in the kitchen. And a painter arrives tomorrow to refinish the furniture, which took a terrible beating, both during our absence and in the accident. He is called a *chi chiang* and works with that wonderful tung-oil-base varnish and paint. Unfortunately, it has to dry at least a month before one can go near it, otherwise one becomes infected with a poison-ivy-like rash. (You remember poor Edna Veals.) If you think all this is fun, you can have it!

☐ *AUGUST 1ST:* This is the first of our summers in China we have not gone to the hills. There is too much to get ready for Fall term. The heat and the humidity, however, are so enervating I have been forced to ease my pace. It seems I can't drive myself in weather like this and stay human. I had been flying into tempers, five minutes later forgetting why. The children are great. Kerry, in particular, is a riot. Yesterday, when I was resting, he assumed the responsibility of keeping me supplied with cookies and glasses of water, while rapidly attaining a well-filled look himself. As I write, he has just come in with a wig of wood shavings on his head, singing a song and a bunch of flowers in his hands, "Just for Mummie." He filches me flowers wherever we go. Carol has a tub of tadpoles outside the back door, the position of which she regularly changes, so I hear a good round of Chinese curses every time someone trips over it. She looks well, pink cheeks, clear eyes, full of beans and happy. (The plastic surgeon at home did a marvelous job.) Dorothy Day lives nearby and they are inseparable. Also Dora Ann Stinson and Judy are great friends, so that is taken care of. Our cook, Chiang Si, has insisted I send a picture of him to my mum so that she will know he will do everything in his power to take care of her precious family. I like his spirit, although I sometimes wish he had not learned his trade in the army.

☐ *AUGUST 30TH* (2 A.M.): It has been blowing a true sou'easter for the last twenty-four hours. The stream at the bottom of the garden has overflowed and the house is surrounded by a shallow lake. I couldn't sleep, so I got up, checked the children, then started putting pots to catch the innumerable leaks. We have no basement (naturally enough, given the high water table) and with the flooding, all sorts of creepy-crawlies are beginning to ooze through the single floor boards. I'd wake Ralph, but he is dead to the world. He did three major operations today and is exhausted. I am disappointed for him. After all his work at home to attain the qualifications necessary to teach general surgery, he has felt obliged to stand aside to make way for a very able Chinese surgeon with a training the equal of his own. He has been asked to teach and develop a program in orthopædics instead, for which he is not so highly qualified. He seems to take these things in his stride, but will have to work very hard if he is to keep on top of his new responsibilities.

☐ *SEPTEMBER 15TH:* The intense heat of the summer is at last waning. People are spending less time at home fanning themselves and are once more on the streets, where the excitement at present is the government's attempt to peg commodity prices while floating a new currency based on silver. (We were just getting used to the million dollar notes.) The people have been given three months to convert their old dollars, which are no longer legal tender, at $3 million (old) to $1 (new). We now have to think again in 10 cent, 50 cent and $1.00 coins. (The international exchange rate is now four silver dollars to $1.00 American.) To add to the confusion, the old metal currency in use during our first term here is to re-enter circulation. This set everyone digging out all the previously worthless copper and nickel coins they had lying about. There is a story going the rounds concerning a man who runs a small shop in town, who some years ago went from door to door buying up loads of the old copper coins for use in the manufacture of metal wash basins. For some reason, however, he never got around to melting them down. He woke up the other day to find himself a multi-millionaire!

Critical to the success of the government's program is its ceiling on the price of rice, etc. We hear that in other parts of China, the authorities have this situation under control. The Szechwanese, however, with their reputation for being "the first to pick up arms and the last to lay them down" are as usual proving recalcitrant. Suspicious of the government's motives and considering the new system unworkable, the merchants have refused all price regulations. And, in the face of a buying spree by those with hoards of old coins, all the shops closed their doors, afraid of getting stuck with money that at any moment might again prove nugatory. That was four days ago. This has created hardship, especially among those whose homes and property were savaged by the recent floods. (We had a drowned child wash up in our garden.) The Generalissimo's son is expected to arrive tomorrow to take the situation in hand. No doubt several people will be shot. Then everything will be business as usual.

Ralph had quite an adventure last week. At noon on Thursday, a wire arrived from Kiating, "Pastor Liu acutely ill. Send Surgeon immediately." It seemed a strange request, in that the Hospital there has a staff of four Western-trained Chinese doctors, one of whom is a very fine surgeon. However, there was no choice but to respond. One hundred miles is a relatively short distance in Canada or the United States, but here the roads are heavily rutted single-lane dirt tracks. What is more, as the road approaches Kiating, it winds through hills notorious for bandits, who have the unpleasant habit after stripping their victims of everything marketable, of leaving them tied by their thumbs to the limb of some tree or, worse, of holding them for ransom. Because the bridge at Meichou, the half-way point, has been washed out, it was decided that Ralph would proceed from there by motorcycle, a means of transportation he had not previously experienced. Alf Day would follow by bicycle and a staff coolie would stay with the Mission truck, which they would leave in Meichou. The motorcycle is a Villiers, small, heavy, and with a number of idiosyncracies. The self-starter doesn't work. The head light only functions at speeds of twenty m.p.h. or more. (The greater the speed, the better the light.) The exhaust cover's gone, exposing a red-hot pipe on which to burn oneself. There is no foot brake, just hand levers. Finally, because the only fuel available here is dirty, the spark plugs regularly foul and the gas line routinely clogs. Otherwise it runs like a dream! It was 6 P.M. before they were able to leave. Averaging about ten miles per hour, they arrived at the wash-out about eleven, where they had to ease the motorcycle across a long, single-plank makeshift foot bridge. The coolie then returned to the truck to get some sleep.

After first walking a hundred yards or so to familiarize themselves with the road, Ralph began to run into the blackness, saying a prayer as he jiggled the cycle's gas and spark controls. Suddenly, the engine ignited and the bike took off "like a bat out of hell" up the bank and over on its side. Alf helped Ralph to his feet and he started again. But this time, when the motor roared, Ralph managed to keep on course. Soaking with rain and sweat, shirt-tail flying, eyes streaming, he says it was the most thrilling ride of his life. Or at least it was, until the engine conked some fifteen or twenty minutes later. The spark plug cleaned and the gas line blown clear, he was off once more . . . until twenty minutes later! At one point, sensing something irregular ahead, he veered into a flooded rice paddy. Extricating himself from the muck, he got out his torch to investigate. Sure enough, another wash-out, with a twenty-foot drop to the rocky creek bed below! Later, around two in the morning, at the top of a hill in the mountains near Kiating, when the damn thing quit for the umpteenth time, Ralph, in utter exhaustion, lay down beside it. Fortunately, he had tended to the gas line, etc. first, because he soon became aware of voices coming up the road. Now no honest citizen is abroad in the Chinese countryside at this hour. The question was whether to hightail from whence he came or brazen it out. He got up, righted the machine and started running towards his unseen companions. With only twenty or so yards between them, the motorbike responded with an unearthly roar and a blaze of light. Obviously taken totally by surprise, the bandits parted ranks. (Ralph saw their guns as he flashed by.) What they must have thought we'll never know, although it is amusing to speculate that Ralph and his fiery charger may now be the Sze. equivalent of "The Headless Horseman of Sleepy Hollow"! It was nearly 5 A.M. when he reached the city gate, where his steed finally died and had to be pushed to the Mission compound. Fatigued beyond belief, soaked and filthy, he gratefully climbed steps he had last seen in 1940.

Partially restored by a hot bath and breakfast, he went to the hospital to examine his patient. Pastor Liu's gall bladder was enlarged and threatening to perforate, so Ralph decided to drain it. The operating room was prepared and everyone ready when the Pastor's old grandmother came limping in. Although she had agreed to surgery when Leonard Bacon, the local Missionary, sent the telegram, she now categorically refused. The *fung shui* (spirits) were not auspicious. And this despite the fact her grandson preached the Gospel! Given the structure of Chinese society, however, her familial authority could not be challenged. There was nothing for it but to cancel the operation and hope Pastor Liu's medication would somehow do the job. As to why Dr. Yang, our surgeon in Kiating, had disappeared from sight, he and the Pastor had had a serious public dispute. Consequently, he was afraid that if his antagonist died under the knife, the Liu family would accuse him of purposely using this method to avenge himself. While Ralph was catching a couple-of-hours sleep at the Bacon's, Alf arrived on his bicycle. In the meantime, Leonard had arranged for their immediate return to Meichou on the postal truck. Bike and motorbike loaded aboard, by nightfall they were back in Chengtu. Had Don Quixote and Sancho Panza been Missionaries. . . !

To matters less exotic, the children started school about ten days ago. The girls are attending the Canadian School. We have enrolled Kerry in a Chinese kindergarten taught by Pearl Chiang who has studied early childhood education in Britain. (You may remember my mentioning Pearl and her sister when we were in Jenshow.) Yesterday morning, I watched from behind a bush as Kerry's class started their day standing at attention in a semi-circle around the flag pole, while Pearl raised the colors, and a little fellow out in front saluting led them in the Chinese National Anthem. You can't imagine the discordant consequences. However, gusto was not lacking and they clapped merrily when the flag finally made it to the top.

□ *NOVEMBER 20TH:* We have been passing through interesting days. With the fall of Mukden (Shen-yang) to the Communists, a near panic developed here. Every kind of speculation was rife. People began to talk wildly about getting out. Commodity prices went haywire. (The Nationalist government had already lost its battle to control the merchants.) The exchange rate is now thirty new Chinese dollars to one dollar American. Rumor has it that the government will move to Canton. One does not talk long with the Chinese here before realizing the Nationalist regime is endured only because not enough people are yet convinced there is anything better to take its place. Despite this, dissatisfaction and anger grow daily. It is reported a delegation is planning to approach Chiang Kai-shek to request that he resign. The notion is that there would then be the possibility of a coalition government. Just why the Communists would choose to cooperate when the entire country is within their grasp escapes me entirely. Besides, the Generalissimo is not likely to yield to such demands.

Last week, our friend Col. Tom McNight and his American Advisory Air Force Group (fifteen families in all) were ordered to Formosa. Before departing, they sold or gave their equipment to various institutions here and generally left a good feeling behind them. Personally, we shall miss Tom and his daughter. It was a handsome gesture on his part to present us with his beautiful police dog, "Lady," when he could have taken her with him. She seems to understand she is now part of our family and has attached herself especially to me. She also instinctively knows who she can accept on the property and who she should not. We too have been advised to leave. Transportation is available, but should we fail to take advantage of this, our Embassy offers no guarantees to our future safety. I have found it illuminating to observe the mental torment of our younger colleagues as they try to decide what to do. One of our single Missionary ladies has had a nervous breakdown. Reminds me of our first term. It looks as though the sick and pregnant will go. We have decided not to . . . yet! Ralph is happy in his work, likes teaching, enjoys the students and is getting a lot of interesting surgery. The children have never been healthier or happier and they love school. However, should it close, we then will have the problem of teaching them ourselves. Also, if for any reason our salaries cannot be paid, we would not have the means to continue. There are so many things to consider.

For myself, I am becoming increasingly interested in Irma Highbaugh's Family Relations Group. Our Chinese students see nothing but very bad American movies, read only the trashiest of Western books and have, in consequence, an exaggerated idea of the looseness of our morals. This would be of little significance if they didn't try to pattern themselves accordingly. I belong to a reading committee perusing material for possible translation into Chinese on relationships within the home and between males and females before and after marriage, all that sort of thing. Irma ("the tallest woman in the world" from Jenshow days) has become upset over the rising divorce rate and general immorality of our graduates and students. She feels that a large part of the problem lies in the tradition of arranged marriages which denies young people the opportunity to get to know one another or to do the things together we take for granted before they wed. Also, a male student may be married when he comes to campus, but while he is learning and broadening his horizons, his wife is living with his mother performing the duties of a maid or field worker. The results are often tragic. On a lighter note, we have started a Saturday Night Club and are putting on Houseman's "Victoria Regina," which is great fun. Ralph is playing the Prince Consort and Marion Manley, the Queen. It is his first dramatic role. I am assistant director, casting small parts, arranging rehearsals, etc. As yet I am too shy to take a part, but will do so after Christmas.

☐ *DECEMBER 10TH:* It has been beastly weather. It's Friday and the week's washing is not yet dry. My sinuses have been kicking up so am taking it easy for a couple of days. Ralph usually takes my illnesses as doctors do, rather objectively and not too sympathetically, but this time he has been at home as much as possible, helping with all the little things he never used to do. Isn't it wonderful that he gets nicer after all these years, when by all odds we should be fed up with one another. I don't talk a lot about our happiness, but I want you to realize that for all the difficulties, dangers and discomfort, there is compensation.

We are going through anxious times. With the imminent collapse of the Nationalist forces, the American and Canadian governments have evacuated all their diplomatic staff and those others of their nationals who wanted to go. The last plane left Shanghai on Tuesday. We chose to stay. Make no mistake, we are not even "pink." However, neither are we here to support the Kuomintang or the warlords. We seek only the liberty to pursue our various jobs. This is particularly the case with the wcuu people. Probably the theologues should go home. The Chinese Christians will be less conspicuous without foreign hangers-on. Ralph and I are going to wait and see how things develop. Don't think we're being noble, it is just that everything here seems to be real and vital when compared to home. Most of our University colleagues feel the same way. Maybe it's because our work is so creative, the building of young lives so important. It is so different from our last term.

□ *DECEMBER 26TH:* Home was very much in my thoughts yesterday as I tried to make Christmas a good day for the kids and the two wandering American Fulbright scholars who are boarding with us at the moment. Carol was into everything beforehand, even the best hidden stuff. There were tears in her eyes Christmas morning, when she realized there was no Santa Claus. But never a word! We had the usual Christmas dinner at noon (goose), then visited friends for high tea. Later, after tucking three tired pups into bed, we went out to finish the day with some bridge. As I write, our lovely golden kitten is asleep on my lap, Lady is at my feet beside the warm stove, the radio is playing "Cavaliera Rusticana," the lights on our Christmas tree are twinkling and the fragrance of Chinese lilies fills the room. The really good news, however, is that the Communists appear to have reversed their policy on the persecution of foreigners.

□ *JANUARY 31ST, 1949:* Our situation remains about the same. In an attempt to foresee what may be in store for us, we collect whatever news we can from those parts of Communist-controlled China where Mission groups and universities are trying to carry on. The picture taking shape is that the foreigner is tolerated, albeit within strict limits, but only because the Communists still haven't decided our importance to their future relations with the West. I get fed up with some of our Missionary colleagues who can hardly wait to sell out everything democracy stands for. Oh well, we hear a new air route is going to be opened from Hanoi to Lanchow, stopping at Kunming and Chengtu. I hate the thought of ever seeing Hanoi again. And travelling aboard those stinking dirty French steamers is not a prospect to which I look forward. But. . . .

□ *FEBRUARY 24TH:* Mike Rogers, one of our brilliant Fulbright students, is now firmly entrenched in a Buddhist Temple (he is a Roman Catholic) and has actually taken refuge in one of its Orders. Although their oath of discipline apparently is much like our Ten Commandments, the one thing he could not bring himself to do was *kao tao* to Buddha, until it was pointed out that he was "kao taoing" to Buddha in his heart. He is finding Buddhist philosophy extremely interesting, although in many instances their faultless logic is based on false premises. He comes to see us about once a month just to prove he is still alive and to have a bath! At the moment, Mike is in Lanchow to visit Tun-huang, where in 1907–08, Sir Aurael Stein and Paul Pelliot discovered a treasure of ancient documents (circa 1000 A.D.), both Chinese and Central Asiatic, in a cave Temple library that had been sealed for centuries. When I was working in the University's Rare Book Department, I was fascinated to learn that among their "finds" was a copy of "The Diamond Sutra," block printed in 821 A.D., six centuries before Gutenberg.

☐ *MARCH 10TH:* We have just come back from two days in Tzeliutsing. Although we had not seen Banyang since our return to China, of course we had been in touch. But she was again pregnant, so we had put off going to visit, feeling she had enough of a handful with five children, three born since our departure in 1944: Hua-di (Margaret), Huei-di (Dora-ann) and at last, a precious son, Ning-di (Ralph). Then came an emergency call, requesting we come to Junghsien. A second son had been born, but something was terribly wrong. Gilbert Hsu felt a congenital fistula joining œsophagus and trachea was preventing milk from reaching the stomach without being inhaled. Ralph and I rode down with Bob Edwards, the University mechanic, in an old jeep. I thoroughly enjoyed the ride, even though the vehicle had two broken springs and an oil leak that necessitated frequent refills of expensive rapeseed oil purchased from farmers along the way. The countryside is at its Springtime best. After fifteen hours on the road, we reached Tzeliutsing, where the jeep gave up the ghost. So Grace Webster put us up. The next morning, Ralph continued on to Junghsien in the local

Mission truck. In the meantime, Bob and Roy worked and worked on that wcuu junkheap, but without success. When Ralph returned with Banyang and the baby, Roy drove us back to Chengtu, dropping everything to accommodate us and of course to save the baby's life. Actually, we put the jeep in the back of the truck and rode in that. The weather had changed and the roads were like soft grease from the heavy rains. The trip was a great strain. We had to feed the baby by nasal catheter and take our meals in the filthiest of mud-floored teahouses. I doubt our godson will survive. All we can do is hope that being away from heavy responsibility for a while will give Banyang a new lease on life. She is without doubt the most beautifully mannered and deeply courteous person I have ever known.

☐ *MARCH 23RD:* Ralph is studying. The children are in bed. Banyang has retired for the night. I am sitting in front of the fire with Lady as usual at my feet. Our godson (we consider all the Hsieh children in this light) died yesterday. An autopsy revealed a malformation of the trachea, which looked almost as if it had been put in backwards, and a missing kidney. The eyelashes of one eye were turned in and one toe was also misplaced. All in all, it is a blessing that Banyang is now relieved of this pain. She is such a brick and says little about her bad luck. The circumstances, however tragic, have served to renew our beautiful friendship and to restore my faith in the Chinese.

The hoedown held at the Canadian School on the eve of my fortieth birthday was great fun. The prize for the best-dressed hayseed was a wee black piglet which squealed its head off. Ralph was so mad at himself for not taking enough time with his get-up to win that bonanza for Kerry. I must say I was relieved. With dogs (we kept one of Lady's pups) and kids tearing around the garden, my poor seedlings take enough of a beating as it is. My birthday breakfast arrived only after an extensive treasure hunt organized by the children which yielded a lovely piece of brocade for a housecoat, numerous little gifts from the children and a beautiful jade ring from Banyang. Breakfast was waffles, bacon (canned) and all the frills. Then the servants came marching in with their contribution: a live chicken and firecrackers! After breakfast, a stream of callers and notes usually accompanied by flowers. We were invited out for both tea and supper so had my birthday cake and firecrackers at lunch. Ralph, dear man, as usual composed a "Love Poem" to celebrate my special day. He may not be Marlowe or Shakespeare, but he is sweet,

> What's the use of minimum diet
> If you haven't got no money to buy it,
> What's the use of financial flurries
> They only give grey hairs and worries.
> So let's chuck it all and drown our sorrows
> And think of todays and not of tomorrows,
> Of the girl of my dreams whose birthday it is
> Who keeps my life full of bubble and fizz.
> She's as lovely by far as the flowers in May,
> Here's wishing many happy returns of the day.

☐ *APRIL FOOL'S DAY:* It has been riotous. The children put baking powder into the salt cellars, salt into the baking powder, sugar into the flour can and vice versa. Chiang Si, our cook, was furious until I carefully explained the reason. He then forgave them. I went out to a flower fair in the country this afternoon where the wares on sale included items of woven bamboo, crickets in small cages and so on. I bought some pansy plants for Carol's birthday and several pairs of lovely carved chopsticks for the house. I am making Carol a peasant blouse to go with a jumper I brought from home and Ralph bought her a pretty green-handled penkife, tiny scissors and a back scratcher.

As to our finances, we live well and are not worried in this regard. It is true that I use our entire salary each quarter. No doubt I am more generous than most with our servants, but because there is such a gap between our standards of living, I can't bring myself to check too closely the supplies they receive. Also, we do a little more entertaining than most, so it all adds up. However, we think hospitality very important in these pressure ridden-days.

□ *APRIL 30TH:* Things are restless, upset and dangerous if the anti-foreign feeling gets out of hand. I am packing a duffel bag with necessities in case we have to make a break for it. But to where? The Hsiehs can't protect us. They themselves will be targets when the Communists come in. There will be no place for feudal landlords in the new régime. We are the lucky ones to have a homeland to which we may return. I have told Ralph I do not want to stay here with the children during the "turn over." I am not afraid for my life, which is my responsibility, but the children are a different matter. They did not ask to be born nor did they ask to return to China, so we cannot place them in a situation of unreasonable risk. At the same time, Ralph is now one of the key men in our Mission and spends quite a lot of time these days in meetings, formulating policies for various eventualities. Because medical men seem to be at least tolerated by the Communists, he will be needed to help protect our property here. He has told the Council Executive that if they will assume responsibility for the children and me at home, he will stay.

□ *MAY 15TH:* Recently, Ralph was called to do some emergency surgery on the leg of a woman visiting from the United States. He had to arrange to bring her down by truck from Kiating, where she was visiting Jean Stewart, one of our WMS stalwarts. During her rather long convalescence, Ralph became concerned about her increasing depression. Of course, she was lonely. Jean, her one friend here, was a hundred long miles away. When Ralph told me about her, I realized we had been introduced some years before, albeit in the strangest of circumstances. This was in New York in July, 1945. We had been transported as refugees from Bombay aboard a Swedish liner, the S.S. *Gripsholm.* I alluded earlier to our being stuck there for over six long, hot, bedbug-ridden months after our flight from Chungking in December 1944. What I didn't mention was that we were treated like pariahs by the Canadian official responsible for securing us passage, who seemed of the opinion that Missionaries were, by definition, cowards and incompetents, who had evaded their duty to face the dangers of the War and weren't able to contend with the real challenges of "making it" at home. (Stupid man!) In any event, we were not many days aboard the *Gripsholm* when Ralph contracted paratyphoid fever. Of course he was put in isolation. The ship's doctor, however, hadn't a clue and disdained even to attempt treatment! Fortunately, Johnnie Lenox, one of our American doctors, was also on board. What a trip! The morning we were due to land in New York, it still wasn't certain that Ralph would be pronounced fit to disembark. Ellis Island was looming large. All I could do was hope. Nevertheless, I was up at 4 A.M. (the only time I could get into the normally crowded laundry area six decks down) ironing the kids' only decent outfits (everything else I pitched out our porthole—somehow hoping to influence the day's events by this act of confidence). I slipped everyone aspirin to get their temperatures down and then waited for the decision of the ship's doctor. When we were all pronounced fit enough to escape quarantine, I dispatched Ralph, of course very pale and wobbly, and the children to the hotel while I went with the other Missionaries on board to get our stuff through customs. Transportation downtown was to be provided "we refugees" by the Red Cross. Well, Ralph waited and waited and along with him Grace Webster and Mary Birtch, each of whom likewise had three kids. (We had become quite the little Missionary colony in Bombay during those six months.) They stood there for hours in the blazing sun in an open storage area. In the meantime, our pristine little angels playing in the accumulated soot, now mixed with the remnants of some chocolate milk purchased from an ice cream wagon, assumed the appearance of ragamuffins. Finally, a station wagon arrived. Mary and Grace piled the nine kids into the back and poor old Ralph, who by this time could barely stand, sank with relief into the front seat beside the driver, forgetting he had Kerry's baby bottle in his back pocket! Naturally, it popped its cap, soaking the seat of his grey-flannel trousers. Then little Eric Webster upchucked, adding his contribution to the mess in the back. You can imagine then the scene when this lot arrived at the King George Hotel to the welcome of various dignitaries, officials, gushing ladies in large summer hats and gossamer frocks and a melee of reporters and photographers. (As the first Canadian refugees to arrive from the Far East after the War, they were *news*!) Ralph had to smile, say the right things, keep a rein on the kids and his back to the wall, all at the same time. He managed somehow until he had to register, at which point the children (all nine) whooped through the lobby, destroying the quiet club-like atmosphere and prompting startled, then generally amused, reactions from the worthies reading their newspapers in over-stuffed chairs. Our kids, who had been too excited to eat breakfast and had had no opportunity for lunch, were starving. As room service was not available, the problem was fresh clothing. They had not been allowed to take anything beyond what they were wearing through customs. Fortunately, Ralph's pants were almost dry and the girls' filthy dresses could be turned inside out, but Kerry's diaper and sunsuit were quite impossible! After bathing the three of them, Ralph fashioned our wee boy a Gandhi-like loincloth from one of the hand towels and they proceeded to the dining room, Kerry with "King George Hotel" blazoned across his bum! When I finally arrived at the hotel after a gruelling day in the customs shed (precipitated by a few of our Greek fellow passengers who were caught trying to smuggle in gold), Jean Stewart and her friend, Jaymin Wilcox, were waiting to greet me. Following our introduction, Jean's friend explained they had been there since early afternoon, when the first of the refugees arrived. "That poor man and his nine children!" she exclaimed. Now here she is a million miles from home. When Ralph saw Jaymin the next day, he began to tell her the above story supplemented with all the horrible detail of our time in India during the monsoon season and then on board the *Gripsholm*. She lay fascinated through it all, until he got to the punch line, when Jaymin recognized herself and burst out laughing. Not only has her depression disappeared, but we have made a new friend.

☐ *JUNE 6TH:* I was talking to our old amah the other day about the Communists coming in. She has had a rough life and supports a blind husband and young children on what she earns from us. I told her she had nothing to fear and everything to gain, that they had promised to equalize society, etc. She replied, "Don't want. No freedom!" I don't think I've ever seen a Chinese with his or her spirit broken. They are so different from the people of the Indian sub-continent. Here, everyone cherishes and loves his independence, from the meanest on up. For this reason alone, I think China will develop something unique under Mao Tse-tung, and perhaps one day there will be as many kinds of Communism as their are cultures.

Everything really goes along pretty much as usual except for an insidious war of nerves. Whispered words that pollute the atmosphere with rumor. Missionaries are being shot. Missionaries are not being shot. Foreigners are being tolerated. Foreigners are not being tolerated. The University will be allowed to remain open. It will be closed immediately. This at times becomes almost unbearable. And from this vast confusion, we must decide our wisest course. We do not want to split the family unless absolutely necessary and are willing to put up with a fair amount of discomfort if we can stay together. Discomfort, not physical danger! We just don't know what we are going to be up against. Ralph thinks the greatest danger lies in a Third World War with Russia.

☐ *JUNE 14TH:* We are definitely staying on. Although my father thinks us absolutely irresponsible, we are at least without illusion. It's just that we can't put our heads in the sand like so many in the West. Perhaps we can be of some influence for democracy before Communism envelops the entire globe. Ralph has had a good year, doing a job no one else around was able to do and doing it well. Lectures at wcuu ended a week ago. The medical students, however, are all out on strike and won't write exams unless guaranteed a pass! Those in the other faculties just refuse to write, period. All this is Communist Party inspired and even our "pinko" colleagues are upset.

The Days have had a series of tough breaks. Marg's baby was due this month and everything went okay until about a week ago when all movement stopped. Upon examination, there was no fetal heart beat and the day before yesterday she was delivered of a dead son. It is an Rh business which I don't quite understand. We should have been alerted, however, by the fact that Diana, Marg's youngest, was very jaundiced when born. Then Alf's hernia ruptured again. This time Ralph fixed it with living fascial suture. Now Diana is down with the chickenpox. And the night after the baby was still-born, their house was robbed. There are a lot of burglaries on campus these days. We have all our windows screened and padlocked, one dog under the house and one in, plus two cats. So surely unless it's an inside job, we won't be caught napping.

☐ *JULY 1ST:* We have had a busy week socially, farewelling various people returning home. The Wilfords, whom we will miss, are taking a trunk of our stuff as far as Vancouver, the third we have sent out to date. Bill Willmott, seventeen years old and en route to begin studies at Oberlin College in Ohio (where his older brother Don is a Senior), is travelling with them. He is a nice lad, clever and Judy's "big moment." She adores him and he is very tolerant and kind to her. The Bacons have left, as have the Websters and Haywards, among others. I will be glad when the exodus is over—it is unsettling. (At least, the postal service is functioning again, thank goodness). Ralph is on holidays, but we can't leave the plain given all the uncertainty (currency, bandits, civil war). Thank heavens for the tiny Canadian School swimming pool! The children swim every day. I am working in the Chinese Research Section of the Library and am finding it intriguing. I am also deep into Upton

Sinclair's books. Ralph and I play tennis every evening, then plunge into the pool to cool off and sleep like logs despite the heat.

The Li Hens were in for tea yesterday. Dr. Li Hen cut his sabbatical year short and returned to China to stand by. He is acting President of the University at the moment and one of the most objective men I have ever met. An astronomer and mathematician of renown, he is also a brilliant conversationalist whether in French (studied at the Sorbonne where he met his equally interesting wife), English or Chinese. Although about fifty, he could be taken for thirty. Mrs. Li Hen is a "dramatic novelist," who also translates English classics into Chinese, and is lots of fun. They seem to like us and we are looking forward to their friendship.

Last night, we went downtown to the movies, which in China are an experience. The picture is usually an ancient Grade B or C American flick. The theater is uncomfortable, dirty, flea and bedbug ridden and the latrines are very high. Although the noise level drowns out the dialogue, it is fun once in a while. We returned about seven and brought the gang in for sandwiches, talk and bridge. Life could be worse.

At a recent conference between Mao Tse-tung and leaders of the Chinese Christian Church, the message was clear, "cooperate 100 per cent or face the consequences." Many wishful thinkers here were disappointed, but as I see it, it could not be otherwise. Earl Willmott, who is staying with us at the moment, feels there has been a mistranslation of the Communist demands, but he is very "pink." He also feels, based on his contacts with "progressive groups," there will be a "turn over" in Chengtu early in September. I am much more conservative in my estimation. We now have occasional blackouts as the city readies itself for possible air raids, but why the Communists would want to turn public feeling against them by doing this is to me beyond reason. Reports from students at Wuhan University near Hankow were at first enthusiastic about their "liberation," then somewhat disillusioned, now guarded. Ralph is interested in the attempts to bring in international aid to help the

Kuomintang. I, however, feel that guns will never combat Communism. The only defense is a higher standard of living for the downtrodden. Devastation and suffering caused by war only serve to make Communism more attractive. And why not? The flooding of the Yangtse and Yellow Rivers has caused unimaginable suffering over the years. If the money used for armies and armaments could only be used to harness the potential of these rivers for hydroelectric projects and irrigation . . . but why dream? You can't imagine what it's like living here. In one sense, it's as though we were sitting on a time bomb. Yet in another, it's so normal. I've just been preserving peaches and making apple jelly.

☐ *AUGUST 15TH:* Reports from "liberated" areas still vary considerably. In Central and North West China, foreigners have difficulty in getting passes to move about, their property has been taken over directly or indirectly through high taxation, troops have been quartered in their houses, their schools have been closed, association with Chinese colleagues has been banned and they are subjected to searches and other harassments. Further to the south, it has been easier and in Kansu (in the north), where fighting is still going on, the Communists had large placards put on the walls of evacuated Mission property, "This property of the foreigners is not to be touched. We would welcome their return." Despite American Secretary of State Acheson stating there is a danger of foreigners being taken as hostages, we see no evidence in Szechwan to support this. For the present, we are not really too concerned about working under the Communists. We have a lot of good Chinese friends and orthopædic surgeons are scarce out here. If it becomes too unpleasant or we are expelled, we can leave with a clear conscience. We are sending out another trunk with the Stinsons who leave shortly for Hong Kong. Most of the conservative (fundamentalist) Missions are pulling out their personnel. I can't help feeling a bit smug.

Lady Banting is staying with the Cunninghams. She now works at a hospital in Hong Kong and is charming. I was able to tell her I had known her late husband, who in 1923 shared the Nobel Prize for isolating insulin. (Friends once tried to interest us in each other, but there was no chemistry on either side.) The most interesting of the many entertainments for her, to which we were invited, was at the Dzu family home. The head of the family is known locally as Dzu Tsai-shen, "The God of Wealth" and their house occupies about a city block. We were entertained in a large Western-style living room, done in excellent taste, with beautiful Peking rugs on the floor and the windows opening onto a perfect garden. Along one wall, open sectional shelving held priceless Chinese vases, each filled with flowers. Every member of the Dzu family has an interest in Chinese art. Two of the daughters paint chrysanthemums after the Sung [Song] manner on silk from Swatow, with colors from Peking made from ground semi-precious stones which never fade with age. One brother paints birds. Another showed us his exquisite jade collection. We wandered around their garden, over an arched bridge to a teahouse atop a small artificial hill overlooking the property. Later, beside the goldfish pool, one of our gracious hosts told me that these were his hobby, and that they answered when summoned. To demonstrate, he banged the side of the pool. Sure enough, a group of the most fantastic fish surfaced.

□ *SEPTEMBER 10TH:* A chastened bunch of university students are back swotting for exams and now realize what a stupid thing they did in June. Our Mission Middle School, reputed to be the most Communist of any in Chengtu, was closed last July by the Nationalist gov't. Our two most avid red sympathizers, Jim Endicott and Earl Willmott, have both taught there. Earl resigned when it was reopened under what he considered a repressive and authoritarian regime, but continues to teach a couple of courses at the University as well as to look after our Mission's finances. I am preparing a paper for the Border Research Society next month (the only non-university graduate to ever be asked). It is on the books I have discovered in the Rare Book Department of the Library. I'll die a thousand deaths before I deliver it! I am also teaching English at the School of Nursing this year and helping with some translation work for a conference in Bangkok. Our Family Relations reading committee is bringing out a book that I am editing and I spend a couple of hours every morning working at the Library. This doesn't leave much time for worry.

I suppose our friends at home think we are at the end of the world and about to disappear behind the Bamboo Curtain. True, if they consider their place the center, but actually we think ours the more important. We wait with mingled feelings, expecting the worst yet hoping to be disappointed. It has been a pleasant year, full of upsets and disappointments, excitements, worry and interest. Our home is really nice. I have had fun making it so and some disgust at having to pack away my nicest things and ship them home (not so many actually, having kept the right thing for the right spot). I think you would like it. The children thrive. They have a bike now which they adore. Truly normal kids.

☐ *NOVEMBER 12TH:* Sun Yat Sen's birthday. Al Ravenholt and his wife have been our guests the last few days. He is a newspaper man for the *Chicago Tribune*, with columns syndicated throughout the U.S. and Canada. A student of the Far East, he has been around these parts the last twelve years, so has seen a lot. Awfully nice, he looks like an early FDR. His wife, Marjorie, was a correspondent for *Time/Life* at one time and is now public relations officer for the Joint Commission for Rural Reconstruction, headquartered in Formosa. She is very intelligent, smart looking and good company.

The local gov't is dispersing, although the police are still on duty. The mayor has resigned and most of the civil servants have pulled out, terrified. Anyone with the means to do so is headed for Formosa. Paper dollars are again in circulation, but yesterday the Central Bank refused to exchange them, causing an immediate devaluation of 50 per cent. As a result, most of the city shops closed. Rice, however, has reached a new low of .70 (silver) per bushel. The landowners and speculators are dumping their hoarded supplies. At several points in the city, particularly the North-East Gate, thousands of Nationalist soldiers have assembled. We hear they are being given $50 (silver) each with orders to make their own way overland to Kunming which is to become the next and last capital of Chiang Kai-shek on Mainland China.

☐ *NOVEMBER 16TH:* Planes continue to shuttle back and forth as General Hu Tsung-nan moves his army to the Kunming area. The province is being deluged with Communist pamphlets and leaflets. It is, however, peaceful and the students with few exceptions have settled down. The garden is picking up, the lovely cosmos in bloom, chrysanthemums in bud. And now after the last couple of long, dull, wet months, we may have a bit of decent weather. The Mission Council is in full session, everyone full of plans for life under the hammer and sickle. Gilbert Hsu has asked Ralph for advice regarding his position in Junghsien. He would like to leave before the Communists come as there has been criticism on the part of malcontents re his administration. We are worried about the Tzeliutsing Hospital as well, where Ralph would like (Edward) Dzen Tze-yao made administrator perhaps with additional responsibility for Junghsien and Kiating. There are even more Nationalist troops in the city. They look to be in good condition and well equipped. The common folk are terrified lest they stay to loot and burn before the Communists come. Everyone is trying to get hold of guns and ammunition for protection. Our Mission has an arsenal of twelve bullets and two pistols with rusty barrels. There is now an 8 P.M. curfew.

It is hard to teach one's classes these days. The student nurses are definitely not in a study mood, so we talk instead. Today they wanted to know why we are staying on despite the uncertainty of our future. I told them we could not leave with a peaceful heart until we knew what the future held for them. I urged them to be hard working and conscientious and said there would be no place in the new China for those who were not. They are good kids. Adoring Ralph, they wanted to know where

Margaret and Ralph on their wedding day, June 17th, 1938, Prince Rupert, British Columbia. Days later, they boarded the Empress of Japan *for Yokohama.*

*Missionary children attended the Canadian School in the Mission compound,
Chengtu, 1938.*

West China Union University had a thriving social scene. A staff wedding, 1939.

The people of the Szechwan countryside: a land of tradition when Margaret first arrived.

*Summer was a time to enjoy the healthy air on the slopes of Mount Omei, 1939
(Top: Margaret at left).*

*The "Wart": a bamboo verandah at-
tached to the Rev. Veals' house was
the Outerbridge home in Jenshow,
1939.*

Margaret with Judy, Jenshow, 1939.

Mothers and babies (from left): Margaret, Banyang and Margaret Day, Junghsien, 1943.

Mr. Liu, Banyang's father-in-law, leaving the Mission Hospital after a successful cure, with Ralph, Junghsien, 1943.

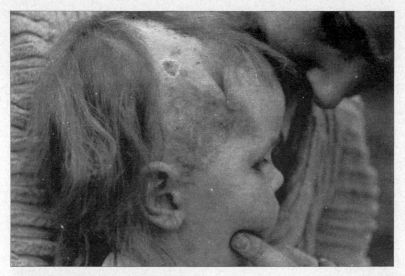

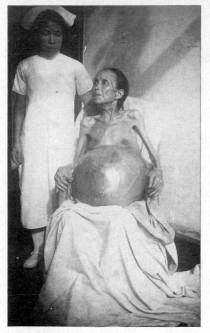

Carol's burn, the result of a kitchen accident, Junghsien, 1943.

Ignorance of hygiene and neglect of medical conditions were common in rural China. Woman with an ovarian cyst half her body's weight, Junghsien, 1942.

Margaret, Carol and Kerry leaving Goa Sh Ti, with their staff, the end of summer, 1943.

Dzan, the Dragon, Fuh and his wife: the Outerbridges' household staff, Junghsien, 1941.

we met, about our engagement and our life at home. This afternoon, we went into the city and found the streets crowded and the theaters doing record business. We passed a long file of school children who shouted, "*din hao*" (you are tops). I found some material in a shop that I wanted but hadn't enough money to buy it. The shopkeeper insisted I take it home and pay at my convenience.

□ *NOVEMBER 25TH:* Tonight, the BBC "World Service" announced the wholesale evacuation of Chungking. The government is moving to Suching. We hear "from a very reliable source" (all rumors we hear these days are prefaced with these words) that there are Japanese "volunteers" with the Nationalist troops at Hsin Gin Airfield! Banyang sent up a Christmas parcel and a message that they would soon be moving to Chengtu. At the moment Robert Hsieh is busy selling his holdings. I sent them a bunch of pretty dresses and outgrown shoes by return carrier. Eugene Chen, the clever Cantonese eye surgeon who is Ed Cunningham's second-in-command at the EENT Hospital, was over tonight with his three little girls. They are beautiful, well mannered and adored by our children. Joy Willmott wrote her parents a long letter from home. She is in psychiatry and her letter was full of it. When she interpreted a ham sandwich as a phallic symbol, however, I felt she was going a bit far.

□ *DECEMBER 2ND:* Barricades are everywhere in the city, placed about every hundred yards or less. We hope there will be no incendiary bombs for they are locked at night. We have made our own preparations. We have enough rice to pay our servants for three months and enough flour, tinned supplies, peanut oil, sugar, salt, walnuts, etc., to last several months. People all over the city are burying their family silver and gold. We are no exception. The few things we have of value are secreted in a bricked-up cubby-hole. We expect that as soon as the Communists take over it will be possible to send letters home again. We hear that Britain (which probably means Canada as well) will recognize the new régime before Christmas.

☐ *DECEMBER 6TH:* At about eleven this morning, Ralph and I biked into the city for news. The night before, we heard the Communists were approaching rapidly from three sides and we wanted to see how everyone was taking it. The streets were filled with jittery people. Cars everywhere, travelling at a furious pace. Normally, cars are seldom seen for everyone travels by bike, rickshaw or wheelbarrow. Several times we were nearly run over, for accustomed as we are to the leisurely pace of things, we did not allow enough time to get out of the way. The roadsides were crowded and particularly so around the old South Gate, where hucksters were doing a terrific business selling used clothing, most of it khaki!

Yesterday afternoon, I went over to Hart College to help get a reception ready for Dr. Shen and his bride. The experience was both interesting and inspiring. Shen, a Shanghai boy, is marrying a beautiful little girl from Jenshow, a nurse. He is, in Ralph's estimation, an extremely clever chap, and Leslie Kilborn thinks he is the best ever to pass through his hands. Because he was strapped for money, his colleagues and chiefs paid for the wedding feast. The bride was lovely in a beautifully cut white satin Chinese gown, a veil and carrying a bouquet of chrysanthemums. In the evening we went over to the Moncrieffs' for a sukiyaki supper. It was great fun and a nice crowd: the Gunns, Sewells, Days and Kilborns (Jean Millar, the pædiatrician, married Leslie following Dr. Janet's death). Leslie told me that the most hated and feared man on the campus, Chou Hsiao-wu, is leaving for Formosa. He has been very active in the Kuomintang Youth Corps, and with approaching "Liberation" his life is no longer safe.

☐ *DECEMBER 10TH:* Very good reports of the Liberation gov't have just come in from the Baptist mission in Sian [Xian]. They are being treated well and courteously. Hospital and OPD busier than ever. And an interesting thing, an English-language newspaper published in Bucharest is now being delivered there every two weeks! Among others, it publishes articles written by the Chairman of the Communist Party in Britain.

We went over to the Phelps' today. While there, Peggy told us that Audrey Honey had finally persuaded Floyd, her husband, to bury a box of valuables late one night in their garden. This morning, she spied a group of workmen digging a ditch within twelve inches of their cache! Ed Cunningham got as far as the attic with some stuff of theirs, then turned to Gladys and said, "What's the use, I don't care whether they take it or not!" "I agree," she replied. Whereupon they marched downstairs. And Marion Donald, who buried her precious belongings in the Mullet garden, was so inexperienced in this sort of procedure, her box is only covered by a half-inch of dirt. Now she worries day and night lest the gardener inadvertently dig it up. Dryden Phelps has just received notice from his government appointing him Acting U.S. Consul in Chengtu. He is very "pink" and insists he is going to put up the Stars and Stripes with a Hammer and Sickle on it!

☐ *DECEMBER 16TH:* We have been given another week or two of grace. Instead of marching on Chengtu, the Communist troops have entered Suifu and Nueichiang. We also hear that Tzeliutsing annd Junghsien have been occupied and that there is fighting in the Lung Chuan I hills. We have no news of the Hsiehs.

We have had a bit of bad luck with our washing machine. We sent it to the University machine shop to have the head oiled. We waited and waited, until this morning when our enterprising gateman went over to see about it. The juniors in the shop said it was ready, so he brought it home and without saying a word to me, started it up. Puff went the motor in a cloud of smoke.

Ralph and I went into the city today, for perhaps the last time before the "turn over." As soon as one enters the New South Gate, one feels the tension. It is almost as if it were floating on the air. The larger shops are all closed. Only a few people were about, but hundreds of U.S. army trucks, jeeps and weapon-carriers laden high with troops were heading towards Kiating. What they will do at Hsin Chin I don't know because the ferry there has only a two-truck capacity. As we progressed down one of the streets, we saw one truck parked by the side of the road with a huge Nationalist flag draped over its tailgate. We remarked on this rather flamboyant gesture, but as we passed, we saw that both front wheels were off, the hood gone and the engine removed. It seemed symbolic.

□ *DECEMBER 20TH:* Our other Fulbright student, Dave Gidman, dropped in this afternoon. The last time he visited he left in a temper, but today he talked for two hours as if nothing had ever happened. He had come to say good-bye as his servant had told him the children and I were leaving. I got a lot of Argyle sock knitted. He is shacking up with a very bad tempered female and it is beginning to get him down. The woman, Portia Mickey, late Missionary, is now collecting erotica for the Kinsey Report and studying the designs of the Miao tribes. Nothing came out of our conversation except that he dislikes our friends the Ravenholts, and that he is putting all his silver in wax and dumping it into his open toilet!

Tonight, Ralph went to a meeting called to create a University self-protection association (the Chengtu police force has collapsed). About 300 students attended and were divided into groups according to their dormitories and given patrol duty from tonight at 9 P.M. 'till dawn. Each group was supplied with a bamboo drum for an alarm and a whistle to signal fire. Armbands must now be worn and passwords memorized by everyone connected with the University. Later, we took our bicycles apart, sent the handlebars over to the Cunninghams and put the remainder in our attic. Ralph then buried a tin can containing our small store of money in the garden. As Irvin Newcomb said the other day, "It will be a pity if the looters don't come after all the trouble we have gone to."

□ *DECEMBER 23RD:* It was rather nice to get up this morning and not hear the distant percussion of heavy artillery and guns. It apparently stopped about 11:30 last night. The city is full of the news that General Hu Tsung-nan, whose army was once 300,000 strong, has fled Chengtu. Dave Gidman reports that yesterday troops on the run were pouring through the city. Certainly, when I was in town today, it was crammed with soldiers who looked as though they had been in active combat. We heard that the old South Gate was being pulled down and that everyone had to have permission to enter or leave the city. So we went to see. Rumors, rumors. No demolition of the gate and no one being asked for passes!

Christmas preparations go ahead. Today my class of twenty student nurses came in for tea. They are dears. They sang, did Sikang dances and even a Communist dance and song for us. It was a good party and practically all the food disappeared. The place looked nice: Marjorie Ravenholt's beautiful tapers on the mantelpiece before two holly wreaths, the tree decorated with lights, which fortunately went on. I should mention that at the end of last month, when the Ravenholts stopped in Hong Kong on their return to Formosa, Marjorie did a lot of shopping for practically everyone she had met during their stay with us. My only request was that, if she had the chance, I would adore something quintessentially feminine. I had rather forgotten about this until a large envelope arrived in the post containing the sexiest of short black lace silk nighties. What a change in self-image. Appears to have done something for Ralph's morale as well!

☐ *DECEMBER 24TH:* A busy day. Ralph just home from the Hospital where he did two more upper-arm gunshot wounds. This makes a total of seven affecting the humerus, but only two of the femur. He feels that this is probably due to the fact that those with leg wounds are still out on the battlefield. A letter just in from Fuling reports a peaceful "turn over" and that the "millenium" has arrived. As I write the children are asleep "all tucked in their beds," their stockings "all hung by the mantel with care." And Santa has come and gone early. The servants gave the children lovely gifts, dolls for the girls and a popgun for Kerry (he didn't let it out of his hand all afternoon). And Chiang Si's son brought in a handsomely decorated cake off the street. The Wilford's cook presented us with a plant and a chicken.

Rhoda Yang sent us a table cloth that she had worked herself and my students gave me flowers and a beautiful card.

☐ *CHRISTMAS, 1949:* As morning broke clear and not too cold, it brought Peace. Seems fitting. Yesterday is history. The fate of the city no longer hangs in the balance. An interim "police" force is patrolling the streets and warnings have been issued that anyone caught looting will be shot. Chengtu will go to bed happy tonight. For ourselves, about 6 A.M. the children came down to a beautifully laden tree and their stockings. After we had presented our servants with their gifts (new gowns all around, plus toys for their children), we started getting ready to receive six guests for dinner which was scheduled for noon. Chiang Si was suffering a ghastly hangover, so Ralph and I set the table. I think 1949 has been the best year of our lives.

CHAPTER 8

Chengtu / The Year of the Tiger

□ *DECEMBER 28TH, 1949:* Yesterday morning, on the out-
skirts of Su Ma Tou, a village some fifteen miles south of
Chengtu on the road to Jenshow, Ralph was stopped at a PLA
(People's Liberation Army) check point. Under the cover of a
heavy-caliber machine gun, two grey-clad soldiers emerged
from behind a barricade of branches, sub-machine guns at the
ready, obviously not taking any chances with what, from their
perspective, must have been an unexpected and pretty unusual
sight: two "foreign devils" and two Chinese, all dressed in hospital whites, in a jeep piled high with medical supplies, flying a
Red Cross flag.

Dr. George Deng, one of the physicians on the Medical
School staff, acted as spokesman. He explained they were a
medical team from the West China Union University (of which
these soldiers from Shansi province had never heard) who had
come to assist the PLA medical corps or the local public health
station should either be unable to cope with any flood of recent
casualties. We had heard that 20,000 of Nationalist General Hu

Tsung-nan's troops had decided against all odds to make a stand somewhere to the immediate south or west of Chengtu. Because we had no accurate information, apart from the renewed thunder of the big guns, our men (Ralph, George, "Lefty" Dong, an intern, and Fred Nelson, their driver) had loaded the jeep with morphine, dressings, splints, etc., and gone out (not knowing what they might encounter) to try to locate those in need of help. Perforce their search had to be confined to the three motor roads leading west to Wen Chiang, southwest to Shuang Liu or south to Su Ma Tou, there being no others.

All this had been Ralph's idea. He had been fretting for days about the University Hospital not carrying its share of the load when the provincial and military hospitals in the city were packed with wounded, two patients per bed. (In fact, the Nationalists had simply declined to make full use of our facilities.) And as an orthopædic surgeon, he was particularly worried about casualties with lower limb injuries being abandoned to rot on the fields of battle. Without the short interregnum hereabouts, however, Ralph would never have been able to seize the initiative to do something useful.

As it was, early Boxing Day morning he went to talk to his two senior medical colleagues, Leslie Kilborn and Wally Crawford, about sending trucks to bring the wounded in to our Hospital from the surrounding countryside. They caught the idea at once and took it to Leslie's successor as dean of Medicine, Dr. Tsao, and to the superintendent of the University Hospital, Dr. Beh Yin-tsai. In turn, they enlisted the support of WCUU President Fang Shu-hsuan, who agreed to lead a delegation to the pro-tem mayor of Chengtu to secure the passes necessary to move around the city and its approaches. The acting mayor was most cooperative. He could hardly have been other, having expressed a similar concern for the well-being of both the Communist and Nationalist wounded in that morning's local newspaper. In the meantime, Ralph was busy organizing transportation and medical personnel. By the time the necessary documents arrived from the mayor's office, Ralph had decided the course of wisdom would be to reconnoiter by jeep until they found what they were looking for.

When Chengtu and its immediate environs yielded no result, they decided to venture further afield, even though they had no authority to do so. Indeed, the acting mayor had warned specifically against this. Thus, running into the advance-line of the Red Army could have put them in a fine pickle. Without valid travel permits, they might well have been shot as spies. The soldier assigned to take them to his company headquarters in the village, an eight-year veteran of campaigns throughout Central China, wanted to know if Ralph or Fred were Americans. When George said no, he seemed very disappointed. He apparently had a few things he wanted to get off his chest about the United States! (Fred, who works with the Scandinavian Alliance Mission [SAM], is an American, but George thought him Canadian.)

When they reached Su Ma Tou, Ralph and George were marched at bayonet point through several courtyards of a large family dwelling, distinguished from its neighbors only by the number of telephone lines running into it. Their guard knocked at a closed door, then proceeded inside, leaving his charges to peer into a dimly lit room where four men sat huddled around a charcoal brazier (presumably senior officers, although dressed in the same plain grey uniform, undistinguished by insignia, as ordinary foot soldiers). Ralph's business card was passed to each in turn. (In China, a personal card carries one's name, nationality, institution, function, etc., and is almost like a passport.) After about five minutes, Ralph and George were ordered inside, where four pairs of stony eyes silently assessed them. They were beginning to wonder what was going to happen next when the quiet was broken by a child's shout from outside, "Yao *yi seng*, Yao *yi seng*" (Dr. Yao, Dr. Yao). A rather fearsome looking little girl burst through the door, followed by her father, and wrapped her arms around Ralph's leg.

At the end of November, when this child had suffered a gunshot fracture of the lower jaw, Ralph had repaired the damage using a Roger Anderson external pin fixation set. Probably there is no other equipment like it in China and the sight of this six-year-old with steel pins protruding from her jaw bolted to a curved steel joining rod, all of it moving as she talked, immediately broke the tension. The Communist officers were intrigued and wanted to know all about this rather spectacular means of splinting a jaw fracture. There was no question now as to the legitimacy of Ralph's bona fides. They, however, had no need for additional medical services. There had been no fighting locally. The officers suggested Ralph look for casualties to the northwest around Shuang Liu.

Returning to Chengtu without incident, Ralph decided they should first check Wen Chiang. The countryside, however, showed little evidence of fighting, and the public health station at Wen Chiang only had six patients and none of them seriously wounded. Apparently, there had been a battle twenty *li* further west, but the path was too narrow for a jeep or truck. So it was home again empty handed.

This afternoon they went off ready for business in Fred's SAM truck: a one-ton with a covered deck, over the sides of which they draped two huge Red Cross flags. They plastered another across the hood and wrote "University Hospital" in large Chinese characters across the windscreen. With Fred at the wheel, Ralph and George beside him in the cab and four residents in the back with all their supplies, stretchers, etc., they drove straight through without once being challenged until they reached Shuang Liu's East Gate, where they were promptly allowed inside the city walls. It was market day and despite the fact there had been heavy fighting round about just a few days before, life seemed to be going along fairly normally. "Happy and gay," was Ralph's description. The streets were so crowded, the truck could barely move. Finally, Ralph and George decided to walk ahead as the Communist Army hospital was across town in a school just outside the West Gate atop a high knoll.

The Medical Officer in charge, a somewhat nervous little man, was delighted when he learned the purpose of Ralph's visit and scurried off to get permission to transfer several of the seriously wounded from his care. In the meantime, he invited Ralph and George to examine his patients and decide the ones they wanted to take. In what had been a large classroom, 25 Communist soldiers, still dressed in blood-stained uniforms, were neatly laid on double-decker beds. Curiously, there was no sign of any surgery, and although dressings covered their wounds, many of these were now soaked through. In some cases, crude splints had been used to repair limbs, but no plaster casts. Eight of the men were in potentially critical condition. It was the better part of an hour before a now acutely embarrassed MO returned with a regular PLA officer who, perhaps not unreasonably given the fact that the Red Army has not yet entered Chengtu in force, gruffly dismissed the whole idea. "The People's Liberation Army looks after its own," he said. When George, at Ralph's prompting, asked if they could discuss the matter with any higher authority, his reply was a curt "No!"

On their way back down the hill, however, their feelings of frustration vanished. The truck now stood in the center of the playing field below the school-cum-hospital. Word of its arrival obviously had spread like wildfire and as Ralph and George watched, wounded Nationalist soldiers came from all directions, including some on improvised litters, others stumbling along between two buddies, still others carried on the backs of peasants. Ralph's residents were all busy doing dressings, splinting broken limbs, giving morphine, instructing those who needed further care but could walk how to get to the University. After sorting them all out, there were twenty who required transportation. Ralph and George then went to visit the local Magistrate to ask his permission to take these men to Chengtu. He proved cordial and grateful. Nearby farmers fetched straw and the patients were packed in like sardines, a second layer above the first on stretchers, the handles of which were rather precariously balanced on the edges of the wooden truck box. The tarpaulin again pulled taut over its metal frame protected this cargo of human suffering from the rain which had just begun to fall. It was now about 5 P.M. and already dark.

Two incidents may be significant to our future here. While the truck was moving slowly down Shuang Liu's main street to-

ward the playing field, one of the residents spotted a wounded
Nationalist soldier on the sidewalk. The truck stopped and two
of our lads got out and began dressing his wounds. When a
crowd quickly gathered to watch, some PLA soldiers came to see
what was going on. "What are you doing?" Young Dr. Shen
replied he was a doctor to whom it did not matter whether an
injured person was Communist or Nationalist. He was just
doing his duty. The soldier rejoined, "You will come to learn
the difference between right and wrong. In the meantime, take
this scum somewhere else. You can't work on him here." Then,
on their way home, they were stopped at a newly erected road
block, just a few miles from Chengtu. The PLA soldier on duty
summoned his superior from under a shelter where he and several others were eating their evening meal. By this time, the rain
was coming down in buckets. The officer (whatever his actual
rank, he was in charge) was not amused. George presented
Ralph's calling card, as well as the Shuang Liu magistrate's letter
with its impressive official seal. The officer looked at these
askance. Although he made a pretence of doing so, he obviously
could not read. (One reads Chinese right to left, not upside
down.) He angrily demanded to know what they had in the
truck. When told wounded en route to hospital, he wanted to
know if any were Nationalists. George explained they had little
experience with such matters and had considerable difficulty
telling one soldier from the next. Whereupon, the guard was ordered to check, "If you find any Kuomintang, shoot them"!
Ralph and George both jumped out to block his path, waving
their permit and loudly denouncing the inhumanity of the officer's decision, etc., etc. Within seconds, the four of them were
shouting at the top of their lungs. In this sort of high drama,
which is typically Chinese (except for the possible consequences
in this instance), it doesn't matter so much what one actually
says, it is a question of volume and histrionics. There wasn't so
much as a cough from the back of the truck until these verbal
combatants reached the tailgate. At which point the four residents leaned out, adding their voices to the protest and preventing the guard, who had forced Ralph back one slow step at a
time by poking him in the chest with his rifle, from further

advance. The officer, realizing the shouting match was lost, regained "face" by ordering them to "get the hell out of here before I change my mind!" Fred had the truck rolling even as Ralph and George clambered in beside him.

☐ *DECEMBER 29TH:* Given the cases brought in last night, a busy day for Ralph's operating team, including several hours sorting through eighty patients one of the military hospitals in the city dumped on our OPD. These were mostly survivors of an internecine battle in early December when General Hu's troops attacked Liu Wen-huei's army to prevent their turning over to the Communists. Representatives of the new government also visited the Hospital this afternoon promising to send transportation to remove all convalescent wounded soldiers to an appropriate military facility, to reimburse our Hospital for the cost of the food consumed by military patients (regardless of side) and to provide such future ambulance service necessary to bring in wounded! Dr. Beh was further informed that the Hospital was expected to send representatives to welcome the Liberating Armies tomorrow morning at ten o'clock. The Hospital Pastor, whom everyone suspected of being a Communist Party plant, has been working very hard preparing banners and pennants bearing words suitable to the occasion.

Alf Day, who is responsible for the Mission Press, also had an official delegation in today, presumably to look over his establishment. When they left, they took Alf's two Chinese assistants back to headquarters where they were given a stiff "Party" lecture and were reminded that they were *Chinese* who had belittled themselves by working under foreigners, all of whom were *spies!*

A letter from Banyang, written on December 22nd, reports the liberation and turn over in Junghsien as peaceful and orderly. Her father, Mr. Liu, organized and paid for an interim self-protection corps. She sounds less fearful than she has for some time.

☐ *DECEMBER 30TH:* This morning while Ralph was again busy operating, Margie Day, the Gunns, Clarence Vichert,

Audrey Honey and I walked into the city to see the Victory Parade. Communist flags everywhere, bright red with five yellow stars. The walls of the buildings posted with multi-colored slogans, drawings and news sheets. One I saw showed a knife dripping with blood and some stuff about the Generalissimo. Another, Uncle Sam with a bag of money over his shoulder being pushed out of China. While there is an active anti-American propaganda drive, there is no indication so far of any bad feeling toward us, although we are always taken for Americans. The streets were crowded with people crushed six deep along the narrow pavement, which resulted in a lot of pushing and pulling. We made our way slowly to the corner of Chuen Shi Lu and Chuen Shi Shi Lu, where we took our stand to watch truck after passing truck filled with PLA soldiers or laden with students (junior, middle school and university) wildly excited and often singing or yelling the words on their colored paper banners. Later, foot soldiers, cavalry and tanks, the whole army seemed to march past! And after six hours it was still going strong. I counted at least 150 Russian trucks, all new. There were also some new Fords and Chevys. Another interesting thing was the presence of Russians who were recording the parade photographically.

□ *NEW YEAR'S DAY, 1950:* A busy A.M. for in the P.M. we were "at Home" to almost 100 people for doughnuts and coffee. It went off well. The Kilborns stayed on for supper. We have just finished reading ten letters from home dated October. And as I wearily type, the dogs asleep at my feet, Ralph is leaning back in the easy chair playing a Chinese flute.

□ *JANUARY 2ND:* At present there is a big bonfire in the middle of the campus showering sparks into the clear night air. Around it crowds of students and others are participating in Communist folk dances, which have suddenly become very popular. They apparently go with the New Order. Yesterday a special instructor was sent to teach them to the Hospital staff and coolies. The evening will probably end with the Generalissimo burning in effigy. Ralph, who now has about seventy Communist soldiers as patients, spent most of the day operating.

☐ *JANUARY 4TH:* Yesterday was one which the people of Chengtu will remember for its Civilian Parade and public holiday. Foreigners were tolerated, but not welcomed, and no one was allowed to take pictures. Not even the Russians were in evidence. No classes at the University of course, where the Theological College seems to be having a most difficult time at the moment. Yesterday morning, signs were posted reading, "Down with Superstition."

Last night we went to a lovely party, long dresses, delicious buffet, twenty-three present. The evening was a complete success for Hash Mullett (a member of the Dental faculty since 1919), whose birthday we were celebrating, until the servants set off firecrackers. Within minutes, PLA soldiers arrived to take Hash in for questioning, marching him down the street with fixed bayonets. Firecrackers apparently are out with the New Order.

The air is again full of rumors. We hear the Nationalists have attacked by sea from Formosa and that the common people have turned against the Communists in Yunnan. We also hear Chengtu has been divided into districts for taxation purposes. The shops, particularly those on Chuen Shi Lu, are to be heavily assessed. In addition, the University, the banks, etc., all will have to pay a special levy to support the "liberation" of Tibet. Not much else today except the arrival of our first copy of the *Ladies Home Journal.*

☐ *JANUARY 5TH:* Among the new regulations is one that all overnight house guests must be registered with the police before 8 P.M. each evening, which probably is an attempt to ferret out former Nationalists. About a year ago, one of our students left her handbag at one of the local tailor shops. The proprietor opened it, no doubt to discover its owner. Out dropped some

Communist literature. So he notified the authorities. Some say her Communist Party card was in her purse, but of this I am not sure. In any event, when she returned to claim it, she was arrested. She was kept in prison with some other students (mostly from the government university, Chuan Ta) until about three weeks ago, when one morning, thirty of these young political prisoners, this girl among them, were taken outside the West Gate and shot, their bodies dumped in a common grave. A few days ago, her mother, while looking for a coffin to give her a decent burial, spotted the Nationalist secret policeman, now dressed in rags, who had arrested her daughter. She at once reported him and he was seized. There are apparently many such people in hiding.

Word comes from Kiating that Communist troops have almost completely taken over the Baptist Mission. Miss Broadbeck, the American field worker in charge, is, however, quite content. She says they frequently ask her to play the Church organ for them, which she does, and that she has never had such opportunity to preach the Gospel!

Of late, there have been cartoons posted about the campus. One shows a raised boot with "United States, England and Canada" written on it, coming down on the members of President Fang's University Council, who are meekly kneeling under it saying, "Yes Sir." And the monthly faculty meeting, at which the affairs of the University are discussed, has been replaced by a new body composed of faculty, students and coolies.

□ *JANUARY 7TH:* Just in from a lovely birthday party at Number Three (the residence shared by some of our younger colleagues). *Mian* (noodles) and music. Ralph was called out to do a Krukenberg operation on a child who had a live grenade explode in his hand. This old fashioned technique is used when no prosthetics are available. It involves separating the two forearm bones, re-attaching the available muscles and covering each of these two new "working fingers" with sensitive forearm skin. Certainly it's better than a stump and some can even handle chopsticks efficiently with the result.

□ *JANUARY 8TH:* There seems to be a very definite and almost studied whispering campaign against the new government. Every day we hear stories or bits of gossip of one disparaging kind or another. One of the most popular is about the Pastor who was forced to get out of his rickshaw and pull his coolie and then pay several dollars for the privilege. What truth there is in stories like this I don't know, but people are afraid to ride in rickshaws now.

□ *JANUARY 10TH:* At a meeting of students and faculty representatives from local teaching institutions yesterday, a Communist official stated that student political agitation would no longer be tolerated. In the past, such activity was right because it was against something wrong, but in the future it would be considered as directed at the present government and therefore is forbidden.

□ *JANUARY 11TH:* A day filled with warm sunshine. I did a spot of work for the Library and then dropped in at Jean Kilborn's for coffee. She had a letter from Stewart Allen in Chungking reporting great joy on the part of the students and general public at the Communist take over. He corroborated the story we had heard earlier that the retreating Kuomintang Army had blown up the arsenal, with no warning either to workers or populace. The factory was operating full blast when its explosion shook the entire city. Stewart reports casualties as high as 2,000.

Ralph came home from the OR for lunch exceedingly tired, so I insisted he take a long siesta. He slept soundly, and after a small tea we went for a stroll out beyond the Middle School through fields which at this time of year resemble a huge market garden as far as the eye can see. Acres of a purplish red-stemmed vegetable, large radishes and so on. Our own garden has been pretty much wrecked by the dogs and children. This evening Ralph went to bed feeling rocky and I went over to the Willmotts' to hear a discussion on Mao's New Democracy. The newspapers today say America is making a large-scale attempt to protect Formosa.

☐ *JANUARY 14TH:* Ralph is still flat on his back, though his temperature is a little better today. I hope he is over the hump. So many reports on the doings of the new régime have been drifting in it is difficult to get them down. One thing seems obvious however: they mean business! Since the take over, there has been amazing activity. At first, everything was returned to the status quo as quickly as possible. Already this phase is almost over. Representatives have been sent to every organization, school, hospital, etc., to study its effectiveness in meeting the needs of society.

Yesterday the faculty, students and coolies were invited to a mass meeting in front of the Administration building. A Hunan man addressed those assembled, complete with loudspeakers, etc. He was not easily understood, but one thing that met with cheers was his announcement that compulsory Religion is to be abolished and that Ethics is to be removed from the curriculum. More cheers.

Prices seem to be coming down a bit. I bought a lovely old dish today and paid too much for it, but could not turn Chen, the old curio man, away. He still comes at noon (as he has since we first arrived in 1938), but now the wares he sells are much less in number and quality. He is an opium smoker and in poor circumstances.

The American Baptists are starting a communal kitchen. They plan to live within the same salary as their Chinese colleagues. Clarence Vichert has been pushing this venture. No move on the part of the Canadians yet.

☐ *JANUARY 16TH:* Poor old Ralph has taken a turn for the worse. It is now certain that he has hepatitis. I have been pretty busy with intravenouses and things. And our dog Lady is attracting all of the available four-legged swain for miles around so our nights are none too good either.

Today, a letter from Banyang, very happy and optimistic. They continue to sell land. Eunice Peters writes that it looks like the Mission Hospital in Kiating will soon be taken over. I am buying in more flour as the Communists have decreed that in future it must all be of one grade so that we will have to eat the same as the poor. Our cook, Chiang Si, tells me the government is going to take over the University Museum.

☐ *JANUARY 20TH:* I've been too uninspired to write. Ralph has been exceedingly ill. Intravenouses every day, unable to tolerate anything by mouth. Today, however, he seems a little better so I will try to assemble some small bits of news.

Ruth West had a nasty experience the other day. When coming out to campus from the city, one of the guards seized her radio. She was told she could not move it without a permit. A permit office, however, has yet to be opened and special passes can only be obtained with great difficulty. And two Catholic Priests were arrested, apparently for being on the street in non-clerical clothes!

If I can believe Chiang Si, there is great unrest in the countryside, particularly around Peng Hsien and Beh Lu Din.

Ralph's most immediate faculty colleagues, Bert Yang, Professor of Surgery, and Clifford Tsao, Dean of Medicine, have urged him to take all the time he needs to recover (at least a month) and have made provisions for his classes and surgery. They could not have been more understanding. And Stephen Shen, who is now Ralph's chief resident, has been doing awfully well. While Ralph has been away, he has done two Krukenbergs on his own.

☐ *JANUARY 24TH:* Ralph is sitting up in bed as I write, feeling much better, but lemon yellow!

Earl Willmott, who teaches a course in Christian Ethics at the University, preached Sunday night on Christianity in the New Era, contending the Church too had been "liberated," that at last it had a freedom to speak denied under the old régime! Christ, he proclaimed, was a materialistic determinist like Lenin and Marx, etc., etc., etc., which left everybody boiling. The part that really burned up Leslie Kilborn was Earl exhorting the

Chinese Communists to have patience with us foreigners and our bourgeois attitudes. We were victims of our backgrounds and would know not what we did unless they re-educated us!

☐ *JANUARY 27TH:* Ralph is still feeling rotten and will be convalescing for some time. He is enjoying his reading though, so I don't feel too sorry for him.

When Gladys Cunningham took the Prayer Meeting Wednesday evening, she spoke of the importance of realizing God was a spirit and not one of the images in our minds. Audrey Honey, who is extremely fundamentalistic, was very much annoyed and told Gladys she was presumptuous to speak thus before theologues. And Kay Willmott and Bill Small so raked Earl over the coals for his sermon Sunday, he now reluctantly admits there might have been something wrong with it.

☐ *JANUARY 28TH:* Quite a day! We started off by hanging the new flag we were obliged to buy ($1.50) over the front gate to celebrate Liberation Day. The servants scurried to get their chores done so they could spend the afternoon in the city. Ralph had a steady stream of visitors all morning for it was a lovely day and no one felt like staying indoors. Each brought news. Preparations for the "liberation" of Tibet are going on apace. Li Anche, the head of Anthropology at WCUU and an authority on the culture of Tibet, has volunteered to accompany the invading armies. He says he is going in the hope he can mediate and help the Tibetans whose hospitality he enjoyed for years. It seems to me a lousy thing to do. Dr. Shen was in looking harrassed and tired. The Krukenbergs have all gone wrong and he is very worried. He borrowed all the literature Ralph has on the procedure.

Outside, soldiers were milling around our compound. Yesterday, when I tried to get rid of an unsolicited guest the gateman had brought to live in their quarters during the fighting a couple of months ago, I incidentally asked his wife what they were doing with my water crock in their room. I told her taking things without permission was the same as theft. She at once sent word to her husband, who was attending a union meeting, saying I had accused him of stealing. He returned in a mad fury, accosted me and figuratively tore me apart with his big voice. This attracted enough attention to result in an official inquiry today. We have put up with a great deal from Chiang Ta-yea in the past because of his family. (We pay him, but he doesn't actually do much work here, just attends meetings and struts about acting important.) Now I will get rid of him on the first pretext.

☐ *FEBRUARY 2ND:* The last couple of weeks have seen the beginnings of a debate between the students and their teachers on the "re-organization" of the University. In the process, however, every petty hatred, old quarrel and ancient slight has emerged in full festering flower. The Communist officials on campus are reputed to have said that in all their experience they have never seen anything like it! The atmosphere is so poisonous that both Vice-Chancellor Lindsay and President Fang last Saturday submitted their resignations to the University's Board of Directors. (These have been tabled, temporarily.) Finally, it was decided the students and faculty of each Department would meet in preliminary sessions to thrash out their problems. Yesterday afternoon, the Medical faculty met with the Fourth Year students and, in the evening, with the Fifth Year. Each had its long list of complaints and suggestions. For example, the students want no examination in the fifth year, but wish to be passed on their ward work. They want to be graduated now rather than in the Fall. They want all lectures given in Bai Hua (the people's or common language) rather than in technical English. Each meeting took four hours.

Canning Yang, an American-trained Cantonese architect, and Grace, his lovely wife, a Kiangsi woman also educated in America, have three children, two of whom are old enough to be affected by all the changes taking place. Their eldest is a student at the University of Hankow who wants to study medicine. For some reason, although wcuu is the best medical school in the country, he refuses to enrol here. Personally, I feel this is because his parents are much loved by and at home with the foreign community and he does not wish to share their conspicuousness. Their second child, who attends the Mission Middle School, is extremely enthusiastic about her Communist indoctrination classes. Indeed, she wants to go with the army to Tibet. Her father, naturally, is opposed. It takes a little longer for the older people to become convinced this new government is sincere. They have seen so many come and go. Grace is quite wonderful and realizes that as the children mature, things will work out.

Still no real news from the Hsiehs. Their carrier was in and he says things are really tough in the country and food scarce. However, for New Year's they sent us a smoked duck and some of her wonderful dates. Banyang's little joke was that the duck being eggless the dates would take their place. Dr. Hsu and his wife sent us smoked tongue and ham.

☐ *FEBRUARY 3RD:* Last night at our Faculty of Arts meeting, one of the students gave a long harangue against Kiang Wen-kang, the head of the Department of History and Philosophy, said he was no good as a lecturer and that none of his students liked him. He then brought up a lot of unsavory stories about Professor Kiang's past life and reactionary ideas and demanded his resignation. Today, Kiang, who was not present to answer these charges, resigned after "confessing" that since "his wisdom did not equal that of his students, he was unworthy to be their professor"!

☐ *FEBRUARY 5TH:* Rice, which remains the index for general commodity prices, has jumped 600 per cent since the arrival of the Communists. No attempt has been made to put a ceiling on things. This will have to be done soon if those on government-regulated salaries (all of which have been radically cut or temporarily suspended) are to survive.

Also, it has been necessary for the government to tax those people with property at a far higher rate than ever imposed by the Kuomintang, which has caused terrific suffering and hardship. I heard about one poor old lady who had to sell her sewing machine, without which she has no means to make a living, to pay her assessment.

Of course, people are slow to accept anything new and it takes time for the machinery of government to get oiled and running. And no doubt part of the problem for the Communists is that the Szechwanese are suspicious and resentful of anyone from outside their province. We saw this during the Sino-Japanese War when the hundreds of thousands of refugees who flooded Szechwan from occupied China were given a very rough time indeed. Well, now there are whole armies here talking in different dialects!

☐ *FEBRUARY 8TH:* This afternoon, I went to a meeting of the Democracy Club. This is a study group on Communism for foreigners which more or less parallels the indoctrination classes which are compulsory for the Chinese. We discussed recent government pronouncements on the family. Parents must not be too possessive, remembering their children now belong to the state. No husband can have more than one wife. There must be utter equality between the sexes. In North China, each family is organized as a productive unit and prizes are given each year for the most successful. In Manchuria, women are now employed in heavy industry. It is a disgrace for anyone to become an economic or social parasite. In Peking, as in Russia, prostitution has been abolished. Each family member must work, earn wages and help the country by paying taxes.

☐ *FEBRUARY 9TH:* Last Saturday, there was a meeting to which all doctors in private practice in the city were summoned by numbered invitation. As each arrived, he was told to take the seat with his number on it (an easy way to check absentees). They were lectured for several hours on their place in the New Society where their sole purpose will be to serve the public and the state. Profits are out. House calls are in, unless of course the patient happens to be a "reactionary." Anyone opposed to the new order henceforth will be denied all medical treatment!

Yesterday, silver dollars officially went off the market. They are to be exchanged at the rate of 1 to $6,000 RMP, which stands for Ren Min Pi and means "the common people's money." Unfortunately, the ordinary citizen does not trust paper money and persists in using silver, despite a threatened penalty of three years imprisonment. Perhaps if the new government's paper lasted longer when buried, it might be more popular.

Although the papers never mention it, we hear former Nationalist troops, in bands numbering anywhere from a dozen to 2,000, have turned to banditry, rendering the roads out of Chengtu unsafe to traffic. The only official word is that no foreigner is allowed to travel beyond the city.

□ *FEBRUARY 11TH:* Today is Chinese New Year's, which begins The Year of The Tiger. The new Government wants to abandon the lunar calendar, but it is very difficult to change the custom of several thousand years overnight. (The Kuomintang tried and failed.) The servants gave a feast at noon, at which we were "honored" guests. The gateman presented us with *mei hua* flowers.

This morning at 6 A.M., Communist soldiers came into our yard to ask how many were living here and other details about us. This apparently is part of a city-wide investigation. Also, there were police on every street corner today checking registration cards. And next week, there is to be what is called a public health drive, when every house is to be inspected for cleanliness. This is probably just an opportunity to check for stores of arms or rice. We still have seventy bushels which we bought before the turn over to make sure we had enough on hand to pay our servants should there be shortages. I understand the new regulation is that only five bushels per person can be stored. Of course we have fourteen on this property counting the servants' children, so that should cover it.

We hear there is a very active black market in foreign currency, gold and silver. The merchants still prefer silver money to paper. In some shops, the only time the price of anything is quoted in RMP is if a Communist soldier is around.

Kerry had a chest X-ray taken today. There is a patch on the left mid-lung, suggestive of Tb! Ralph is beginning to get up for short periods in the morning and afternoon.

☐ *FEBRUARY 13TH:* A letter in from Banyang. They have built a small house outside Jungshien's North Gate and are planning to move out of their grand old Chinese home. She is going to do spinning and weaving and Robert, her husband, is going to raise chickens and ducks and help teach the children. He was, as you remember, a banker. Old Mr. Liu, Banyang's father, the leader of the local Elder Brothers Society, has been chosen as a representative of the progressive gentry on the new municipal council, so they feel a certain security. Nevertheless, their position is a precarious one and we are worried about them.

☐ *FEBRUARY 15TH:* The doctors got together today over Kerry's disturbing X-rays and have put him in bed flat on his back for three months. It was quite a blow to have his suspected Tb confirmed, for I feel we could have avoided this with care. He is running a slight temp. at times, but has no other symptoms and is so far enjoying the unusual attention. His playmates, however, are not allowed to call. Poor darling.

☐ *FEBRUARY 17TH:* If one is sensitive to the atmosphere around one, the strain is pretty severe. One has no way of knowing what is true. It is said an advance unit of the army to "liberate" Tibet has been wiped out by ambush, that an attempt to use a thousand coolies to repair the Hsin Gin airfield for use by large Russian planes has been blocked by the local people who are having none of it. This is probably the sort of thing whispered by Kuomintang agents to keep the populace stirred up. Gunfire, however, has been audible all day today to the south. And when Yang Jing-guo, one of our surgical residents going on rotation, and a nurse who had been doing post-graduate work up here went down to Tzeliutsing last week, their truck was stopped by bandits five times and the passengers robbed of all they possessed. He arrived in Chungking completely naked and she in a pair of wool panties. The Communist Army is called the People's Army of Liberation. The guerillas fighting in the countryside have turned the characters slightly around (as the Chinese love to do) and call themselves the Army to Liberate the People.

☐ *FEBRUARY 18TH:* Another lovely day. The children are upstairs playing with a Meccano set the Willmotts lent to Kerry. Dr. Meuser is visiting Ralph. Clarence has been in. And because I have a few spare minutes, I'll take the opportunity to record a thing or two.

Money is very expensive. The exchange rate is now $16,000 RMP to $1.00 U.S., but it takes a million dollars to buy two sacks of flour. Our diet would be reduced to a minimum were it not for our foreign supplies (purchased in advance) which supplement so well we hardly notice. Conseqently, we are in a much better position than our Chinese friends for whom things are getting pretty tough. If we have to cut down to the point of risking the kiddies' health, I want to go home.

Ralph is working on a book on fractures, "The More Common Fractures And Their Treatment," for his students, which, if we have to leave, will at least be a small contribution toward their future. The students cannot afford to buy textbooks either in Chinese or from abroad. This little book is being printed by our own Mission Press on grass paper (the kind we use for toilet paper) and will cost about fifty cents. He is writing this in simple English with extensive hand drawings to demonstrate both the variety of fractures and the necessary remedial techniques, and hopes young doctors will find it a useful guide.

☐ *FEBRUARY 19TH:* In former times at Chinese New Year's, the government gave rice certificates to the poor. None have been issued this year. We heard several little children on the street chanting, "Last year we had meat and cakes at New Year's. This year we have rice gruel."

Today, Ralph felt strong enough to walk the hundred yards over to the Cunninghams'.

☐ *FEBRUARY 22ND:* Turnabout is fair play. Ralph is up and I am spending the morning in bed. My back is on the fritz. Grace and Canning Yang came in for tea yesterday. I have mentioned all the petty hates and jealousies that have come to the surface around here. Many of the meetings called to re-organize the University have turned into gripe sessions where everyone has taken the opportunity of airing personal complaints against the administration and faculty. Some of our finest professors, even a couple of world renown, have been dragged through the mud and are thinking of leaving, Canning among them. He has had an offer from the University in Canton to head up their Department of Architecture. Both he and his wife will be greatly missed. Grace is an example of radiant Christianity and a complete darling.

Yesterday, several hundred hungry people swooped down on the large truck gardens behind the Women's College and picked the vegetables clean while the farmers stood wringing their hands and cursing.

☐ *FEBRUARY 25TH:* The head of the Dzu family, now the "God of Wealth" in name only, was arrested yesterday.

Chiang Si reports guards at the city gates frisking people for illegal silver and gold. A story circulating concerns one man, who had $10 silver confiscated at the Marco Polo Bridge. He became so indignant when the soldier in charge threw his money into the river, he demanded the right to search the soldier. He was backed up in this by the crowd of passersby who gather for every street drama. As it turned out, the soldier likewise had $10 silver, which the man, to the delight of all and sundry, promptly hurled over the bridge to join his own.

Kerry continues fairly happily and gifts pour in from all our neighbors and friends. People are remarkably thoughtful and kind. His prayers now end, "God bless Mummy, Daddy, Judith, Carol and Kerry and make him better soon, and bless all the little sick kids in the world." He has astonished me with his fastidiousness and good manners while in bed. Perhaps his usual lack of them is because he has never before felt the leisure to indulge in amenities.

A few days ago, three second-year medical students called on Leslie Kilborn. They said they had just had a class meeting at which each had presented a detailed account of his or her economic situation. Twenty-nine of the eighty were completely destitute and needed help to earn their way. Leslie took up their case and it was decided to give each Year a plot of the Hospital's lawn for a vegetable garden, to be tilled, planted and looked after entirely by the students. The Second Year is very enthusiastic and today reported they have already planted 1,500 cabbage seedlings. They are also going to raise fish in the Hospital pond. Some of the boys have been given jobs looking after the animal house. And others have begged for work of any kind, even cleaning out toilets. Surely a new era has arrived when the so-called intelligentsia are willing to soil their hands!

☐ *FEBRUARY 28TH:* Today, a new low. The student nurses went on strike because there was no rice for breakfast. Apparently, school funds are so short that last week they had to borrow rice from the Tb Sanitorium. In the meantime, they tried to get money from the Mission, the Hospital and the University. All three institutions were strapped. Therefore, no breakfast. Later this morning, they were able to borrow two more *dan* (5½ bu.) from the San., but this just shows the fleecing our Institutions have taken as a result of the terrific inflation.

☐ *MARCH 2ND:* I started a letter home today, but got no further than the date when I was interrupted and we have been having guests and doing chores ever since. The student nurses are back on duty. Their Superintendent is going to take each girl aside unofficially and suggest that if she is unwilling to go through the tough times ahead, she had better leave now. There is a possibility the Nursing School may be closed.

When Barbara Arnup saw Carol coming home from school the other day blowing up a French safe, she stopped her to ask where she had obtained such a thing. Carol replied, "Oh, Lan gave it to me. She found it in her very own drawer and doesn't know where it came from." Lan is the little English child who shocked the guests at a party on Mount Omei last summer by announcing, "I know how to have babies and how not to have them." She is eight!

□ *MARCH 4TH:* Harrison and Bee Mullett were over the other night to have a cup of coffee. Hash hadn't seen me for ages and as we were walking up the stairs, he put his arm around me, said how glad he was I was up and about again and kissed me. Well Judy saw this and ran to tell Carol. I had to face two pairs of accusing eyes at breakfast the next morning. I explained that Uncle Hash is old enough to be my father and on rare occasions kissed me as a father would his daughter. They thought this pretty feeble!

The ditches have not been cleaned out this year nor has the water been dammed at Kwanhsien, which will mean floods and an upset in the economy of the entire province. We have it on reliable authority, however, that more troops are being brought in to rectify this and other forms of resistance. Returning from the Hospital yesterday, Ralph saw a water buffalo coming along the campus road with one of our female medical students riding on its back and another leading it. They had borrowed or rented its services to plow up their ground at the Hospital. Here at least, the revolution is alive and well.

At the Mission Executive meeting, Alf opposed our cost-of-living bonus. The poor kid felt pretty badly when I jumped him about this, but he feels a Missionary cannot accept bonuses when his Chinese colleagues are being reduced to starvation. Ergo, we either get out or accept the same relative drop in standard of living.

☐ *MARCH 12TH:* Listened to a cracking good sermon by Dave Gunn, who has been mad all week because the Theology students said his teaching was not sufficiently progressive to meet the challenge of this new day and age. They asked that Dryden Phelps and Earl Willmott give them all their lectures. Dave decried the split in our community. He maintained that there is no one here who is not progressive in his thinking, in that each of us believes passionately in the betterment of oppressed classes, although we may not all agree that Communism is the answer. Therefore, he objects to being labelled "reactionary" and feels the Dryden/Earl faction is limiting our Christian message.

Word from I Pin that the passports of foreigners have been taken away. Miss Broadbeck in Loshan [Kiating] writes she has dismissed all her servants telling them that it is wise for them to leave a sinking ship. In the same letter, she asks Clarence to have a new will made out for her. We hear as well that the Baptist Station in Yaan have turned over the Middle School and one of the foreign residences to the new government, together with the annual appropriation for their Mission. No explanation comes with this.

Bill Arnup was over this morning and could hear nothing amiss in Kerry's chest. His temperature remains around normal and he has been gaining weight each week, so we are feeling quite happy about him. Marg Day, who is again pregnant, gave us a scare yesterday. Her ankles began to swell, her blood pressure was up and Gladys could not hear the fetal heart. Marg, after her experience of last summer when she lost a full-term boy, was naturally frantic. Today, however, things are back to normal.

☐ *MARCH 14TH:* A couple of weeks ago, there was a patient in Hospital, a peasant woman of about thirty-five, who had attempted to cut out a piece of her own liver with which to make a medicinal broth to cure her sick mother. In the event, not knowing the exact location of the organ she wanted to slice, she made her cut far too low and a piece of bowel was extruded which became gangrenous.

So far as we know, this is the first reported instance of this particular sort of self-mutilation since the 1920s, when Dr. McCartney reported two similar cases in Chungking. Interestingly, the only one of those to successfully cut out a piece of her liver survived. Both, however received tremendous public acclaim. And the one who died had a *pai fang* (gateway) erected in her honor!

The belief that filial loyalty demands a son or daughter use a part of his or her own body to prepare a medicine for an ill parent is derived from a basic precept of Confucian teaching. Indeed, it is one of the twenty-four forms of filial piety. And although this usually doesn't go much beyond the burning of hair, nail clippings or bits of skin so that minor ailments can be treated with the ash, one of our wcuu professors, Chung Lo-yuin, has a badly scarred arm from slicing off strips of flesh to make a broth for an ailing parent when he was a young man. The potency of the medicine prepared is thought to be in direct proportion to the degree of the donor's suffering. However, this practice has been forbidden by law since early in the Ch'ing [Qing] Dynasty (1644–1911 A.D.). And a visit to four of the city's leading herbalists or traditional doctors revealed that none had ever heard of anyone in their profession prescribing vital human organs as medication.

The question, then, remained: where did this illiterate peasant woman learn about "liver soup"? Her village was typically isolated, where ninety per cent of her neighbors would never have travelled more than ten or twelve miles from their homes. Her world was one without education, newspapers, magazines, books, radio or motion pictures. In that she seemed incapable of explaining herself, Ralph concluded there were but two possibilities. The only important contacts with the rest of Szechwan in her meager life were the drama and the storyteller.

The Szechwan drama is in fact opera. Troupes of players tour from village to village, often stopping for a two- or three-week stand in one of the local temples, during which they run through their entire repertoire. Traditionally, the actors are all males (female roles are sung in falsetto). Typically, their plays are full of romance and remote from reality. But a couple of WCUU scholars, well versed in this subject, knew of no libretto depictions of filial piety of the sort Ralph was curious about.

The travelling storyteller, on the other hand, equally popular throughout West China, is the master weaver of tales which run the gamut of raw emotion, damsels in distress, dæmons and færies, bravery and adventure, magic and tragedy. And unlike the dramatic players, his material knows no restraints.

Consequently, when Ralph learned eighty professional storytellers were gathered for Communist indoctrination in the city park, he sent his resident to tell them about our patient. Initially, everyone denied ever having used a story in which a brave person had cut a piece from one of his or her own vital organs to cure an ailing parent. They were so adamant, it was apparent they were afraid to answer truthfully lest they be branded as engaging in practices unacceptable to the New Order. Finally, one of the storytellers admitted that each had told such tales, which were immensely popular with their audiences. This then was how the faithful daughter learned how to cure the mother she loved.

□ *MARCH 16TH:* The surrounding countryside is again aflower with rape and bean and the air is beautifully fragrant. I biked in from the city today, realizing only after I got home, that when the guard at the Gate waved his red flag, he was not being friendly but wanted me to stop, probably to show my resident's certificate. I just smiled and whizzed on by.

Clarence reports there were no Christians selected for the People's Congress. Also that one of our leading local clergy suggests foreigners take a back seat in the months to come. Things are going to get pretty tough and the sooner administrative positions in our hospitals, schools and churches are taken over by Chinese, with whom they properly belong, the better.

I found everything under control at home, except for Kerry's big fat tree worm. It's disappeared and we don't know whether Mike the dog ate it or whether it passed through a hole in the floor. I had just changed to go to the Prayer Meeting when Mrs. Meuser came over to get my enema kit. Poor Margie Day is in more trouble. There is little hope now for the baby.

□ *MARCH 17TH:* As I write, Ralph is downstairs looking around for a midnight snack. I spent a million dollars today—a little lard ($12,000 per pound), the electric light bill ($350,000), needy students $18,000, etc., all of which represents $25.00 American.

While the children were playing in the ditch this afternoon trying to catch fish by hand, they were approached by a stranger who grabbed Judy and started to molest her. Fortunately she got away. It strikes cold into my heart. Frankly, I am terrified these days. If it isn't one thing, it is another.

□ *MARCH 24TH:* An article in the newspaper yesterday, datelined Peking, said *spy* schools are being organized in various parts of the Far East by English, American and Canadian Missionaries. According to this tirade, each of us has been instructed not to leave China under any circumstance and to organize anti-Communist cells from among our wealthy Church members and other reactionary remnants of the Kuomintang. One does not have to think far to see how much these damnable statements can ruin our work. Isn't it pathetic there cannot be more faith and less suspicion in the world today! One other thing, this article particularly mentioned the Catholics as front and center in all of this. One reason may be their penchant for acquiring tracts of local real estate.

We went to be registered today. They took our passports, various completed forms, four photos each, our old resident certificates and $20,000 RMP apiece. Then we were each questioned in detail on all sorts of things. "Who are your friends? What party do you belong to? Why are you out here?" While they were very polite, they were also very firm about some of the answers they required. For example, our "party" is "Christian," which perhaps means that one could not be a Communist as well.

Another letter in from Banyang. All their rice has been seized for taxes. Robert carries the water, feeds the poultry and helps *Lao tai tai* with the children. Banyang is taking a teaching job at a neaby public school. The whole family are working hard to stay alive and, naturally, report themselves as being happy and healthy.

☐ *MARCH 27TH:* Floyd and Audrey Honey were here for a supper of beans and fruit. Floyd wanted to take a wire recording of some of our gramophone music (the Weniewski 2nd Concerto), but before he did so we all had fun talking into the microphone and hearing it played back. I was surprised my voice is as nice as it is.

Kerry is running a temperature again.

☐ *MARCH 28TH:* The Methodists are having a hard time. Their Board at home has refused to pay taxes on Church property in China. This, they feel, should be a local responsibility. The government here is equally adamant that they must and is criticising them for trying to oppose the New Order. But when questioned about the fairness of a huge retroactive levy, one Communist official replied, "We wish to destroy you!"

☐ *APRIL 2ND:* Dr. Li Hen, head of Astronomy and, as I've mentioned, an internationally recognized scholar, received a venomous open letter a couple of weeks ago, in which he was accused of all sorts of things and told he was not fit to remain on faculty. There are certain elements in the University who are laying for him because of the April 9th "Bloody Massacre" incident two years ago, when a female student was slightly injured during a demonstration parade against the policies (no cheap rice for students) of Wang Ling-chi, the then governor. During a scuffle with Wang's police, this girl was kicked or hit in the perineum. She was brought to the University Hospital where she was treated by Dr. Gladys and confined to bed for a few days. Reports got out she was mortally wounded, that she had been bayonetted and was at death's door. One student wrote an article in the *China Weekly Review,* describing the incident as, "The Bloody Massacre of April 9th." The thing just grew and grew. Finally, public sentiment worked itself up to such a pitch, the University had to issue a report on the actual extent of the injuries sustained by this girl, to which Li Hen affixed his name as Dean of Arts. Instead of calming the situation, it almost caused a riot. Li Hen's statement was not believed. Nor is it today. The anniversary of this "event" is now celebrated as a day of resistance on the part of the students against the old régime.

☐ *APRIL 4TH:* The city is groaning under taxes, of which there are to be four this year: 1) a tax for cleaning out the ditches, 2) a property tax, 3) a victory bond drive which is not voluntary and therefore may be considered a tax and 4) an income tax which hasn't yet been announced, but is supposed to be the heaviest of the lot. Educational institutions are taxed at a very low rate or are exempt. Our hospitals, however, have been very heavily hit. For example, the Leper Hospital (a completely charitable institution which gets every cent of its money from abroad) has been assessed five hundred bushels of rice. The same for the Tb San, which is an old converted farmhouse off among the fields, with twelve patients, not one of whom is paying. The University Hospital, seven hundred bushels. The Eye, Ear, Nose and Throat Hospital, the same, which amounts to about $2,400 (American). And it is said the property tax is about double this. The obvious is that the hospitals will have to close. A few years ago, when the Leper Hospital was threatened with unfair taxation, the patients marched in a body to the government offices where they simply sat down. The officials all fled and the question was never raised again.

☐ *APRIL 5TH:* Margie Day's baby was born dead. The victory bond drive is under way. Apparently, Mao Tse-tung has said nothing since his return from Moscow except that the next few years will be only "sweat and tears," which has the Chinese wondering.

☐ *APRIL 12TH:* A few days ago, Dr. Beh came back from a meeting in Chungking at which representatives from the four western provinces met with the new government to discuss the future of medicine in this area. Medical education apparently is going to be put under the Ministry of Public Health instead of the Ministry of Education, which will be much more satisfactory, as in the past many problems of a professional nature arose which the officials in the Education Department did not understand. Also, to meet China's need for doctors at the present time, there is a proposal to establish a number of new medical schools in which a short course of two or three years will be given. Only one university will continue to train medical researchers and professors. Ours is recognized as the best medical school in China and apparently they would very much welcome an offer from us to co-operate in this scheme. It is not outside the realm of possibility that we may drop our entire Arts program and continue with only Science, Medicine and Dentistry.

Ralph has just received a note from his students in Orthopædics saying, "We are so sorry we cannot come for our examination tomorrow. We are too tired!"

☐ *APRIL 20TH:* A man with four children came to the door of one of our colleagues and begged for enough money to buy arsenic to poison himself and his family. With some difficulty, he was persuaded to think it over.

Our mission in Chungking wired Earl today telling him that they had been taxed the equivalent of $1,000 American on the Hospital and other buildings and that if they did not pay today, probably it would be doubled or the property seized. Poor Stewart Allen had such faith in the new set-up and expected duck soup, telling us how cordially disposed the Communists were toward Canadians and their work because of Norman Bethune. "All the Communist hospitals in the North are named 'Bethune Memorial Hospital,' " he kept repeating.

□ *APRIL 21ST:* This morning, after giving the cook $50,000 to buy cherries if the farmers had managed to bring their fruit to market, Margie Day and I went over to give Win Gunn a permanent. She told us a friend had just returned from Junghsien with the news that Robert Hsieh is in prison and that Banyang and her five small children are in sore straits, with nothing but rice congee to eat and not enough of that!

Earlier today, Ralph talked to Li Hen, who reported that Mr. Wen, the Communist party representative on campus, had inquired as to why he had signed the now infamous "Bloody Massacre" letter. Li Hen replied, "because it was the truth and as a scientist, I believe in the truth." Wen rejoined, "Do you not realize that besides truth and falsehood, there is good and bad. To have signed that letter was bad. I am sure that if you were aware of the difference, you would never have done so. You scientists must learn that anything that supports Chiang Kai-shek and American imperialism is bad, but following the Communist party line is good." Li Hen's observation to Ralph was, "It looks as though the future of Chinese science is Lysenkoism."

□ *APRIL 24TH:* Word has come that Robert Hsieh was only in prison for a few hours. Thank Goodness!

Saturday was a big day in our house. Ralph made his violin debut that evening at the students' concert. He played beautifully and we nearly burst with pride.

Tuesday the tailor came. I now have a new summer dressing gown and three dresses just about complete. They are nice but unexciting.

We applied for exit permits yesterday. It was thought better to apply in a group and, as there is little hope for action in under six months and more likely a year, I thought it wise to put our names in. Golly, I hope we don't have to go.

Last week, all radios were checked to make certain no one had a transmitter. Tomorrow all bicycles and rickshaws are to be registered.

Yesterday, a couple of Communist soldiers came to ask

permission to dig up the plot in front of our gate. They were told it belonged to the University and that they would have to check with the appropriate authorities. They then gathered our servants together and told them they were dogs to work for the foreigners, etc. This went on for about an hour. Our servants are pretty loyal and even if not, know on which side their bread is buttered.

☐ *MAY 1ST:* I have spent the day wandering around seeing my friends and shamelessly collecting news and gossip. I started with Mrs. Lindsay and heard that Bill Small, who has been very left-wing in his views, actively blocking our attempts to get a salary bonus and urging us to buy bonds, has been trying to get the University to bring in a trained Chinese accountant so that he can teach him the ropes of the Bursar's Office in case he decides to leave!

The Days are becoming quite cynical, Alf swinging like a pendulum to the extreme of disillusionment. The action of the central committee of the YWCA in excluding foreigners from the executive staff has cut deeply, especially Margie's mother, Mrs. Meuser, who has given them years of service. She has lent Alf her copy of Igor Gouzenko's *I Chose Freedom*. A story going the rounds is about the child who was told his father was Papa Stalin and that his mother was the great USSR. When asked, "And what do you want to be, my dear, when you grow up?" He replied, "An orphan."

☐ *MAY 5TH:* Marx's birthday today, all day.

Five-year-old Diana Day fell in the irrigation ditch and floated down to Willmott's where their cook fished her out badly scared and full of filthy water, but otherwise okay.

☐ *MAY 7TH:* A story came to us rather illustrative of the times. A man of moderate means had bought a hundred bonds. His two children told him they thought he should buy three hundred. He said he couldn't possibly. The children pointed out he had some money put aside. He agreed, but explained he had been saving it for them. "You wouldn't have me use that would you?" he asked. They told him yes. And when he refused, they reported him to the authorities.

☐ *MAY 12TH:* This afternoon, Ralph and I rode our bikes into the city, where the sidewalks along Chuen Shi Lu are now lined with small stalls at which one can purchase almost anything. A number of these outlets are watched over by well-dressed people who look as though they are ordinary citizens trying to sell off personal possessions. Others are definitely offering goods from the big shops, many of which are closed. Apparently, most buying and selling in the city has shifted to these kiosks as merchants try to escape the severe taxes imposed on their businesses. Also, beggars, more numerous than ever and much bolder, grab at your bicycle or clothing and yell for their colleagues to help make you stop. This is because the police not only refuse to control them but take their side in a dispute, forcing you to give them money. I slap them away when they clutch at me, regardless of the consequences.

Something I have noticed and keep forgetting to mention is the degeneration in the grooming of Chinese girls. They now practically all wear poorly cut blue or black slacks of some cotton stuff, hair sloppy and no make-up. Those in the army are absolute messes. Shocks of black, short, sawed-off hair stuck under ill-fitting red star caps, ugly uniforms and a general toughness of appearance that is all quite new in my experience here.

☐ *JUNE 2ND:* A letter from Banyang:

"My dearest Margaret:
  "Robert sent your birthday gift and he wrote Chinese letter to you. Because when I was in school learning the new knowledge and very busy for my school work, I only ate and slept at home, so he wrote.
  "Your letter came a month ago. We were very very busy to finish our taxes of our land, so I did not write you for the long time. Thank you very much for all your concern about us.

"Also many thanks for Ralph asked about us in Dr. Hsu's letter. Yes, Robert was in custody for a short time. Because the man who bought our land did not pay the tax, the soldiers wanted Robert to pay for him. But it was not our duty and we have not enough to pay ours, so Robert refused it. So put him in custody one night. Tell me, how did you know? My dear!

"We used our rice, cotton, silver, gold, all we have and borrowed some to pay our taxes. Now the worry is over. We are peaceful again.

"I am teaching in the primary school which beside our gate. I have [some] rice every month. I am very lucky and very enjoy my work. And the pupils love me. It is very convenient that so near my home, and that is so good?

"We eat some rice, wheat, beans, vegetables; no eggs, no meat, no sugar. We are very poor. But I am so very happy that I am real free now. Because there are no guests, guests' children, guests' servants etc. to stay our home for a long time. Also, 'Lo Ti Ti' [*Lao tai tai*] is better to me.

"I remember Carol's and Kerry's birthday in April. Also remember last year I was at your home, so happy, so interesting.

"The Hsus are all well. They are very good to us.

"My father is very well to. He loves us and help us too. He has the simple food to feed his family, and my brother who return to Hankow sends money home.

"The children are all sweet. They like their simple food and feel very strong, very interesting. They are so proud of the beautiful clothes that you gave to them. The Hsu girl is also very happy to get hers. The shoes just fit for Jennifer, so she wears it. Of course this help us a lot, no one notices to dress in Chinese way or not. Everybody are very busy for get food, have not money to buy clothes. That is the good way for help. Thank you again very much.

"I hate to hear perhaps you want to go, darling. If you go, I don't want something. But, please remember me, my old dear.

"Yes, a lot of doctors and engineers went to Northeast. Mr. & Mrs. Chang (my friend remember?) with their children went to Peking. Mr. Chang is a engineer.

"I am so busy my dear. I cannot write more longer now. Love to you all. Regards to the Days and Cunninghams. Please write me soon."

☐ *JUNE 3RD:* These public apologies are something else. Mr. Wang, the head of one of the dormitories, discharged a servant the other day, not realizing that before doing so one must now notify the police. Apparently, there had been an announcement in the paper about this. In consequence, this reputable, very nice citizen was hauled in, insulted at length, grilled and finally was made to write that he had been told about the new ruling, had read it many times, but even so had disobeyed deliberately and had failed to support the government, etc., that he was very, very sorry and would never do it again! Well, just as he was finishing, Canning Yang was hauled in for the same offence. Canning thanked Wang for writing his apology for him. He would simply copy it and avoid all argument!

We heard yesterday that all American citizens will have to be out by September. I wonder.

In the evening we went to a wonderful party at Clarence's. He and his friend, Art Stupee, who was a cook in the American army, put it on. They really went to town with a smorgasbord of ham, bologna, chicken, potato salad, sardines, duck and countless other dishes, all wonderful. Clarence was dressed in white trousers and black coat and Stupee in a scarlet mess jacket. We found our partners by matching lines of Robbie Burn's poetry. The menu was a masterpiece in French, Latin, German, Greek and Chinese. I shall keep it.

☐ *JUNE 5TH:* Marg Day and I took rickshaws into the city to see about buying American-made velvet which is now selling at bargain prices. We found the Great South Street only half open for traffic, the other part lined solidly with old men, women and children breaking hard river rock to give the street a new bed. And outside the West Gate, we saw a chain gang of former Nationalist generals, important officials and gentry also breaking rock.

At the Hospital, the students say they are not going to write exams. They probably won't as they in effect control the new University Council.

During the last few days, volunteers from our Hospital have gone out to help the provincial authorities give cholera inoculations in the countryside. These are now compulsory and soon everyone will have to carry a vaccination card signed by a reputable doctor. Also mandatory under the new regime is the inoculation of cattle against anthrax and rinderpest.

□ *JUNE 10TH:* Katharine Hockin (Lily's daughter), who comes out each week to campus, had supper with us last night. She was born in China and teaches at the Middle School level where they are up against their own version of all the new problems we are experiencing in teacher-student relations and government control. Although hers is a Christian school, the study of Christianity is no longer compulsory and considerable peer pressure is being put on the Christian pupils not to attend religious classes.

We went to a cocktail dance at Harry Simons' place on the 8th to celebrate the King's birthday. I wish he could have seen us standing at attention, drinking to his health while the piano (very out of tune and badly played) drummed out "God Save the King." The irony of our situation here came so close to home I had difficulty suppressing my tears. Harry is an Englishman working on ancient Chinese drama, music and poetry. He is very keen and a nice person. He takes out a little Chinese girl, the former wife of the Nationalist ambassador to Belgium.

□ *JUNE 22ND:* We have been somewhat upset by reports that the Church here has been ordered to cut itself off from abroad, both in support and personnel. No foreigner is going to be given a re-entry permit. As our terms end, we will leave China and our work behind. I suppose we cannot, consciously or unconsciously, but be "agents" for our individual countries so far as disseminating our culture is concerned, which apparently alarms the present government. Following a meeting between

Chou En-lai and our leading Churchmen, a "Manifesto on the Direction of the Work of Chinese Christianity" was issued in the names of Y. T. Wu, Cora Den, Y. C. Tu, H. H. Tsui, etc., which reads in part, "Christian churches and organizations in China should exert their utmost efforts, and employ effective methods, to make people in the Churches everywhere recognize clearly the evils which have been wrought in China by imperialism. . . . Christian churches and organizations in China should take effective measures to cultivate a patriotic and democratic spirit among their adherents in general, as well as a psychology of self-respect and self-reliance. . . . At the same time, self-criticism should be advocated, all forms of Christian activity re-examined and readjusted, and thorough-going austerity measures adopted, so as to achieve the goals of a reformation in the Church."

□ *JUNE 23RD:* Today, Ralph's book came off the press. He had his last class with the Fourth Year and presented each of them with a copy.

There was a farewell tea at Jean Kilborn's in honor of the first graduate of our Nursing School who is retiring after more than thirty years of truly devoted service. She was presented with approximately $100 (American). We all shared in providing the food and everyone had a good time. Among the many speeches made, Cora Kilborn's was outstanding. (Cora, Leslie's sister, is an RN and herself has been on Faculty since 1922.)

Clarence told us of Stupee's latest classic. The city Baptist Church, a lovely little Chinese building with exquisite lattice, has among its congregation two mental cases, one an epileptic, the most faithful in its flock. Stupee has been turning out for Service every Sunday. When someone asked him why, he replied, "I wouldn't miss it for anything. It's the best floorshow in town!" He is so different from the rest of us out here, a footnote is probably in order. Stupee, a former American GI, made a bundle playing poker because of a particular "dextcrity" with cards. Apparently, he saved every dollar he won until he had enough to go AWOL. He finally made his way to Chengtu, where he sort of dropped in on the foreign community. He wanted to study medicine here, but could not meet the entrance requirements. So, to make money, he got a job at the government Obstetrical School teaching Chinese nurses gynecological and obstetrical English! At the moment he claims to be falling in love with Mary Kilborn, Leslie's daughter and herself an RN, but is being sued for breach of promise by a couple of Chinese girls. A real character!

☐ *JUNE 26TH:* The Sunday Service yesterday was the last before the gang starts to break up. Dryden led it and did so beautifully, but when he announced with reference to Christ and His disciples in the storm on the Sea of Galilee, "that all their vested interest was in the equilibrium of a rocking boat," Ralph nudged me so hard, I almost choked. That evening, however, none of us were listening to the radio, so we missed the news of North Korea invading the South!

Today there has been little talk of anything else. We have been holding our breaths wondering what such an outbreak may mean for us. It has a very nasty potential.

☐ *JUNE 29TH:* This morning we heard President Truman's speech and his announcement that the 7th Fleet is going to Formosa to preserve the *status quo* and that the American Air Force is fighting in Korea. This started a proper flap.

Clarence takes a very serious view of things and thinks we should leave immediately. The problem is we cannot leave without a visa or permit. And while I recognize that we will be in a very uncomfortable spot indeed if the fighting turns into a world conflagration, I can't help feeling optimistic, although there are few others who do.

Our gateman is out nearly half of every day getting indoctrinated. I think Communists must be a bit like my grandmother of whom Mother once said in a fit of exasperation over not being able to hear anything over the radio on Sunday but sermons, "Some people seem to require an extra amount of Church to keep them good"!

Chiang Si says the Chinese newspapers claim that North Korea has already overrun the South. We listened to a Moscow broadcast which, naturally, seemed to confirm this. Margie Day has started to pack.

□ *JUNE 30TH:* So much has happened today, I had better take things in order. Breakfast on the screened porch, with sunshine streaming through the ivy and the children gently bickering. Ralph off to work. Then the police arrived to deliver our exit permit. Chiang Si translated it for me and was rather a dear, for he looked as though he would weep. I immediately sent it over to Ralph as we had to report this morning and I knew he would need time to think. After I cleared up the household messes, fed the cats and let the rabbit out into the garden, I biked over to Jean Kilborn's. She was in the depths of despair over something Bee Mullett had let slip. Bee, still smarting from Gladys' suggestion yesterday that she was "too old" to be of any further use here and should be going home, had gone over to Jean's for sympathy. Apparently, in course of their conversation, Bee said that Gladys had never forgiven her for encouraging Jean's marriage to Leslie in 1947 (Dr. Janet died of coronary occlusion in 1945) and that Gladys' friendship was only pretended. There is a fair amount of truth in all this, but it set Jean into a tailspin, which is dangerous because she has had two nervous breakdowns already! So I took her in tow for the rest of the morning.

While I was doing this, Ralph and Bert Yang were at the Foreign Office, where they were very courteously received by Mr. Wang, the official who interviewed me for my residence permit. Bert explained it would seriously embarrass the surgical wards if Ralph were to leave when there is so much work piled up, and that it would take some time to break in a successor. Mr. Wang was sympathetic and put our permit aside for the time being.

□ *JULY 2ND:* Margie Day and I spent the morning, or part of it, fooling around Jade Street to see if we could find a nice piece reasonably priced. She did. I am harder to please. One of the *ku dong* (antique) dealers brought around something he called emeralds not so long ago, wanting fabulous prices, but they were beautiful and exactly the color I look for in jade. Perhaps it is emeralds I like after all.

Ronald and Stella Sung and Dorothy and Edward Dzen came for lunch yesterday. We had a lot of fun, wonderful food. Ronald is going to a conference in Peking shortly, along with other representatives of our medical school. He is a plastic surgeon. Dorothy is going as well. While Alf Day is officially in charge, she practically runs the Mission Press and has not been away for years and years so is taking this opportunity. They suggest we send the children home. Wish we could.

The Baptists are getting their Missionaries out of the small Stations. Clarence plans to accompany them home and feels very strongly we should do the same.

Jean Roland who is visiting for a few days from Jian Yang, a distance of about forty miles, has the words "VERY DANGEROUS SPY" stamped on her papers. She not only looks like an angel, but is one.

Our gateman is being very quiet, but we hear he is now one of the leaders in the servants' union. He is off most of the time, but is more polite. Yesterday, when we were entertaining our friends, however, I noticed him slip beneath the dining room window to listen in. Fortunately, we were speaking English, not that we were discussing anything more than flowers and food. Golly, there is so much commendable about this régime, but how can the good survive when there is so much hatred and suspicion?

A little friend of ours told us people were being executed for spreading news of the North Korean reverses. I don't believe it! But I do know the local papers and "The Voice of America" are completely opposite in their reports.

□ *JULY 8TH:* I wish we were going home. The Meusers have gone. The Days are packing. And the Newcombs have requested exit permits (Fran is pregnant and if she doesn't travel soon, she can't unless her obstetrician goes with her). Ralph did an intussesception on Patsy, their little girl, a while ago and she is threatening another.

Today, there was a meeting of the Canadian School Board, at which it was decided to turn over the buildings and land to the University and dispose of the furnishings. This will be done at a terrific financial loss. However, there is a lot of feeling against foreigners (damn that word!) having property. All our houses will shortly be filled with our Chinese colleagues, which is a good thing.

There are anti-American demonstrations and processions in the city today. I, however, have heard so much anti-American propaganda lately that I'm fed to the teeth with it. Coincidentally, our department of Western Languages is to be abolished. In other words, English is out and Russian is in.

□ *JULY 9TH:* Last night, Harry Simons, Jane Chen, Clarence, Mary K. and Dave Gidman came in for bridge. The snacks were lousy. Chiang Si has a mad on. Probably, all the anti-American propaganda is breaking down his confidence in us. I don't know.

I took the children out for an early morning walk and we were lucky enough to see the Snow Mountains of Tibet in the distance. This is possible only a very few times each year when the air is particularly clear. Then Marg and I went to Church. It was Baccalaureate Sunday. The whole Service, hymns, readings, etc., centered on the idea of the responsibilities of the intellectual Christian. It was truly thrilling. The gymnasium was full and everyone seemed to enter into the spirit of the occasion. The norm is to present each graduate the gift of a Bible. This year, each received a letter asking if he or she would like one. Two hundred of our three hundred and fifteen graduates answered in the affirmative.

□ *JULY 18TH:* Another letter in from Banyang, dated July 13th:

"Dearest Margaret:

"Your kind letter arrived yesterday.

"The carrier came to Chengtu before yesterday. I told him I want to send you a little thing, and he had come to my home. But I was in school, did not meet me, and the next early morning, he had gone!

"Thank you very very much that you are worry about us. And wish to help us. We are a little better now, and the famine of all the people is going almost to be over. The new rice are coming out in the field. And the government is selling old rice very cheaply. And we sell some of old things that Robert's father and grandparents had used. You know Robert's ancestors are country people. They had a lot of cloth clothes which Lo Ti Ti keeps them very carefully.

"Margaret dear! please don't return the jade ring, that is the remembrance of your special birthday (forty years old). If you return to me, that means you want to leave or stop our friendship, so never return it, my dear! You must keep it to remember me! And I hope we will send you more when you are fifty years old.

"The Hsus are all well. They are much better than us, because they are not wealthy, so they can do very good to us. You know 'Kuo Ti Ti' 'Chang Se Ti' 'Lan Ti Ti' . . ., etc. They are the same like us and we can not help each other.

"I am also writing to the carrier, and ask him to come to get the things that you want to give me when he leaves Chengtu, about a few days after.

"Yes! It is the good way to send some powdered milk to help the children. I need soap too, have you some? And what you want to give me. Please don't send too much once, wait to the next time or the other best way. You may send some to try first, this is not very cheap dear.

"The children are all well. I never think they are so easy to feed, for you know they were so spoiled and change to the hard time.

"I am very happy. I am thinner and look nicer, and I am free now.

"Love to you all as always."

☐ *JULY 22ND:* The servants told us we had so many people coming and going in our compound, we were again under suspicion as spies. Indeed, last night after our weiner roast, they had been taken separately and questioned about us. I told them next time to please invite the authorities in to search the place.

I have prepared two large boxes about the size of steamer trunks full of lovely woolens and used but not worn out clothes to send down to Banyang.

☐ *JULY 23RD:* We got up at 6:30 this morning to see off the Crawfords, the Liljestrands, Walter Small, Miss Clare, Cora Kilborn, Ruth West and Lillian Taylor. And last night we went to a farewell feast for the Days and the Newcombs.

☐ *JULY 24TH:* Carol got so fed up today at being asked to pick up her things she told me she was leaving home. In five minutes she was back, tears streaming down her face, asking me to forgive her. She is a darling kid.

We were talking today about how the Christian Church throughout history has survived periods of stress and challenge. In the Soviet Union, when Churches were converted into dance halls and clubs, people came on Sunday mornings to worship nevertheless, even if they had to kneel in the street outside to do so. In North China, we hear there is a growing movement called the *Chi Tu Jia Tin* or "Jesus Homes." Groups of five or six or ten Christian families join to form a sort of communal cooperative. They pool their incomes and energies, help one another in every way possible and meet for worship in one another's homes. As one Chinese friend said about the Communists, "They can never reach our hearts."

Next week begins a month of indoctrination classes, when 7,000 middle school students arrive to camp in the University buildings.

☐ *JULY 27TH:* Today has been one incredible rush. We are torn about going home. Ralph feels that if he could just spend a little more time with Stephen Shen, the future of his orthopædic work would be secure. We, however, may have to leave regardless. There are three considerations: 1) the international crisis, 2) the internal attitude toward foreigners and 3) the children's schooling (their teacher has applied for an exit permit).

In relation to the latter, Ralph took the girls aside and talked to them about the possibility of their spending the next year in Spokane with Connie and Clarence and their three boys. After which he said, "The decision is not up to you girls, but we don't want to proceed without knowing just how you feel. I would like you to think about it, talk it over for a while and then let us know." Later, Judy came to me and said, "Mother, we have weighed all the pros and cons and have come to the conclusion that we would like to go. Of course there are certain advantages and certain disadvantages. For instance, one advantage is that we would not have to take medicine all the time. Also we could walk in bare feet and not be afraid of hookworm. The disadvantage would be that we would miss you and Dad very much."

☐ *JULY 30TH:* A quiet, hot Sunday morning. The last couple of days have been madly busy getting the Days packed and ready. Their house is a complete shambles of good furniture, stuff scattered all over and really a terrific amount of useful *tza tza* (miscellany) for anyone who takes the trouble to pick it up. "Frik," their lovely police dog, an offspring of Lady, is disconsolate and forgotten. We are taking her until a suitable new home can be found.

Poor Calvin Bright is on the carpet at the Museum where he has been working like a Trojan for the last year or so, getting its many thousand pieces in order, filing, cataloguing and generally handling everything well. He has had to keep close watch on its treasures and has tried not to antagonize any of his Chinese workmates. He was born in China and has spent a lifetime specializing in Chinese history and the artifacts of its various dynasties. However, a couple of the Museum staff have whispered that some precious items have gone missing and this is being taken up by the authorities. Yesterday, at one of the Lindsays' wonderful Chinese feasts, I heard Dryden Phelps making deprecating remarks about Calvin's knowledge. I went to his defence and discovered a Dryden I had never known before. He was despotic and unfair. It was very disillusioning. Calvin accepted work at the Museum on a half-time basis as a favor to the University. He is a Bishop in the Church of the Brethren and here to do Mission-related work. What is more, attempting to straighten out the mess Dan Dye left on retirement took all his leisure time as well. Consequently, had he not done a good job, which he has, even had he been terribly misinformed about everything, which he has not, criticism is not merited, for he is the most modest of men and one of the most helpful!

There is a glorious full moon tonight and the campus is alive with strolling bands of middle school students singing Party songs.

☐ *AUGUST 8TH:* I have been too busy to write letters or diary. As usual, life proceeds apace with never a dull moment. We have decided to send the girls to Spokane, but as Clarence has yet to receive his exit permit, this gives me time to get all their things in order for school.

As I write, Jean, Leslie, Clarence and Ralph are playing bridge in the living room. It is the first day of Fall, according to the Chinese calendar, and it seems a little cooler in the mornings and evenings. Even so, it runs well over 90 degrees during the day. The news of Calvin's difficulties broke today and even the servants are discussing him. It is so unfair!

☐ *AUGUST 10TH:* The case Ralph is working on tonight is a woman of fifty-two who felt she could not carry on and jumped off the Marco Polo Bridge, but unfortunately survived.

Earlier, when I was at the University gate waiting on my bike for the kids to catch up in their rickshaw, a Communist guard started asking questions about Canada. Bystanders joined in. They wanted to know if Canada was the same as America (which is now anathema). I said no, we were just good friends.

☐ *AUGUST 14TH:* This morning I had breakfast in bed attended by a loving husband. (My back went on the blink again.) But when Chiang Si arrived with a pot of hot coffee Ralph somehow tipped it over. A generous amount ran between our twin beds and through the wide spaced floor boards. The children were eating immediately below and when Ralph shouted a warning, Judy yelled back, "Yes Dad, it is coming through. Do you want me to save it?"

Chiang Ta-yea has been causing more trouble. As I've mentioned, he simply walks off whenever it suits him, with never a by your leave. A gateman is supposed to watch the gate, deliver messages, do the odd chore and keep the garden in order. Besides, whenever I speak to him about anything, his face contorts with rage. And this despite all we have done for him, including saving his son's life. We hope to relieve him of his job at the end of the month. Even with paying him an extra three months wages, he may try to take me to the People's Court. But he has gotten on my nerves so badly, the other night I dreamt he killed Ralph and Kerry and only by Clarence's maneuvering were the rest of us saved.

□ *AUGUST 20TH:* I hear the land reform program in Szechwan is to begin shortly. I believe the Communists are counting on this to consolidate the support of the peasants who constitute 85 per cent of the population. As one of the indoctrination class leaders said the other day, "This may take a few years, but after it has been accomplished, we may look forward to a hundred years of peace."

□ *AUGUST 24TH:* Ralph received letters from some of his graduates who have gone to work at hospitals in the Northeast. They find the equipment wonderful, but standards low and reading material in English nil. (We hear that there is now an agent in Hong Kong buying up all the English texts he can find for use in these institutions.) One of these lads ended his letter with, "I need your help and encouragement in the future and I need your kindness to teach me either by letter or your newly printed book. Your book gave me a lot of help. I want to preserve it as my most delicious thing."

□ *AUGUST 27TH:* The China Inland Mission has sent word to their people to remain no matter what. If they pull out, it will be on the understanding they pay their own passage home and consider themselves no longer Missionaries. No one else has taken this position, except of course, the Catholics.

☐ *AUGUST 28TH:* A further word about the Mukden Medical Center from one of our boys. He says they do not use gloves when operating and that the same holds for obstetrical work. The women are delivered squatting on a very high chair with the doctor standing below!

☐ *AUGUST 29TH:* Clarence and Dave Gunn in tonight for a game of bridge, Clarence very depressed. Dave was bucked up because at last, after eight months of negotiating and frustrations of every kind and description, he has been able to get off the load of drugs to Dr. Clow at their Sian Station. As the men loaded the trucks, they shouted "Up Mao Tse-tung," each time they heaved a heavy box.

The other day the Lindsays' cook died. The servants' portion of the Workers Union were canvassed to contribute towards a fund for his family. This is certainly a new thing and a very good one, a form of insurance in time of trouble. Previously, only the employer paid.

☐ *AUGUST 31ST:* This morning, one of my Chinese friends came in with a diamond ring she needed to sell to help pay taxes. I took her around to see Clarence who has been acting as a middleman to help people in great need. While there, he showed me a four-carat yellow diamond that is quite something. The Willmotts have offered $400 (American) for it as an investment, but feel that when the next round of taxation hits, they will be able to pick up better bargains. I hate this scavengering instinct on the part of our "worthy Communist brothers and sisters."

☐ *SEPTEMBER 8TH:* At last, detailed reports are back from the big National Health Conference in Peking (600 plus delegates, meeting over 13 days) which was held during the middle of last month to formulate policy for the future of medical and dental education in this country. Questions related to Missionary Hospitals, foreign funding, etc., were also discussed at length. It was generally recognized that our hospitals were well equipped and staffed and had contributed materially to the medical welfare of the Chinese people. It was urged that something be done to stop the political pressure on our institutions. After much discussion, it was accepted that the government had a definite responsibility towards us. Unfortunately, it will take some months for any official policy to be put into effect. In the meantime, several of our hospitals will close.

It is interesting that Norman Bethune, the Canadian doctor who served some 18 months with the Communist Eighth Route Army before he died of blood poisoning at Wupai Shan in Shansi province in November 1939, holds such a high place in the esteem of China's new leaders. He is almost worshipped. Indeed, at the conference in Peking, his picture was framed above the door of the main hall. There were a few who argued that many of the Missionary doctors had made far greater contributions to China than Bethune. Party spokesmen, however, disagreed. They consider all Missionaries to be the tools of imperialism and capitalism. Bethune, on the other hand, belonged not to Canada nor any other country but was "international," etc., etc.

☐ *SEPTEMBER 9TH:* Ralph has now had a chance to explain our personal difficulties to Clifford Tsao, saying we would be obliged to take the girls home ourselves unless Clarence got permission to leave within two weeks. He was very understanding and said he would speak to the University president.

☐ *SEPTEMBER 10TH:* The weather continues cool. I've spent a couple of days with a tummy upset.

Calvin's situation looks brighter today. They found enough of the missing stuff to satisfy the rest of the Museum staff.

Kerry's x-ray films are now completely negative.

☐ *SEPTEMBER 13TH:* Public show trials are becoming a regular feature of Chengtu life, as are arrests in the middle of the night and public executions. One never knows who will be next among one's Chinese friends. One of our University Admin. officers was dragged off two months ago and hasn't been heard of since.

We are just back from farewelling the Lindsays. This winds up forty-two years of service for Dr. Lindsay. Few are blessed with the opportunity of seeing so much accomplished before they die! Wherever he looks he can see the fruits of his labors— dental graduates scattered through every province in China and a dental college unsurpassed in this country. Yesterday, sitting through the formal tea in his honor, I thought of the man, his strength of character and the sheer dogged stubbornness which have carried him and the University through many a difficult period. A few years ago, Jim Endicott remarked that, come the turn over, the only thing that would save Ashley from being shot was his technical ability. Instead, this send-off which warmed my heart.

When I passed through the Medical Building today, a high ranking PLA officer was sitting in one of the dental chairs. Outside his cubicle stood three armed guards with bayonets fixed. I don't know what they expected, but they were ready for it.

□ *SEPTEMBER 14TH:* It was a lovely P.M., and about 5:30 Ralph and I strolled out into the countryside, meeting Clarence Vichert on our way. As we were walking, we saw Marion Manley coming from the cemetery where her sister is buried. She was very upset. She has had a dreadful time with the authorities and feels she can no longer carry on. She has spent practically all her life here, building up her school of midwifery and supporting it by writing plays and books.

The landlords have been ordered to refund their former tenants all the rental money ever collected. This assures the financial liquidation of what remains of the Szechwanese gentry. I don't know what the Hsiehs or Mr. Liu will do in the face of this.

□ *SEPTEMBER 17TH:* Gilbert Hsu arrived a couple of days ago and was in for lunch. He is in trouble. At a Junghsien teachers indoctrination meeting in July, one of those attending became ill and was taken to the Mission Hospital. To make a long story short, he died of respiratory paralysis. When Gilbert was called before the teachers to explain, he couldn't offer a definite diagnosis. A Communist officer then swore he had seen Gilbert give the patient poison and threatened to have Gilbert, Chloe and their three children shot unless he signed a paper confessing full responsibility for the death of this man. Gilbert signed. He also had to promise a written confession for publication in the local paper. As it turns out, what they now are demanding so discredits him that it would be impossible for him to continue practice. He managed to get permission to come up to Chengtu to explain the situation to the Mission executive. He says he will not go back and is waiting an opportunity to get his family out. The Hospital in Junghsien will probably have to close.

☐ *SEPTEMBER 20TH:* I used the fact the girls are returning home as an excuse to fire Chiang Ta-yea, but he wouldn't leave! Then I figured that since the Workers Union was taking all the prerogatives of the employer, they might as well have my headache as well. So I turned the whole thing over to them. They discussed it from every angle, with the police and a Communist Party representative present, and have now decided he must leave and that if he does not, he will never be allowed to hold another job around the University. I think this union is a fine thing.

☐ *SEPTEMBER 25TH:* A lot has happened this week and time seems to be suspended since we went out to the air office on Tuesday to see the children and Clarence off. I was very touched at the way the two girls supported and looked after one another. It augurs well for the future. With their very different personalities, it might have been that as they grew up they would grow apart. I am betting this experience will knit them together for their lifetimes, regardless of what fate has in store for them or the different paths their feet travel.

Gilbert Hsu is looking much happier. It seems a couple of government doctors happened through Junghsien shortly after he left. When informed of the allegations against him, they undertook a thorough investigation and found Gilbert had been done a great injustice. They since have submitted their report to the Communist party central district office. Things like this make one realize that very often we cannot see the forest for the trees and that petty officialdom, whatever its political stripe, is the curse of mankind.

☐ *SEPTEMBER 26TH:* It appears that the Communist indoctrination "schools" are pretty tough. I heard about one near Chung Lai which involves a three-year compulsory course for the sons and daughters of the wealthy and other former Nationalist supporters. They get up at 5 A.M. to begin a daily program that doesn't end until midnight. Sleep is bourgeois! Two meals a day are considered sufficient. I hate to think of the incidence of Tb in this group at the end of their sentence.

☐ *SEPTEMBER 29TH:* Ralph talked by telephone to the girls, who are in Chungking, waiting with Clarence to begin the next leg of their journey by air to Hankow. For those few of us left, we have started our own school, with each Mother teaching her own kids. We do this every morning from nine until twelve.

☐ *OCTOBER 1ST:* Today is the glorious first of October, the anniversary of the proclamation of the People's Republic of China in Peking last year, the biggest and best national holiday of them all. Already four days have been set aside for the festivities. Great was the general disappointment therefore when it rained last night and the paper flags, lanterns and decorations began to smudge and run. Ralph and I went into the city this evening to see the torchlight parade. The police on their elevated stands used megaphones to keep the pedestrians, the most aimless in the world, to the sides of the street. They did this courteously, however. And although there were soldiers armed with tommy-guns everywhere, they did nothing to interfere with the revellers. Nor was there comment on the fact that we were watching, despite a day of speeches cursing America.

☐ *OCTOBER 4TH:* Yesterday, Marion Manley, who is over sixty, was sent to jail for five days for removing a picture of Chairman Mao from the wall of her school (and making some glib remark in the process). This is her second offence. The original, some two months ago, was settled by a letter of apology in the press. Unfortunately, this time it's a totally bum rap. A disgruntled student set her up. Another case where an unbending personality caused bitterness! We have been advised a) not to make any public speeches, b) not to get into any arguments and c) never to be derogatory about any aspect of the New Order.

We received word Clarence and the girls should be in Hong Kong tomorrow.

☐ *OCTOBER 9TH:* Marion Manley got out of prison yesterday. Through a misunderstanding, she was handcuffed for a while, but otherwise treated fairly. There were twelve in her room. No furniture, but many Chinese sleep on the floor and she was allowed to take her bed roll. The food was adequate and they were allowed to keep clean, wash their clothes and do some jobs around the place. Compared with some of the jails I've heard about in China. . . !

I hope our affair with the gateman is settled. The Workers Union decided he should be given a three month bonus (which is now the custom when a servant is discharged) plus tea money amounting to $200,000. This is simply extortion, but I paid it at once (to the union).

☐ *OCTOBER 13TH:* The days are full to overflowing. Our morning school time is always broken by something and I am afraid Kerry will not make the proper or required progress.

Despite his exoneration, Gilbert Hsu has decided not to return to Junghsien. He was in this afternoon and stayed late into the evening. His wife, however, is not allowed to leave until the

Mission sends a doctor down to replace him. The Hsiehs cannot leave at all. The division of land will take place next year. If the now established custom is followed, the peasant farmers have the right to dispose of their former landlords (all of whom were executed around Sian or so I'm told). I fear the worst for Banyang.

There was no unpleasantness about residence certificate renewals. Ours is for a year. Non-medical personnel, such as teachers and preachers, are for only six months, except for the Willmotts, Phelps and Sewells, whose permits are also for a year. Of our Protestant group, there are about 63 left as compared with 200 in 1949.

Chiang Ta-yea has finally moved off the place. Left the day before yesterday and actually cleaned up after himself! Poor guy, for all his meanness, I felt sorry for him, for he got an attack of malaria that morning and was awfully sick to his tummy. We gave him a course of medication. I was going to keep him here the night to make certain he was alright, but Chiang Si took me aside and told me he would be far better off in his new home. The garden has perked up and everyone in the house seems happy for a change.

☐ *OCTOBER 22ND:* It has been a good day, evening now, and supper is being spread in front of the living room fire. Kerry is whooping it up in his bath. Through the fading light, I see sheaves of cosmos in the garden and just outside my window a bed of red roses in bloom. Chrysanthemums half out are already blending their autumn spiciness to the garden perfumes. And leaves are beginning to fall from the young plane tree by our sleeping porch.

This morning, John Kitchen, who has taken over Alf Day's job at the Mission Press, came in. He says he has been followed and spied on for several months, but only realized it lately (and he an inveterate reader of whodunits!). Secret police enter his home or the Press at odd hours, looking for goodness knows what, he is never told. He has been asked questions like, "What were you doing at so and so's house last July 5th?" A Chinese, with whom he has worked for twenty-five years, is under suspicion because occasionally they had a spot of tea together. Now, they dare hardly speak.

☐ *OCTOBER 28TH:* A letter in from Banyang sounds quite optimistic. She has "made good with the new Government" and is working hard at her school. Old Mr. Liu, her father, is dying of Tb and is now at home. She says so little, I have to wonder what their situation really is.

I am told the five stars on the Communist flag represent farmers, laborers, petit-bourgeoisie, national capitalists and the Party. The national capitalists are a small group of industrialists. Because the country cannot get along without them, they are accepted and allowed to live in luxury. In this province, most of the wealthy put their money into land.

Omar Walmsley's picture is in the Shanghai papers among a group of foreigners come to help China celebrate her October 1st holiday. He was representing Canadian youth.

☐ *OCTOBER 31ST:* This afternoon, I attended a meeting called by members of the Chinese Church here to explain the stand of those who signed last June's Manifesto. In some ways the effort was pathetic. And yet, I wonder if I would not be the same in a similar situation. They are desperately trying to trim Christianity to fit the government's policy and it seems they are having to do some tall rationalizing. They speak of making the Church self-supporting but claim the Manifesto does not mean quite what it says and that foreign funds must be continued! However, their "objective" must be self-support. They have jumped on the bandwagon in decrying "imperialism" and say it must be eradicated from the Church. One hears this cry daily. When you ask for a definition of imperialism, however (what is it, where is it found in the Church—bring it out so we can know and get rid of it), they cannot answer. They cite the Church's connection with the Unequal Treaties of the last century, but that is long passed, thank heaven! They talk about the use of funds, personnel, etc., by one country to force its aims on another. If this was so, it certainly cannot be said of the Church here today. Wallace Wong got up and gave as his example the Missionary who, when visited by a Chinese at lunch time, insists his guest wait while he finishes his meal. Well, this properly may be described as rudeness or discourtesy in any country, but "imperialism?" When asked if it would not then be better for the Chinese Church if we much-resented foreigners withdrew, they strongly urged us to stay. Ironically, just as it was being pointed out that Bill Arnup had been advised not to hold the Medical Journal Club meeting at his house lest it be wrongly interpreted, a policeman arrived to disperse us for not having a permit for our gathering!

☐ *NOVEMBER 1ST:* Dryden Phelps, Bill Sewell and Earl Willmott all tried to join the Workers Union at the University. Bill and Earl were accepted, but not Dryden. When he asked why, he was told preachers belong to the same class as "soothsayers and fortune-tellers"!

☐ *NOVEMBER 3RD:* It is about eleven o'clock and Leslie and Jean have just left after a couple of rubbers of bridge. Very pleasant. Finished up with coffee and chopped-egg sandwiches.

The world news doesn't sound very encouraging, what with the attempt on President Truman's life and Chinese "volunteers" fighting in Korea. Should China become an "official" combatant, we are likely to be arrested immediately and interned as "enemy aliens"! Locally, the paper gave prominence to a diatribe against the Missionaries by the younger brother of Helen Yoh (one of our faculty colleagues), labelling us spies and goodness knows what else. Helen is feeling pretty low about this.

Our coolie, Chiang Si's elder brother, leaves the house every evening at seven for night school. I suppose he is studying politics as well, but the fact is that for the first time all servants can go to classes to improve themselves and are encouraged to do so. This is one of the exeedingly fine things this government has done.

Now, not only are we obliged to obtain a permit to hold a meeting of any kind, but foreigners can no longer attend Chinese meetings without special permission from the police.

□ *NOVEMBER 6TH:* We had just received word, on good authority, that the government's attitude toward foreigners was hardening further, when Dr. Li Hen slipped in to see us. After the usual exchange of courtesies, I excused myself realizing this was not a social call. He begged Ralph to get us out as quickly as possible. He too had heard the news and sensed a rising anti-foreign hysteria all around us. (In similar times past, especially during the Boxer Rebellion and the Civil War period of the 1920s, some rather nasty things happened to Westerners who were not evacuated.) Nevertheless, Ralph and I thought, before we decided one way or the other, that he should talk things over with Bert Yang and Clifford Tsao, both of whom are very good friends. Each agreed the time to leave had come. Dean Tsao then and there wrote a letter to the Foreign Office releasing Ralph from his duties at the University.

□ *NOVEMBER 10TH:* To our utter surprise, permission to start proceedings to leave came through yesterday. We began immediately to advertise our departure. Under present regulations, this must be done five times so that anyone who wants to *gow* (make a claim or lay a charge against) us can do so. The problem is that the newspaper will not guarantee to run the ad. in consecutive issues. Consequently, we may not know until the last minute whether we will be allowed to leave or not because, if someone does *gow* us, the matter will have to be thoroughly investigated and settled in the People's Court. (Calvin Bright to date has been held up for more than six months, with no resolution in sight.) In addition, Ralph has had to obtain the necessary shop guarantee (a merchant who will pay any claims against us after our departure) and a clearance from the bank. As to the sale of our household things, we have decided to put this entirely in Chiang Si's hands and hope for the best.

☐ *NOVEMBER 14TH:* We are holding our breaths. The feeling against foreigners mounts with each passing day. We hear that Olin Stockwell has been jailed in Chungking on trumped up charges. Only the dearest (and bravest) of our friends dare do anything to help, among them Ronald and Stella Sung and, of course, the Li Hens, who sneak over at night to try and help me with the packing. Others slip in with messages or letters for us to take out. Unfortunately, we have had to turn down those who want us to deposit money for them in the U.S. We could never get it past the personal searches and baggage checks en route.

Posters are up around campus that the foreign gifts of hospitals, teaching institutions, etc., are but a very clever plot to control the life and thought of the Chinese by American imperialists, through the agency of "foreign barbarians" like us, each of whom is a spy school graduate! The West and the Church are vilified by the most abominable accusations and in caricatures of Cross-carrying Missionaries with horrible faces distorted by avarice and carnal desire! Even Earl Wilmott is accused of being a hypocrite, of preaching Communism but living the life of a petit-bourgeois. Only the Cunninghams and ourselves have so far escaped personal calumny.

☐ *NOVEMBER 16TH:* Dave Gunn and a couple of other foreigners drafted a manifesto to be presented to the Foreign Office for publication in the local press stating our position as non-political and offering the government every aid the Western community here might render it. We hesitated, but signed. The Foreign Office received this politely. We shall see if they publish it.

Some of Ralph's students have started to cut him in the halls, even a few of the staff doctors. And when I ran into one of the servants' daughters for whom I had solicited a job and for whom I had interceded when she was about to be fired, my greeting to this child was met with the frozen gaze of hatred.

I am afraid to write to Banyang lest I increase her problems by bringing our friendship to the attention of the authorities.

☐ *NOVEMBER 18TH:* Calvin came over this morning greatly upset. He said, "Come into the garden and pretend to be discussing plants while I tell you something important." Of course, I did as he suggested. He then continued, "Don't ask me my source, but last night at a University student meeting, Rosalie Den was asked to testify against you, to name an example of imperialism as demonstrated by the Outerbridges." Rosalie is the needy medical student we hired to help our girls with their Chinese language studies, and for the last month, she's come to take Kerry for walks, stayed for the odd meal and so on. According to Calvin's informant, she said she asked Judith and Carol why they were going home to America and they replied that their Mother and Daddy "do not like Communists" and that they were going home "until the Generalissimo comes back"! If we are charged over this, we won't be going home for some time.

☐ *NOVEMBER 20TH:* So far nothing has come of Rosalie's tales out of school. We can only hope Ralph is sufficiently liked by those who count to have this nonsense squelched. The Fifth Year Med and Dental students, including our old friend Gordon Chiang (the Hospital Registrar in Junghsien and now in his final year in Dentistry), managed to put on a simple farewell for us tonight. And most of them attended. We had a plain meal, played some games, but very little was said. Nevertheless, it was a good brave effort on their part and I for one shan't forget it! They really seem to love Ralph, as by jingo they ought! I suppose even the most rabidly anti-foreign among them paid him a compliment of sorts when they demanded he not be allowed to leave until he had finished his lectures for the year, which has necessitated three times his normal teaching load.

☐ *NOVEMBER 22ND:* We are scheduled to fly to Chungking on the 28th, but only two of our newspaper announcements have appeared. So far as we know we have no enemies to *gow* us, other than our ex-gateman and we have stuffed his big mouth with money. The only other possibility is a patient whose leg Ralph had to amputate. To forestall any attempt by Party zealots to put her up to mischief, Ralph dispatched one of his two loyal residents to her home with money to pay for the artificial limb now under construction at the University machine shop (the first to be made in Chengtu I think). So that is that, I hope.

□ *NOVEMBER 24TH:* With only four days to go, the tension is almost unbearable. It is like walking through an unmarked minefield. Earlier today, Ralph did a spinal fusion on a young woman, allegedly the wife of a senior Communist official, who was suffering from Tb spine. Because this patient has not been in hospital long enough for the course of antituberculosis medication to achieve sufficient remission in the activity of her disease, she was considered a very poor risk indeed. Her "husband," however, was adamant Ralph go ahead. And when his demands at the Hospital yielded no result, he came around to the house literally to beg Ralph to operate before we left for home, as none of our residents has ever attempted this procedure. I wondered at the time why, given his Party rank, he could not have arranged an air flight to the Peking Union Medical College for his "wife" early in the New Year when her chances would have been greatly improved. In any event, Ralph finally yielded to his pleas and accepted his assurances that he personally would assume all responsibility should the operation not be a success. Only later did we begin to think Ralph was walking into the lions' den. If she died (and it seemed on sober second thought that the calculation here was that she probably would), Ralph likely would be subjected to a lengthy show trial before the People's Courts, where his character and professional reputation would be ripped to shreds by Party prosecutors determined to destroy such public esteem as we Missionaries have left. No verdict other than guilty could be expected and years of imprisonment would follow. Only by the Grace of God have we escaped this fate! The fact is that the patient almost died before the surgery began due to what, all reports and suspicions to the contrary, we are prepared to believe was a genuine error by one of the residents with the rather tricky and very dangerous chloroform-ether combination we are forced for reasons of economy to use for anæsthetic. When Ralph, after scrubbing up, checked to see what stage she was in, she had entered the fourth and was about to breathe her last. They got her back through artificial respiration, but it was a near thing. The operation itself, I am relieved to report, went off without a hitch.

This afternoon, in desperation, we sent our poor coolie around to the newspaper office with Ralph's card as a gentle reminder about our ads. *Ai yah*, what an uproar! He told us the manager of the paper spent a good half hour calling him names for being a foreign slave. Nothing seems to augur well.

☐ *NOVEMBER 26TH:* These last few days have been complicated by the fact Ralph had promised the Music Department he would put on a recital before leaving. They advanced the schedule to accommodate our departure and this evening, he, with Peggy Phelps at the piano, put on a darned good, well-attended show. Someone tried to make it a little less enjoyable by running a noisy machine in the vicinity, but this was ignored and the evening passed without mishap.

☐ *NOVEMBER 27TH:* Excluding our fridge and generator, which we sold to the University's Biology Department, our net receipts from the sale of all our furniture and household effects is a mere $60 American, which represents at least a thousand dollar loss. In addition, I've had to write off about $200 American in canned foods and staples. It's too bad there isn't insurance for this sort of thing. Then, I engaged a painter to do over the kitchen, bathroom and john so the house would look its best. The boys went over all the woodwork, dusted down all the walls and the attic is clean as a whistle for the first time in its history. I wasn't going to have those damn Communists coming in and saying, in addition to everything else, "Those *dirty* foreigners!"

☐ *NOVEMBER 28TH:* Our final notice of departure appeared in the newspaper yesterday and we left our barren house to spend our last night in Chengtu at Kay Willmott's, where we had a small farewell dinner of roast squab with all the trimmings.

And today, we are homeward bound. At the Air Office in Chungking, a soldier tried to create an incident by asking Kerry to agree the Communists were "bad" people. But bless his six-year-old heart, he had learned from our experience with Rosalie and replied, "No, I like them. They are fun!"

As I wrote to Judy and Carol, "The only time I wept was when I had to say good-bye to our dog Lady. We sent her to Dr. Bert Yang's place. Aunt Dorothy Chiu and Uncle Edward are living with them so they will help look after her, and Mrs. Li Hen will call to see her once a week and bring her cookies. So I think I can lay down my heart." *Fang hsin lo.*

E P I L O G U E

In truth, Margaret's heart was hung up when she left Cheng-tu. So it would remain. For although she had reason to fear the worst, she did not know what fate had befallen Banyang.

Among the various unconfirmed reports drifting out of Sichuan was one in a letter dated February 22nd, 1951, from Dr. Gladys Cunningham, who had arrived in Hong Kong with a party of West China Missionaries two days earlier, that Banyang's father had been shot and others of their acquaintance tortured and killed. "The Hsiehs," she continued, "were reported when last we heard to be in grave danger of death, so we do not know how it is with them." In other news, she reported Stewart Allen had joined Olin Stockwell in prison in Chung-king; Marion Manley was having more difficulties with the authorities; Earl Willmott had been forced to write a letter of public apology for having a cache of American currency; Calvin Bright had been arrested and put to breaking rock and study "to get his thoughts corrected"; and, generally, all foreigners (Dryden Phelps included) were now being "treated as criminals" by the Communist Military Commission which had taken over the wcuu campus on January 5th.

If, when still in Chengtu, Margaret had deemed it inadvisable to write to Banyang, to do so now would have amounted to irresponsibility. Indeed, returned Missionaries were admonished in Church newsletters "NOT to write to any Chinese in China," lest the very people they were concerned about be placed in jeopardy (double jeopardy if these were already identified as Christian brothers and sisters or belonging to some other "reactionary" class). Margaret could only hope that someone else would bring out news.

On August 5th, 1951, Margaret Brown, who ran the Church Guest House in Hong Kong, wrote Margaret that she had just been told by Florence Fee (one of the long-time Woman's Missionary Society workers from Junghsien) that Robert Hsieh had been executed and Banyang "arrested . . . still in prison and the children . . . starving on the streets."

Following the formal (as opposed to *de facto*) takeover of West China Union University by the Communist government on October 5th, 1951, the few remaining foreigners on faculty had their contracts cancelled and departed. The last of the Missionaries *per se* would not be far behind. Then the Bamboo Curtain closed. There would be no further word from Junghsien.

In the meantime, the Outerbridges settled just outside Vancouver, in New Westminster, where Ralph began a very successful practice as an orthopædic surgeon. Finally, Margaret would have her beautiful home, prized possessions and elegant clothes. Likewise would her children mature and prosper, each graduating in her or his chosen field: Judy in social work, Carol in nursing and Kerry in medicine. In due course, grandchildren would grace Margaret's world. Yet, she could never again be as she once might have been. She continued to pray (and perhaps believe) that somehow, somewhere, Banyang survived in more than loving memory. And this despite all "evidence" to the contrary, including news reports, again unconfirmed, that executions of the former gentry in China continued en masse. Only on January 10th, 1984, did her worry cease. This was the day Margaret Outerbridge died. It has since been established that

Hsieh *tai tai* preceded her by twenty-two years.

We also now know that in 1962, one of Banyang's sisters arranged for the Hsieh girls to get a fresh start in life in a commune outside Xi'an in Shaanxi province. As to Banyang's circumstances in those last years of her life, especially after the death of her much cherished son, "Ralph," aged fifteen, in 1961, we have no knowledge. Her eldest daughter, Hong-di (Jennifer) died in 1967, aged twenty-eight, leaving two children, a son and daughter. Ying-di (Marilyn), Hua-di (Margaret) and Huei-di (Dora-ann) survive.

Ralph, of course, did not discover any of these facts, despite repeated enquiries after the "thaw" in China's relations with the West in the late 1970s, until 1986, when he, Judy, Carol, Kerry and Judy's husband, Evan Walker (a prominent Australian politician), were free at last to travel to Chengtu. After an absence of more than thirty-five years, however, it seemed improbable any trace of the Hsiehs would be found. To make a long story short, although it proved impossible, given travel restrictions on both sides, to make personal contact, a correspondence with "Margaret" (Hua-di), on behalf of the three sisters, began.

For Ralph, this represented a welcome, indeed heart-rending, reprieve from a fate that seemed destined to deny him ever the opportunity of fulfilling even a portion of that promise made so long ago before the god shelf in the Hsieh home in Junghsien. The reader of Margaret's diaries will recognize the greater obligation in Ralph's words to Hua-di and her sisters in a letter dated August 15th, 1986, "Your Aunt Margaret would have been so excited to have been a part of our renewed connection as well! She loved your Mother so very deeply." One may only hope that for the sisters the re-emergence of this strange foreign figure from their past did not prove a mixed blessing. Heaven knows, Hua-di's letters, while providing no detail of their lives, showed they were touched by the sincerity of "Uncle Yao's" regard for them and this renewed memory of their mother, father and grandfather. One may hope further that the publication of this intimate account of Margaret's life will cause them neither embarrassment nor inconvenience.

Hsieh *tai tai* will live forever in these pages, as will Margaret,

Ralph and various of their friends and associates. Of course, the picture is not complete, nor can it be. Perhaps as profound an aspect of Margaret's and Ralph's view of their lives can be found in the special place of remembrance they created in the early 1950s among the towering Douglas-firs atop a high bluff over-looking British Columbia's Strait of Georgia. Inspired by the Japanese Shinto shrines in which large and beautiful trees are venerated and often hung with *Shime-nawa* (little pieces of paper at the ends of rope of plaited straw telling of the tree's divine quality), each tree in the Outerbridge memorial bears a copper or brass plaque engraved with the name of a particular friend or pair of friends or relatives. The list of those who significantly influenced their lives is not long: Margaret's father and mother, Wil and Fran Kergin; Ralph's father and mother, Howard and Edna Outerbridge; Syd Johnston, Margaret's childhood friend from Prince Rupert; Mac Pugsley and Frankie Hueston, two of Margaret's life-long girl friends; Janet and Leslie Kilborn; Gladys and Ed Cunningham; Lewis and Constance Walmsley; Mil and Gordon Campbell; "Ba'Niang" Hsieh *tai tai*; and Henry and Nancy Li Hen. Banyang, I should point out, is thrice commemorated on the same tree. To a degree, this shrine became the Outerbridge equivalent of a Buddhist god-shelf. Indeed, as one approaches this grove of spirits, one is met by a variation of the message contained in the prayer wheels of Tibetan carriers: *Om mani padme hum* (O thou Jewel of the Lotus), from the Lotus of the Good Law. In a phrase, "Man and the Universe are One." Margaret's ashes lie beneath a granite stone in the midst of this perhaps appropriately eclectic creation. Her dedication (Ralph's adaptation of Mark Twain's "Homeward Bound") reads:

> Great Giants Guard Her Peaceful Rest,
> Gentle Winds, Blow Softly Here,
> Brown Sod Above, Lie Light,
> Lie Light,
> Good Night, Dear Heart, Good Night,
> Good Night.

J.A.M.

I N D E X